MORAL INFIDELITY

REBECCA WARNER

Black Rose Writing | Texas

The author grants the final approval for this literary material.

First printing

This is a work of fiction. Names, characters, businesses, places, events, and incidents are
either the products of the author's imagination or used in a fictitious manner. Any
resemblance to actual persons, living or dead, or actual events is purely coincidental.

ISBN: 978-1-68433-933-4
PUBLISHED BY BLACK ROSE WRITING
www.blackrosewriting.com

Printed in the United States of America
Suggested Retail Price (SRP) $19.95

Moral Infidelity is printed in Cambria Math

*As a planet-friendly publisher, Black Rose Writing does its best to eliminate unnecessary waste to
reduce paper usage and energy costs, while never compromising the reading experience. As a result, the
final word count vs. page count may not meet common expectations.

To my husband, Jason,
who keeps me thinking and laughing.
Strength to Strength

MORAL INFIDELITY

FOREWORD

Roe v. Wade (1973) placed the government's interest in protecting women's lives and health care above the government's interest in protecting the potential life of a fetus.

In the following years, the Court heard various challenges, which were largely ineffectual. But on July 3, 1989, in *Webster v. Missouri Reproductive Rights*, the Court issued a ruling that reversed course and demonstrated that *Roe v. Wade* was not necessarily settled law that restricted future revisions.

Justice Blackman, speaking for the minority, wrote that the ruling made clear that, for those who support *Roe,* "a chill wind blows."

Some state governors construed the Court's 1989 *Webster* ruling as an invitation to begin enacting stricter abortion laws.

And here our story begins . . .

"We establish no religion in this country, we command no worship, we mandate no belief, nor will we ever. Church and state are, and must remain, separate."
–*Ronald Reagan, 1984*

"Most Human affairs come down to depending upon whose ox is gored."
–*Martin Luther, 1521*

1

July 4, 1989

MICHAEL ROMANO PULLED the front right and back left ends of his bow tie apart to loosen it, then pulled the front left and back right ends apart to tighten it. There. It had only taken him two tries tonight. He was pleased.

Governor Romano had several other reasons to be pleased this particular evening. A record-breaking political fundraiser for his re-election was taking place tonight in the downstairs salon. Caroline was getting the house in France ready for a short vacation. And yesterday the Supreme Court had finally ruled in *Webster v. Missouri*. In a 5-4 decision, the Court had voted to uphold a Missouri law that could mean the beginning of the end of *Roe v. Wade*.

With a gratified smile, Michael refocused on his image in the mirror. Every strand of his dark, thick hair was in place. The gray cummerbund accented his flat stomach, and the cut of the tux jacket enhanced his broad shoulders and tapered waist. The hands that adjusted the bow tie were strong and well groomed, and the even white teeth looked dazzling set in the tanned olive complexion of his face.

He couldn't help noticing that also reflected in the mirror was the vivid play of moonlight on the ocean. Michael turned away from his unabashed self-admiration and crossed the wide expanse of the bedroom, where he opened the French doors that led out onto the balcony overlooking the ocean. He stepped outside and observed that the tide was in, and that the pungent, salty smell of the ocean was strong. He looked up, hoping to see stars, but they were obliterated by Palm Beach's own glittering lights, though the full moon cast enough light on the ocean to illuminate the waves that broke gently onto the shore.

Michael was grateful for the luxurious haven this estate of his wife's father provided for them. The ocean was a sight he never tired of, the privileged view one he never took for granted.

As he stood there, peering out over the ocean and recalling the words of the Supreme Court ruling he'd read just that afternoon, he felt deep satisfaction that the Supreme Court had upheld Missouri's law requiring doctors to determine if a fetus was capable of surviving outside the womb before aborting it .

Yes, the justices had finally done it. Upholding Missouri's law was the beginning of the end for the *Roe v. Wade* decision that had been handed down in January, 1973—almost seventeen years before. Michael didn't want to think about the millions of babies that had been aborted in those years.

Instead, he considered that the true significance of this whole thing was that the Supreme Court, in the same ruling, was giving each state the right to limit abortions. While he was disappointed that the *Roe v. Wade* ruling was still intact, he felt that the justices had made a sharp turn from defending abortion rights.

"About time," Michael said aloud. He knew that since the landmark *Roe v. Wade* decision, nineteen states had repeatedly enacted legislation designed to limit access to legal abortion services. Many of the laws had been struck down by the Court, and those few upheld were ineffective on the whole.

But this...this was a clear statement, a turning of the tide, and he would now have to determine the best means of coaxing his own Legislature to enact the same restrictive laws for Florida.

He wondered again at this place and time in life to which fate had brought him, to this pivotal time in history when he was in a position to do something about the killing of innocent babies. Millions of babies had died at the will of the mother and the sharp instruments of doctors, solely because they were unwanted. Unlike him and Caroline, who had wanted a baby more than any other single thing in their lives. But it hadn't happened, and it never would.

Shaking off the melancholy these thoughts brought, he instead acknowledged, as he often did, the abundance of the good things that had come his way. "God, I'm a lucky son-of-a-bitch," he mumbled to himself for the ten-thousandth time. It was his way of giving thanks without being too humble, but it needed to be said often so that no jinx was laid upon him. Michael was too superstitious to take any chances. Life was just too dicey. The tide could go out as quickly as it had come in.

A sense of duty pulled him back inside. He crossed the bedroom and stopped in front of the mirror for a last inspection.

At that moment, the greatest triumph of his life walked into his dressing area. She looked stunning in the long white sheath of a dress that clung lightly to her body and emphasized her trimness and soft curves. Her tall, strappy silver sandals brought her to within a couple of inches of his six-foot height.

The light tan that she had gotten from spending some time by the pool gave her a glow that set off her bright blue eyes. Her blonde hair fell in a chic cascade to her shoulders. She was holding a jewelry case in her hand, and as she approached him, she held it out to him, smiled and said, "Need your help, darling."

From being married to her for seventeen years, he instinctively knew what jewelry she would be wearing tonight. He opened the case she handed him and saw that he was right. White diamonds, red rubies, blue sapphires. It was a Fourth of July celebration, after all.

"My pleasure. You look so beautiful, Caroline."

"And you look so handsome," she said, giving him a quick kiss before turning away from him and sweeping up her hair with one hand, offering him the back of her neck. But instead of clasping the necklace around her smooth and lovely neck, Michael set the jewelry case aside and put both hands on her shoulders. He kissed her just below her left ear, and felt her light shudder of pleasure.

"New dress?" he murmured, as he continued to lay tender kisses upon what he knew were particular points of arousal for her.

"Um hmm," she answered, as his hands moved down her bare, toned arms, caressing them gently.

"It's lovely," he said softly, still kissing her neck. Her skin was warm and soft and fragrant. He turned her around, and Caroline dropped her hair and put her arms around his neck, meeting his expected kiss with enthusiasm. He pulled her closer and kissed her with even more passion.

"Yum," Caroline said, disengaging from the kiss. "Such delicious kisses. I'll look forward to more of those later."

Michael was already slightly aroused. Even after all these years, his physical response to his wife was palpable. "Maybe we have time for..."

"A quickie?" she finished for him, giving him a mischievous smile.

"What do you think?" he asked, lowering the spaghetti straps of her dress and kissing one shoulder, then the other.

"I think I would love to, darling, but guests will be arriving any minute. So unfortunately, even a quickie is out of the question. Let's save it for later, after the party."

"I'll look forward to it," he said, looking into her eyes, conveying his love and lust.

"I will, too. Now help me with the necklace so that I can finish getting ready."

After he had clasped the necklace, she turned to him and said, "Meet you in five." Then, with a devilish grin, she snagged his bow tie and undid his handiwork.

"Hey!" Michael said with mock anger.

"And you had it almost perfect," she teased as she left the room.

Michael turned back to the mirror and started the tedious process of tying the bow tie once again, smiling at the thought of the lovemaking to come.

"Lucky son-of-a-bitch!"

Caroline was waiting at the top of the staircase when Michael walked out of the room. Their eyes met in mutual admiration as they quickly assessed each other's appearance. They never assessed each other in a critical way. There was nothing to criticize. It was always a matter of dual satisfaction at having found such an attractive, accomplished mate. Each took as much pleasure in the attractiveness of the other as they did in themselves. It helped to keep the spark alive.

He liked the system Caroline had worked out from the beginning of their marriage. Here in the Palm Beach house, they each had their own dressing area, separated by their bedroom in the middle. Caroline knew Michael appreciated the space a separate area provided, and she appreciated the privacy.

Michael appreciated the separate areas for reasons much the same, but different. He could take his time in the bathroom, steam it up as much as he wanted, do a few exercises in front of the mirror without feeling silly, and take time grooming that might be considered excessive by some. Michael was aware of this, but he was also convinced that his looks were at least fifty percent responsible for getting him this far, and he wasn't about to take them for granted at this point.

The best part of the arrangement, however, was just what Caroline had predicted when she set up the system seventeen years before...the pleasure in beholding a perfectly-finished package. Always the surprise and pride in seeing each other like this.

Oh, they knew they were vain, but few others knew it. They were so comfortable with their position in life, their good looks and good fortune, their love, that they had absolutely no pretentiousness about themselves. Their unaffected manners and genuine interest in other people immediately put everyone they met at ease.

"Let me say this again," Michael said, beholding his perfectly coiffed wife. "You look absolutely beautiful."

"And you look good enough to devour," Caroline responded with a playful smile.

"I'm holding you to that later," he laughed, taking her hand and giving her a light enough kiss so that he didn't smudge her lipstick.

"It will be my pleasure," she assured him. "Now let's go, Governor Romano, our friends are waiting. This should be a fun evening."

"You're right," Michael agreed. "This is a good crowd. You know David and Andrea are back from Cote d'Antibes, which should give you two ladies a lot to talk about."

"Maybe she can lend me some of her domestic help," said Caroline.

"No luck getting help for the du Cap house yet?" asked Michael.

"No, Michael. You know how difficult those French employment agencies are to deal with. They pretend they don't understand me."

"What? With your perfect French?" exclaimed Michael. "They're just trying to extort a bigger fee, and..."

"Excuse me, darling," Caroline whispered to Michael as she saw their good friends, Victor and Julia Chambers, approaching. Victor and Julia always arrived a bit early so they could spend some private time with the Romanos.

"Victor, so nice to see you," said Caroline, lending him her cheek for a soft kiss. "Julia," she said, opening her arms for a hug from her best friend.

Michael watched Caroline and Julia begin their ritual of sharing confidences and giggles. He took Victor's extended hand and gave it a hearty shake.

"Julia's looking wonderful, Victor, and so are you," Michael said. "Looks like the trip to Martha's Vineyard was good for you two."

"Great vacation," Victor said. "A little biking, golfing, beach time. My inadequate nod to the great outdoors, but it sure was relaxing."

Victor had always been one of Michael's great supporters, and not just because of his family's long-term friendship with Caroline's. Victor had admired in Michael that first year of law school what so many others, including voters, had come to admire in him—integrity, brilliance, and a drive that could only translate into good works. He had supported Michael's rise in politics, both financially and personally, and the two men were close confidants.

They looked at their wives. Caroline and Julia had grown up within a mile of each other, each in her own family mansion in Palm Beach. Victor was from the same neighborhood, though his family had lived in Palm Beach only since the sixties. His family was originally from Charleston, and had moved to Palm Beach after his father had sold the family shipping business and taken an early retirement.

Since Caroline and Julia were being educated in Europe, Victor had not met Julia until the same summer Michael met Caroline. Victor and Michael had been roommates at Columbia Law School, where Michael attended on a scholarship. At Victor's urging, Michael had come down on their summer break to stay with Victor's family in Palm Beach and to work at the Palm Beach Country Club. He had been assured by Victor's father that solid contacts with vaunted law firm partners could be made there, and they had been. But the contact he had made that summer with Caroline Fulton had been the one that really charted the course for his future. Victor and Julia had fallen in love also, and the marital fate of both men was decided.

Caroline and Julia had gone back to France in the fall, while the men returned to New York to finish law school. Both couples became engaged at Christmas, and both were married the following summer. The foundation for a lifelong friendship had been laid.

Julia became pregnant during the second year of the marriage and had a son, quickly followed by two others. Michael and Caroline had not been as lucky.

More people were beginning to arrive, and Michael said, "Sorry we didn't get more time together, Victor."

"Me, too, but let's try to have dinner soon."

"Great. We'll let the ladies set it up."

The men shook hands and parted at the same time Caroline and Julia exchanged cheek-kisses and parted.

Michael and Caroline merged in perfect, unplanned unison, taking each other's hand as they did, and moved forward to greet arriving guests. Each guest had contributed one thousand dollars to be here, and the Romanos were truly appreciative of their support.

The dinner party had been a huge success, with friendship rather than politics being the focus of the evening. A spectacular fireworks display—put on annually by the city of Palm Beach—had been enjoyed, along with countless bottles of Champagne, on the beachfront of the Fulton estate.

The women had kicked off their strappy designer sandals and the men had discarded their jackets and bow ties as the evening turned into a raucous celebration when someone replaced Beethoven with *Sgt. Pepper's Lonely Hearts Club Band*.

Everyone was delighted to have been invited, and sorry to be leaving.

As the last guest said goodnight, Michael turned to Caroline and pulled her to him. "Thanks, baby, for making everything so perfect."

"Oh, Michael," she answered, "you don't have to thank me. You know this is as important to me as it is to you."

"I know it is," Michael said, pulling her even closer, "but I don't want you ever to think that I don't appreciate you."

With a Champagne-induced giggle, Caroline said, "Oh, yeah? Show me."

He did.

2

IT WAS THE end of a long day, and Michael was tired. The long July Fourth holiday at the Palm Beach estate had been great, but he was paying for it now. His meeting with his Chief of Staff, Henry Thomson, and his Lieutenant Governor, Dennis Becker, had lasted longer than anticipated after Michael shared his plans for calling a special session to pass restrictive abortion laws in Florida, based on the Supreme Court's ruling.

Henry had expressed doubts, and they had argued. It ended when Henry extracted a promise from Michael that he would hold off making a definitive decision about a special session until Henry could present him with the information, analyses and views Michael was obligated to consider.

Dennis promised his support for the governor's agenda, and agreed to step up his duties to compensate for the time the governor would have to devote to getting the bills written and advanced if there was going to be a special session.

Michael's day wasn't finished yet. He poured himself a Scotch and picked up the folder on his desk.

Though he had read the Court's decision as soon as Sally had faxed it to him two days before, he wanted to read it again. After all, it was what he would be building upon to enact stricter abortion laws for Florida.

Michael wondered if any of the other forty-nine governors had waited for this decision with the same anticipation that he had. He doubted any of them had as much of a personal motive as he did in wanting to see *Roe* overturned.

He read the Court's ruling again, and then he read both the majority and dissenting opinions. The Supreme Court had been only one vote away from overturning *Roe*... but it didn't happen because of O'Connor. Scalia was angry *Roe* wasn't overturned, while Blackmun, in contrast, feared for the future of *Roe*.

For now, *Roe v. Wade* was still the law. So it would be up to the states to put enough restrictions on abortion—restrictions that rationally related to promoting potential life—until abortion was no longer a legal option for women who weren't victims of rape or incest, or in danger of dying.

And he, Michael Romano, was going to lead the way.

This was the defining moment of his life. To become the leader of this movement, he would need divine guidance and imbued strength. He bowed his head and prayed for both. Then he turned off the light on his desk and went to find Caroline.

The next morning, Michael looked at the notes his press secretary had given him. Come on, he thought. Does he really expect me to take a noncommittal stand on this?

"Andy," Michael snapped as he pressed the intercom button to his press secretary's office, "come in here."

Andy didn't answer. He rose from his seat slowly, fully aware why Michael's voice had an edge to it. He had known the governor would not agree with his suggestion on how to handle the press conference.

As he entered Michael's office, he was surprised to see that Michael was really angry. Michael normally fenced with him from a devil's advocate position, not from emotion.

"Hey, Michael," was all he said as he came in. This didn't seem like a good morning for the two minutes of bullshit they usually shared. Andy was silent, waiting.

He watched as Michael got his temper under control before he spoke. He had always been impressed with the governor's self-control. Andy had been writing media copy and political speeches for eleven years, but had yet to meet anyone as cool or analytical as Michael when it came to handling the press. When Michael finally spoke, Andy heard a disturbing chill in his voice.

"If you think I'm going to wimp out on this issue, you're wrong, Andy. I'm sure you think you know what's best here for handling the press, but I won't go along with this."

Michael held up his hand as Andy started to speak, and said, "You know my personal feelings on abortion. I watched this whole Supreme Court session with the hope they would do the right thing, and they did. They upheld the Missouri law and they gave the states the power to enact the same law. And by God, we're going to do it. The press has to be told my intentions now if—"

"Michael," Andy interrupted, sitting forward in his chair. "Hold it. Sure, I know how you feel about this. Who was at the hospital with you when Caroline lost your baby three years ago? I know life is sacrosanct to you, but I also know that there are myriad voters out there who don't agree with your position."

"I don't give a damn whether they agree or not," Michael barked.

Andy met Michael's outburst with momentary silence. He knew this was a hot issue for him, but it was a hotter issue for the media. Michael's personal stand on abortion could affect the Party vote by as much as thirty percent, if he took action. Previous, recurring polls showed that Florida voters were strongly in favor of keeping abortion legal, and Michael couldn't afford to ignore those numbers.

"Michael," Andy sighed, "you have to give a damn. Henry and I have discussed this. He's gathering information. He's initiating some new polls. You've got the latest ones. Florida voters want to keep abortion legal."

"Plus, we're already into serious campaigning for your re-election, and we have some really vulnerable Republican legislators coming up for re-election, too." After recapping the polls for Michael, Andy added, "Their re-election and yours is going to be jeopardized if you ignore those poll results."

"The new polls may be better. A Supreme Court decision like this one can influence attitudes," Michael countered.

"Maybe, but I doubt it. What I don't doubt is that an issue as hot as this one can blow the Party apart, just trying to support you. There aren't enough Republicans in this state for you to alienate even a single one."

"I have the power of the national GOP on my side, Andy. Look." Michael tossed the morning edition of the *Tallahassee Democrat* across the desk to Andy. "The White House agrees with me. The president says that 'the Court appears to have begun to restore to the people the ability to protect the unborn.' Are you trying to tell me that the president's opinion counts for shit?"

Andy smiled to himself, knowing that Michael had quoted President George H.W. Bush verbatim, from memory. He had an incredible memory. "Of course the president's opinion counts, Michael, but I'm telling you, the polls come out strongly for pro-choice in this state, and I can't let you endanger the balance of the Party by letting you cut loose on this one."

"You can't let me?" Michael laughed, in a lame attempt to instill some humor into what was becoming a very tense conversation. "When I looked in the mirror this morning, I was still the governor."

Andy laughed with Michael, though he was still uncomfortable with the tone of the whole conversation. "Look," he said, "I have another meeting with Henry at nine o'clock. Take a few minutes to re-read what I've written. You're only saying that you're agreeing with the Supreme Court's decision to allow the states to govern themselves on this one. The media know your feelings on abortion. You don't have to give them any ammunition by saying you're going to act on the ruling right away. All you have to say is that you're going to explore the issue to determine what's best for this state."

Michael knew Andy made a good point. "Okay, Andy. But whatever I say today has to leave wide open the possibility of a special session. I don't think this will keep until the spring session when the Legislature reconvenes."

"Don't worry," Andy sighed. "Nothing in that speech prohibits any future action you might take. But I would strongly advise against announcing any plans for a special session, at least until we can get some further poll results, based on the Court's decision."

Andy was right. Michael would wait. Besides, he needed time to plan.

Michael watched Andy leave, then turned around to look out the window. He stared past the magnificent gardens. He had too much on his mind to notice. Dammit, he couldn't take a neutral stand on something that meant so much to him and Caroline.

God, how they had wanted children. Caroline had been an only child, but Michael had two brothers and a sister. Even in the roughest times, when there wasn't even enough money to buy the two-day-old fish at Cassio's Market in Brooklyn, there had been family. Strong, supportive, tight. Family was what really counted in this world, and he and Caroline hadn't been able to have a family of their own. It was his deepest regret in life.

Michael rubbed his tensed-up forehead and thought about Caroline's third and last miscarriage. The doctor said Caroline shouldn't get pregnant again.

So he had a vasectomy right away, saving Caroline any further physical trauma that surgery might cause her. It had been the scariest thing he had ever had to do in his life. He had felt almost emasculated, and the worst part of it was that he couldn't share that feeling with anyone, not even Caroline.

For three months afterwards, they had used a condom when making love, to make sure that the remaining live-sperm downstream from the vasectomy site was completely flushed out of his system. It made the act of making love more remote, when he needed closeness more than ever.

At the time Caroline had enough to deal with herself. So he got over it. She helped, even if she didn't know it. She made him feel like so much of a man in every way that she had dispelled the insecurity.

He lit a cigarette and took a long drag as another painful memory pushed its unwelcome way to the surface. Alison Ledford. His first love; and before Caroline, his only real love. Alison would have been his wife, instead of Caroline, if she hadn't made the terrible decision to abort his baby. Sure, things would have been difficult. Michael had no money. Hell, without a full scholarship, he would have never seen the inside of a college. Alison's family was comfortable, but she had been sure they would disown her for getting pregnant, even if Michael had married her. And he would have. Both were working hard for a degree at NYU, but they would have managed.

When he had learned she was pregnant, Michael had been elated. He was going to have a child with the woman he loved. Hardship was nothing new to Michael, he could handle whatever came. But Alison didn't feel the same. Besides the scary prospect of her family's disapproval, she didn't want to be married and saddled with a baby at the age of nineteen. So she had arranged for an illegal abortion behind his back.

Michael had been devastated. He had loved Alison. He wanted to marry her and have a family. Then, in a single afternoon, she had shredded those dreams, torn out his heart, and tossed away his child like a used tissue.

He couldn't believe that the Supreme Court had declared such a murderous act legal just four years after his unforgiving heart caused him to walk out on Alison.

Though he had converted to Episcopalian when he married Caroline, Michael had grown up Catholic, and the Roman Catholic Church had long criticized abortion as a form of infanticide. Due to this indoctrination, Michael had believed an abortion should be illegal under any circumstances, except if the mother's life was in danger. But Caroline had tempered that opinion with some salient points.

"What if your sister, Rose, were violently raped and became pregnant? Would you expect her to carry that baby to term, and to look at that baby and see its cruel father's face for the rest of her life? Or would you understand if she wanted to abort it and attempt to put everything behind her, so that she could have a chance at a normal life with a loving husband and children that are wanted?

"Or what about your cousin, Angela? You told me that there was a major scandal in her family, though you never gave me details. But let me guess that it had to do with incest. That brother of hers who went to jail for rape? Wonder if he raped her, his own sister, and got her pregnant? Is she supposed to bear her brother's child?"

Both scenarios caused Michael to feel physically ill with repugnance, so much so that he had to concede that Caroline had a point. He had admitted to himself more than once that his personal pain had laid the foundation for his strong anti-abortion stand.

With *Roe v. Wade*, the Supreme Court voted overwhelmingly, 7-2, to support legalized abortion in the United States. Ironically, five of those seven majority justices had been appointed by Republican presidents. While that should have solidified Michael's loose affiliation with the Democratic Party, it did just the opposite. It made him think that Republicans were headed in the wrong direction, and he was cocky enough to think that he could somehow make a difference in correcting that. As a result, he became the first Republican in his family's history.

Yet hadn't fate worked out much like he had planned? Now, as a Republican governor, he was in a position to do something about abortion. He was in a pivotal place at a providential time, and he couldn't let this opportunity slip away. He had a calling.

There was a short rap on the door, and Andy came in. "Ready, Michael?" he asked.

Oh yeah, Michael thought. I'm ready.

"And so we are faced with addressing the same issues the Supreme Court chose to uphold in the *Webster v. Missouri* case," Michael concluded in his speech before the media.

"Questions, ladies and gentlemen?" he asked.

Andy tensed in anticipation of the onslaught.

"Governor! Governor!" It was Debra Stanton, a reporter for Channel 3, a station owned by a left-winger with a chip on his shoulder, in Michael's opinion, calling for his attention.

"Yes, Ms. Stanton?"

"Governor, are you aware of the recent polls which indicate the people of this state are three-to-one pro-choice? Why do you feel it necessary to address this issue at all?"

"The opinions of the people of Florida govern me in the true sense of the word, but the most powerful court in this country found reason to uphold stricter abortion legislation, and we will need to study their basis for doing so. That's all I plan to do at this time."

Andy breathed a sigh of relief. That sounded good. Sure, he and Michael had practiced it, but Michael's delivery was so effective, so sincere.

"Governor, are you planning to call a special session to address this, or will you wait until the regular session next spring?" asked a reporter from the *Tallahassee Democrat.*

Damn, thought Andy. That was a big point he had gotten Michael to concede, not announcing a special session at this time. Where did these people get their information? He held his breath and crossed his fingers.

"I'm not announcing a special session at this time," Michael replied, "but I'll take it into consideration. Thanks for the suggestion."

The crowd chuckled. So did Andy.

"Governor Romano," a young reporter unknown to Michael spoke up. "Are you waiting to call a special session until the State Supreme Court's decision on the challenge to Florida's 1988 law requiring parental consent for abortion to minors comes down?"

"That's a separate issue from those we're addressing today," Michael replied, "and it will have no effect on any action I might decide to take."

In response to a question regarding the support of the state's GOP, Michael answered as he and Andy had prepared. "The GOP, unlike the Democratic Party, has always made its position against abortion clear, though it hasn't been an issue on tickets in recent years. I expect the Republican Party to support my position."

What he expected and what he was actually going to get might be two different things, but the answer was just ambiguous enough to cloud the possible truth.

"Ladies and gentlemen," Michael said before the next question could come, "that's all I have time for today. Thank you."

Those in the crowd emitted a small groan, but they recognized the end of a press conference.

Andy stood up as Michael turned around, and gave him a smile and a handshake. When they were safely in the back of the limousine, he said, "You did a great job, Michael, just great."

"Let's hope Henry thinks so," Michael mused. "I'm going to need his support if I decide to make this the top item on my priority agenda."

"True," Andy said. "And as your chief strategist, he's going to have to oversee the process of you campaigning for a special session, if you really plan to push for that. Plus coordinate with the budget director the dollars that are going to be necessary. Somehow I don't think he'll be happy about it."

"Can't blame him," Michael concurred. "He's got a hell of a lot to do as it is with overseeing the daily operations and the gubernatorial staff. Not to mention the state agencies. But this will have to become a priority for him. And for you, too, Andy. Are you up for it?"

What else could Andy say? "Sure, Governor."

3

MICHAEL WALKED INTO the brightly-decorated banquet room at the Tallahassee Hilton, where the kickoff fundraiser to re-elect him was going strong.

He had been told that the room held up to four hundred people, but the crowd was spilling out into the hallways. The sight of such a throng ignited a spark in Michael, propelling him through the crowd to bestow handshakes and thanks to the volunteer campaign workers.

Michael really appreciated these people. Few were paid to be involved in his re-election effort, and the thousands of combined hours the volunteers gave to his previous election, and now his re-election, were priceless.

Michael studied the crowd as he passed through, aware of the fact that there were a number of people who would not have been here if not for his pro-life position. He knew full well that if he had taken the opposite position, there would be only a token representation of that side; but with a hot issue like this on the platform, he had aroused the passion and loyalty of anti-abortionists.

Pro-lifers had a distinct fervor, unlike those mandating pro-choice, because they were intent on change, and change took action. Recognition of the need to act spurred on those who were willing to champion a cause. Action wasn't called for, to the same degree, to keep things as they were. The pro-choice people had to reorganize and gather strength against the assault on *Roe v. Wade*. That would take time.

"How's it going, Michael?" asked his campaign chairman, Les Jenkins, coming up behind him and giving him a good-old-boy slap on the back.

"Hey, Les, how are you? Nice job on this event."

"Yeah, pretty good crowd, huh?" Les responded enthusiastically. "I was a little worried about doing it a couple of months earlier than we planned, but I think we made the right move."

Michael neither agreed nor disagreed. He trusted Les' strategy and his decisions and showed up when and where he was told to.

Les was a good-old-boy, but he was bright as hell and knew his business. He had run some of the most successful campaigns in the country, including Michael's own initial tough run for governor three years before.

"Hey, Governor Romano," a very familiar and boisterous voice behind him penetrated the other voices in the room. Michael turned to look for the owner of the boisterous voice, his friend Gary Williams, but instead he found himself looking into a pair of captivating eyes. The din of the room faded slightly as Michael stood there, staring at a woman he had never seen before. He would have remembered her if he had.

Her eyes were silvery-gray clouds ringed by a deep, dark blue. They were actually sparkling. If anyone had told Michael before this moment that eyes really sparkled, he would have accused them of reading too many cheap romance novels.

But there was something more. It was vague, to be sure, but there was a resemblance to his college sweetheart, Alison. Although the eyes were silvery-gray, rather than hazel, there was something about the shape of her dark brows, the thickness of her lashes, the tilt of her head, and the soft but intelligent expression in those eyes, that evoked memories of Alison.

After an unseemly and lengthening pause, Michael found his voice. "Uh, hello." Well damn, was that all he could manage? Why did he feel so off kilter?

"Hello, Governor." She seemed shy, maybe even a little awestruck.

He wondered if she had picked up on the effect she was having on him. Did it show? No, he decided. In reality, only a few seconds had passed before he had spoken.

"It's such a pleasure to meet you," she said in a soft, sultry voice. Michael took in the total face, as a whole and not in parts, as she spoke. He thought she was a damn good-looking woman.

He was staring. He knew he was staring, but he couldn't help himself. He had never seen eyes that color. And what made them even more appealing was the strange yet suitable way they were offset by a shock of silver hair along the front of her hairline. It stood out, yet it blended with the rest of the luxuriant locks of her raven-black hair. Alison's hair had been raven-black, too, but she had worn it in a long, thick braid most of the time.

"I'm sorry for staring," Michael said, pulling back from the memory of Alison, "but you look like someone I used to know."

"Really? No one has ever told me that before. Just the opposite. 'You don't look like anyone I've ever known' is much more familiar to me."

Was she playing with him, Michael wondered? No, she seemed sincere, not a trace of sarcasm in her voice.

"Well, just a resemblance, really." And it was just a resemblance, he decided. He was being prodded into comparison by a memory of Alison that recently had been taken off the shelf and lightly dusted. Besides, Alison had been a very pretty girl, but before him stood a very beautiful woman.

Kristin Long watched Governor Romano as he spoke. She was confused by the way he was looking at her. She knew men found her attractive, but unless she was very wrong, this man found her very attractive.

What confused Kristin even more was the emotional pinwheel on which she suddenly found herself. It wasn't just that he was devastatingly handsome, either. There was something absolutely magnetic about him.

"Well," she volunteered, "I'm Kristin Long."

"Kristin Long," Michael repeated. "It's good of you to be here. What brings you to this event? Are you a campaign worker?" The comparison to Alison was wearing off. Now Michael found himself interested in the woman standing before him. She really was damn good-looking.

"Why, a number of reasons, really," she answered, "but mostly because of your strong position on the abortion issue."

He had been right, then, in assuming he had won new support because of his position. Michael felt someone touch his elbow.

"Hello, Gary," he said as he stepped out of his trance and into conversation with Gary Williams. "Was that you calling me from across the room?"

"Yeah, and it was tough working through this mob to get to you," Gary laughed.

"Great turnout, huh? Oh, Gary, I'd like you to meet Kristin...Long, right? Kristin, this is Gary Williams."

Michael had paused between her first and last name to make it clear to Gary that he had just met this woman. He wondered why he had done that.

"Yes, Kristin Long," she said to Gary. "It's nice to meet you."

She gave Michael a sweet but sly smile that told him she knew what he did, and why. He returned her smile with a slight shrug of concession.

"Nice to meet you, too, ma'am," Gary replied.

"Uh, Michael, excuse me, but have you got a minute?" Gary asked, indicating his apology to Kristin for the interruption.

"Sure, Gary." He looked at Kristin and found it hard to look away again. "Well, Kristin Long, it was nice meeting you. I thank you for your support."

"It's been my pleasure, Governor," she replied. She turned to Gary, giving him a slight nod as she said, "Gary."

"Ma'am," he responded, clearly not recalling her name.

"Well, good luck, Governor," she said as she held out her hand for Michael to shake. He automatically took the hand, one of thousands extended to him over the years, but he was completely unprepared for the tingling quiver that coursed through him when he shook Kristin's hand. He pulled his hand away—too quickly, he realized—and stepped back.

Kristin turned and walked away. Michael's eyes followed her. She was wearing an expensive blue knit dress, one that, thanks to his wife, he recognized as a St. John. It was sexy and classy at the same time, showing off a luscious figure and shapely legs.

"Hey, what's the matter, Michael?" Gary asked in amusement. He could tell Michael had the hots for that one.

"Nothing, Gary. She just reminds me of someone I knew years ago," Michael answered, a half-lie at this point. No doubt her resemblance to Alison had caused him to give her, at least initially, more consideration than he might have otherwise. But in doing so, he had opened a vulnerable part of himself. He was attracted to her. He realized this with a stab of genuine surprise.

Gary shrugged, not really interested in any explanations. "Nice-looking gal," Gary muttered, closing the subject. He had more important things to discuss.

Michael was glad to change the subject, and he made an attempt to give his full attention to Gary when he began to speak. It wasn't easy. He had a compulsion to seek out Kristin Long, but he overcame it and listened as Gary complained about the Florida Department of Environmental Protection, which was giving him a hard time over how he was disposing of some chemicals. Could Michael help?

Gary Williams and his corporation were healthy contributors. Although Michael sometimes resented getting involved with their issues, he knew it came with the territory.

"I'll have someone call the FDEP on Monday, Gary. We'll find out what their beef is, and then I'll see what I can do. But if you do have a problem, you'll have to take care of it—understand?"

"Believe me, Michael, there are no problems, except with those tight-ass inspectors."

"Okay, then. I'll see what I can do."

"Thanks, Mike, I'd appreciate it. Say, where's that beautiful wife of yours? I haven't seen her tonight."

Michael felt a twinge of guilt at the mention of Caroline. He hadn't thought of her at all over the last few minutes, which was unusual under these circumstances. Although he was more than capable of going into any situation on his own, he liked having Caroline with him. She always made conversation flow more smoothly, and was even better at working a room than he was. People were absolutely charmed by Caroline.

"She's home with what she calls a summer cold. Didn't want to pass it around. I'm sorry she couldn't be here. She loves these things, believe it or not."

"Yeah, well, Caroline's a peach. Anyway, you give her my regards and tell her to feel better, will ya? And thanks again for your help."

"Sure, Gary. Now I better get my ass in gear and greet a few hundred other people." He could see that people were waiting to speak with him.

As the two men shook hands, Michael gave in to the impulse to scan the room for Kristin Long. He didn't see her, so he moved on to greet others.

As the party was breaking up, Michael searched the room for her once more. He caught himself, and was surprised by his irrational desire to lay eyes on her again.

It was just as well she wasn't here, he thought, because he was damned confused about his feelings. He had never deliberately sought out another woman since he had married Caroline, and although he had plenty of women before Caroline, there had been none since.

Oh, sure, there had been temptations. He still got horny looking at pretty girls sometimes, like when they vacationed in St. Barths, where the women sunbathed either topless or totally nude. What man wouldn't, looking at those hot, young bodies? But that horniness had been saved for when he and Caroline returned to their room, and had resulted in some of their best lovemaking ever.

He left the party with a happy feeling of anticipation at seeing his wife. And then the image of Kristin Long popped into his head. Michael shook his head resolutely, clearing away the cloudy, intermingled images of Kristin Long and Alison Ledford. Besides, he concluded, he'd never see her again anyway.

Kristin had left the party five minutes after walking away from the governor. She had felt a shortness of breath, and her heart was racing.

This was not a familiar feeling for Kristin, and it unnerved her. Since her husband had died of cancer two years before, she had not even had a real date. She had a few male friends who accompanied her to social functions, but no one interested her enough to take it any further.

It had been a difficult period because she loved and missed Ted so much, and because she found herself totally alone in the world again.

Her parents had died six years ago, and the grief during the period from the time of their deaths to the time she met Ted had been overwhelming. Ted had filled a void and taken away the pain.

Kristin was scared of loving ever again. Everyone she had ever loved had been taken from her, and the fear of more pain had caused her to build a fortress around her emotions.

Now she was feeling something she had never felt before—not even with Ted. It was a feeling she did not know she was capable of, and she could not describe it.

As she sat in her car in the dark parking lot, trying to understand her feelings, she became aware of her sexual excitement. It had been so long since she had felt any sexual stirrings that she had actually failed to recognize them.

But then, it had been a long time, all the way back to the year before Ted died. His deteriorating condition had taken away the sweet lovemaking they shared, and Kristin had learned to suppress her desires.

To actually feel this way again caused another kind of excitement in her that she welcomed. It made her feel alive again. She suddenly realized she had been holed up with her grief far too long.

But this was the governor of the state, for heaven's sake. He was married, and happily so, from what she remembered hearing and reading. The state's first couple was a favorite of the press. A beautiful, rich, philanthropic couple; and with him being the governor, they were often in the news.

Kristin conjured up a picture of the governor's wife. Caroline was her name, wasn't it? A tall, stately blonde, beautiful and classy. Rich, too. Palm Beach rich. Had she even been here tonight?

But the governor had been attracted to her, Kristin was sure of that. Perhaps she had misread, in the confusion of her own emotions, the degree of his attraction to her.

She had never been attracted to a married man. She automatically rejected any inkling of interest in them because, old-fashioned as it was, she respected the sanctity of marriage. Besides, too many headaches, judging from what her girlfriends who had been unfortunate enough to fall into that trap, had experienced.

But this man, married or not, had introduced a new and exciting kind of energy into her static life.

When she finally started her car and pulled out of the parking lot, she knew one thing for certain: she would see Governor Michael Romano again.

4

JAKE MILLER TURNED away from the scene he was watching in Central Park from his apartment window. A father had lifted his son high in the air, causing the boy and his mother to laugh. A family. It was a beautiful sight to him, even though it induced a touch of melancholy.

He sat down and picked up the packet of information the Ackerman Investigations agent had delivered only an hour before. Given enough time and money, Ackerman's had found his sister—a woman named Kristin Marks Long. A sister he had never met because she had been adopted by different parents than his own. Marks had been her adoptive parents' name, and Long was her married name. But, Jake was sorry to discover in the documents, she was a young widow. Ackerman's had included a dossier on her late husband. Maybe she's lonely, too, he thought. Maybe she'd like to know she has a brother.

He was glad to learn he did indeed have a sister. He had always known, just known, that he had a sibling out there somewhere. The fact that he had a twin sister had surprised him, though.

When he was nine, his parents had told him he was adopted. He smiled as he thought about his reaction to their news. "I knew that," he had responded, between bites at the dinner table. Most parents would have laughed at that remark, but not his parents. They had long ago recognized the special gift their adopted son possessed, a healthy dose of a sixth sense. By age four, when he could articulate, he would answer his parents before they even asked a question. He could tell his mother where to find misplaced objects.

"Now where did I put my car keys?" his mother might mumble. Jake would nonchalantly answer, "In the pocket of your blue coat," as he continued to stack his Legos. In a short time, her amusement had turned into dependency. She was always misplacing things, and he could often tell her where to find them.

His parents hadn't treated it as anything special, though. They didn't take him to the nearby university for testing, as so many parents were doing around that time. It was around the beginning of the ESP craze. They just accepted it, and neither encouraged nor discouraged him, except in the case of deliberately "reading our thoughts" because, they explained, that was disrespectful. That was the best thing they could have done for me, Jake thought. Everything just kept developing naturally, and his sixth sense had diminished into what now would be better termed as sharp instincts, or keen intuition.

His thoughts came back to his recent discovery of his sister. Why hadn't his parents told him about her? They must have known. His adoption papers were from the same agency as hers. Hell, he had given Ackerman's a big head start with just that one piece of information—the name of the agency. So his parents had to know about his twin sister, for God's sake. Why, then, had he spent so many years in the dark? Dammit, he had asked his parents straight out if he had a brother or a sister. He had been surprised by their reactions, the startled looks on their faces. After a slight pause, his mother had simply answered, "No, dear."

It hadn't taken a sixth sense to know that they were hiding something. He should have pressed them, but he never would have done that. He knew they sometimes chose to ignore or avoid certain topics, and if he had pressed them, they would have gotten upset. After all, they had to make lots of exceptions and adjustments because of his "special ability."

But the feeling that there was someone else out there, someone close to him, had stayed on his mind through the years. He had always intended to pursue it, but he had just never gotten around to it. Until now. So many years lost. Who knows, if it hadn't been for his accident, he might never have looked into it. He would not have had all this time to think about it.

Accident. That word still bugged him. It didn't truly describe such a traumatic event, one that had changed everything about his life, did it?

The thought of the accident seemed to send a message to his brain, which transmitted it directly to his body in the form of pain. Damn. He was usually good at controlling the pain. It had sneaked up on him this time.

Jake stood up slowly, pulling his body upright until he felt he was standing straight and tall. He knew he wasn't really straight and tall—not yet. But he was getting so much better.

He walked over to the refrigerator to get a beer. Right there on the top shelf, so he didn't have to bend over too far. He silently thanked his housekeeper, Lucy. She took care of everything for him. He felt especially fortunate that she had been with him for nine years, because no one else would have taken care of all the things she had, with the level of devotion that she had, while he had been laid up.

He enjoyed the first rush of the ice-cold beer going down his throat. He walked back over to the sofa and sat down, picking up the packet and thumbing through it again. His sister had been six weeks old when she was adopted. He knew from the adoption papers he had found in his parents' safe deposit box that he was also six weeks old when he was adopted. Had each set of parents wanted just one baby? Why would they separate twins?

Studying the picture of Kristin more carefully, he thought that, as fraternal twins, there should be more dissimilarity. But there were striking similarities. The facial structure was certainly different, but she had the same dark hair with a shock of gray, and her eyes were so close to his in color and shape that he could have been looking at a reflection of his own eyes. With those eyes and that hair, she had no doubt heard the same kinds of comments as he had over the years.

The phone rang, and Jake was glad for the interruption of his solitary thoughts. It was his ex-partner, Vic Salinas.

"Hey, Vic, good to hear from you," he said happily.

"Yeah, how ya doing, Jake? Listen. Grogan is getting married, and we've thrown together a last-minute bachelor's party for him tonight at the Rampart Room in Midtown. Can you make it?"

"Sure, I'll be there. What time?"

"Eight. Hey, you want me to pick you up?"

"Nah, no need for you to fight the traffic. Besides, I might want to leave before you, and I wouldn't want to cut into your good time."

"You think I'd let you? But hey, that's okay, that's good. I'll see you there."

"Thanks, Vic." There was a touch of gratitude in Jake's voice. He would really be lost if his buddies forgot about him.

"Hey, for what? You always were and always will be my best partner."

"Yeah, right. Enough already. Later."

Jake smiled as he hung up the phone. A bachelor party for Grogan. With him married, Jake was now officially the last bachelor in the old rookie group. Had it really been thirteen years ago that they had all joined the force? Geez, that sounded like such a long time. Hell, it was a long time. But it had gone by so fast.

He looked over at a picture of himself and his parents taken on the day of his graduation from the academy. They were smiling, but they weren't happy. They had wanted him to be a doctor or a lawyer. They certainly could have afforded to send him to any college, and his grades had been excellent. But after only two years of college, he had decided to join the police force. His parents had been disappointed; but more, they had been afraid for him. They didn't like the idea of his being out on the streets of New York.

It hadn't taken long, however, to get off the streets and into homicide. His intuition, instincts, whatever they were, had helped the department in solving crimes. And while no one openly speculated about his uncanny ability to come up with new leads in dead-end cases, his talent was widely acknowledged. That, plus his affinity for getting along with practically everyone on some basis, whether friendly or professional, had fast-tracked him within the department.

As hackneyed as it was, he did it for the love of his job and justice. He had always had a strong sense of right and wrong, and he believed he could do more as a cop than as a lawyer to keep crime in check. But as with all cops, his dreams of catching all the bad guys died quickly. It became a push just to stay even, though trying to do so was a big part of the excitement of the job.

Despite all of his training and instincts, which had served him so well in keeping him out of harm's way on more than one occasion, he had been caught off guard and had paid dearly for it.

He couldn't resist rolling the tape in his head again. He had done it a thousand times. Each time he asked himself, "What if...?" knowing damn well how useless it was. It led nowhere, but it was a compulsion. Talking to a shrink had helped get rid of a lot of the anger and regret, but not the second-guessing.

Maybe if he hadn't dropped the grocery bag as he started to reach for his gun, maybe if he had just laid it down quickly, not making so much noise, with the wine bottle shattering, he wouldn't have been a target for the robber's bullet. He knew that his sudden action had caused one of the robbers to panic and fire. He recalled the hot, shattering pain in his back right before blacking out. When he woke up in Columbia Presbyterian Medical Center thirty-six hours later, he saw Vic Salinas standing there.

They had gotten the bastards, Vic told him. One was shot and wounded, the other surrendered after a chase. Both were alive, and they'd make sure the bastards burned.

Jake hadn't felt any better knowing the punks were in custody. Lying in the hospital bed, he could only speculate about his own injury. He had figured that the body cast he was wearing was meant to keep him immobile. He remembered being shot in the back, but he couldn't feel any pain. That scared him. He thought he was paralyzed, but it was only the pain blockers numbing the pain, and everything else.

Jake reflexively rubbed the large scar where the bullet had rocketed into the mid-portion of his body. The doctor had told him it had caused a burst fracture to the vertebrae body. He had assessed his paralysis incorrectly. The fracture to the vertebrae body had, in fact, caused the spinal cord to swell and hemorrhage, and he had suffered a temporary loss of feeling in his lower extremities. That had been the toughest thing to hear, because even though the doctor had said there was a very good possibility that it was only temporary, there was the possibility that it could be permanent.

Thank God, that wasn't the case. With time and a strenuous rehabilitation routine, he had come back, though not all the way. Fortunately, the bullet had missed his spinal cord, or he would have been paralyzed for good. But the bullet had not gone directly into his back. It had entered from more of a flank position, hitting the vertebrae body instead of the spine. The body of the vertebrae had burst into many pieces, some of which had lodged into the spinal cord.

Jake winced at the thought of his upcoming surgery. He had already endured three surgeries, the first one from the front and a second one from the back, to remove the bone fragments on the spinal nerves. Both of those had been brutal.

The third surgery to stabilize his spine with plates and screws had been the worst. Now he was coming up on the time when those plates and screws would have to be removed. But he would be almost normal after that operation—almost being the operative word. Never again good enough, though. Not good enough to be a detective.

Here he was, thirty-three years old, and on disability for the rest of his life. The real irony of it was that he wasn't even on duty at the time. He was cooking dinner for a woman he had liked a lot—someone he had only been out with three times, but was feeling good about. He had stopped to pick up a few things that Lucy hadn't gotten at the market...a special bottle of wine, a nice triangle of brie cheese. Then he ended up lying in broken glass and spilled wine.

Ah, well, he wasn't bitter—not really. More like disappointed at his fate. He'd had such high expectations, expectations he would never realize. The only thing he could expect from the city of New York now was a disability check each month.

Jake looked around his comfortable apartment and acknowledged the one thing for which he was immensely grateful—the inheritance from his parents that had made it possible for him to continue living well in Manhattan. Of course, if he could have traded the money to have his parents alive, he would have done so, a hundred times over.

He was left completely alone at the age of twenty-six when they had died in that car crash seven years ago. Though he had dated plenty, and even been in love a couple of times, he had never married. His career had been a top priority, and marriage was always something for the future.

His only consolation, and it was a small one, was that they had not lived to see their fears for him realized. They would have said he got shot because he was a cop, even if he wasn't on duty when it happened. Well, so they were right. If I hadn't been a cop, he thought, I wouldn't have reacted like a cop. Nothing to be said or done about that now. Just move on. And now there was a place to move on to, at least for a visit— Tallahassee, Florida—where his sister lived.

He was excited, and yet somewhat anxious, at the thought of meeting his sister. Sister. How nice to be able to say that word, and know it applied to him.

But what if she doesn't want to meet me, he wondered. He knew there were some problems, some serious problems, with kids finding their parents. But siblings finding each other...what kind of problem could that be?

Well, first of all, asshole, he admonished himself, it could be her parents never told her she was adopted. What a shock that would be, huh? Where was it her parents were living? Was it Pensacola, Florida?

He reached for the stack of files and shuffled through them until he found the dossier that he had only glanced at earlier. Father a CPA, mother a teacher. Jake skimmed the page, taking note of their lifestyle. Active in their church and numerous civic associations until their deaths...

Their deaths...both had died instantly when hit head on by a drunk driver...

Jake's parents had died in a car crash in 1982. Kristin's parents had died in a car crash in 1983. Christ, talk about coincidence. How weird was it that both sets of parents had died the same way, in a car crash, and within a year of each other?

Jake was certainly aware that weird coincidences occurred all the time, but this one was way up there on the scale of holy-shit.

He lit a cigarette and thought about the numerous other weird things that had happened to him, and how each one had some significance. He wanted to meet his sister, but now he considered that—besides causing shock if she didn't know she was adopted—he could also cause her pain. He would want to discuss this uncanny coincidence with her, but in doing so, he might cause her sad memories and more hurt. He knew all about those feelings.

Ah, hell, he mused, I'm not fit to travel anyway. Maybe I'll just wait until I'm over this last operation. That's only two or three months. Maybe by the beginning of November, I can go. That'll be a good time to get out of New York.

He looked at his watch. Time to get ready and meet the guys.

He closed the files and put them inside his desk drawer. He'd come back to them later. After all, it had waited this long, so what difference could a few more months make?

5

MICHAEL MET THE maid outside the bedroom door and took the breakfast tray from her. He had called down from his dressing room and asked the kitchen to bring up some fresh orange juice, some hot tea, and two pieces of toast and jam. There was a white rose from the garden in a small crystal vase, and Michael thanked Ann for her thoughtfulness in adding that extra touch. The staff Caroline had hired when they moved into the Florida Governor's Mansion was really superb.

Caroline was sitting up in bed and brushing her lovely blonde hair when he went in with the tray.

"Good morning, sweetheart. Are you feeling any better?" he asked as he set the tray down and gave her a kiss.

"Some better, but another day in bed should completely cure me."

She looked down at the tray. "How sweet. Thank you, Michael," she said, as she lifted the glass of orange juice to her lips. She took a sip, then asked, "So how was the kickoff last night? Sorry I was asleep when you came in."

The image of Kristin Long came to Michael, surprising him and causing him to feel guilty. Man, he hadn't done anything. Why was he feeling guilty?

"Pretty good, actually," he responded. "There were over four hundred people there and it seemed like a pretty enthusiastic crowd. I think this abortion issue has driven a few sleepers out of the covers. I just hope they don't get fanatical about it. There were a few there who definitely looked like they could," he laughed, as he brushed his fingers through her hair.

She laughed with him, and thought how much she loved him. He was always so cheerful in the mornings. They were alike in that way, as in many others. It was a rare day that they didn't greet each other with smiles and kisses.

There was something a little off about him today, though, and Caroline pondered it as she ate her toast and watched him.

"Anything special happen last night?" she asked.

Michael started. "Special? What do you mean, special?"

She laughed. "My goodness, it was just a simple question. It doesn't require any specific answer." She paused and looked at him more closely. "What happened?"

It was on the tip of his tongue to tell her about Kristin Long. But what could he say? He looked closely at her face to see if she knew something. But what was there to know? It was obvious that she was merely interested in the campaign party, and that she wasn't sensing more.

He decided to answer her with a different truth—his assessment of the people who were there. "Just a different kind of crowd than usual. The abortion issue came up a lot last night, lots of questions about what I'm going to do next, questions that I don't have all the answers to. Just put me on edge. I'm feeling a little strung out. God, I'm looking forward to that week in France."

"Good, because I've just about finished arranging for prepping and staffing the house, thanks to Andrea. She put me in touch with a top-notch agency."

"An agency where the employees understood your French?" Michael teased.

"Mais bien sûr! My accent may not be what it was when I lived in Paris, but the language has not been lost to me. You know, I think the woman I was speaking with at the first agency was drunk. Honestly, she's the one who was slurring words. It was I who couldn't understand *her.*"

"Hey, I trust you on that. You and I need to start speaking it on a regular basis before we go. I'm the one who's gotten rusty with my French." Michael had relaxed with the turn in conversation, relieved that she suspected nothing more had happened at the fundraiser. He realized that he was deceiving her, though, and with no real reason. He had never had a reason to be this way. He didn't really have a reason now, except he knew that he couldn't just tell his wife that he had felt a physical attraction for a woman with whom he had spent only five minutes— though she might understand. Hell, she had understood that women had been attracted to him before. But why chance alarming her when nothing more would come of it?

31

"Okay, I've got a lot to do today," Michael said, standing up to leave. "I'll see you this evening. Je t'aime."

"I love you, too. Now go on about your day, and I'll see you for dinner this evening. We'll have dinner up here in the salon, if you'd like."

"Sure, I'd like that. I hope you'll feel like dessert, because I'm very hungry for some *sweet Caroline*," he teased as he leaned over and ran his hand under the sheet and up Caroline's long, toned leg.

"Oh, Michael," she admonished, pushing his hand away in mock disgust. "You know I can't stand that song. You're lucky the offer is still open, but it is, because I can't resist you. Now go," she commanded, but with a forgiving smile.

Michael leaned down to give her a kiss. She was so lovely.

He left the room feeling that his wife's sunny aura had dispelled the shadowy guilt he had been feeling. Everything was back in place, and he felt pumped, ready to face the demands of the day.

Michael looked at his watch and realized that despite his secretary's escalated prompting, he was going to be late for a luncheon at which he was the guest speaker. He and his chief of staff had just hashed out what would be involved in calling a special session. Henry hadn't hesitated to voice his all-around misgivings, but he had agreed to make it the top item on the governor's agenda. That meant action, and Henry was already overburdened with his massive efforts to keep the governor's office running smoothly. Michael couldn't blame him for not wanting such a controversial issue on his plate, but he trusted Henry to handle it as well as he did everything else in the governor's office on a day-to-day basis.

His thoughts switched to the wonderful evening he had spent with Caroline. She sure didn't let any illness get her down for long. Their lovemaking had been tremendous.

As the limousine pulled up to the entrance of the Billiard Club, he began searching for Caroline. She had planned to meet him here, after her morning appointment at the beauty salon. When he spotted her, he saw the beautiful results. She was chatting with a couple of their friends, and he thought how gorgeous she looked.

His chauffeur, Manny, opened the door and Michael popped out of the limousine. Only then did he notice that there was an unusually large crowd outside of the club. He wondered why. Normally they would be inside at the bar, getting primed for chicken surprise and a political speech.

He looked questioningly at Manny, who pointed to a news truck that was parked on the side of the building. Behind it was a second news truck from a different station. Michael was confused. This was just a simple luncheon. Why were the media here? No sooner had he asked himself that question than a group emerged from behind one of the trucks. They were carrying pro-choice signs. *Aw, shit,* he thought.

Michael turned to look for Andy and spotted him coming out of the front door of the club. As he approached, Michael stepped up to meet him and hissed, "Why didn't I know about this?"

"Because I'm just your press secretary, not a goddamned clairvoyant!" Andy hissed back.

Michael apologized, but he still wanted some answers.

"I just got off the phone with the police. They're sending a couple of cruisers to make sure everything stays cool. But I'll be damned if I know why the fucking press would show up here today."

Michael raised his eyebrows at Andy, as if to say, "Oh, really?"

"Yeah, who am I kidding?" Andy said in response to the unstated sarcasm. "These people called the press. They need the exposure. Doesn't do much good to demonstrate unless everybody knows about it these days, does it?"

Michael nodded, and then looked over to see Caroline waving at him. Manny stepped in and started leading him through the crowd towards Caroline. It was a precaution Manny didn't usually take, but in a heated crowd, there was no sense in taking a chance.

When he reached her, Caroline said, "Michael, let's get these people inside quickly. We don't need to encourage *them.*" She inclined her head towards where the pro-choice people were congregated.

Michael looked over to where she indicated, and was startled to see Kristin Long. She was talking calmly and confidently to a man in a green golf shirt who held a sign saying, "It's All About Choice."

Michael saw that the man was becoming agitated. Without thinking, he moved towards Kristin and the man, leaving Caroline standing at the entrance of the club. Manny moved quickly to stay with him.

As he approached, he saw Kristin shaking her head in apparent frustration in response to whatever the man was saying. She turned away from him, and as she did, her eyes met Michael's.

Of course, she knew she would see him here. That's why she had come. Her husband had been connected everywhere within the GOP, and as his widow, she was often invited to GOP functions. Before two nights ago, she didn't have a reason to go; and although she expected to see the governor, she didn't expect to feel the sexual stirring she felt when she did.

Michael's head buzzed slightly at the moment their eyes met, but he quickly gained control of himself and the situation. He realized he had just walked off and left his wife standing so that he could intercede on this woman's behalf.

In a concerned yet impersonal voice he asked, "Are you okay, Ms. Long?"

Manny was confused by Michael's actions, but he was more confused as he watched the play of emotions upon this woman's face. He had never seen her before, and as far as he knew, neither had his boss. But Michael had spoken her name.

Kristin was not as adept as Michael at concealing her feelings, or in gaining such quick control. She stopped short as she opened her mouth to speak. She closed it, then found her voice and said, "I'm fine, thank you, Governor Romano."

Caroline was watching with no small amount of curiosity. She had never seen that woman before, but Michael obviously knew her. How? She thought how very attractive the woman was, and for the briefest moment the worst possible thought flashed in her head. But no, she would know if something was going on with Michael and that woman. She didn't know how she would know, but she would.

She watched Michael nod his head before walking back to rejoin her.

Before she could ask, Michael volunteered, "I met her at the kickoff the other night." He dropped his voice to a whisper and said, "Remember the anti-abortion fanatics I told you about?" Caroline nodded, and he continued. "Well, she was one of them. I just wanted to make sure nothing got started."

Of course. That made perfect sense. Although she had been sure there was nothing between her husband and the woman, she was nevertheless relieved. She looked over at the woman again, and when she did, she saw a fanatic. She was glad Michael had interceded and perhaps kept an embarrassing situation from starting.

"That was wise, Michael," she said, taking his arm and turning him towards the entrance of the club. Everyone else was moving inside under the urgings of Manny and the club manager.

The relief Michael felt was at the same time unnerving. He had always been good at coming up with plausible excuses, but that had always been for everyone else's benefit. He had never had to do that with Caroline. He didn't like it, but he was still relieved.

He could see that Caroline was completely at ease about the situation, and she had already turned her attention to other people. He could feel the sweat under his armpits, though, and knew it was from more than just the heat. He wouldn't be able to take off his jacket.

Caroline was perfectly satisfied with Michael's explanation, but she couldn't refrain from turning around to look at the woman again. When she found her, she saw that she was surrounded by several men, and held each one's attention. Caroline watched her for a few seconds to see if she would look at Michael, but she was caught up in conversation with those men.

Caroline then turned to speak with someone standing next to Michael, so that she could observe whether he was looking at the woman. No. He was facing in the direction of the woman, but he never even glanced at her. Caroline thought she must be getting paranoid as she approached forty. There was obviously nothing going on. She was being silly.

Her fears being put completely to rest now, she gave Michael's arm an affectionate squeeze.

He put his mouth to the hair covering her ear and whispered, "I love you," so that only she could hear.

As he did, he had an impulse to look at Kristin. He knew where she was and to whom she was talking. He had grasped the total image with the briefest glance, when he knew Caroline had been looking at Kristin also. It took real willpower now to keep from giving into his impulse. It was a good thing he didn't. Caroline looked into his eyes at the same second he might have been looking at Kristin Long.

Instead, his eyes met hers, and he felt the strength and love of his wife. He could never hurt her.

Michael was addressing a politically active group this day, and the questions which followed his economic development speech turned, not surprisingly, to the abortion issue.

"Governor," a well-known Tallahassee attorney asked, "is it true that you plan to call a special session of the Legislature to address this state's current legislation in respect to abortion?"

Michael was caught—and caught off guard. He had not planned to announce the special session until he could hold a press conference in the next day or two. The media would jump all over the cost of a special session if he answered this question truthfully, which he would have to do, because he couldn't afford to make enemies of these people by lying to them today.

Andy moaned to himself, again wondering where people got their information. But he knew how Michael would answer, and he was comfortable.

"Several members of the media asked me that question just a few days ago," he began. He took a deep breath and continued. "At that time, I had not made up my mind about a special session. I have now, and I am planning to call a press conference in the next day or so to announce my plans.

"Since we're here today, however, and since you've asked, I will tell you that yes, I do plan to call a special session to address the abortion laws of this state. We now have the responsibility of deciding the laws of this state which will directly affect the rights a pregnant woman currently has to use public employees and public hospitals for abortions. We may look further at the possibility of requiring doctors to administer the necessary tests to determine whether a fetus can survive outside the womb before it is aborted."

Michael's statement was met with murmurs throughout the room.

"But Governor," asked Judge Moore, a man whom Michael had known for years, "do you really think that is what the Supreme Court intended?"

"Yes, Judge Moore, I do. I'm convinced the Supreme Court, in upholding Missouri's right to limit abortions, has virtually invited state Legislatures to pass legislation that restricts abortion."

Michael stopped to take a drink of water and look at Caroline. She gave him a supportive smile, and he continued. "I'm going to attempt to get the Florida Legislature to pass several bills that will put certain restrictions on abortions, restrictions that are in accordance with the Supreme Court's latest decision.

"And I feel," he continued, "that the high court has sent a clear signal that it is no longer committed to the milestone *Roe v. Wade* precedent, which first gave women a constitutional right to abortion."

"Just how restrictive are you talking about?" came a woman's voice from the back of the room.

Michael looked in the direction from where the question had come and answered, "One of the dissenting justices of the court sees that the plurality of that court implicitly invites every state Legislature to enact more and more restrictive abortion regulations. Such action will then provoke more and more test cases in the hope that sometime down the line, the court will return the law of procreative freedom to the severe limitations that generally prevailed in this country before the *Roe* decision."

What he didn't say was that he also intended to address life at conception and a seven-day waiting period. He'd push that agenda closer to the special session.

After answering a few more questions on that and other topics, he thanked them, and asked for their support. And he congratulated himself for his control in not even looking toward Kristin Long, although she was in clear view.

Caroline and Michael settled in for the ride back to the Mansion, and as the limousine pulled away from the club, he looked out of the window and quickly searched for Kristin. He spotted her. She was putting on her sunglasses as she watched the limo pull away. He was disturbed and confused to see the disappointment in her eyes before they were hidden behind the darkness of the glasses.

6

MICHAEL READ THE various newspapers with disgust. Besides pointing out that he was the first governor in the country to act upon the Supreme Court's decision, each one harped on the same note—namely that he was overplaying his hand in a state that had a majority Democratic Legislature. He couldn't win with the press. The fact that they were negating the session one day after it was officially announced was what really concerned him most. He needed the voters of the state behind his decision. The way it was being presented, however, was certain to foster anything but accord. He was also being touted as a crusader, albeit a deranged crusader, who was being totally self-serving in calling the special session. He was being held up to scrutiny based upon the media's speculation that his purpose was more aligned to furthering his political career than to his true interest in the rights of the unborn.

More than anything else that might be said, this was the one thing that disturbed him the most. His political aspirations were healthy, though not all-consuming. To tie the special session to a pursuit of greater power was almost blasphemous.

Where did they get off making such an assumption? Wasn't it enough anymore simply to be a moral man? A man who was willing to fight for the rights of the unborn, even at the risk of alienating voters?

It was true that if the legislation he planned to propose were to pass, he would receive a great deal of recognition. So what? If that recognition served to promote his political career within the GOP, well, that would be a fine bonus.

But the real issue here was one that spoke to his heart. He believed in the rights of the unborn, and it was his obligation to move to protect those rights. He was certainly in a position to do something about it. He had no doubt that fate had a hand in his being here in this office at this pivotal point in time. It was inconceivable to him that he could ignore his obligation to fate. Fate, which had been so good to him, now laid at his feet this demanding task. Consequently, he was compelled to follow that task through to the finish. He would make that clear to the press over the next few weeks. He should discuss this with Andy to make sure that message was imparted. His hand was in mid-air, reaching for the phone to call Andy, when the line that connected his office with Caroline's buzzed.

He pressed the button, but before he could say anything, Caroline's unnaturally panicked voice came over the receiver with just one word: "Michael!"

The alarm in her voice shocked him. "I'll be right there."

He sped out of his office and met Caroline in the foyer outside her office suite. She was very upset, but without saying a word, she took his hand and led him back into her office, past her secretary, who was looking quite concerned. She closed her office door behind them and collapsed against it as she did.

Michael quickly reached for her, just in time to keep her from slipping to the floor in her overwrought state. "For God's sake, what is it, Caroline?"

"It's father," she said, tearful but fighting for control.

"What?"

"A stroke."

"Oh, God, no. Sweetheart, I'm so sorry. How is he?"

"Critical. Intensive care. Michael, I have to go to him."

"Of course you do. I'll have Lynn arrange to have your father's plane fly up and take you back to Palm Beach. Ann can pack you, and Manny will drive you to the airport."

Caroline was bolstered by Michael's strength. He was always so even, always able to think and to react to a crisis with logic and calm. She acknowledged again how lucky she was to have this wonderful man for a husband.

Then her grief and anxiety overwhelmed her, and she broke into uncontrollable sobs. Michael held her close, wishing he could take her fear and her pain away. If by some sort of magic he could transfer it all from her to him, he would gladly do so. As it was, he was helpless to do anything about it. He wasn't used to feeling helpless, and he didn't like it.

"Oh, Michael," she sobbed, "I still haven't gotten over losing mother. I just don't know what I'll do if father dies."

"I know, Caroline, I know. It will be okay," he reassured her. Despite the dire circumstances, Michael thought about their obligations for the weekend.

"Look," he volunteered, "why don't I call Janice and ask her to postpone the dinner party tomorrow night so I can go to Palm Beach with you?"

"No, Michael. We just can't do that to Janice. It will be enough of a disruption that I won't be there. You have to be there."

She was right, of course. "Okay. But I'll be down first thing Sunday. Will that be okay?"

"That would be great. You're sure you can come?"

"Of course I can. And in the meantime, you'll call me regularly to let me know how he's doing?"

"Yes, of course, but..." Caroline choked on her sobs, unable to finish her thought.

Michael knew what she was thinking. "If you need me, if anything happens, you know I'll be there in a flash," he said.

Grateful, she laid her head on his shoulder. He held her tight, trying to pour some comfort into her. She pulled away and looked up into his eyes.

"I'm so glad you're here. I need you, Michael."

He met her eyes and smiled reassuringly. "I'm here, baby. Always."

She laid her head against his shoulder again, and with a deep sigh she whispered, "Thank God."

Michael, how is Mr. Fulton?" asked Janice Asheton, his hostess. Janice and her husband, Landon, were good friends. The condition of Caroline's father was of genuine concern to them.

"Still in some danger, I'm afraid, last time I talked to Caroline."

"When was that? And how is she?"

"About two hours ago. She's holding up, Janice."

"Well, really, Michael, we could have called this off if you needed to be with her." Janice was so real, so sincere. She really would have thrown away many thousands of dollars and weeks of work if he had asked her to.

"Thank you, Janice," he answered, pressing her hand. "But she wanted me to be here."

Janice looked at Michael closely, then smiled and nodded her head, satisfied. "Good. I'm glad you are here."

"Actually, Janice, I wanted to be here. I'm grateful to you. Your formal dinners are always so elegant and traditional. No one does it better."

"Why, thank you, Michael; but it's an honor, and a pleasure. You know how I love to entertain. And it's so much more fun when it is in honor of someone as special as you."

"I hope this change didn't cause you too many problems with the seating arrangement," Michael said. He was well aware of the complications involved in arranging a formal dinner, and of how any small change could ruin weeks of planning.

"Not at all, dear. Another guest was suggested just this morning. That made alternate arrangements quite simple. I trust you're satisfied with your dinner partner?" she asked, with a look of mischief in her eyes.

Michael was embarrassed to say he had not looked in the envelope he held in his hand to see who his dinner partner was. He would have to do so and seek her out before dinner. He didn't want Janice to know he had not bothered to look at the card.

"Perfectly fine," he answered. "And I really do appreciate everything, Janice."

"Oh, but you're quite welcome, Michael. Please allow me to say that I'm awfully sorry about Mr. Fulton, and if there's anything I can do, anything at all..."

"Thank you, Janice. I'll be certain to pass that on to Caroline."

Michael looked around, aware that guests were looking at him and expecting him to mingle.

"Uh, Janice." He hesitated, then decided Janice was a good enough friend to understand what he was about to ask. "I promise to be a charming guest of honor, but I would appreciate a little respite from a certain someone."

Janice knew exactly who he meant. She had arranged the seating to accommodate him in that respect, and she had been surprised he hadn't commented on his dinner partner. "Well," she said, "since it is my house, I guess I can steer the guests anywhere I want *before* dinner, now can't I?" She gave him a conspiratorial wink.

"Meaning, away from me?" Michael asked.

"If that's what you want."

"You're a gem. And you know exactly who, don't you?"

"Indeed I do. Here she comes now. Go. Meet and greet. I'll handle her. These fine people are contributing quite a bit on your behalf to experience my cuisinière's considerable skills. Now go," she said, giving him a small push.

With that, she turned to greet Mallory Wain, who had been headed straight for Michael. Mallory never missed an opportunity to socialize with him. She was at least thirty years older than he, but it was obvious to everyone that she had a terrible crush on Michael, and she maximized her contributions by attending every function she could, even traveling to do so. Her generosity was appreciated, though, and she was given the special recognition she sought within the Republican Party.

"Mallory, so nice to see you," Janice said, taking her arm. "Come with me, dear. I must show you the Dalí I just acquired." She deftly steered Mallory away from Michael.

"Delighted," Mallory said, though there was obvious disappointment in her voice as she turned to look back over her shoulder at Michael, who was walking away from her.

Michael almost burst out laughing when he opened the envelope and saw that his dinner partner was none other than the lady Janice was spiriting away. What a brilliant move on Janice's part. If Caroline had been with him, then she, as the dinner partner of the guest of honor, would have sat across from him. Then, most likely, because of her august position among his supporters, Mallory would have ended up sitting next to him. He would have been stuck talking to her for at least half the evening.

Janice had outdone herself. She had elevated Mallory to an even higher position in the seating arrangements by making her Michael's dinner partner, which meant she now had to sit across from him. There was no way Mallory could be offended, even if she was disappointed. It was perfect.

Michael wondered who would be sitting to his right. It didn't really matter. With his delightful hostess on his left, he would manage just fine.

He was working his way through the cocktail-drinking crowd, enjoying himself, when the call for dinner came. He was surprised that the time had gone so quickly. He had wanted to say hello to everyone.

He watched his host, Landon Asheton, offer his right arm to Mallory Wain and lead the way into the dining room. The other guests followed, with Janice and Michael entering last. Michael hadn't paid close attention to the procession, so that as he approached his chair, he came very close to faltering in mid-step as he saw Kristin Long standing by the chair next to his. Since she was to his right, it was he who would have to seat her.

His mind was racing almost as fast as his heart, but he kept his emotions in check. He showed no signs of discomfort as he cordially greeted and gracefully seated her. When all the other women were seated, he turned to seat his hostess, and then sat down himself, along with the other men. He was determined to get his breathing completely under control, to subdue the pounding in his head. What in the hell was she doing here? And what was it about this woman that caused him to feel so at odds with himself?

He didn't look at her until she said in her soft, deep voice, "I'm as surprised as you are about this seating arrangement, but I'm also delighted."

He found himself drawn in by those amazing eyes. She must have sensed the effect she was having on him, because she gave him a sly smile much like the one she had given him before, when he had pretended to forget her last name. He said a silent prayer of thanks that Caroline wasn't here to see his behavior. He may fool the other guests about how shaken he was, but he knew Caroline would have seen right through him.

He noticed his palms were moist, and he was tempted to wipe them on his napkin. He resisted the impulse. He wondered to himself at the irony of it all. Here he was, the unflappable politician, a level-headed man who could deal with virtually anyone, on many levels, with total confidence. From his days at the law firm, to his tenure in the state Legislature, to his office as governor, Michael had always been known for his composure. Now he was reduced to clammy palms and a racing heart by a virtual stranger. He felt uncommonly unsettled.

He had to answer her. He had to say something. "It's a pleasure to see you again, Ms. Long," he said casually. He couldn't look at her. He looked around the table to see if anyone was watching him. If so, they might wonder about his odd behavior.

But no, he was just being paranoid. Why was that? He had nothing to be paranoid about. No one could read his thoughts, and he was pretty damn sure his actions were subtle enough not to draw attention. He found he couldn't help himself. As if she were willing it, he turned his head to look at her. Her magnificent eyes met his. He felt the blood pounding in his temples, and he forced himself to look away.

He turned his attention to the footmen, who were being discreetly directed by the major-domo as they served truffle custard with crab and caviar and poured a vintage Dom Perignon. He knew these footmen were brought in for the occasion, and he was impressed by how well Janice's major-domo of so many years handled the young men.

One had to have someone like that even to consider hosting a large, formal dinner party. Dinner parties of such grandeur were virtually extinct in America, but the Ashetons seemed to do it with little effort. Their English ancestry and tradition had been preserved and carried forth with grace.

His and Caroline's dinner parties were considerably less formal, with Caroline directing the staff herself, though her father's major-domo was always available to help them.

He turned to Janice on his left to compliment her on everything, and chatted with her as much as he politely could. He did have an obligation, however, to the woman on his right—Kristin Long.

Besides, Janice kept getting drawn into conversation by Mallory, who was always eager for attention.

"You can only ignore me for so long, Governor Romano, or you will draw attention to yourself," Kristin said, interrupting his thoughts.

"I'm sorry," Michael said. "I didn't mean to ignore you."

He paused before asking the question that had been on his mind since he saw her. He didn't bother to try to phrase it politely.

"What are you doing here?" He tried to keep his voice low, though it was difficult, since they were seated the customary one foot apart and the chatter around the table had grown louder.

Kristin laughed, an enchanting laugh, the laugh of one who is delightfully surprised but not offended by such a straightforward question.

"My, you are direct, aren't you? All right, I guess I should be truthful with you. I snagged an invitation from Janice through Betsy and Oliver St. Vincent. I've only met Janice twice, and I would not have been invited under any other circumstances, I'm sure, if a guest had not canceled. I didn't learn until tonight that it was your wife. I was obviously at the top of the list for replacements, thanks to Betsy and Oliver. I saw you speaking with them earlier. They really are wonderful people, aren't they?"

Michael wondered how he had missed her when he was circulating earlier. She looked so stunning that he should have noticed her right away. It occurred to him that perhaps she hadn't wanted him to see her before dinner.

He was even more puzzled about how she seemed to know so many of the same people he knew, and yet he had never run into her before. After all, Tallahassee was a pretty small town.

"How do you know Janice...and the St. Vincents?"

"Through my late husband."

Michael was surprised. She was a widow? She was so young that he had just assumed she was either divorced or single.

"Your late husband?" he repeated.

"Yes. I know you must have known of him, though you haven't made the connection. Ted Long?"

"Sure, Ted Long. Of course. I remember hearing he had passed away. I am sorry."

"Thank you."

"Ted was, um, in plastics, wasn't he?"

"What an excellent memory you have."

"Yes, well," Michael paused. His curiosity was peaked.

"I met Ted a couple of times. Why didn't I meet you?"

"Because, before two weeks ago, I had no interest in politics, and frankly, neither did Ted, though he contributed enough to the GOP that he was invited to everything. I bet you met him at a business function, not a political function."

"I honestly don't remember."

"Well, no one knows better than you that in this town, there's a strong mix of socializing and politicking. You're more likely to see the people we both know at political functions. I'm more likely to see them at social functions. Ted was involved with the GOP mainly through his contributions and his friendships with highly-placed people in the Party."

Michael pondered the logic of that as the next course, broiled bay scallops, was served with an outstanding Wehlener Sonnenuhr Auslese. He found he didn't have much of an appetite, though the food and wine were delicious.

After several minutes of silence, Kristin decided to speak her mind. After all, what did she have to lose? She felt confident that Michael Romano was as attracted to her as she was to him. Men didn't get nervous and avoid eye contact with her if they weren't attracted to her. Taking a deep breath, she looked at him and softly cleared her throat. When Michael turned to her, she said quietly, but in a voice audible to him, "Governor, I'm confused. I've never felt this way, and I don't know what to do about it."

Michael picked up his wine glass, took a sip, and looked away from Kristin. His lack of response almost inhibited her from saying what she had planned to say next.

No, no backing down, she reprimanded herself. Go for it, she thought. "I'm willing to find out, though."

Michael was stunned. He wasn't sure he had heard right. Assuming he had heard correctly, he turned to her with a nonchalant smile and said, "Not happening, Mrs. Long."

Kristin was taken back. She had known she was being bold, but she had gambled that her bold approach would elicit a desired response. His response was equally bold, all right, but not what she had hoped to hear. And damn, wasn't he a cool one? She was embarrassed as well as hurt, and she fought to gain control of her emotions.

"I'm sorry you feel that way. I suspected that you were feeling what I am. I see I was wrong."

It was on the tip of Michael's tongue to agree with her that she was indeed wrong, but when he looked into her eyes, he found that he wasn't able to say it. He wondered why. Was it just because he didn't want to hurt or embarrass her any further?

She turned away from him and began a conversation with the couple on her right. Michael was reeling from Kristin's brazen approach. He began thinking about what he would say to her when she turned her attention back to him, but after a couple of minutes it became obvious she didn't intend to.

He focused his attention on both Janice and his dinner partner, Mallory Wain. He engaged the ladies in harmless, flirty conversation while he savored the Scotch grouse with wild rice, served with a delightful Chambolle Musigny.

Mallory's eyes were sparkling with pleasure from both the wine and the attention Governor Romano was paying her. She picked up her wine glass and exclaimed, "I can't imagine anyone having so much beautiful china and crystal. Why, it's like royalty!"

"Aren't you astute, Mallory," Michael responded. "The Ashetons are descendants of royalty, on both sides."

"Michael, really. That's ancient history," Janice playfully scolded.

"Oh, my dear," Mallory said, practically swooning. "You really are too modest." It was evident that Mallory was impressed. She raised her wine glass to Janice and Michael.

To Michael and Janice, her enthusiasm seemed silly, but they acknowledged her gesture with kind nods.

Michael noticed Janice's faint smile as she brought her glass to her lips.

Mallory turned her attention away from them in response to a question from another guest, and Michael, against his will, turned once again toward Kristin Long.

Her eyes met his as he did, and he felt his pulse quicken.

The other thing he felt, which both annoyed and surprised him, was a stirring in his groin.

"You know, Governor Romano," Kristin said, her voice taking on a business tone, "I've checked with my accountant, and it appears that I can contribute up to forty-five thousand dollars to your campaign."

Michael was taken aback. The maximum allowed contribution per person or corporation was three thousand dollars. That much could be contributed for the primary, again for a runoff—which wasn't likely in his case—and again for the campaign. Although there were those who wanted to contribute more, and certainly could afford to, that was the allowed contribution amount, which meant only nine thousand, maximum, she could contribute. Was she confused about that?

"That's extremely generous of you, but..."

"Not really," she interrupted him. "I can afford more, but my accountant tells me that I can contribute only nine thousand personally—six if there isn't a runoff—and the same on behalf of each of my corporations."

Michael quickly did the math. "So you have four corporations?"

"Yes."

"All plastics?"

"Yes. All in different cities, however—Tampa, Orlando, Clearwater and Miami. Miami is the largest manufacturer."

"Do you take an active role in running those companies?"

"Not an active role. I'm on the board of directors, and I'm an officer, so I receive a salary. I don't take dividends, so the companies can reinvest most of their profits and grow faster. There are very competent people in place who run them. I do have an independent auditor go in for surprise visits, as my accountant suggested. The companies are doing very well."

Michael was momentarily at a loss for words. He had no idea this woman was so well off. Sure, she looked great and dressed expensively, but not everyone had an extra forty-five thousand to contribute to a campaign. Unwittingly, he reassessed her and her motives. He found he was more puzzled than ever.

"Well," he finally said. "I can hardly thank you enough for your proposed generosity."

"Oh, there might be a way," she teased, but Michael knew she was casting her line again. Persistent woman.

He didn't bite. He ignored the comment, silently cursing himself for giving her an opening.

He didn't speak with her again as the party reached its peak over the strawberry pineapple kirsch compote, served with a delicate Niersteiner Kanzbert Beerenauslese.

The chatter started winding down with the coffee, which was served with a side of rare and delectable Chateau de La Grange, Jonzac Charante Cognac, which Michael knew was close to a hundred years old.

Even the very wealthiest people in Palm Beach rarely served such wines and brandies as had been served here tonight; and when they did, it was only among a small party of intimate friends. Michael could only guess at the cost of such generosity. And the Ashetons did it out of pure friendship, neither needing nor wanting anything more than to see their friend re-elected.

At what he thought was the appropriate moment, Michael nodded to Janice and then rose to address the guests and his hosts, brandy snifter in hand.

"I can't think of a finer Cognac," he began, "with which to toast our extremely generous and gracious hosts, Janice and Landon Asheton."

He turned to them and raised his glass. "Thank you for the absolutely finest dinner party I have ever had the pleasure of attending."

A chorus of "Here! Here!" rang out as Michael lifted the snifter to drink. The Ashetons accepted the thanks with their usual modesty and grace.

Michael continued. "My friends, and I do not use that term lightly, I appreciate your support more than words can say. Not only your tremendous financial support given this evening, but your moral support as well. I promise to justify your faith in me in every respect, both personally and as governor of this state.

"I'm sorry my lovely wife, Caroline, is not here to share this wonderful evening with us, but she went to Palm Beach yesterday to be with her seriously ill father. Many of you know Mr. Fulton. She asked me to relay her apologies, along with her heartfelt thanks to each of you for being here.

"And so, here's to four more years!"

The guests roared a chorus of "Four more years!" Michael smiled at the wine-flushed, admiring faces around the table, including Kristin's. Hers was the most admiring of all.

7

THE NEXT MORNING, Michael boarded his father-in-law's private jet, a Cessna Citation, grateful for this privilege that Pierce Fulton's wealth afforded him. Caroline had flown down on it Friday, and the jet had returned to take him to Palm Beach this morning. He had the use of one of the state's planes, a Gulfstream g200, for official travel, but he had never used it for personal travel.

Manny, always the vigilant chauffeur and bodyguard, watched as Michael boarded Mr. Fulton's plane. He was not happy about being excluded from the trip. He guarded Michael with a vengeance, fearing for the man whenever he wasn't with him.

Manny knew Michael was a self-sufficient man, but that didn't lessen his concern. He would unwaveringly, if not gladly, lay down his life for the man. His loyalty went back a long way, and it went deep.

He watched the plane ascend, and only then did he return to the limo. He told himself that he couldn't stop a plane from going down, and that's about the only thing that could happen to Michael. Old man Fulton's bodyguard would meet Michael on the other end, and he would be safely delivered to West Palm Hospital. Still, Manny preferred to be with Michael wherever he was.

Michael looked down and saw Manny getting into the limo, and he smiled to himself. Manny was a helluva good friend, besides being the best bodyguard Michael would ever find. Michael personally compensated Manny way above what the state allowed. He had a wife and six kids to care for, and although he said he owed Michael a big debt, Michael knew who really owed whom.

Manny had saved Michael's life back in New York, and all that Michael had done for Manny in return was take him away from his life of poverty. In his mind, he still owed Manny a big debt.

Michael settled back and sipped the orange juice that he had been served. He reached for the over-stuffed briefcase on the seat next to him, but then changed his mind. He didn't feel like working. Instead, he leaned back and closed his eyes, hoping to relax, but too many thoughts intruded.

Kristin Long. Now there was a woman who could really intrude on a man's thoughts. He started going over last night's events. Weird how things worked out. Caroline couldn't be with him, and Kristin just happened to show and end up sitting next to him. He pictured her again. Those startling silvery-gray eyes, soft and expressive, even as they penetrated right through him. She was a lady, but she had a wild streak. For Michael, those traits in a woman had always held a lot of appeal.

It had become obvious to him that she knew all about the good life. She had seemed very comfortable in elegant surroundings, very sure of herself at a formal dinner that would have made any number of people feel self-conscious. Michael could remember the time when he would not have even been asked to serve at a formal dinner, let alone be the guest of honor.

He lit a cigarette and sipped his juice. He exhaled the smoke slowly, enjoying it. He didn't smoke often, but he still found it an incomparable way to relax. He smiled to himself as he recalled how one of the guests at last night's dinner had asked for an ashtray between courses. Being the gracious hostess that she was, Janice hadn't flinched as she signaled for an ashtray. He could smile because he recalled the first time he had almost committed the same faux pas at his first formal dinner with Caroline's family.

He had reached into his jacket pocket for his cigarettes, but Caroline's hand had restrained him. He looked at her questioningly, but she just gave him a short, terse shake of her head. He had refrained, though he was annoyed. Her family knew he smoked, so what was the problem?

He found out in short order. After dessert, ashtrays had magically appeared, and about half the table lit up. He had raised an eyebrow to her mockingly, as if seeking permission for him to do the same, and she had smiled and nodded.

As so often happened in their marriage, Michael had learned another little etiquette trick from Caroline. Caroline didn't need to explain to him later that no ashtrays were kept on the table at a formal dinner, and that the end of dessert signaled it was okay to smoke. Michael had just figured it out and catalogued it away, the same way he had catalogued thousands of little details over the years.

It hadn't been easy to come up to well-bred standards, coming as he did from a poor Italian family that lived in a low-income tenement building on Mulberry Street in Little Italy. But he had known early in life that he wanted more, and that he was capable of getting it.

When, he wondered, did he really become aware that there was more? It must have been around the time he read his first James Bond novel. Later, on screen, Sean Connery had made Ian Fleming's suave hero come to life. And as many young boys did, Michael started identifying with 007—the sophisticated, dashing, brilliant figure of a man who had caused Michael to fantasize about becoming a secret agent. Bond was also multilingual, which had intrigued Michael. He learned that the Bond character was fluent in French, Italian, German and Russian, was conversant in Greek, Spanish, Chinese and Japanese, and had a degree in Oriental languages.

He hadn't known where to start, but he knew that the first rule to becoming a secret agent was to become smart about everything. So he had turned to the only source of knowledge he had ever known—books. Nothing in the Catholic school library addressed secret agent-ing, so he would regularly make the three-mile trip on his beaten-up bike to the public library near Midtown to check out books that he thought would help him, especially books about intrigue and espionage.

When he had his fill of Bond and spies, he moved to self-taught language books. He would quietly enunciate the words, not knowing if he was saying them correctly or not. He already knew Italian, of course, so Spanish came pretty easily. Within two months, he felt that he was fluent enough to use it, so he started speaking Spanish with the Puerto Ricans he encountered around Brooklyn. It was different from the textbook Spanish he had learned, but he was able to pick up the nuances and slang words almost effortlessly.

French had proven to be more difficult for him, however. It wasn't until one of the librarians, Mrs. Potts, had approached him and become aware of his interest in foreign languages that he had learned of the tapes he could listen to that would prove invaluable in helping him learn the language.

Mrs. Potts. Michael owed her a great deal. She had seemed so old to him then, but Michael realized she must have been only in her forties at the time. She dressed like the older ladies at church, though her face wasn't wrinkled like theirs. She had worn her hair in a bun, and she wore glasses that seemed to make her eyes look very large. He had been more than a little intimidated by her before he had gotten to know her.

There had been many "Mrs. Potts" in Michael's life. People who had tried to help, those who had made a real difference. Like Mr. Tissot, a French immigrant who owned a bakery on Grand Street.

Mrs. Potts had sent Michael there with a sealed envelope. Michael tentatively handed it to the gruff, flour-covered, bearded man, and though he never knew what it said, he knew it must have pleaded his case, because the baker became a mentor. He began by speaking simple French phrases with Michael, and in time quickly moved on to speaking that language exclusively. Michael struggled to keep up, but that was just what he needed to really master the language. Mr. Tissot seemed happy to have someone he could converse with in his native tongue, since his wife had died a few years before and his children had moved away.

Mr. Tissot encouraged Michael each time he saw him, telling him that he spoke the language like a native Frenchman. He admitted that his was not the same French as that of aristocrats. Had Michael ever heard a rich person talk? Mr. Tissot had asked. Michael had, and he understood the difference Mr. Tissot was speaking of. He had always been attuned to the differences in Brooklyn-speak and Manhattan-speak.

Michael leaned back in the plane's soft leather seat and closed his eyes. He recalled how embarrassed he had been the first time he had gone to one of the fancy buildings in Manhattan, where even the doorman, in a navy blue coat with shiny gold buttons, had sounded different.

He was delivering a large order of salmon to a Mrs. Silverman. He had stood outside the revolving brass doors, shivering in the cold, while the doorman stepped inside the warm building to call the Silverman apartment. He had made Michael feel small and dirty before he stepped out of the door and started to direct Michael to the back of the building where the service elevators were located. But he had taken pity on the shivering boy, and instead, after a quick scan of the lobby, pointed to the lobby elevators. "Twenty-third floor. Make it quick."

Michael's older brothers had been delivering seafood to those fancy places for a couple of years already. Cassio's Fish Market had become very popular on the Upper East Side because the fish was fresher and cheaper. Michael couldn't imagine it could be very much cheaper, because the cost of sending a driver and delivery boy up from Little Italy to deliver in the area was, according to Mr. Cassio, added to the price of the fish. Mr. Cassio laughed about charging the rich people extra. He said they didn't really mind the small uptick in price. They valued quality more.

He had never been in an elevator with plush burgundy carpet and mirrors. With a shaking finger, he had pressed the button for the twenty-third floor. He was afraid to move as the elevator went up, though there was none of the shaking or rattling he had previously experienced in elevators. Although his brothers had bragged about being in these fancy buildings and had described the wealth and luxury, Michael's limited experience could not have prepared him for what he saw and felt.

His fear turned to intrigue as the elevator ascended, and by the time he had reached the twenty-third floor, Michael's intrigue had turned into desire which virtually shouted, "I want this, too!" all the while acknowledging that the only way he could have it was if *he* made it happen.

He had found the apartment he was looking for, and as he rang the bell, he had a strange premonition.

A man wearing a fancy black jacket cut all the way down to his waist answered the door. "But why are you at this door?" the man asked brusquely. Michael didn't have an answer, and after a few seconds the man sighed and said in an irritated voice, "Mon Dieu. Through there, young man," pointing down a long hallway toward what Michael figured must be the kitchen. But he had to pass by the dining room on the way, and he had seen three pretty ladies in black dresses, wearing frilly aprons and hats, bustling about and setting the table. He couldn't help himself. He stopped to stare.

"But why are you stopping here, little boy?" one of the pretty women had asked. "Go on, go on," she said, pointing to a white door.

Michael had been delighted. Although she spoke in English, she had an accent like Mr. Tissot's. Michael followed through on a hunch by saying, "Merci, mademoiselle."

"But what is *this*," she had exclaimed, laughing with the other two ladies in surprise. "Parlez-vous Français monsieur?"

"Oui, je parle français, mademoiselle."

"Est-ce que vous êtes français?" she had asked. He had almost laughed at that, her asking him if he were French.

"Non, mademoiselle."

"Mais, où est-ce que vous avez appris parler français?" one of the other ladies asked.

Michael was enjoying himself. "Les livres dan la bibliothèque," he had answered.

The ladies looked at him in disbelief, doubting that he had learned to speak their language merely from studying books at the library. Michael continued, "Aussi, je parle français avec mon ami de Little Italy, Monsieur Tissot."

The ladies had giggled, and one had clapped her hands in delight. "Quel charmante," she had said. "Tu es un garcon très sage et tu parles très bien le français."

Michael had been so pleased to be told he was smart and spoke the language well, that he had blushed and stammered his thanks in English.

Just then a woman who was to become one of the most important people in his life walked in. She was a very tall and imposing figure of a lady, but she was also beautiful, Michael had thought.

"Why have you stopped?" she had asked, looking at the three maids who were obviously doting on a delivery boy. "There is so much more to do."

As she said this, she looked at Michael, and then gave one of the maids a questioning look.

"He delivers fish, Madam, but he speaks French beautifully," she had said in answer to the unasked question. "Listen.

"Monsieur, comment vous appelez-vous?"

"Je m'appelle Michael Romano."

"Et, s'il vous plaît, dites madam où est-ce que vous avez appris parler le français."

Michael had repeated to her what he had told the maids: that he had learned French from studying books in the library and by speaking it with Mr. Tissot.

Mrs. Silverman had given him a smile that had warmed him all the way through, then said, "Bien. Maintenant, s'il vous plaît, emporter aux-la à lu cuisine—là bas." She pointed to the kitchen.

Michael nodded and said, "Mais bien sur, Madam, et merci pour votre amabilité."

"He really is a darling," Mrs. Silverman was saying as he made his way to the kitchen.

He was ecstatic! He had never spoken French to anyone except Mr. Tissot, and he had begun to wonder if anyone else would understand him. But these women had not only understood him, they had told him he was smart and charming.

He was walking on air as he handed the package to a man in a tall white hat. The hat had looked sort of like Mr. Tissot's baker's hat, but the man didn't look like a baker. He was giving directions to several different men who were cooking, and he didn't even look at Michael as he took the bundle from him.

"Ah, bien, le saumon," he said, but not to Michael. "Vit, vit... prepare this immediately," he said, handing the package to one of the men.

Another French person. How exciting it must be to live like this, Michael had thought. He was prepared to dazzle the man in the hat with his French when he was lightly shoved towards a door in the rear of the kitchen. He had looked questioningly at the man, but the man just waved him away.

Michael opened the door and found himself in a hallway by different elevators. These had a sign by them saying, "Service Elevators."

He had no idea where he was, but he figured these elevators could at least take him down to the ground floor. He was right, but as he stepped off, he realized he wasn't in the lobby, but in the back of the building. A door which had a sign saying, "Exit Only" was in front of him.

He had pushed it open, and with no small amount of regret, had stepped into the cold air.

"Governor," **the voice** on the intercom woke Michael. "We're getting ready to land."

Michael didn't remember dozing off. He had been lost in thoughts of the past, the last he remembered. "I must be more tired than I thought," he said aloud to himself as he sat up from his slumped position.

He recalled what he had been thinking about: Mrs. Silverman, and the first time he had met her. "Dear Edith," he said softly. She had been dead for years now, but he still held a big place in his heart for her. That fish delivery had been the beginning of what turned out to be the most interesting and educating years of his life. He had returned to her beautiful East Side apartment many times over the years, first as a delivery boy, then as a student, then finally as a friend.

Edith Silverman had taught Michael lessons he never could have learned from books. She taught him proper enunciation of English and French words. She had encouraged him to learn German. Though she didn't speak it fluently herself, her grandparents had immigrated to the United States from Germany, and she considered it the language of life. She taught him manners and social graces, and she taught him about the evils of prejudice.

He had been shocked when he learned that she was Jewish. Even in his neighborhood, the basic iron kettle of immigrants, Jews had been among the most mistrusted by his family. There were references to double-dealings in the old country, followed by colorful language, whenever the topic of doing business with Jewish-owned businesses was raised.

He had heard degrading slurs throughout his young life, and he was ashamed of himself for his initial feelings towards Edith when she told him she was Jewish.

He had been so confused. The woman was perfect in his eyes. But how could she be so perfect and be Jewish, too? He hadn't had to say anything. She understood his confusion and she had taken his hand and led him through years of history to help him understand.

That understanding had helped him deal with the cruelty and prejudices he had experienced as he grew up. After all, lowly immigrant Italians often felt the sting of racial slurs, too.

He had been devastated when Edith had told him that her husband had taken a position heading up a law firm in Philadelphia, and that they would be leaving.

"Et vous, mon cher," she had said, "You will become a lawyer, too, and you will be a great lawyer. In fact, you will be a great man."

Michael reflected again on how no one in his life had ever given him more of everything, including encouragement, than Edith Silverman.

REBECCA WARNER

He wondered for the millionth time at the lucky breaks he had been given, and as he unfastened his seat belt, he mumbled his thanks to the Big Guy upstairs who had made it all possible by saying, "Lucky son-of-a-bitch!"

8

THE HOT AIR hit Michael in the face as he stepped off the plane. He saw Hanes, Mr. Fulton's chauffeur, waiting at the bottom of the steps. He had hoped to see Caroline there, too.

"Hello, Hanes, how are you?" Michael asked as he extended his hand. Hanes took it, but Michael knew he was embarrassed to do so. Chauffeurs didn't usually shake hands with their employers, but Michael had long ago drawn the line for standing on what he considered stupid formalities.

"Fine, sir," Hanes replied. "Miss Caroline was sorry she couldn't be here, but she felt she should stay with Mr. Fulton." He paused before he could continue. "He is very ill, sir," he said, unable to hide his concern behind his clipped British accent.

"Then we'll be going straight to the hospital?" Michael asked.

"Yes, sir. Miss Caroline is expecting you there."

Hanes led the way, looking to his left and right as he did so. He was not as big as Manny, nor nearly as scary looking, but Michael knew that Hanes was a top-notch trained bodyguard first, and a chauffeur second.

He sighed. Sometimes he wished life was simpler. Money and power offered special privileges, sure; but with those privileges came some pretty heavy restrictions.

He climbed into the back of the cool limousine, which was still running. In less than ten minutes, they had arrived at the hospital. Hanes pulled right up to the front. He came around to open Michael's door.

"Shall I accompany you, Governor?"

"No need, Hanes, but thanks."

"Right. Room three five eight, sir. When you exit the lift on the third floor, turn to the right and go all the way to the end. But you'll want to stop by the nurses' station on the way. I'll be right here when you return."

Michael gave Hanes a smile, along with a mock salute. "Very good, thank you," he said. Hanes returned the smile and the mock salute.

Michael followed Hanes' directions to the intensive care unit. He stopped by the nurses' station and spoke quietly to one of the nurses on duty.

"I'm Michael Romano. I'm here to see my father-in-law, Pierce Fulton."

The nurse recognized him immediately and said, "Of course, Governor Romano, your wife told us to expect you. I'll take you to her."

Michael nodded and followed the nurse down the hall.

Caroline was sleeping in a chair next to her father's bed when Michael walked into the room. She looked so tired. Michael's heart went out to her, and to her father, who was connected, it seemed, to every machine modern medicine and his money could justify.

Although Michael had been quiet upon entering, Caroline woke up within seconds, as if she knew he was there.

"Darling!" she exclaimed in a loud whisper, as she rose to hug him.

"How is he?" Michael asked as he held her close.

"Not well, and getting worse."

"Is that what his doctor said?"

"No, that's what I say. I've been sitting here with him for two days, and his breathing seems to be even shallower."

"You can't judge by that, sweetheart," he said, kissing her hair. "He's in a coma. Now please tell me what his doctor said."

"He said father had a cerebral hemorrhage. He warned me that massive bleeding strokes are fatal about forty percent of the time within the first month. That's why I have to stay with him. There's nothing I can actually do, but I feel better just being here with him."

"Of course you do." Michael looked into her eyes, hoping to reassure her. "He's going to be fine, Caroline. He's made of strong stuff."

Caroline sighed and put her head on his shoulder. "I'm glad you're here."

"Me, too. I've missed you."

"I've missed you, Michael."

Caroline gave him another hug then went back to the chair. She looked exhausted but glad to see him. "How was Janice's dinner party?" she asked.

"Superb. Just one flaw, though."

"A flaw? What?"

"You weren't there."

Caroline smiled. It was a tired smile, but an appreciative one.

"I hope my not being there didn't cause too much of a problem for Janice?"

"It didn't seem to. Not at all. You were missed, but lovely Mallory Wain took your place as my dinner partner."

"Oh, no."

"Yes, but I survived. She really is a very nice woman, you know."

"But a pain in the..." Caroline didn't finish. She let Michael.

"...ass," he said, laughing with her.

"So who sat beside you?"

He knew she wasn't asking about who sat to his left. Of course that would have been the hostess. She wanted to know who was on his right, since Mallory had been moved from that spot. But why? Did she hear something? Did she suspect something? How could she? No, she was just curious.

"A woman who neither of us knows, really," he hedged. "A wealthy widow, who plans to donate quite a bit to my campaign," he added, assuming she would draw the conclusion that widow equaled old.

"Lucky you," she kidded. "Seems you can't help attracting old ladies who want to give you money."

Michael thought it best to leave it there and not invite any more questions.

"Anyway, it was a very successful party. Everyone asked about you and your father. People really care."

Caroline's eyes watered. Michael went over to where she was sitting and bent down to give her a kiss on the top of her lovely blonde head.

"Have you eaten?" he asked. He was concerned about how tired she looked, but didn't want to tell her so.

"Yes, they brought me some lunch a while ago. Are you hungry?"

"No, I just thought you might need a break."

"I just want to stay with father. You understand, don't you?"

"Of course. I'll stay with you for a while. Do you think we could get another chair in here?"

"I'll go ask."

"No, I'll ask. You stay here."

Michael stayed for about an hour, but then felt he just had to get out of that room. The monitors, the nurses, the smells...they were making him crazy.

"Sweetheart, I better go," he said, giving her hand a squeeze.

"I know. I'm so glad you came. Thank you, Michael."

"Why do you always thank me for things? I love you. I do things because I want to."

"I know that. But wonder if I never said thank you? Wonder if I never told you how much I appreciate everything you do for me? You do the same thing, you know. That's what makes us want to keep doing for each other, knowing the other appreciates it. It doesn't hurt to say it often."

Michael thought about what she said and realized she was right. It did make a difference in the way he wanted to do things for her. If she had taken him for granted, he might still do things, but grudgingly. No, he did things because he loved her, and because he knew she appreciated them.

"You're right," he said, leaning over to kiss her. "And you're welcome. I love you, Caroline."

"I love you, too, darling." She stood up and gave him a tired hug. "Have a safe flight back."

"I guess you don't really know when you'll be back in Tallahassee."

"No," she sighed. "I have to stay with him, at least until he comes out of the coma. *If* he comes out of the coma," she finished with a weary sob.

"Of course he will, sweetheart. He will."

He held her close, and when her sobs stopped, he gave her a kiss. "Call me later?"

"Yes, but probably not until tonight," she sighed. "I may go back to the house for a couple of hours."

"Good. You could use a break from here."

"But wonder if..."

"I know. But take care of yourself, too, Caroline. You won't be any good to him when he does wake up if you're worn out. Okay?"

"Okay," Caroline agreed with another tired sigh. "I love you."

"Love you, too. Call me this evening."

It was with real relief that he climbed into the back of the frigid limo that was waiting right where Hanes said it would be. He loved Caroline and wanted to be with her whenever she needed him, but like most people, he couldn't stand hospitals.

After he had settled into his seat on the plane, he took out his calendar and began checking off the events which might have to be moved or canceled, depending on when Caroline might come back to Tallahassee. Some he had to attend whether she was with him or not. Others really called for her to be there. What a mess. He would have Lynn handle it. Caroline would probably be back within a week. Lynn could juggle the schedule for that short period.

Michael sighed when he realized he would be a whole week, at least, without Caroline. He was going to miss her. His schedule, he could see, wouldn't even allow for half a day to get back down to Palm Beach. But he understood that she had to stay. He knew that her father was, next to him, the most important person in her life.

Man, he hoped Mr. Fulton didn't die, for all the right reasons of course, but for some selfish ones, too. He didn't know if he could handle Caroline's grief, the special session, and the re-election campaign circuit all at the same time.

He was inexplicably bushed. He slept through the remainder of the flight, and was glad to crawl into bed after a quick dinner and shower, and a short phone conversation with Caroline. And as is so often true of a man with a clear conscience and a tired body, he slept a very sound sleep.

If he had known that night that it was to be his last sound sleep, he might have appreciated it more.

9

MICHAEL WOKE UP a half-hour early. It was only five o'clock, but he felt totally refreshed. He quickly went over in his mind what he had to do today, then got out of bed to start his morning exercise regime. Forty-five minutes later, he was on his way down to his office.

Breakfast was waiting for him when he got there. That was always the case. No matter what time he got up, his breakfast was ready on time. He wondered again how the kitchen staff always knew he was up when their quarters were in a separate part of the Governor's Mansion.

He took a sip of hot coffee and then sat down with the *Tallahassee Democrat* to eat his breakfast. There was a short article in the bottom right-hand corner of the front page announcing his meeting that day with six female legislators who were planning to ask the governor to reconsider calling a special session. They hadn't wasted any time in requesting the meeting. Though the papers had announced the special session only three days ago, these women were obviously prepared for that announcement, and had no doubt planned to ask for this meeting as soon as it was announced.

He had to hand it to them. They had bullied their way into his schedule as few others could have. Michael wondered if his secretary, Lynn, was sympathetic to their cause and had arranged his schedule so that an extra hour was squeezed in to accommodate them. He had been somewhat surprised to see their names on the revised schedule that Lynn had handed him Friday afternoon. But it didn't matter. No preparation was necessary. Of course Lynn knew that, or she wouldn't have scheduled the meeting in the first place.

Michael finished breakfast and walked over to his desk to pick up the stack of messages that was waiting for him there. He felt his heart leap as he read the third message in the stack. It said, "Mrs. Kristin Long. Important." He looked at her number.

Why would Kristin be calling him? Michael had no intention of calling her back. He crumpled the message and threw it in the garbage can. *Fini.*

He finished going through the other messages, but since it was too early to return any of the calls, he put them aside and sat down to dictate. But he found he couldn't think clearly, couldn't dictate in his normally articulate manner. Images of Kristin kept popping into his head, and no matter how he struggled to get on with the business of the day, she kept coming to mind.

Thoughts turned to fantasy. He wondered what kind of a lover she would be. She had a great body. Sexy. Would she be as aggressive in bed as she was out of it? He gave in slightly to the fantasy, until an erection cornered him, causing a fresh wave of guilt to wash over him.

"Dammit," he said out loud. He had to get this woman off his mind. But how? Only one way. Tell Caroline about Kristin. She knew the scenario well—women who threw themselves at her husband. Yes, that was it. He wished she were here right now so he could go and tell her, and neutralize the situation before it became troublesome.

But she wasn't here. Michael found he felt better, though, for having made the decision to tell her.

With that burden seemingly lifted, he proceeded to get a lot of work done, and was surprised when Lynn buzzed him to let him know that Les Jenkins was here. Was it eight o'clock already? Lynn must have just arrived herself.

"Hey, Mike, sorry to hear about Caroline's father," Les said as he came in, extending his hand. "Anything I can do?"

"Thanks, Les, but there's not much anyone can do right now except wait and see. I'll be sure to let Caroline know you asked."

"You do that. Give her my best. Tell her I'm praying for him."

Michael knew Les was sincere. Les was a deeply religious man, but he didn't let his religion get in the way of running an effective, if not exactly squeaky-clean, campaign.

Michael simply nodded his appreciation.

"What do you think of my latest report?" Les asked, getting down to business quickly to prevent the mood from turning maudlin.

"Very interesting, especially your prediction that Chuck Garner will get into the race. Where did you get your information?"

"Where do I get any of my information? From one of my many sources. In this case, the source happened to be a close, mutual friend," Les confided.

"Reliable?" Michael asked.

"You bet."

"Well then, Les, this is serious stuff. If he looks like a real contender for the Democratic Party nominee, this race will take on a whole different tone. He's a popular senator. And he's a Florida Gator from the 6th District. Lot of money in that area around Gainesville. Plus he's likeable, damn likeable. Hell, I like the man." Michael gave Les a smug smile. "Just not in this seat."

"Everything I know so far is in that report," Les told Michael. "I wouldn't include anything that I hadn't confirmed. So you can be ninety-nine percent certain, based on info from my sources, that's he's going to run."

"Who's going to primary against him? Until now, Ken Rolland was the only Democrat's name I heard."

"Democrats are backing Ken Rolland pretty strongly right now, but when Chuck officially lets his interest be known, I have a feeling that they will drop Ken like a hot potato and back Chuck. I don't expect him to announce his intentions for another two or three months, though."

"Why would he wait so long?"

"His wife had breast cancer. She's still doing chemo, and they're not sure how she's going to make out right now. My guess is, if she responds well to chemotherapy, he'll run. If not..." Les' voice trailed off.

"God, I'm sorry to hear that. I've met Florence. I haven't heard a thing about her having cancer. Distressing news."

"I can appreciate how you feel, but you've got a lot riding on her health, I think."

"Les, don't be crass. Look, let's say he does announce his candidacy three months from now. That gives us an awful long lead time. We can lay a lot of solid ground work in that time."

"Sure we can, but we can tear up some solid ground, too. Like with that special session you're so intent on calling."

"Not you, too? Hey, that's one area we won't get into today. I've got my share of problems with that already. You know about the six female legislators I'll be seeing this morning?"

"Of course. They're not going to come at you easy."

"I know. But I also know that if I just stand behind my principles, I'll make them see things my way."

Les hesitated, about to say something more, then changed his mind. "Whatever, Mike. Now listen. I've got something else to discuss with you that's just come up."

"Shoot," Michael said, relieved he wasn't going to get into any arguments with Les about the special session.

"Well, I got a call yesterday at home from this lady named Kristin Long," Les started.

If Michael's reaction showed, Les didn't seem to notice, because he continued without pausing.

"I knew her husband, Ted Long. Good man, but cancer got him early. Anyway, she told me she's a big supporter of yours. So far, it's only been in thought. Now she wants to do it in deed."

Michael was amused to think Les should know just what kind of deed Mrs. Long really had in mind.

But he didn't let his thoughts show. "Yes?" was all he said, with a studied nonchalance.

"The lady owns four corporations. That means she can contribute twelve thousand for the primary right there, along with three more personally."

"Not bad." Michael didn't tell Les that Kristin had already told him the same thing. She obviously hadn't told Les, or he would have said so. Les thought he was the original bearer of good news.

"Not bad, my ass. It takes our volunteers and campaign workers a lot of time and energy to accumulate that much money, based on your average contribution of twenty-five dollars. I'd say her kind of contribution should be rewarded."

"Rewarded? How?" Michael asked, continuing to be secretly amused with his own private jokes.

"I'm talking about a special fund-raising dinner. Very private, very exclusive, where she would be the guest of honor."

"The guest of honor? Really?"

"How many other people do you have lined up that are willing and able to make that big a contribution? Or even to raise that much on your behalf?"

"Okay, good point. Who else do you plan to invite?"

"Well, the way she and I figured it, we've got about a dozen people who have committed to raise ten-to-twenty thousand for you. Plus, we have five others who have already raised that sum, or more. I think we could go ahead and reel in some other people willing to raise that kind of money if we made this dinner real special. Send out engraved invitations, saying that, in acknowledgment of their generous contributions and pledged support, Governor Romano and Mrs. Romano request the honor of your presence at a private dinner party, to be held at the Ambassador, et cetera, et cetera. You get the picture."

"Why not here at the Mansion?"

"We could do that, but for what I'm thinking, you'd have to bring in extra staff. The Ambassador is well-equipped to handle something like this."

"True. Let me ask you, was this your idea, or Mrs. Long's?"

"Both, really. It just started growing as we talked. She's a sharp lady. Really nice, too. But you met her. Didn't you think she's a nice lady?"

"Yes, she's a nice lady. How well did you know her husband?"

"Pretty well, but I didn't run in his social circle. In fact, I first met Kristin at Ted's funeral. Why?"

"No reason, really. Anyway, I like it. It won't hurt to go ahead and get those contributions on the books. The campaign fund will pay for it?"

"It would, but Mrs. Long volunteered to underwrite the cost of it. I suggested that her contributions could be better put to use in other ways, but she wanted to do this, in particular."

"That's certainly generous of her to offer."

"It is, it sure is. So, do we go with this?"

"Yes. What date did you have in mind?" Michael asked as he reached for his calendar.

"How about Saturday, August twelfth? That's about three weeks from now. Your campaign schedule doesn't show any conflict. How about your personal schedule?"

Michael sighed. "You'll remember that Caroline and I planned to go to the house in France that week, though we hadn't decided on a specific date. But that was before this thing with Pierce. I'm sure she'll be back here by then, but she won't want to leave the country while he's recovering. So the twelfth is good."

"Okay. The invitations will go out this week. We need to get this booked as soon as possible."

"That sounds fine. I'm pleased about this, Les, thank you. And would you give my thanks to Mrs. Long?"

"Don't you think you should do that?"

"I don't know how to reach her."

"I've got her number."

"Okay, give it to me. I'll call her."

He thought it was ironic that he should end up calling her anyway. But if he had made an excuse, Les might have wondered why.

Les copied down Kristin's number, and after handing it to Michael, he stood to leave. "You might try to call her today, if you have time. If you wait, she might think you don't appreciate her efforts. No need to discourage a new patriot."

"I'll call her today," Michael promised as he walked Les to the door. "And thanks again. I appreciate your ideas for keeping the campaign coffers filled."

"Just doing my job," Les said, as he left.

Michael stood and walked over to the picture window. He liked to look out at the gardens when he thought.

He knew for sure now that Kristin Long was serious about bagging the prize. She was a surprisingly resourceful woman. Well, wouldn't she be discouraged when Michael showed up at the dinner with Caroline firmly planted on his arm? Surely no woman could imagine competing with Caroline for his attention. Their marriage was strong, and that was obvious to everyone who saw them together.

Michael shook his head in confusion and amusement. Again, he vowed he would tell Caroline about this woman's game. That would certainly serve to neutralize any guilt or any threat.

He stood at the window for several more minutes, allowing thoughts of Kristin Long to roll around in his head. He found himself becoming aroused again.

By the time he returned to his desk, for reasons still unclear to him, any thoughts he had of telling Caroline about Kristin Long had been dismissed.

10

LYNN BUZZED MICHAEL at exactly nine o'clock to let him know that all six of the pro-choice legislators had arrived. He had just finished discussing with his chief of staff the points he wanted to make. Michael relied on Henry to advise him on a wide range of policy issues, and he was glad he had sought his advice before the meeting. He thought Henry should stay, but Henry felt otherwise. Michael acquiesced.

"Send them in please, Lynn," he said, rising in anticipation of greeting them. Out of the one hundred sixty lawmakers, only twenty-six were female, but they could be a powerful voice when united in cause.

He greeted each one individually as she came in. They sat down quickly, as if anxious to get on with business. No small talk ensued. They came right to the point.

The first to speak was Representative Jane Rey Thompkins, a Republican senator from Sarasota. Jane was a petite, attractive woman in her mid-fifties, who had earned a lot of respect during her fifteen years in the Legislature. She used to say, "I'm small, but powerful—concentrated!" Michael had always liked her, and they had become good friends during his first year in the Legislature. She had been very supportive of him in his campaign for Governor of Florida. As a Republican, she should have been on his side now.

"Governor," she started, "every indication is that the people of this state would prefer to leave the abortion law just as it is."

"Current indications may seem to lean that way, Jane," Michael replied, "but we're finding that support for change is swelling."

"Not among my constituents."

Michael glanced at the faces of the other women. "Is that true for all of you?" he asked.

They answered in the affirmative in one voice.

"Governor," said Sarah Beeson, a second-term senator who had earned significant recognition for her ability to get key pieces of legislation passed or killed. "We just don't feel it's necessary to call a special session for this purpose. None of us is too pleased with the idea of showing up for a special session that's intended to change a very acceptable law."

He smiled at her, and nodded his head to indicate that he understood what she was saying: she didn't want to be bothered with a special session.

"Well, Sarah, you may not be pleased about showing up, and I understand that. Really I do. We're all very busy. But the law, of course, requires you to be there, and you might just want to help make it a productive session."

Sarah felt the governor was being condescending. "Governor Romano, this session can be nothing but counterproductive. We may be required to be there, but a majority vote can end the session in three minutes. Wouldn't it be better for you to reconsider—in light of the fact that we are here, representing many of our peers—even calling this special session? Surely you know your announcement was not well received by other legislators?"

"Some, of course. Others, many, are supportive."

"What about Senator Campbell?" Sarah challenged, referring to the President of the State Senate.

"He has expressed some concerns, but he's overall supportive."

"I don't think so, Governor."

"Sarah," Michael said, "I have heard none of the overwhelming negativity about this session that you are referring to."

"Well, now, Governor, why do you think *we're* here?"

Michael smiled. She was right about that. They were here to give their negative points of view about the special session.

"For precisely that reason," he replied with a wan smile.

Sarah returned the governor's smile, but she was here for a serious purpose.

"Yes. And if you think we're alone on this, well, you might need to crack your window a little more to hear what's really being said."

Michael started to reply, but was cut off by Representative Eleanor Ferguson, a Democrat from Orlando.

"Governor, if you have to address this law," she said, "why not hold off until the regular session next year? That certainly makes a lot more sense."

"Eleanor, this needs to be addressed now," he responded.

"Why does it have to be addressed now, Governor Romano? The law as it stands has been in effect since 1973. What's the urgency?"

He kept getting cut off. Before he could answer, Sarah Beeson charged him with "striking while the iron was hot."

He admitted to them that the Supreme Court's ruling indicated that they were more willing to tamper with the *Roe v. Wade* decision, and that, indeed, he felt that was an indication that the general population was ready to address it in more serious ways, too.

"Really, Governor," Eleanor countered, "I think that the population, so to speak, is more concerned with providing access to safe medical abortions for women. Surely you remember how it was before *Roe?* Women died as a result of abortions that were so-called 'banned,' but that didn't prevent them from having abortions anyway. You know what happened when they went to backroom butchers, and you must believe they have the right to have safe clinics and hospitals available to them."

Michael calmly answered her, "The unborn child's rights have to be the first consideration, Eleanor."

"You can't really set aside the law and a woman's rights like that," Eleanor replied, shaking her head in disbelief.

The other women vigorously echoed her sentiments.

"Eleanor, the rights of the unborn are not just a woman's concern. The rights of the unborn transcend either male or female concerns. It's simply a concern for life, period."

Eleanor was not to be deterred easily. She was a formidable opponent, and she wasn't afraid to pull out the stops.

"A concern for *life,*" she mocked. Gathering momentum, she continued. "Don't you think it's just a bit ironic, Governor Romano, that you are both pro-life and pro-death?"

"I beg your pardon?"

"Pro-life for the unborn, pro-death for convicted murderers. For one who holds life in such high esteem, you sure haven't backed down from the death penalty. In fact, you've *escalated* that effort."

"There's a difference, Eleanor," he replied resolutely.

Eleanor bit her tongue to refrain from sarcasm. Instead, she said in a calm, controlled tone, "Perhaps you could explain that difference to us, sir."

Michael responded with what he felt in his heart. "A convicted murderer has had a chance at life. Like everyone, he is born with a clean slate. What he chooses to write on that slate leads him down certain paths. As a murderer, he has chosen a dead-end path."

He paused and smiled, "No pun intended."

Since there was absolutely no response from any of the women, he continued. "He has taken a life he had no right to take. In doing so, he forfeits all of his own rights—even the right to live.

"But an unborn child...to take his life, even before he has a chance to make his first mark on his slate, well, it's just not fair. He deserves a chance. Sure, he may screw up. But he might be someone who is meant to change the world for the better. If he's aborted, the world never knows. With a murderer, the world does know, and it has passed judgment. The death penalty only serves to carry out the laws of this country. And of God. 'An eye for an eye.'" Michael concluded. He indicated he was finished by putting out his hands, palms turned upward, and shrugging his shoulders.

The women said nothing at first, nor did they look at each other, though they were all thinking the same thoughts. Eleanor voiced their thoughts.

"Michael," she said more sympathetically. "We believed that you wanted to call this special session for selfish reasons. I believed that you were using the wrong issue to make headlines across the nation, and to enhance your political career, which just might happen, if you were successful.

"I had no idea that you had such strong *personal* convictions about abortion. And while I can admire the strength of your convictions, I must also warn you away from them. There are opinions you must consider other than your own." She stopped to look at the other women, who were nodding their agreement with all she had said.

The next to speak was Justine Holloway, a representative from Tampa. She was the only black female legislator, and she had suffered prejudices, Michael knew. But he also knew that she didn't have a chip on her shoulder, and that she was there to get a job—any job—that needed to be done, done.

"I agree with Eleanor on that point, Governor. I understand you may personally feel passionate about this, but you have an obligation greater than your own personal agenda."

Michael acknowledged there was some merit in her words. Before he could respond, she continued. "You know, some might say that I have a special interest in being here because I'm black, and that I have something to say about the situation of the blacks in this country, who represent the fastest growing portion of the population. But the fact is, I'm here because *all* women are going to lose if there is any change in the law as it now stands."

"Justine," said Michael, "I understand your point, but I don't agree with it. Let me say this again. It's the rights of the unborn I'm concerned with. It's impossible to straddle the fence. But you—all of you—need to know that I am not opposed to abortions in cases of rape or incest. Or to save a woman's life. That shows I'm being fair about this."

"That's all well and fine, Governor," Justine responded. "Because if you didn't include those exceptions, you'd be labeled a zealot." She smiled a benevolent smile in response to Michael's raised eyebrows and continued to speak. "But there's another extremely important issue to address here. If you try to ban counseling and abortions in public hospitals for women who are too poor to pay for private care, then you're going to find yourself with a lot more problems on your hands. This whole country is. Do you know what I'm talking about, sir?"

"I think so, but please go on, Justine," Michael said.

"I'm talking about the number of crack babies that are being born by the thousands here in Florida alone. These are babies whose care is completely dependent on public money for survival.

"There would be many more born if counseling and abortions were not available for indigent women. Did you know, that among blacks, there's an attachment of social status to teenage motherhood? How can we hope to change that attitude if no counseling is available? And that attitude needs to be changed, because teenage motherhood is an expensive proposition, emotionally as well as financially."

"I agree with that point," Michael said.

"I'm glad you do, because I want to put a question to you. Do you know what it costs the government to treat and provide for a crack-addicted baby until his eighteenth birthday?"

74

Michael had seen the numbers. "Yes, I do."

"Then you know it's over a quarter of a million dollars. And do you know what the cost of five counseling sessions or one abortion is to the government?"

"About five hundred dollars?" he answered cautiously.

"Right. Now you tell me, Governor, if a woman wants to be counseled, or wants to have an abortion, but she can't, because she's poor, and always will be, and there are no public facilities available to her, what chance does she—or her baby—have to draw pretty pictures on *their* slates?

"Really, Governor," she continued, gathering even more steam, "how can we talk about the rights of a fertilized egg, when we don't care enough to see that every child is born into a stable, safe, and nurturing environment? It seems to us," Justine continued, nodding to the other women, "that once a baby is born, there is no concern for the peace and security and love of that baby. As it is, one in five American children lives in poverty, including a third of all Hispanic and two-fifths of all black children. Almost one in seven children is born to a teenager."

Without allowing Michael to respond, Justine continued. "And let me throw some more figures at you. There are five hundred and seven babies born in Florida each day. Of those, one third are born to mothers who did not receive adequate pre-natal care; seventy are born to teenagers; thirty-nine are low birth weight babies who are at much greater risk of health and development problems as they grow. And way too many are born to mothers addicted to drugs." Justine leaned back and let out a long sigh, indicating she was finished.

The silence in the room was one of respect, and one of sorrow. Michael was sensitive to her issue, and he was giving her words the weight and consideration they merited. But his heart, and consequently his expression, remained unchanged. Justine knew she had failed to change the governor's mind, even a little.

The silence was broken by Beverly Marks, a Democratic senator from Miami, who had said nothing up to this point. She had watched these remarkably bright, dedicated legislators swing their weightiest weapons at the governor's thick wall for three quarters of an hour now, with no advance. She doubted that any group of legislators, male or female, would be able to change his mind.

Beverly was a real political veteran. Almost twenty years in the Legislature had taught her to be especially tough and unwaveringly strong. Some chose to label those characteristics as bitchy. Beverly didn't mind, because she knew that despite the derogatory reference, she was respected. When she spoke she was right on point, and she seldom wasted words.

"Okay, Governor, then you are not going to change your mind about calling a special session. Right?"

"Right, Beverly," Michael said, unconsciously squaring off to the woman.

"And it's obvious that you are not going to be swayed by anything we say, or by the results of the polls."

Michael realized she was pushing him into a corner, where he would be forced to admit that nothing said here today had carried any weight. That would make him look totally unreasonable. He didn't want that.

"Now, Beverly, I..."

"*And*," she escalated the attack, not giving him a chance to respond, "We know the election is only fifteen months away, and you intend to use this issue in the hopes of gaining political momentum. We think this action will do the exact opposite for you. We're actually trying to save you from yourself."

Michael leaned forward in his chair. "Save me from myself? I don't see that as your role, Beverly. I have good people in place to advise me, and none have predicted as dire an outcome as you."

"Dire outcome," Beverly repeated. "I'll tell you the dire outcome. This abortion issue will be your undoing. You won't have the support of your own Party, because everyone knows this is a volatile issue. And polls clearly show you won't have the support of the great majority of voters in this state.

"And I promise you, Governor," Beverly continued, "that we will use every maneuver available to us to make sure your bills never even make it out of committee. They will die a quick death because we won't let them face a vote of the full Legislature."

There was a virtual roar of agreement from the other women.

Michael was livid to think they would pull such a stunt. "That's a counterproductive scheme, Beverly, and one I doubt you'll be able to pull off," he postured.

"Don't underestimate us, Governor. We women may be only fifteen percent of the legislative body, but we know our way around and we know our own power. And, we are doing the will of our constituents, unlike you."

Michael struggled to tamp down his temper. He forced control into his voice as he tried another approach. "Have you women ever even considered the rights of an unborn child? Has any one of you asked yourself, 'What is an unborn?' Do you think that, just because you can't see it and touch it, it's not real, not alive? Have you considered that, at only eight weeks, when it's called a fetus, it has all its organs in place? That its heartbeat is detectable? That the limbs and hands and feet have taken shape? And, most important, that the neural cells in the brain have begun to connect? It moves at that point, ladies. Can you really, in good conscience, ignore the fact that there is, indeed, a *life* to be considered, and that *that* life has just as many rights as the mother? Even more, perhaps, because it can't beg for its life, and so someone must do so for it."

Michael took a deep breath at the end of the uninterrupted, impassioned monologue, and asked with all the commiseration in his heart, "Can you really, truly, have so little regard for *that life*, ladies?"

"You've done your homework, but you've cherry-picked your points, Governor. Allow me to put a medical spin on this," said Angie Jennings, a senator who was also an M.D, and who was widely acknowledged for her mental acuity. "At twelve weeks, although the fetus is certainly starting to look like a little human, the neural circuits responsible for conscious awareness are yet to develop. We know that the brain structures necessary for conscious experience of pain do not develop until twenty-nine to thirty weeks, while the conscious processing of sounds is only made possible after the twenty-sixth week. Those are scientific, medical facts. You talk of life in the abstract, whether you realize it or not."

She took a deep breath before continuing. "Let's talk about life in the real sense. What's really at stake here is a woman's right to choose what to do with her own life and her own body. That fetus cannot survive outside of her body. It is a part of her body. It cannot breathe on its own. It is not viable.

"And I'm going to take this opportunity to put a religious spin on it, because I'm a Christian, and I studied theology while I was studying medicine. I've brought you something I want you to read," she said, handing him a sheet of paper.

She handed copies to the other women as well, and began reading out loud:

"In 1968, <u>Christianity Today</u> published a special issue on contraception and abortion, encapsulating the consensus among evangelical thinkers at the time. It featured numerous articles dealing with reproduction, including abortion and contraception. The issue contained what was called "A Protestant Affirmation" that stated: "Whether or not the performance of an induced abortion is sinful we are not agreed, but about the necessity of it and permissibility for it under certain circumstances we are in accord."

She continued reading:

"In that same issue, in the leading article, professor Bruce Waltke, of the famously conservative Dallas Theological Seminary, explained the Bible plainly teaches that life begins at birth: 'God does not regard the fetus as a soul, no matter how far gestation has progressed.'

"The magazine, <u>Christian Life</u>, agreed, insisting, "The Bible definitely pinpoints a difference in the value of a fetus and an adult.

"And the Southern Baptist Convention passed a 1971 resolution affirming abortion should be legal not only to protect the life of the mother, but to protect her emotional health as well."

Michael was stunned. "But the Catholic Church..." he started to say, but Angie interrupted him.

"Has long held that abortion was against God's law. That it is tantamount to infanticide. But the Protestant Church didn't believe that, as you've heard and read here, until televangelist Jerry Falwell spearheaded the reversal of opinion on abortion in the late 1970s. He led his Moral Majority activist group into close political alliance with Catholic organizations against the sexual revolution, and especially against *Roe v. Wade*."

"I just find this difficult to believe," Michael said.

"But you can't ignore it, because you have the evidence in hand. And you're relating to the Catholic doctrine, not the original Protestant doctrine, by giving a fetus' rights more weight than a woman's rights."

Beverly Marks jumped in. "If you really want to understand the difference, Governor Romano, consider this simple fact: fetuses can't vote. Women *can*." Beverly had gathered a head of steam, which no doubt propelled her next stinging volley. "And we all know *that's* really what is most near and dear to your heart."

This last jab stunned them all into a collective silence. Michael was fuming at the attack, but he responded in a carefully modulated voice. "Thank you, ladies, you've made your points, and quite well, I might add. But we are at an impasse. I'm still going to call the special session, you're still going to be compelled to attend, and we'll have a vote. This is an issue that the Supreme Court's latest ruling has put in the spotlight. Opinions on abortion rights are shifting, and I'm going to give it the sunlight it needs to clarify where things stand in Florida."

Their continued, smoldering silence made it obvious to Michael that they had made their choices, just as he had made his, and nothing said here today had changed that. And so, with no hope remaining for reconsideration on either side, the meeting between these powerful foes was essentially over.

Michael initiated the end of the meeting by standing up and saying, "Ladies, we've seen here today how emotional an issue this is. That's why I can't wait until the regular session to address it. An issue as emotional as this deserves attention on its own, and it's my job to make sure it gets it."

It was obvious to everyone in the room that any further discussion was pointless.

"Well, Governor," said Michelle Stevens, a less experienced but quite respected senator from his own back yard, Palm Beach. "We'll see you there. But don't look for smiling faces in their places. We're going to fight you on this, and hard. I know you haven't set a date for the session yet, but you'll need at least two months. You better believe we're going to use that time to our advantage."

And so the line was drawn, the sides chosen. Nothing either side could say would improve the situation.

Few words and fewer courtesies were exchanged as the women rose and left the room. As he watched them go, Michael had an eerie premonition. Beverly's words came back to him: "This abortion issue will be your undoing, Governor." And for the first time in his charmed life, Michael Romano came face to face with the possibility that he just might be vulnerable, and that there might be a situation he could not control.

That thought sent an unexpected and unfamiliar shiver down his spine.

11

MICHAEL FOUGHT BACK the feelings of resentment that were beginning to surface yet again. Caroline was spending too damn much time in Palm Beach.

Although he had pleaded with her to fly back to Tallahassee for tonight's dinner, she had begged off, saying that her father seemed worse.

Pierce Fulton had been home for over a week now, and around the clock, he had two of the best nurses his money could afford. Michael could see no reason why Caroline should have to stay by his bedside for days on end. The pace of going back and forth between Palm Beach and Tallahassee over the last month had proven to be a terrible strain on both of them. That, plus the pressures that had been building over the special session, had caused him to become tired and irritable. He hadn't slept well in weeks. Dammit, he wanted his wife at home.

This was one of the most important times of his career. Surely Caroline understood how important these fundraising events were during this re-election year, especially with the special session pending. It was a crucial time, he had reminded her. She had reminded him that her father's well-being was much more crucial at this time.

Michael wondered what was really bothering him. Could it be that he had been looking forward to wearing his "trophy wife" on his arm tonight, for Kristin Long's benefit? He hadn't thought of Caroline as a trophy wife before, though she was a real prize. Maybe he did need her for that purpose tonight.

As he tied his bow tie for the third time, he realized he was nervous. He knew it was because he would be seeing Kristin. He had stopped admonishing himself for thinking about her. The thoughts and feelings just crept in, and he couldn't push them away easily. As long as they were just that—thoughts—there was no harm being done, he told himself.

Was he kidding himself, he wondered, thinking that showing up with Caroline would neutralize everything that was evolving in relation to Kristin? It had worked before. He could think of several women whose arduous advances had been thwarted when Caroline had become a player in the game.

He had always brought her into the game, telling her what was going on. At first, she had teased him about being egocentric for thinking that other women were hot for him. It wasn't her fault, really, that she couldn't see what he saw. It was just that she was so secure in their marriage that she failed to notice. Not that she took him for granted, she had assured him. She was just sure of *him*, so that she didn't give any thought to what she saw as harmless flirtations by other women.

Once she became a player, though, she recognized the same signs that he did. There were some women who didn't care if a man was married or not, they made a play for him. Some made bigger plays than others, as Caroline had learned. There had been relatively few times that called for her to get involved. Michael was very adept at rebuffing advances, but some women just didn't get the message, or didn't want to. That was when he would bring Caroline into it, and she never failed to annihilate the opponent, with absolutely no effort or malice.

Caroline had a way of befriending women, so that any decent woman didn't want to continue the flirtation with their new friend's husband. Others weren't so decent, so Caroline and Michael had stood united with an invisible fortress surrounding them that no woman could possibly penetrate. All had eventually given up.

He hadn't told Caroline about Kristin Long, though. He wondered again why he hadn't. He had continued to dismiss the obvious answer. Instead, he blamed it on Caroline's already strained mental state over her father's health. He told himself he didn't need to bring up some petty flirtation. Besides, she wouldn't be inclined to care about something so minor in comparison to her dear, sick father, now would she?

There was that resentment again. Hell, a man could go just so far in fighting it. He would have liked to think he was above it, but he wasn't. He missed his wife, plain and simple. And he missed sex. He and Caroline usually made love two or three times a week. There always seemed to be time and energy for that.

But since her father's illness, the sex had been infrequent. And lately, when they had made love, it had been strained because one or both of them were exhausted; she with the vigil she kept, he with the travel and pressures of his office.

She had been back to the Mansion only four times in the last three weeks, and then for only one night each time. Even then, she had been so exhausted with the worry and care of her father that she had little energy to give to their usually fantastic lovemaking.

It had gotten a little old, too, explaining to people why she was never with him anymore. Oh, people pretended to understand, even feigning sympathy over and over again. But Michael felt that they must have thought it strange, too, that the governor's wife was so often absent.

He had attempted a few times, with various friends, to explain Caroline's devotion to her father. He was beginning to hate the sound of his own canned monologue, however, so he eventually quit trying to explain.

Maybe he was being too hard on Caroline and everyone else. Maybe others really were sympathetic. They might be even more sympathetic, he thought to himself with a touch of amusement, if they knew how little sex he was getting. The men would certainly be in his corner.

It wasn't just the sex, though. It was also the closeness of her. Her scent, her smile, her touch.

He pictured his wife naked, lying invitingly on their bed, beckoning, wanting him to make love to her.

And then the face and body morphed into that of Kristin Long. Michael struggled to push it away, but found himself too absorbed in the fantasy to let it go. It was nice...and arousing. He pictured Kristin's legs opening up, knees raised, as he lowered himself onto her.

He unzipped his pants and pulled out his penis, and watched himself in the mirror as it grew rigid. He closed his eyes and delved deeper into his fantasy. He was running his hands up and down her body. Now he was sucking her breasts. And now he was inside Kristin Long, looking into those remarkable eyes. His climax within his fantasy occurred at the same time his own climax brought him back to reality.

He knew for certain now, with no more excuses, why he hadn't told Caroline about Kristin Long.

Michael felt a heightened sense of sexual stimulation as he anticipated seeing Kristin again. He hadn't seen her since the Ashetons' party, and had only spoken with her professionally and briefly on the phone to thank her for her participation in tonight's dinner. But he had not been able to put her completely out of his mind, and the fantasy he had indulged in earlier that evening had only heightened his attraction for her. He knew he had to watch his step, though. He believed fantasies were fine as long as they remained just that.

Manny did his bodyguard thing, looking around as he escorted Michael into the Ambassador Hotel. "You're a great looking date, Manny. Think we can get together again later?"

"Yeah, you faggot. About three hours from now, when I pick you up at the front door."

Michael laughed. Manny was one of the few people who could get away with insulting him. He liked that Manny hadn't changed since the old days in New York.

"Wear something sexy for me," Michael joked in return.

"Man, you're getting weird. I better call Caroline and tell her to get her ass back up here."

"Hey, if you can get her ass back up here, you're a better man than I am."

"You just realizing that?"

"Asshole."

"Faggot."

Michael had made sure that he, along with Les, was the first to arrive. It was going to be important to greet people personally tonight. Man, he wished Caroline were by his side.

How could he go back and forth like this? He loved Caroline so much that he ached when she wasn't with him, yet he was looking forward to seeing another woman.

Michael enthusiastically greeted each guest. Many came from privileged backgrounds; others had made their own fortunes. It was a crowd of haves and have mores. Michael was in his element.

Les' wife, Jackie, was doing a wonderful job playing the hostess, greeting people along with him and Les. Michael looked at her admiringly. She was, he knew, responsible for rounding out any rough edges that Les had. Oh, Les still played the good-old-boy to the hilt, but Michael knew that he did that only so that his opponents would underestimate him. They were learning, though, that Les was not to be underestimated.

He was comfortable and genial in greeting each guest. The line was thinning when he turned to see that Kristin Long was next, and that she was with a date. As the guest of honor, Kristin should have been standing in the receiving line; but she had declined that tribute, despite Les' entreaties.

Seeing her with a date, Michael experienced a bewildering sense of disappointment. Her date was a damn good-looking guy, he noted with disquiet—and a surprising tinge of jealousy.

Kristin introduced Preston Thomas to the governor. Michael couldn't help liking the guy. He seemed easy going and self-assured. He looked Michael in the eye as he firmly shook his hand, smiling affably as he told Michael it was a real pleasure to meet him.

Michael was embarrassed as he shook Kristin's hand, because his earlier fantasy slipped back in as he did so. Her sparkling eyes looked into his as their hands touched, and he felt that she sensed his discomfort. Her eyes held his and seemed to be looking for more from him. Michael held her gaze, but offered nothing more as he said, "Thank you again, Mrs. Long, for your tremendous support."

"My pleasure, Governor Romano. And please call me Kristin," she replied with a beautiful smile. "Les told me your wife, Caroline, wouldn't be here tonight. I'm sorry that's the case. I was really looking forward to meeting her."

Before Michael could gather his wits to respond, she took Preston's arm and moved on.

Every guest had arrived on time. Being late to something like this wasn't fashionable. You didn't keep the governor waiting, even if there was a cocktail hour before dinner. Besides, everybody here wanted to get as close to the governor as he or she could. There weren't many such intimate opportunities like this for them to do so.

Michael gave one hundred percent of himself to everyone during that cocktail hour. Les and Jackie were especially magnanimous, and Les confided strategies to those who asked. He knew it made them feel important to be so close to the inside of the governor's campaign. He also knew that people wrote checks, and encouraged others to write checks, when they were feeling that way.

The Ambassador Hotel was Tallahassee's most luxurious venue for any event. The ballroom that was used for private parties was one of understated luxury. Dinner was delicious and elegant. Based on the garnered donations and pledges of fundraising, the party was an even bigger success, Michael surmised, than he and Les had anticipated. He had to hand it to Les, again. And to Kristin Long.

His eyes strayed to the end of the table, where she and Preston were sitting. Although he couldn't see all of her, he found he couldn't take his eyes off what he did see. She was such a feast for his eyes.

Each time he saw her, his attraction grew. He appreciated the way she dressed. Her clothes were always tasteful and expensive, and she wore them with a sexiness that delivered, to him anyway, a knock-out punch. Tonight she was wearing a strapless white dress that hinted at the lushness of her breasts, which were enticingly, yet modestly, on display. His eyes were drawn to a stunning sapphire drop necklace that stopped just above her appealing cleavage. Michael guessed the stone to be about five carats. She wore her hair up in a soft, feminine style, so that her sapphire earrings, which were smaller than the necklace but identically cut, set off her beautiful face and eyes.

From a purely egotistical standpoint, he couldn't help being disappointed that she didn't seem interested in him tonight. She rarely even looked his way, and when she did, she failed to meet his eyes. He found himself growing unaccountably agitated as she flirted with Preston, inconspicuously pressing her breast into his arm as they laughed together. He wished for the hundredth time that Caroline were at his side. That would sure diminish Kristin's sexy self-assurance.

As he said good night to the guests, Michael kept an undetected eye on Kristin. He was pleased when she approached him, sans Preston, who was talking to Jackie. She held up a "one second" finger to Preston as she drew near to Michael.

Later on, Michael wondered at the timing that allowed the opportune moment to occur. Les was turned slightly away from him, saying good night to someone, while other guests were lagging at the precise moment Kristin reached him. As she shook Michael's hand, she placed a small card in it. Michael, though bewildered, had the presence of mind to slip the card into his jacket pocket without looking at it. A quick assessment of the crowd assured him that the exchange had gone unnoticed.

"I'll be alone," was all she said, as Preston caught up with her. He shook Michael's hand and uttered all the proper words of appreciation.

As Michael saw it, fate had intervened in the form of perfect timing, making the exchange possible. And, true to himself, he didn't take fate lightly.

"You okay?" Manny asked from the front seat of the limousine.

"Fine," Michael answered. Not caring to get into any conversation, he said, "Just resting. Long night."

Just as Michael knew he would, Manny said nothing else, leaving him alone with his thoughts.

He closed his eyes and put his head back on the seat, further ensuring that Manny wouldn't bother him.

He had to sort this out. She had practically ignored him all evening, and then she had stuck a card in his hand, inviting him into sin. He had to admit that he wanted to see how it would play out. After all, the elements of the chase were more important than the victory. Or were they?

So many things could go wrong. He was already nervous as hell and full of guilt at the mere contemplation of the act. And who knows, he thought, this woman could turn out to be a crazy person who could get me into a lot of trouble. She could have any man she wanted. Why was she pursuing him?

One time with her, and he would know for sure. But what if he got caught, for God's sake? His marriage would be ruined, not to mention his political career.

She had been careful, though. She had come to the party with a date. That was smart. Anyone who bothered to think about it would assume she was taking her date home. Michael had been nowhere near her all evening. She had been very discreet in handing him the card. She seemed as concerned about being careful as he did.

But then, of course, there was Caroline. What about her? God, he had never even thought about being unfaithful to her. But in thinking about it, he realized that maybe those times that he had told her about other women, he was really just scared, and he had used her to make sure he wouldn't stray. Could that be true?

He recalled one particularly tempting morsel of a woman, Bridgette, who had been the guest of one of their friends at the house in Cap d'Antibes. Hadn't he had a few choice fantasies about her, too? He recalled her sunbathing topless on the stretch of beach in front of their home, and how he had avoided her not-so-subtle advances when Caroline wasn't around. But Michael had been more tempted than he wanted to admit, so he had told Caroline about Bridgette's advances, and she had handled the situation beautifully. She had gone swimming with him that afternoon, going topless herself, showing off her own beautiful breasts and body. Their ardent play in the water in front of Bridgette had given her the message—he was not a man who could be seduced.

He had always exuded that hands-off message, even though he now realized it might not be true. Certainly Kristin Long didn't think it was true. Why? What was different? He realized he must be giving her a different message. He went over everything in his mind, every detail of each moment he had been in her presence. He knew he had said nothing to encourage her, but he also knew that he was attracted to her like he had never been attracted to any other woman since Caroline. And somehow, Kristin damned well knew it.

What made her so tempting to him? Sure, she was beautiful, but so were a lot of women. But this was different. He knew it, and she knew it, and there was no denying it.

He had to see her tonight.

12

MICHAEL TURNED RIGHT off Tennessee Street and stopped at the sign at the bottom of the hill and checked a map. He hadn't driven around Tallahassee himself, and he was usually so busy in the back of the limo that he paid little attention to how Manny always got him to where he was going.

Good old Manny. He had sure been pissed when Michael wanted to take his own car out, all alone. Maybe he shouldn't have told Manny he was going out. But no, this way he knew Manny would cover if anything came up, though nothing should come up since Caroline wasn't likely to call this late. Manny had been a bit of a problem, though. He was just so damn protective.

He couldn't let Manny drive him tonight, so he had gotten into his car and taken off too quickly for Manny to argue. He hadn't even taken time to change out of his tux. Well, Manny didn't need to know anything. After all, Michael didn't really know anything himself, except that he was driven by an impulse he couldn't control. Michael Romano, out of control. The thought made him smile.

Michael's good instincts for directions kicked in, and he made another right, realizing he had shot past where he should have turned off Tennessee Street. He followed the road about a quarter of a mile before making a left, taking him up a hill and around a curve. He followed that road for another half mile before coming to a walled-in area. He looked at the name of the apartments again, and at the address written on the card Kristin had given him: Bent Tree Apartments.

This was the place, but it looked very average, nothing like where he would have expected a woman like Kristin to live. He turned into the apartment entrance and maneuvered his car over speed bumps and around the turns in the apartment complex. He was looking for Building

H. Of course it would be the last building, he thought when he finally found it.

But now that he had found it, he was able to stop concentrating on directions and to look at the location of the building.

It was on the far north corner of the complex. To the east and south, it was surrounded by woods. There were no other apartment buildings in sight, as there had been on the north side. He checked the card she had given him for an apartment number. Number nine. His car rolled along slowly as he looked at the apartment numbers. It was the last apartment on the end—remote in respect to the rest of the complex.

He pulled his innocuous dark gray Monte Carlo into a guest space directly in front of number nine, next to a silver Mercedes. It had to be hers. The other cars were mostly older model Fords and Chevrolets and VWs. Just knowing it was her car sent a shiver of misgivings through him. What was he doing here? His chest was tight, and his stomach was doing flips.

"Fuck," he said aloud, "I can't do this." With the relief that comes with making a morally righteous decision, he put his idling car into reverse and backed out. Putting the car in drive, he pulled forward about ten feet, and then stopped.

He was here. He had come for a reason. And that reason, although base and immoral, had a grip on him.

Admit it, he thought to himself. You want to fuck this woman. Isn't that why you're here? You can't kid yourself about that. So just go on in and do it. Get this damn urge out of your system. With any luck, it will be totally disappointing. What's one fuck? Caroline won't know. Caroline. He loved her. He loved her enough to have been faithful to her all these years. He loved her no less now. So what had made the difference?

He was uncharacteristically confused, tormented with doubt and guilt. He asked himself why he wanted this woman. Was it pure physical attraction? Of course it was. But what else, he asked himself? He was hot for her, sure. But it was more than just physical, wasn't it? Was it her resemblance to the other great love of his life, his college girlfriend, Alison? What? *What was it?*

"Enough," he said out loud. He was going home. He would put this behind him.

A faint tap on his window startled him. It was her. His pulse raced at the sight of her.

He lowered the window. "I'm sorry, Kristin, I shouldn't have come. I can't stay."

She didn't try to hide her hurt and disappointment. "Why, Michael? You're here. Please stay."

She was wearing a casual skirt and blouse, and from her bent position of looking at him in the driver's window, he could see the enticing swell of her breasts. A primal male response rose up in him.

Their eyes met and locked, and Michael felt as if he were being pulled into the ocean by a rip current.

He was without a choice, giving into a force much greater than his own willpower. He was, after all, just a man.

He followed her into the apartment and was surprised to see that the inside was as pedestrian as the outside. There was a flat gold carpet, brown furniture and tables, and plain white walls with cheap pictures.

Kristin read his thoughts and said with a teasing smile, "The landlord has excellent taste, don't you think?"

"Landlord? Oh, you're renting this place?"

"Signed the lease yesterday," she replied. "After all, I couldn't exactly have you driving up to the front door of my home, now could I?"

Michael was confused, but then caught her meaning. "You rented this place for..." He didn't finish. He was at a loss for words.

"Exactly."

"But how did you know...?"

"I didn't. But I hoped. And I wanted everything to be in place, just in case." She pushed back her thick hair with a gesture which Michael recognized as nervousness, but it had a strangely seductive quality at the same time.

He was nervous, too. He felt like a fly in the spider's den, but there was something about this woman that made him wonder if this wasn't unusual behavior for her, too. He looked around the apartment and asked, "You wouldn't have any Scotch, would you?"

"You bet. And glasses to drink it from," she joked. She went into the kitchen, and Michael heard the clinking of ice falling into glasses.

This is it, get out of here, he told himself. But then she walked in, holding two glasses of Scotch, and he lost that train of thought. Man, she had a sexy walk. She walked closer to him, but she didn't hold out the glass to him. Instead, she paused and she set the glasses down on a table.

She hesitated only a couple of seconds before she stepped right into him, putting her hands on his shoulders, melding her upper body into his. It was such a strong, sexy move that it caused Michael to audibly catch his breath. His arms automatically moved around her waist. She pressed her entire body into his. She was tall in her high heels, so that her pelvis met his groin.

Michael expelled a breath of excited pleasure at the sensation of her lithe body pressed against his.

There was nothing tentative about their first kiss. Their lips met with equal ardor, and both felt that tingling sensation unique to a thrilling first kiss.

Michael's impatient hands slid down her back and caressed her buttocks. She felt his hardness, felt that his desire matched hers. He pulled her skirt up and slid his hands under it and into her silk panties. He caressed the smooth flesh of her buttocks, so smooth that he wasn't sure where the silk ended and where her skin began.

Her head was tilted back, her lips slightly parted, her eyes closed. She pressed harder into Michael's groin as she seductively rotated her hips under his hands.

His right hand slid up and out of the back of her panties, and he brought it around to stroke her thigh. She lifted her leg and shifted against him, offering him access. He moved his hand up and around to catch the edge of her panties with his right forefinger. He nudged them aside and plunged two fingers into her, finding her warm and silken and welcoming.

His fingers moved inside her with dexterity and intention, until Kristin gasped and clenched Michael's shoulders as she tensed and released with orgasm.

Kristin sighed with deep satisfaction, and then roughly pulled his mouth down to hers. Michael's arousal exploded when her tantalizing tongue found his.

He had never tasted a kiss like this before, never had such a desire to explore the lust of a woman's mouth in this way. Caroline's mouth was supple and yielding, but Kristin's insistent and probing. It was an exciting contrast.

He had no idea how long their lips, their mouths, their tongues searched and tasted. A primal hunger gored him. He was hungry for a different taste... the taste of forbidden fruit. He needed to sate his hunger.

He pulled away, astonished by his undeniable desire for more. He quickly unbuttoned her blouse and pushed it off her shoulders. He slid the straps of a pale blue silk camisole down her arms, and she shimmied out of both so that they fell to the floor.

His hands encircled her breasts, and he was delighted by how lush and full they felt in his hands. He started to compare them to Caroline's, but stopped himself. Instead, he bent his head, and his mouth found the rigid yet yielding nipple of her breast. Kristin moaned as he gently bit down on the nipple. A surge of greedy ardor shot through Michael, and he increased the force and breadth of his bite.

Kristin's sharp intake of breath caused Michael to pause, ready to retreat. But when Kristin said in her sexy, sultry voice, "Oh, yes, God yes," Michael inflicted even more pressure. He gauged her response—a sharp cry—before moving to her other breast. He teased the nipple with his tongue, then bit down and sucked with increasing vigor, testing the limits of her response to the pain she must be experiencing. He was sucking and biting with a gusto and roughness he had to fight to keep in check.

Kristin felt faint. She had never known any man with the physical forcefulness of Michael, yet he was exquisitely controlled, pushing her to an edge of pain and excitement she had never known. She cried out in surprise when she had an orgasm. She had never known there was such a thing—an orgasm through her breasts! It had sent an electrifying tingle all the way down through her stomach and into her groin.

"Michael, wait. Please, I..."

"The bedroom," he demanded.

"Wait," she panted. "You have to use a condom. I...I have some."

Michael thought for a second and asked, "Is there a health issue?"

"A health issue? No, a pregnancy issue."

"Kristin, I'll use one if you want me to, but I had a vasectomy. So if pregnancy is the only issue...."

"Then it's not an issue," she finished for him.

They wasted no time in reaching for more of everything from each other. He lifted her off the ground by her waist and planted her against his hip. She wrapped her legs around him. Her skirt was still pulled up and he could feel her moist heat against him, even through his slacks. Her naked breast was pressed into his arm. He carried her like that into the dark bedroom and tossed her onto the bed.

Michael fell on top of her, taking no notice of the expensive, hand stitched down comforter or the fluffy down pillows Kristin had brought into her lair. He was a man consumed with sating his pulsating lust. He kissed her again, deeply and roughly. He was still fully dressed, she half-so, but he could feel every heated sensation of her body through his clothing. It awakened a memory of erotica, of teenage explorations of bodily pleasures through the shield of clothing.

He pushed up her skirt and pulled off her panties. He ran his fingers enticingly along the soft folds of her labia, then pushed two fingers into her and deeply probed her silky-smoothness again.

Kristin pressed her face into Michael's neck to stifle a scream as an orgasm, her third now, ripped through her. "Michael," she gasped, "please...stop. I...I need to catch my breath...I've never..."

"You have until I get undressed."

He rolled off the bed and hurried to get out of his clothes. He heard one of the studs from his tux shirt flip off and hit the floor, but that didn't slow his progress. Kristin was now fully naked and stretched out on the bed. Michael gave an appreciative moan at the sight of her trim but curvaceous body.

He lowered himself onto her, and the flesh to flesh contact was exhilarating for both of them. He greedily took her nipple into his mouth again. He loved the sensation of her hard nipple and rounded flesh filling his mouth. Instinctually knowing that Kristin craved the painfully exquisite sensations his mouth could bring, he bit down harder.

Kristin's dual pleasure and pain soared, and she cried out in delight at Michael's ardent demands on her body and her senses. She ignited under Michael's manliness. It had been so long, and to feel this strong, demanding, powerful man's body taking control of hers nearly brought her to tears.

Michael had no desire to explore the more intimate parts of Kristin's body. There was no love or tenderness he needed to impart. His desire for her was strictly carnal. His sole intent in coupling with Kristin was to satisfy his own voracious sexual appetite.

He rose up over her. His throbbing penis was flush against the outside flesh of her vagina, where her heat and wetness melded them together. He drew back, and Kristin's knees rose in invitation.

Michael drove his entire considerable length into her in one shatteringly hard, thrusting stroke. When Kristin gasped, he pulled out almost entirely, and paused. But Kristin raised her hips higher and commanded, "More!"

Michael slammed into her again, and again, fast and then faster, each thrust jarringly hard and roughly demanding. Kristin took each plunge with a lusty, guttural moan that said she wanted it just this way, challenging him to strike even harder, to plumb even deeper.

Michael was overwhelmed by the astonishing pleasure he was feeling— pulsating lust and unchecked, deep, driving penetration like he had never known. It linked him, in a most profound way, to this woman he barely knew.

Their sexual union was so extreme that it was like diving into a vortex. With a level of intense pleasure and pain reserved for first time lovers of a most unique sort, they became lost in their coupling.

It lasted a minute, it lasted forever. Lost in time, lost in lust, they absorbed each sensation, moving in a hammering rhythm as those sensations soared. Fueled by the raw sexual power of their bodies pulsing in unison, they were propelled towards the ultimate, joint gratification.

In their final, equally demanding thrusts, they consummated the deepest, most primordial gratification either had ever known. Breathless and stunned, they collapsed into each other's arms.

Michael rolled to his side, keeping his arm around Kristin so that her head settled onto his shoulder.

"What the *hell* was that?" he murmured.

"You tell me," Kristin replied, sounding exhausted.

"No words for it," Michael said.

After a silent moment, Michael spoke. "That was fucking *amazing*, is what it was."

Kristin stroked his chest and snuggled closer to his side. "Oh, God, for me, too, Michael." She hesitated before speaking again. "I had no idea sex could be like that. I've never had so many orgasms. And it's been so long for me, I guess I just let every pent-up sexual desire pour out."

Michael was puzzled. "What do you mean, *it's been so long?*"

"Three years. That's why I'm not using birth control pills."

"Three years! A beautiful, sexy woman like you? Are you kidding me, Kristin?"

"No, Michael, I'm not. It's been three years. Since the year before Ted died. That was two years ago, and the year before that he was...well, he was dying from brain cancer. It was a long and painful fight for him."

Michael was at a loss for a response. It was unbelievable that this beautiful, sexy woman had not had sex since before her husband died. He had just assumed that a woman like her would have plenty of lovers. The realization of the boldness of the moves she had made to get him to this point suddenly struck him.

"My God, Kristin. The way you came on to me, I just assumed...well, that you were very sexually active."

Kristin rose up and looked at him. She could make out his handsome features in the dim light, but she could not read his eyes. She was glad for the dimness in the room, for she knew she was flushed, and not just from the aftermath of lovemaking. She was embarrassed.

"Michael," she said in the same shy voice which he had heard when he first met her, "I'm telling you the truth. I don't know what made me do what I did to...seduce you. If someone had told me that I would ever do something so bold, so scary, I would have thought they were crazy.

"But," she continued, "what about you? You know something drove you to be here. You're not exactly known as a philanderer. In fact, your marriage has been fairly canonized by the media and the social magazines. Is that a mistake?"

He paused before he answered. She had verbalized what he had been thinking. He could not have said what had happened to him to cause him to be here tonight.

"No, that's not a mistake. I'm very much in love with my wife."

In the darkness, he couldn't see the dismay upon her face.

"And I know you'll believe me," he said as he stroked her silky hair, "when I tell you that this is the one and only time since I married Caroline that I have been unfaithful."

Kristin took a deep breath to steady her voice before she spoke. "I believe you. Do you feel terribly guilty?"

"Of course I do." He paused, weighing what he was about to say to Kristin.

"I feel guilty, but at the same time, this sex was incredible. But I didn't have to tell you that did I?"

Kristin shook her head. Her long, luxurious hair shimmered in the faint light as she did. "No," she said. "You didn't have to tell me, but I'm glad you did. Words are important to me."

She laid her head back on his shoulder. They were silent for a few moments. Both were lost in their own thoughts and feelings.

Finally, Michael spoke. "Kristin, as fantastic as this was, I can't see it happening again. I'm already regretting it."

She felt a stab of pain. She knew she had no claim on him, but she hadn't taken this lightly, either. She swallowed hard to keep her threatening tears in check before she spoke. When she finally did, it was with a calm and reassuring voice.

"I understand, Michael. I know your wife has been out of town a lot. People talk. I took advantage of her absence to pursue this, I'll admit. I don't know why, exactly. I just found you so damned attractive from the first moment I met you. I guess I got what I wanted from this. I really don't expect more."

Michael was relieved. He had feared a scene. But this woman was taking it for just what it was—a one-time fling with a married man.

"Thanks for that, Kristin. Under other circumstances, I'd be back for more of this amazing sex. A lot more. But I can't let it happen again."

"And that's what it was, wasn't it, Michael? Sex, not lovemaking."

"Yes, it was just sex, Kristin. I only make love to my wife."

"I know the difference, too," she said with a sigh. "I made love to Ted, and it was wonderful. But I had fantastic sex with you tonight. Unbelievable sex, actually. I didn't know my body was capable of doing what it did. I never knew a man could go so deep, or that I could have so many orgasms. I never knew there was actual pleasure to be found in pain. Speaking of which...God, I'm sore," she said, rolling away from him and laughing.

"Do you want me to apologize?" Michael laughed with her.

"Oh, sure, apologize for giving me multiple orgasms," she teased him.

Michael laughed and pulled her to him. His body automatically responded to her sexy body against his. He was getting hard again. As long as he was here...

Kristin felt his ardor, and she was astounded. Does he really think he'll get to have sex with me again tonight, she wondered.

She moved to get up, but Michael tightened his arm around her shoulder.

"Kristin, could we..."

"No, Michael. You said it yourself. It can't happen again."

"But I'm here," he entreated. "It's still the same night, and you're so damn beautiful, so exciting."

Kristin lowered her head and smiled to herself. "Thank you. So are you, Michael, but I'd just like to remember it like it was. It was so perfect, I don't think it can ever be repeated."

She moved to get up again. He wanted to pull her back, but he stopped himself. He wasn't going to beg. He squelched a surprising tinge of hurt, mostly to his ego, and told himself it didn't matter.

He watched her silhouette in the dimness of the light as she walked into the adjoining bathroom. She moved with such grace. She really was a beautiful woman.

But he knew he had been given a cue to get up and get out. She came back in as he was putting on his shirt, which was minus a stud. He was about to suggest she turn on a light so he could search for it, but he was mesmerized by her approaching silhouette, which was backlit by the bathroom light. She was wearing a dark silk robe that clung to her curves and flowed with her movements.

She walked over to Michael and put her arms around his neck.

This was more like it, he thought. His amorous hopes were dashed, however, by her words. "I'm still going to support your campaign in every way I can, Michael. I believe in you." She kissed him then, tantalizing him once more.

His impulse was to grab her and throw her on the bed and take her again, but she pulled away and walked into the living room. He followed her, resigned to leaving. She had made it clear now that nothing more would happen.

He watched as she went into the kitchen adjoining the living room. He saw her set a teakettle on the stove. He didn't see her hands shake as she did.

Kristin didn't turn around. She felt awkward, unsure of how to end the evening with any dignity. I can't cry, she told herself. I can't. When she finally turned to him, she was wearing a smile.

Michael had been holding his breath, wondering if she would become uncomfortably emotional. He was relieved to see that she was so calm. He was certain now that she wouldn't do anything to embarrass him, here or in public.

She moved towards him slowly, and he opened his arms for her to step into a comforting embrace.

"Goodnight, Michael," she whispered, with a slight tremor in her voice.

He heard the tremor, and he understood it. It saddened him to think that he might have hurt this lovely, lonely woman.

"Goodnight, Kristin," he responded, releasing her from his arms.

She stepped back and turned toward the door. He followed her, and then stepped around her and opened the door himself. He turned to look at her as he did. She was so beautiful, so exotic. He gently touched the silver strands of hair that lightly crowned her abundance of raven-black tresses.

She had been looking down, but now she raised her head until her remarkable eyes met his. They were glistening with unshed tears.

He bent to kiss her, a quick goodbye kiss, and then, with no regret, he closed the door behind him.

Manny watched as Michael backed out of the parking space. He slid down in the seat as Michael's car went by. When he was sure Michael had turned the corner, he sat up.

He looked at the door of the apartment Michael had just left. He saw no sign of anyone else, but there was a silver Mercedes parked right in front of the apartment. What the hell was going on?

He wondered if Michael was in some kind of trouble. What would he be doing, coming to a place like this? He wouldn't know anyone who lived here. Only students lived here.

The obvious answer kept kicking him in his gut, but he just couldn't believe it. Mike with some other broad? Sure, Caroline had been gone a while, but Mike never screwed around on her. He was as sure of that as he was of absolutely anything. In fact, he had always envied Mike a little for his perfect marriage. This wasn't like Mike, not at all.

Okay, he didn't understand it, but if it was what Mike wanted, hell, he didn't care. He *did* care that Mike had been so stupid to take a risk like this without his help. He was with Mike to make sure nothing happened to him. Didn't Mike realize that? Especially now, when there were people upset with him over this abortion thing. Luring him out alone could have been some kind of a trap, or an ambush.

But Manny had to admit that he was also a little hurt, knowing that Mike didn't trust him enough to tell him the truth. Didn't he know by now that he could trust him with his life, let alone some fling?

Would Mike ever be pissed if he knew I followed him, Manny thought. The schmuck. Anybody could have followed him. It had been obvious that Mike had been too busy trying to find where he was going to even look behind him. Hell, it hadn't even been necessary for Manny to take nearly as many precautions as he had. He could have followed Mike in the limo, instead of his own black Olds, and Mike still wouldn't have noticed. He hadn't followed him into the apartment complex right away, though, or he might have been spotted. It had taken him almost ten minutes to find Mike's car after he had doubled back to the complex.

Manny sighed. Next time, he'd tell Mike he was going to drive him. He'd tell him he knew about the broad, and that he didn't care. He just wanted to keep Mike out of trouble and safe.

The stupid bastard.

13

THE RINGING OF the phone brought Michael completely out of his sound sleep. He had always been able to wake up instantly, with a clear head, ready for whatever was happening.

"Oh, shit," he said out loud to himself, at once recalling the previous evening spent with Kristin Long. "What the hell have I done?"

He picked up the phone, apprehensive about speaking to Caroline, and also annoyed that he had to deal with her at this moment.

"Morning, Caroline," he said. He heard the edginess and defensiveness in his voice.

"Michael?" Caroline asked, confused by his abrupt tone. "Is everything okay?"

"Of course everything's okay—why shouldn't it be?"

"What are you so testy about this morning?" she asked with unmasked hurt in her voice.

"I'm sorry, Caroline. Sorry, babe. I guess you know you woke me up, though?"

"Well, I'm sorry about that, Michael, but I don't think you should bite my head off."

"I know. I guess I just woke up on the wrong side of the bed."

"I guess so."

"Okay. Let's start over. Good morning, darling. I love you madly. I miss you terribly. And why the hell are you calling so early?" he finished, laughing now.

Caroline laughed too, and the tension was broken. "I'm calling to tell you that I'm going to be here for the rest of the week. I don't think I'll be able to get home until the weekend."

"Another whole week? Dammit, this is getting old, Caroline."

He instantly regretted his harsh words when he heard her begin to cry on the other end of the line. "Oh, Michael, why are you being so dreadful about this? Do you think this is fun for me? I'm exhausted. I'm scared. I miss you. What do you expect me to *do*?" she finished, her sobs heavier now.

What a son-of-a-bitch you are, Michael Romano, he thought to himself, feeling sorry to have caused his already stressed wife any more stress.

"Baby, baby," he soothed. "I'm sorry. I just miss you, and I'm a real son-of-a-bitch for talking to you like that. Forgive me?" There was no sound other than her sobs, so he continued, "Sweetheart? Please don't cry. I'm sorry. I wish I could be there with you right now, so I could hold you, tell you everything is going to be fine. Do you want me to fly down today?"

He sure hadn't planned to say that. Where had it come from? He held his breath, hoping she would say no. He really needed this Sunday to take care of some personal chores and to catch up on some reading. He continued to hold his breath, hoping she would tell him she didn't want him to come to Palm Beach.

"Oh, Michael," she hiccupped, her sobs subsiding. "Would you?"

Damn. Well, it was his own fault. He had to admit that he felt damn guilty about what had happened last night. That was why he had been so short with her in the first place, wasn't it? And that was the reason he was now in this position. Already a price to pay, he thought with annoyance.

"Sure. If you can get your father's plane here in the next couple of hours, I can be down there before noon." He hoped he had kept the aggravation out of his voice.

"Of course. You're so sweet, Michael. Thank you."

"You're welcome, sweetheart. Please make sure Hanes is waiting for me."

"He will be."

"Okay, got to get moving. I love you, Caroline," he said with more compassion.

"I love you, too, Michael. I can't wait to see you."

Michael took advantage of the time in the air to read the first of the three papers he always read. He always read the *Tallahassee Democrat* first. That was where news of him and his colleagues was most likely to hit the front page. Just as he expected, there was nothing significant of a political nature today. He quickly covered the front section before he gave into the temptation to read the social page. He read the social editor's comments about the guests at last night's dinner. He was glad that there was no intonation as to the real reason for the party—to rope in the really big contributors' dollars. It was reported as just another fund raiser.

If Gloria Goodman, the social editor, had guessed at the level of support, she had been gracious enough not to mention it. Good old Gloria. Such a classy lady, perfect for writing the social column, and always careful to shed the best possible light on him and Caroline.

He finished the *Democrat* and moved on to the *Miami Herald*. He hated the *Herald*. It was so left-wing and liberal, supporting practically any Democrat who signed his name to a ticket, no matter how unqualified to hold office he or she might be. But the *Herald* had the largest circulation in the state, and he had to care about what was written in it.

He saw there was much of the same world news, so he moved on to the always fascinating "Local" section of the *Herald*. It was a gloom and doom section, always quick to point out social ills and corrupt causes, usually with a biased slant. How many more cops were going to be accused of stealing, killing and drug dealing? Which local politicians were going to be burned at the *Herald* stake today?

He certainly felt that any crooked politician or public figures should be exposed. But the *Miami Herald* could do it in a way that no other paper could. They used a tenacious—even vicious—tack. Vicious, all right. Look what their reporters had done to Gary Hart. Good riddance, as far as Michael was concerned, but they sure had played dirty.

What was this? A mayor of one of the many incorporated cities within the city of Miami, living way beyond his means? Yep, it sure looked that way. Hard to have a nine-hundred-thousand dollar home on the ocean with a salary of only sixty thousand. He had to admit they did a good job of exposing the guy.

Another murder on North Biscayne Boulevard, the second one in the same area in the past month. Police were reluctant to say they were linked, though both of the victims, known prostitutes, appeared to have been killed in the same way. Nasty business.

Michael read on, fascinated with the gore. Local HRS officials were being criticized for mishandling a child abuse case. Good God...broken bones, ruptured kidneys. The parents had been arrested after the child had been taken to Jackson Memorial, where he died. Bastards. He hated child abuse almost as much as he hated abortion.

Damn depressing news. He turned to Dave Barry's column in the *Tropic Magazine* section of the *Herald*. Dave was always good for some real laughs.

Michael felt better after reading Dave's column, and moved on to the rest of the paper. He picked up the *Orlando Sentinel*. He wished he had time to include the *Palm Beach Post* in his daily readings, but he knew Caroline had a direct pipeline to everything happening in Palm Beach, and she could keep him informed of anything he needed to know.

He was having trouble reading the *Sentinel*. His eyes were fatigued, and he realized it was from the lack of sleep. His mind wandered back to Kristin Long. He could not find respite from those thoughts. He thought he could still smell her alluring sexual scent. He could feel her lissome body against his. And he couldn't help but remember the unbelievably exciting sex. He pictured it and started to relive it. With effort, he pushed it away.

Nothing that a good dose of Caroline won't cure, he told himself as the plane landed.

The music enveloped the two lovers in the soulful and romantic swell of David Sanborn's saxophone.

They clung to each other, hungry in their passion, anxious in their coupling.

This is where I belong, Michael told himself. His lovemaking was especially tender. The familiar feel of Caroline's body inspired a passion in Michael that surely no other woman could ever rival. In acknowledging this, Michael swept away lingering vestiges of Kristin Long. Caroline's delicate perfume replaced Kristin's sexual scent in his memory of smells. Her familiar and welcoming body became one with his again. The passion of their lovemaking far overshadowed the lust he had felt with Kristin the night before.

He held Caroline close in the sweet aftermath of lovemaking. His fling with Kristin Long, he realized, had enhanced his ardor for his wife. He didn't understand it, nor did he really care to. Everything just felt right, and he was at peace.

103

He smiled the smile of a man totally fulfilled as he and Caroline drifted off to sleep. As he fell into the lap of slumber, he thanked God once again for his good fortune.

"Lucky-son-of-a-bitch!"

For a Monday morning, Michael felt particularly fine. He was glad he had gone to Palm Beach yesterday. He and Caroline had a wonderful afternoon, making love and taking a nap in each other's arms. When he was with her, he was whole.

True, guilt had intruded once or twice during their lovemaking, and there was a brief, surreal moment when the two women were juxtaposed. But what was done was done, and since it would never happen again, Michael made an uneasy truce with his sole infidelity.

Getting down to business, he sifted through the letters, faxes and phone messages that had piled up on his desk. Henry had left a note, written in bold red ink, which said, "Five to one against the special session." Too bad, Michael thought. As long as he had the power to call a special session, which he did, he would do it. These pro-choice people had just gathered up a bigger head of steam than he had anticipated. The tide would turn before the session.

Andy knocked a short rap before entering Michael's office. "Morning, Andy," Michael greeted him.

"Morning, Michael."

"What's up?" Michael asked, leaning back in his chair.

"We need a quote for the press," Andy said.

"How about, 'Go fuck yourselves,'" Michael replied, laughing.

"Eh, well, they might just censor that," Andy responded in a mock-serious tone. "That's really how you feel, huh, Michael?"

"Nah, not really. There are just some misguided people out there. They just need to become better informed, and the press isn't doing such a good job of informing them."

"Informing? Or brainwashing?"

"Which is easier?"

"Brainwashing, of course."

"All right, you're my press secretary. Brainwash them."

They laughed together with the intention of setting a smooth course for the issues they would be addressing this morning.

"Look," Michael began. "Henry has started this ball rolling by focusing on published reports detailing a series of botched abortions and false pregnancy tests down in Miami."

"Did he say how he's going to handle it?"

"I thought a surprise visit to the offending clinics would do the trick. But Henry tells me there's a standing agreement between abortion providers and the state that inspectors have to be announced in advance. Those clinics have the right to deny the inspectors entrance on the basis of that agreement."

Andy nodded, honing in on Michael's strategy. "Some might. Others will get caught with their pants down," he said.

"Exactly," Michael said. "Could be whoever runs the clinics won't know about that caveat, and they'll let the inspectors in. But they do have the right to refuse entrance. Then the inspectors would have to get a court order, and that could take hours or days. Plenty of time for them to clean up the place and bury some records."

"Are we just trying to fuel the special session fire with this?"

"Damn right," Michael snapped. "But you must see the need for women to know if the clinics they might be using to kill babies are unsafe."

"Michael, you're getting off track. Abortion is currently considered a legal, safe, medical procedure. You can't go around talking about 'killing babies.' The focus has to be on the danger of getting an abortion in an unlicensed or substandard clinic."

"Which will cast an ugly shadow on the whole abortion procedure, I hope. I know I'm on the right track here, Andy. And you've got to figure out a way to bring the need for more restrictions on abortions into this story, tie the two together. The media aren't going to connect those dots for us."

"Michael," Andy expelled a breath. "The media aren't going to connect the dots because the dots don't connect. Let's say a hamburger joint was serving meat with roaches in it, and FDA inspectors found out. They'd close the joint down until the problem was fixed. But they wouldn't outlaw hamburgers, just because one or two burger places were in violation.

"You see what I'm getting at? It's legal to sell hamburgers, but you have health regulations to follow in providing them to the public. It's legal to get an abortion, but abortion providers have to follow health regulations, too. The most you can hope for is to get people thinking abortions are overall unsafe, though that's not true. So you have to be really careful about how you use this."

"You make a good point. So we're going to have to settle for putting the emphasis on 'unsafe' and 'abortion' but we won't be able to tie them together unless we say 'unsafe abortion *clinics.*' Is that right?"

"Maybe those three words will carry enough weight to get people concerned about the safety of abortions overall, but we can't say outright that abortions are unsafe. It just isn't true."

"I think you can do better than that, Andy," Michael countered.

"You have me here because you can trust me to help you impart accurate information to the media, while putting your own agenda in play. My job is also protecting you from making statements that will leave you with egg on your face. If you don't listen to me, you're going to get embarrassed.

"This is a prickly issue, Michael. But you know that. I don't know if Henry's told you, but even some of your staffers are grumbling about the special session. And it's not because they mind the extra work. They just don't like that you're trying to put any restrictions on abortion. Your own staffers, Michael. Women *and* men, I might add. As loyal a group as you could want, and they're unhappy."

Michael was disturbed to hear that there was dissension in the ranks. "They have a right to think what they want, Andy, but they don't have a right to disparage my agenda in public. That's not happening, is it?"

"No, Michael, it's all in house. But that's not the point."

"I get the point, Andy. But this special session is going to happen, despite what they think, or what the polls say."

"You always say you like the truth, Michael. Well, the truth is, you're absolutely blind on this one. I'm close to giving up on convincing you of that."

"A smart concession on your part, Andy. You'd just be spinning your wheels otherwise."

"So I gather. So, what do you want to convey to the public that wrote you all those love letters?" Andy asked, indicating that he meant the letters and faxes on Michael's desk.

"You're the press secretary. What do you suggest?"

"How about, 'The governor is taking the opinion of the people into consideration and will be re-evaluating his position on the special session.'"

Michael burst out laughing. "Do I seem like that much of a hypocrite to you, Andy?"

"No, you're not a hypocrite, but you are a politician." He paused and smiled at Michael. "Most people think they're synonymous."

Michael smiled back at Andy, appreciative of the joke. Andy continued. "As a politician, you have an obligation to consider the opinions of those you govern. Or at least pretend to. You can't safely take any other position."

"Safely? Since when did I play it safe?"

Andy raised his eyebrows in response.

"Okay," Michael said. "I know I don't come across as a gunslinger, but you and I both know that I go after what I want. If I'm adept at looking benevolent while doing it, then I've reached the pinnacle of every politician's dreams."

Andy shook his head and raised his hands in a conciliatory gesture. "Okay, you don't like my suggestion. So what's your suggestion?"

"How about, 'The governor will not be influenced by the opinions of a few vocal opponents who he does not believe reflect the true sentiments of the people of this state.'"

Andy was amazed that Michael could be so naïve. Maybe stubborn was a better word. Michael had seen the polls, but he was deliberately choosing to ignore them. As Michael's chief of staff and chief strategist, Henry had to have told him the same. At any rate, the quote could do Michael no good. But Andy was quite certain he would never convince Michael of that.

"Okay, Michael. I don't like it, but if that's what you want, that's what I'll do."

"Good. We need to stay on track."

The phone lines to the mansion were so busy the next morning that Michael finally asked Lynn to quit putting calls through and just take messages. Even senior legislators couldn't get through after the first hour. All were demanding to be called back.

It was finally beginning to sink in. Michael had to admit that he was up against much stronger opposition than he had originally anticipated.

Andy's statement to the press that the governor would not reconsider his decision to call the special session—even while acknowledging public sentiment was running five to one against it—had created a major furor. Still, Michael thought, I know I'm supposed to be doing this. It's *fate*.

Despite instructions that he not be given any more calls, a buzz came over the line. "What?" he snapped into the line.

"Sorry, Governor Romano, but I have a Kristin Long on the line. She says it's urgent and of a personal nature. She also said something about Les Jenkins."

Michael's heart raced with a dreaded mixture of excitement and fear. How could she call him like this? And what was this nonsense about Les?

"I don't want to talk to her or anyone else. This abortion issue seems to be personal to a lot of people, so don't let that line get to you again. Okay?"

Damn, one thing after another was happening to cause his overall feeling of well-being to evaporate. Why was she calling? He had made it clear that nothing more was going to happen. She had seemed resigned to that. Had she changed her mind?

He poured a glass of chilled water and drank it in one large gulp. Despite his reluctance, he couldn't help but think about the sex with Kristin. After a wonderful Sunday afternoon of lovemaking with Caroline, he had succeeded in quashing the thoughts and the inevitable feelings of lust when reliving sex with Kristin. Being with Caroline, realizing again how much he loved and desired her, had certainly helped. Nothing good could come of speaking with Kristin again.

The intercom buzzed again. "Governor, Manny is here to take you to your luncheon. Leon County Republican Party. The Hyatt," she reminded him.

Hell, was it that time already? Michael felt like he had just sat down at his desk. He had gotten nothing accomplished. "Thanks, I'll be right out, Lynn."

He straightened his tie and smoothed his hair. He looked in the mirror behind the closet door. He was pleased to see that getting up at five o'clock that morning, plus dealing with the stress of the numerous phone calls, including Kristin Long's, had left no mark upon him.

"What's up, Manny?" Michael asked from the back seat of the limousine. Manny was unusually quiet.

"Huh? Oh, nothing, Mike. Two of the kids have the chicken pox, got the household in an uproar." This was true, but it had nothing to do with

108

Manny's silence. Manny was still upset that Mike hadn't trusted him enough to tell him the truth.

Michael accepted the explanation. "Sorry to hear it. They're going to be okay, the kids?"

"Yeah, sure."

"Good. I guess I thought you still might be upset by my taking off on my own Saturday night."

"Well, you know I didn't like it. It's my job to take you where you want to go, to see you get there safe."

"I know, Manny, but I was just restless and missing Caroline. I just wanted to drive around a while, by myself. And as you can see, I came back safe."

Manny hadn't exactly expected a confession from Mike, but he was stung by how easily Mike had lied to him. For the first time since he had known Michael, he wondered if he really knew him.

When Manny didn't respond, Michael continued. "Besides, the great thing about that plain gray Monte Carlo is that no one would bother to look at who's driving it. That's why I drove it instead of the Jaguar."

"I realize that, boss. I was just worried."

"Manny, don't get overprotective." Michael saw the flash of resentment in Manny's eyes reflected in the rear view mirror. He hurried to neutralize it.

"Manny, you know I appreciate your concern. And I don't know what I'd do without you. It's just that sometimes I get tired of living life in this bubble. I was Mike Romano, the guy who could do a pretty good job of taking care of himself, before I was the governor. You understand?"

Manny understood more than Michael gave him credit for, but he couldn't say so. He just answered, "Okay, Mike."

"Okay, then." Michael knew Manny was still upset, but that couldn't be helped. Since it wouldn't happen again, there would be no reason to upset him in the future. They'd be back to normal soon enough.

In the meantime, Michael contemplated what to do about Kristin Long. Do absolutely nothing, he told himself. Let it lie. If he wouldn't pursue it, and if he wouldn't allow her to, she'd give up, just as every other woman had. Granted, this was different. Very different. He hadn't had sex with any of the other women. But he was still counting on history to repeat itself.

14

MANNY PULLED UP to the entrance of the Hyatt and put the limousine in park. He got out and opened Michael's door.

But Michael didn't move. He was planted in his seat, stunned into inertia by the sight of Kristin Long going into the hotel lobby. Judging by the timing, he knew she must have seen his limo.

What the hell was she doing here? He quickly deduced that she belonged to the Leon County Republican Party. A state trooper was standing by the entrance of the hotel, waiting to escort the governor inside. He was looking at the limo, confused about why the governor hadn't gotten out.

"You okay, Mike?" Manny asked, for what Michael realized was the second time.

"What? Oh yeah, sure, Manny. Just some last minute wool gathering."

"Well, come on. The trooper and everybody else are waiting for us."

Michael got out of the limo slowly, making a pretense of being delayed by assembling some papers on his lap. Flashes of sex with Kristin were dancing around in his head. Seeing her again had an effect on him he could not have anticipated.

The state trooper held the door for him and Manny, and when he entered the lobby, he saw that Kristin was off the left side of the main entrance, seemingly holding court, with four men surrounding her. Well, why not? She was a beautiful woman.

Andy was waiting for Michael. He had gotten there early to answer the media's questions, but was standing alone when Michael saw him. Where was everybody, Michael wondered. He had expected a large crowd, but there were only fifteen or twenty people milling around the lobby. As Andy approached him, he answered Michael's question without being asked.

"Most of them are inside already, ordering drinks. These Republicans sure like liquids with their lunches, don't they? Anyway, the press is inside, too. I told them you wouldn't be available for questions until after lunch. They're pretty fired up, and they're ready with questions about the majority of legislators not supporting you on the special session."

Michael groaned and rolled his head to the left. As he did, he caught Kristin's eye. She smiled at him and looked away.

The small group she was with moved towards him. Manny and the state trooper stood close by. Manny didn't know these people, even if Michael did, and from what he could tell, Mike had more than a few people mad at him right now.

Michael shook everyone's hand, including Kristin's, which sent a sexual barb through him. Images of sex with her swam to the forefront of his brain. She looked striking in a beige Chanel suit and a matching, luxurious silk blouse.

"Let's go on in," Andy suggested, urging Michael and the remaining people towards the banquet room. Kristin fell back from the group. Michael noticed, and he turned to speak to Manny, deliberately slowing his stride.

In response to Michael's whispered request, Manny nodded and started to walk ahead, but not before he saw the dark-haired woman touch Michael's sleeve. He had noticed her, of course, as soon as he had walked into the lobby, and had immediately recognized her as the woman Michael had defended at the Billiard Club a few weeks before. He started to wait for them, but then changed his mind. He walked on ahead, but not too quickly.

With feigned indifference, Manny stretched his neck to look ahead, while out of the corner of his eye, he saw the woman slip Michael a piece of paper before she turned away and headed toward the lobby elevators.

Michael's eyes followed her. Manny was disturbed. Didn't Michael know that people were always watching him? He scanned the group to see who else had seen what he had.

To his relief, no one seemed to have noticed. They were finding their seats and squawking away. Manny avoided meeting Michael's eyes. He stopped at the back of the room and watched Michael walk to the front, to the speaker's table. With an unhappy sigh, Manny settled into a chair in the back of the room, where he could keep an eye on things. The state trooper was right outside the door.

REBECCA WARNER

Michael felt comfortable. He was in his element. Here was a group of men and women that embodied the conservative doctrine. He felt they were here today to find out how they could lend support to his cause. He had planned to talk about Florida's economy in relation to businesses, but he and Henry had decided to address the very hot abortion issue.

Andy had notified the media, which were lining the back wall, waiting for the chance to grill him.

The chairman of the Leon County Republican Party addressed the group before lunch began, letting them know that Governor Romano would be speaking towards the end of the meal. The speech would be followed by a fifteen minute question and answer session. With good wishes for a hearty appetite, he sat down next to Michael and proceeded to bend Michael's ear with his familiar sentiments on how business and government should be more separated. Michael amicably agreed with him, assuring him that he would continue to support those same sentiments.

He had little time to give to the reverend on his right who had said grace before lunch. Soon enough, the chairman was tapping his glass with a spoon, calling the group to order. After a standard, inane introduction, which was nevertheless appreciated, Michael approached the podium.

"Ladies and gentlemen, thank you for inviting me here today," he began. It was a large, respectful, and respectable crowd of about seventy. There was none of the usual side chatter going on as they finished dessert and accepted refills on the coffee.

"Although there are many things I could talk about today, I'd like to address my decision to call a special session, and to ask your support for that decision."

He took a sip of water and continued. "Despite what you may have read in the papers or heard on the news, I am not seeking self-gratification in calling this session. I think you folks, as taxpayers, need to feel comfortable with the fact that we're going to be spending a considerable amount of your tax dollars to hold the session."

He took the sputter of comments in stride and continued.

"As you know, the Supreme Court upheld a Missouri law which restricts the use of public facilities and employees for counseling services or for performing abortions."

The short spell of applause interrupted him only momentarily.

112

"In addition, it requires doctors to determine if a fetus can survive outside the womb before an abortion is performed."

There were a few coughs in the room which told Michael that some of the attendees were uncomfortable with the subject matter.

"I know this is a difficult topic for many of you. Whether it's because you're uncomfortable with the subject, or whether you have a strong opinion one way or the other, I can't be sure. But I am sure that it is a matter that needs to be addressed, as soon as possible, to ensure the rights of unborn children.

"I look around here today, and I see fathers and sons. Would any of you, I ask you, wish that your son had never been born?"

Michael saw some nods acknowledging agreement, others of humor. "Okay, Warren, I'll grant you that you may have wished that son of yours had never been born when he beat you in court last year," Michael joked, addressing Warren Cates III, a well-known attorney from a legacy of attorneys.

The crowd, all familiar with the notorious case, laughed appreciatively.

"But seriously," Michael continued, "I want you to know that I am compelled by my conscience and by my sense of moral obligation to the unborn to address this issue in the state of Florida. The Court's decision to uphold the Missouri law is a clear indication that more restrictive legislation on the parts of other states will be tolerated by the Court."

He paused, weighing what he was about to say, then decided that this group would allow him to take the strongest possible position.

"It's time to stop the senseless murder of unborn children in this country, and if Florida's lawmakers have to be the ones to pursue the cessation, then so be it. I hope that I can count on your support in the face of those who would oppose it."

His sincerity and deep conviction had resonated throughout his speech, and the audience responded to it with applause.

"There's much more I could say, but I would rather answer any questions you might have."

With the sincerity of his convictions ringing in his voice, Michael answered the questions from the audience, though many were more statements than questions, agreeing with him in their context.

The questions from the media—not surprisingly—were not so agreeable, but Michael was unshaken by the barrage of intimidating questions which bordered on accusations. He was feeling at the top of his form, and by the end of the questioning, he knew no one could possibly leave that room without feeling that he was a powerful governor, one to be reckoned with. A surge of adrenaline pumped through him as he congratulated himself on a job well done.

He didn't need Andy or anyone else to tell him he had done well, but he reveled in the praise and promises of support from those who came up to offer it.

As the group filed out, Michael shook hands and offered his thanks. He looked for Manny and saw him waiting in the back of the room.

Andy was saying something to him, but Michael wasn't listening. He was trying to *think*.

It had not escaped him that Kristin had not been at the meeting. Although he didn't know for certain, he was pretty sure that the piece of paper she had slipped him had a room number written on it. He hadn't chanced a look yet. He wasn't so sure he cared to. But he felt so good, and he was pumped. To see her right now would be icing on the cake.

He had started walking out with Andy, who was still talking. *Think,* he commanded himself.

"Just a minute, Andy," he said. "I think I forgot my pen."

Before Andy could offer to retrieve it for him, Michael turned and walked back to the speaker's table. He slid the piece of paper out of his pocket as he walked and opened it. Nine one five was all that was written on it.

Think, dammit, he ordered himself again in the short time allowed for him to reach the table. He made a pretense of looking for his pen. He didn't look up to see if anyone was watching. He simply continued the act by looking confused, and then embarrassed, upon discovering it inside his jacket pocket.

With what he hoped was a chagrined smile, he waved it at Andy, then walked back to join him. He formulated a plan. He looked towards the back of the room then said, "Excuse me, Andy, but Manny's motioning to me. Hold on."

Andy's eyes went to the back of the room, where he spotted Manny, who didn't seem to be beckoning Michael. Instead, he was scanning the crowd. Maybe Manny saw something that had disturbed him and he wanted to tell Mike.

"Sure, Michael," Andy answered to the back of Michael's retreating head.

"Manny," Michael said, "find out pronto where the service elevators are and come back to get me. Make it look like I need to take an urgent phone call. *Hurry.*"

Manny didn't ask any questions, and Michael hadn't expected him to. Manny was back before the crowd had completely cleared the room.

He saw Michael talking to a couple of people, and though Michael seemed to be absorbed in the conversation, Manny didn't hesitate to interrupt.

"Excuse me, Governor Romano. There's a phone call for you. It's urgent. They've forwarded the call to a private conference room. You better hurry."

Michael looked convincingly surprised and concerned. He turned to see where Andy was. He was right behind him. Andy nodded to Michael, indicating he had heard and understood. He looked concerned.

"Hold them off for a few minutes, Andy. I'll be back as fast as I can."

"Okay, Mike. Everything okay?"

"I'm not sure. I'll let you know."

Manny let the state trooper, who was standing just outside of the room, know that everything was fine, and that he didn't need to follow. The trooper was well aware of Manny's connection to the governor, and his true function. He respected Manny's ability and judgment. He went to wait by the front doors.

Michael's excitement at seeing Kristin was heightened by the sheer audacity of what he was doing. He followed Manny past the thinning crowd and around a corner. He liked the set-up. Once he had turned the corner, he was in a corridor of meeting rooms. He could be in any one of them, if anyone cared to look, which wasn't likely.

At the end of the corridor he saw the service elevators. "Good job, Manny. Thanks. And wait here."

"No. I'm coming with you, Mike."

"No, you're not. Get lost in one of these rooms somewhere." He pointed to what looked like an empty conference room across the hall. "There," he said. "I'll get you when I come down."

The two men looked at each other. Michael couldn't tell what Manny was thinking, but he suspected that Manny knew what was up. Manny wanted to tell Mike he didn't care if he was going upstairs to pop some broad, he just wanted to make sure things went smoothly. Neither said anything, however, as Michael stepped into the service elevator.

As the door closed, Michael raised his hand in a conciliatory gesture which said thanks, everything's fine.

When he reached the ninth floor, he swung out of the elevator with the gait of a man in a state of uncontrolled excitement. He was charged more than ever now, knowing what was about to happen.

He knocked softly. Kristin opened the door immediately, almost as if she had her hand on the knob. Michael grabbed her the second she closed the door.

He pressed his mouth to hers, and was flooded again with the exciting sensations her mouth provided. After a long and hungry kiss he said, "I haven't got long."

"I know."

She was still dressed except for her jacket. Kristin sat down on the bed and reached for Michael. She unzipped his pants and extracted his penis. It was ready for whatever Kristin had in mind.

She took his penis in her hand and then slid her mouth over it, taking in nearly all of him. Her mouth moved up and down the shaft with deftness, and she moaned with pleasure as she swallowed as much of his penis as possible. She slowly sucked upward, using her tongue on the length of his shaft, then running it over and around the head before swallowing him again, deeper and faster.

Michael had to fight to keep control. Kristin Long had one fucking talented mouth. It was with some regret that he pulled away from her, but he was here to fuck her. He wanted to be deep inside that tight, hot place again. Kristin lay back on the bed and raised her shapely legs, giving him a stellar view.

His excitement was intensified when he saw that under her skirt, she wore no panties. He leaned in and drove two fingers deep and hard inside her, delighted to find her so hot and ready. He moved his fingers in and out of her, probing more deeply, more roughly each time, watching her beautiful face intensify in pleasure, until she shuddered and moaned with an orgasm.

He withdrew his fingers, dropped his pants, and drove into her in one long, hard, insistent stroke, laying claim to her in the same primal way as before. She responded by raising her knees and hips higher, wanting him to go even deeper.

His mouth covered hers so that their moans of rising pleasure were muffled. Just like before, they found themselves in a place neither had ever been before. It was as if they had discovered the one other person who could awaken, and then fully arouse, this aspect of their previously unknown, unexplored sexual desires. Until now, they had not known those needs existed within them. Their coupling provoked a previously-undiscovered level of pleasure in its absolute intensity.

The pounding was merciless, and as she raised her legs and hips even higher, Michael reached a depth inside Kristin that seemed infinite. She had the tightest pussy he had ever known; so tight, in fact, that with each deep, hard stroke, he felt that his penis was being clenched in a silken vice.

Their bodies locked into a rhythm so synchronized that it belied their brief familiarity with each other's bodies. It was *their* rhythm, fast and forceful, driving them to climax in a few short, but exquisitely fulfilling, moments. Michael continued to pump his still hard member into her spasming depths until she cried out, losing herself in the second wave of the tide that broke over her.

He stopped then and rested lightly on her. He kissed her eyes, her mouth, her neck. She had the slightest glisten to her skin, which was radiant from the flush of sex. Her long, shining hair was spread out about her, framing her beautiful face and quicksilver eyes.

"You're fantastic," he whispered into her ear, gently biting the lobe as he said it.

"Oh, God, so are you, Michael," she said with a quivering sigh.

He was still inside her, and could feel himself growing hard again. He would have liked another round, an extended round, of the same electrifying sex. He'd also like to ravage her succulent breasts; but the clock in his brain, which kept very accurate time, told him it was time to go.

He kissed her again, allowing enough time to savor her. He had never tasted anything so delicious as Kristin Long, and for the pleasure of that mouth alone, he could be a goner.

"I have to go," he said, as he reluctantly pulled out of her and rolled over on the bed. "I'm sorry."

117

"No, it's okay," she said, though she sounded disappointed. "I was afraid you wouldn't come, but I knew I had to try. I tried to call you to give you some warning, but you didn't take my call."

Michael started to respond, but Kristin spoke before he could. "That's okay, it worked out. It's just that I can't stop thinking about you. About this. I've thought of nothing else since then."

"Christ, I know," Michael said with a deep sigh. He rolled off the bed, pulled up his pants, and headed towards the bathroom. Kristin heard water running and the toilet flushing.

Michael looked remorseful when he walked back into the bedroom. He looked into her eyes and said, "God, this was fantastic, but Kristin..."

"I know," she interrupted. "It's fine, Michael. I don't expect any promises. I just wanted to see you again, to see if this was really as fantastic as I remembered. It was."

Michael turned and looked in the mirror. He straightened his tie and smoothed his hair. His eyes met hers in the reflection.

"I wondered the same thing," he admitted, turning to her. "It is unbelievably fantastic sex, Kristin, but I'm feeling guilty as hell again. I've told you that I love my wife, and this is just wrong. I'm going to ask you not to get in touch with me again. Okay?"

Kristin was more disappointed than hurt. She loved the wild and demanding sex they shared, and she wanted more. She had acted so out of character in pursuing him, starting with renting an apartment for just that purpose. But it had worked out just as she had planned. Today had, too—just like she'd planned. Why stop now?

Kristin had felt shame for so blatantly pursuing a married man. But after that first time together, she knew she had to have him again, despite what he had said. After all, the sex on Saturday had been so damned perfect for both of them. What were the chances of finding any other person who could give you exactly what you wanted and needed? She couldn't imagine he wouldn't want to do it again, and she had been right. After all, here he was.

But now he was repeating what he had told her Saturday night—that he couldn't see her again. Nothing like this had ever happened to her, and she had no experience in dealing with it. She would just have to accept it.

"Okay, Michael. I understand."

118

Michael was grateful and relieved. He pulled her off the bed and gave her a strong hug and a quick kiss, then opened the door to leave.

"Thank you, Kristin—for everything."

Kristin nodded and held up her hand in a goodbye gesture as he closed the door behind him.

She chained the door and slowly moved to the bed, where she laid down and curled into a fetal position, and cried.

Michael looked at his watch. Incredible. Nine minutes—exactly the same as the clock in his head.

Manny was waiting by the service elevator when the doors opened. His expression was neutral.

Surprised to see Manny standing there, Michael asked, "Everything okay?" Manny heard the concern in Michael's voice.

"Everything's fine. Let's go," Manny answered, his neutral expression unchanged.

A few members of the group, and quite a few members of the press, were still in the lobby. Michael spotted Andy, who was motioning for him to join him and the group.

"Everything all right, Michael?" Michael was pleased that Andy had unknowingly given him a perfect cue.

"Caroline's father," Michael lied, and loudly enough so that those around could hear. "I have to get back to the Mansion. I may have to fly down tonight."

Nods of sympathy and understanding surrounded Michael, and he felt like a real jerk for lying. But he wasn't in the mood for any more questions, especially from the press. Caroline's father's illness was well known, and it made for a perfect excuse.

"I'll let you know," he called over his shoulder to Andy, as Manny led him out the door and to the safe and quiet womb of the limousine.

Michael considered discussing the obvious with Manny, but decided against it. They rode in silence back to the Mansion, with Michael lost in his thoughts of sex with Kristin Long.

15

AT THE SAME TIME his sister, Kristin, was engulfed in the pain of losing a man she never truly had, Jake Miller was engulfed in the pain that was pulling him out of his anesthetized state. It was the same wrenching pain he had felt after the other operations. He had almost forgotten it. Who was it that said that if humans remembered pain, a woman would never have a second baby?

Well, at least a woman had that choice. He hadn't had a choice about having the pins removed. He would have to start the recovery process all over again, and he became morose at the thought.

He simmered in his thoughts for what seemed like a very long time before a nurse came in. Should he ask for a shot for the pain? He didn't want to seem like a wimp who couldn't handle pain.

He was relieved that he didn't have to ask. She was holding a needle, and said, more than asked, "Bet you're really looking forward to some relief from the pain, aren't you?" She wore a sympathetic smile. He hated sympathy, but he would take a dose of it willingly if it came with the shot.

"It's not so bad," he lied. Always playing the tough guy, aren't you, he sneered to himself.

"Well, if you don't want it..."

She was teasing him, and rightfully so. He smiled at her and said, "Well, as long as you bothered to bring it, stick it to me. I can tell you're pretty good at that, aren't you?" She caught the double-entendre and shared a laugh with him.

Within minutes, the pain began to subside. As he fell into a dreamy sleep, a hazy figure of a beautiful woman walked into his dreams. She looked so familiar...so familiar. He couldn't see her very clearly, but as she got closer and closer he wanted to reach out to her. Her eyes were closed, and he wondered how she knew she was walking straight towards him.

When she got close enough for him to touch her, she tilted her head higher and opened her eyes. They were silvery-gray, like his. He was looking into a mirror now, and the person looking back was him, but it wasn't him, because it was a *her.* Her eyes were sad, but when she spoke, he heard his own voice coming from her: "*Where have you been, Jake?*" Then she was gone.

When he awoke, he tried to recall the dream. Normally, he could recall an entire night's dreams with no problem. He figured the drug was fogging his recall ability. He struggled with the image, only slightly aware now of his persistent pain. He closed his eyes and willed his mind to reveal the dream to him.

He thought back about the few prophetic dreams he had. Some of the things he dreamed about had happened, and he hadn't realized until he was almost six that they didn't happen to everyone. His parents had basically ignored him when he would casually state, "Oh, but I already dreamed that this was going to happen. Didn't you?"

Those prophetic dreams had lessened in frequency and clarity as he grew older. His sixth sense became more of a finely-honed intuition once he joined the force. His cop buddies called it "great instincts," and he guessed that fit just as well as anything else.

Great instincts...like when they had searched for the ten-year-old kidnapped girl in a suspect's home, and they were ready to leave when Jake got what he had started calling, "a hit."

He had gone back into the bedroom and searched the small closet again, until he found the seams of a trap door. Behind it was the girl, bound and gagged, but okay.

Great instincts...like when he had deliberately and rudely bumped into a woman who was waiting to cross at Fifth and Madison, causing her to drop her shopping bags. As she cursed and joined Jake in bending to pick them up, an out-of-control car careened into the intersection where she would have been walking.

Great instincts...like spotting the wet and frightened puppy that huddled against the curb in the rain. Jake had picked it up and stood waiting for the owner to show any moment. And there she came, jogging in the rain, wet, distressed, searching...and ultimately relieved.

Yes, those instincts had served him well in life and with the NYPD. He'd always had a strong sense of right and wrong. He hated cruelty and he hated that people were hurt—mentally, physically and emotionally—

because of someone else's cruelty. After becoming a cop, he had seen so much cruelty, so much wrong, so much pain caused by people in the name of love and hate, that he had considered giving up police work. But he knew that someone had to help keep hope alive. And when hope was gone, someone had to help pick up the pieces. He had felt a calling to be that person.

But now he didn't have to worry about that any more, did he? It was no longer his job to mop up messes. He had been good at it, though. He was proud of his time on the force.

The relief brought about by another pain shot made him drowsy, and he started to slip off into the wonderful world of pain-free sleep once again. As he began to sink into a dark bliss, his dream came back to him in full, unfolding in surreal passages, piece by piece, until he was sure he would recall it again when he awoke. But he had no memory of it as the pain brought him out of his sleep hours later. And when the next shot took effect, he fell back into a deep slumber until morning.

As if there were some warning to be heeded, his mind chose to let him dream, but not to remember. When he awoke the next morning, he faced once again the frustration of not remembering. As far back as he could remember, he had dreamed every night of his life, and he had always recalled his dreams. He cursed his need for the pain shots. The drugs that had dulled the pain had again taken away his ability to recall.

He was exasperated that he couldn't remember this particular dream, because it had seemed so significant. There was a message in it he felt he had to heed, but he couldn't recall even a portion of it.

He wanted to shake off the effects of the painkiller so that he could recall it more clearly. But he still felt intense pain, and he knew he would, in fact, need another shot soon. It came right after breakfast, and he looked forward to slipping back into a sleep state. He was almost there, almost engulfed in the warm darkness when he heard his (her) voice again.

"Find me, Jake."

He fought to get to her, whoever she was, to answer her cry for help. But the tides of sleep washed over him, and he gave into the undertow that pulled him back down into the murky depths of sleep.

16

THE RINGING OF the phone in the limousine brought Michael out of his reverie. He had been reliving every short, sumptuous moment he had just spent with Kristin. Annoyed by the interruption to his daydreaming, he picked up the phone with a quick, terse movement, barking "Michael Romano" into the receiver even before it reached his ear. It was his secretary, Lynn.

"Governor?" she asked more than said, obviously surprised at the discord in Michael's voice.

"Yes, Lynn?" he answered, with no apology or explanation.

"Governor, I have Mrs. Romano on the line. I told her I thought I might be able to reach you in the limo. Can I put her through?"

That's weird, he thought. He had just staged an urgent call from her back at the hotel, and here she was, really calling him, with something important enough to have Lynn reach him here. An increasingly familiar pang of guilt stabbed at Michael now, but he quickly pushed it aside and asked Lynn to put the call through.

"Caroline?" he said when he heard the connecting click, "Is everything okay?"

"Not really. That's why I'm calling. I just wanted to catch you before this evening. I know you're expecting me tonight, but I just can't get away yet." She heard Michael's audible and annoyed sigh.

Caroline didn't wait for a response before she continued. "There's been a spike in his blood pressure that no one can explain. They're keeping an eye on him and giving him injections to make sure he doesn't have another stroke. This is bad, Michael, and I just don't feel comfortable leaving him right now."

Although he was annoyed, Michael found he was also relieved. He had to get things straight in his head, and he was really rather glad to know that he would be able to work them out before seeing Caroline.

Benevolence replaced annoyance as he said, "I understand, Caroline. I'm really sorry to hear it. He'll be okay, though. You're there to make sure of it. No idea, I guess, when you think you might be headed back?"

Caroline was relieved that Michael was so understanding. Of course, even if he hadn't been, she would have stayed with her father. But she felt a rush of tenderness towards her husband as she said, "Probably by Saturday afternoon."

Michael felt his annoyance returning, but suppressed it. "Caroline, we're supposed to be in Tampa on Friday, remember? Abe Gilbert, who you damn well know is one of my biggest contributors, is counting on us to be there for the ground-breaking on his new office complex."

"I know, Michael, I know. But couldn't you go alone? Do I really need to be there?"

Michael decided that no, she didn't really need to be there, and told her so in a way that reassured and comforted her.

Michael hung up the phone and looked out the window. They were approaching the Mansion. He thought about Kristin again and wondered if she liked Tampa.

After returning several phone calls, and a meeting with Henry, Michael picked up the private line in his office and dialed Kristin's number. She answered on the third ring.

"Hello," she said in her soft, evocative voice. Even the sound of her voice caused a sexual stirring in him.

"Kristin," he started, but before he could identify himself, she exclaimed, "Michael!"

"Yes. Um...how are you?"

"I'm fine. But I'm surprised to hear from you."

"I know, Kristin. I know I told you not to get in touch with me. But I was thinking about...well, about being at the hotel with you earlier. And I *do* want to see you again."

Kristin closed her eyes and pictured having sex with Michael. She smiled. "I'm so glad, Michael. When?"

"Well, I'm going to be in Tampa on Friday. I'm going to be the guest of honor at a ground-breaking ceremony." He stopped, aware of the hesitancy and nervousness in his voice.

"Yes?" she said, encouraging him to go on.

"Well, my wife was supposed to go with me, but she has to stay in Palm Beach. You know about her father?"

"Yes," she said, "of course."

"Right. Well, he's not doing so well so she's going to stay until Saturday." Damn, he sounded like a teenager calling up for a first date. Hell, he *felt* like a teenager calling up for a first date.

"Oh, I'm sorry," was all that Kristin could think to say. She waited for him to continue.

"Well, I know it might be damned inconvenient, but I was wondering..." Michael paused to pull himself together before taking the plunge.

"Well, I was wondering if maybe you could get to Tampa," he blurted out, then rushed to continue. "There's an Omni Hotel about a half a mile from where I'll be, and I thought maybe I could get over there..."

"And?" she said, encouraging him to finish what she hoped he was about to ask her, her heart beating fast in anticipation.

Michael took a deep breath and said, "Look, Kristin. I'd like to see you again. I know you're not a desperate woman who sits around in hotel rooms waiting for the married man to find time for you. I know you're better than that, and that's why it's hard to ask you this. You know my situation, though, and that's not going to change. But I want to see you again. This might be a chance to do that without worrying about...about anything," he finished.

There was a long pause on Kristin's end of the phone. Although he had said what she had hoped to hear, that he wanted to see her again, she was put out with the idea that she would have to fly to Tampa to have sex with him.

"Why can't you just come to the apartment tonight, Michael? Or tomorrow night? Why wait until Friday, in Tampa?"

"I'm busy every single minute between now and Tampa, Kristin. And, well, even though the apartment is pretty clandestine, it's still here in Tallahassee. It's just riskier."

More silence from Kristin's end of the phone. When Michael could stand the silence no longer, he said, "Forget it. I'm sorry. I shouldn't have asked. It's wrong of me to expect you to do something so ridiculous."

"I'll be there," she said softly. She wanted to see him again. She wanted to see him more than anything else, and if it had to be in a hotel in Tampa, then that's where it would be. She wondered at the force of this man. How could he have such an effect on her, so much so that she was willing to be a participant in such a...a...*compromising* affair? She had no answers, only desires.

"Ah, great then," he said, his relief obvious.

"Well, I wish things were different," she said, with honest regret in her voice, "but I'm not in a position to make any rules. And frankly, Michael, I don't think this affair can have any rules. We'll just take it as it comes."

"Kristin, I...well, I'm appreciative that you understand that, and I'm also glad you want to see me again."

"Oh, yes, Michael. I want to see you again...and again," she said pointedly.

A faint alarm went off in his brain. He turned it off.

"I'm glad," he said quickly. "Look, we're going to be flying down on the state's plane and using a friend's limo, not a rental. It has a private line. Could you call me at exactly one forty-five and let me know your room number?"

"Of course. Give me the phone number in the limo."

He did, and she repeated it back to him, promising to call the number at one forty-five.

"Good." Michael's nervousness abated somewhat. "I'm really looking forward to seeing you again."

"I'm looking forward to seeing you, too, Michael."

"Friday, then."

"Friday."

Kristin seemed to float over the thick white carpet to the custom-made black marble bar, where she stopped to pour a Dewar's over ice. She sipped it slowly, and took a deep breath, attempting to calm her racing heart. She knew she was falling in love with this man. She couldn't believe she had actually agreed to meet him in a hotel room in another city for what was obviously to be another short lovemaking session. Oh, but what lovemaking. She refused to think of it as just sex. To her, it was so much more.

Michael had told her that there had been no other women since he had married Caroline, and she believed him. She knew that she held an attraction for him that was causing him to step out of his cautious and

126

predictable world. She supposed she should be flattered. A man like him, so damned good looking, and the most powerful man in the state, for heaven's sake. But his power had nothing to do with her attraction for him. No, she just knew that from the first moment they had met that she had wanted him.

What did that kind of want really add up to? Did she just want him for the lovemaking they so obviously enjoyed with each other? Or did she want more of him? His love? Maybe she could have that. She was quite sure, though, that for him it was pure lust at this point.

Could he fall in love with me, she wondered. And if he did, would he be willing to leave her for me? She didn't think so. He had made it clear that he loved his wife very much. But how much could he really love her if he was willing to cheat on her, and to go to such lengths to do it?

Kristin bent down to stroke Amos, her golden Persian who was demanding her attention at the moment by rubbing against her calves. She put her glass down and picked him up.

"Oh, Amos," she cried as she buried her face in his soft neck. "How can I make him love me?"

Governor Romano smiled for pictures with various Tampa businessmen and politicians.

He glanced at his watch. One thirty-nine. He nodded at Manny, who hurried over to where he was. "We have to be going, Governor Romano."

Right on cue. He nodded to Manny as he reached into his pocket for his sunglasses. "Ladies and gentlemen, I'm afraid I have to be leaving. I have another meeting scheduled before I return to Tallahassee."

After a few more well wishes and handshakes, and a hearty thanks for coming from Abe Gilbert, he was gone. Manny ushered him into the borrowed limousine, and a state trooper flanked the car. It was fine that the trooper would follow him to the Omni Hotel. He would wait outside the hotel until the governor was ready to be escorted to the airport. It was generally acknowledged within every law enforcement office in the state that the governor's chauffeur was also his trusted bodyguard, and their duties were light when they were assigned that particular detail. It had become a courtesy, really, rather than a necessity.

Michael had not yet told Manny why he was going to the Omni Hotel, but he knew he had to tell him now. He would have been surprised to learn that Manny instinctually knew why he was going there.

"Manny," Michael started, "I'm going to be meeting someone after..."

Just then the phone in the borrowed limo rang. Michael picked it up quickly. "Yes?" he said, cautious in answering a phone in someone else's limousine.

"Hi, Michael," she said. His nerves jangled a little, but he was also relieved. Until this moment, he wasn't sure she was even going to follow through. The thought occurred that she might not be in Tampa, after all.

"Everything's okay? You're here?"

"I am. Room seven nine three. How soon will you be here?"

"I'm not sure. Just a minute. Manny..."

"Five minutes, boss," Manny answered the question before it was asked.

"Five minutes. But I'm going to have to take a few minutes to see someone else. I have a friend meeting me in the lounge. I have to take a short meeting with him to make it look like that's the reason I'm there. It shouldn't take long. I'll see you in twenty minutes or so."

"Shall I order some Champagne?" Kristin knew it was a silly question, but she was hoping Michael meant to spare her some extra time. Some element of romance would be nice, after all.

"No good, for two reasons. Time, and discretion. Why would a pretty lady in a single room order a bottle of Champagne with two glasses?"

"I'll order one glass, and you can use the one from the bathroom," she laughed.

"Clever, but no. Please don't. I'm sorry about the time constraints, but I really won't have time to enjoy Champagne *and* you. "You understand, don't you?"

Kristin sighed softly and answered, "Yes, Michael, of course I understand."

"Good. Okay, we're pulling up now. See you soon."

"I'll be in touch soon, Michael, and let you know what I think of this project. I appreciate you giving me the chance to look it over."

"Glad to, John. After all, I trust your opinion more than anyone's when it comes to doing anything that might upset the EPA. I'm on their side most of the time, you know."

"Yeah, I know that. Nixon might have been a son-of-a-bitch, but he did a good thing, establishing the EPA. But it's evolved into a monster of over-regulation. That's why you need an objective opinion from me, isn't it? You don't trust yourself to be objective, do you? You must have a soft spot for trees and birds," John chided.

Michael laughed. "You'd think so, right? Yeah, I like trees and birds well enough; but in this case, I just don't want that over-regulation you just mentioned to come back and bite my friend in the ass."

"An even better reason to get me involved," John said. "I'll make sure it doesn't."

As Michael started uttering the words that signaled the end of the meeting with his friend, Manny turned and, following Michael's earlier instructions, approached the concierge's desk at the Omni.

"Excuse me," Manny said to the concierge. "Is there a private area where Governor Romano can make a phone call?" Manny emphasized *private* in an effort to ensure Michael wouldn't be interrupted during the call.

The concierge looked past Manny to see the governor, who was now approaching the desk.

"Of course. There are several meeting rooms on the third floor. Let's see. Yes, the Orange Blossom room is free this afternoon. Off the elevator, to the left, end of the hall. Will that be okay?" he asked, directing his question more to the governor than to Manny.

"Fine, thank you," Michael answered graciously.

"The elevators are..."

"Thanks, I spotted them earlier," Manny said before the concierge could finish.

Turning to Michael, Manny said in a formal tone, for the benefit of the concierge, "Let me get you to the Orange Blossom room, Governor Romano, and then I'll go let the state trooper know we'll be a few minutes longer."

They didn't speak on the ride to the third floor. Manny got off and said, "I'll be waiting right here." Michael nodded at him as the elevator doors closed. He rode up to the seventh floor, uninterrupted.

Michael's excitement and anticipation escalated on the ride up. Was it just six days ago that he had fucked Kristin for the first time? Christ, and again on Tuesday. Now here he was, only three days later, and he was going back for thirds. He acknowledged that opportunity had played a part in his infidelity, but sheer lust for the new and the different was the actual driving force. His appetite for Kristin had become acute, he realized with a sense of disquiet.

Kristin opened the hotel room door wearing a sheer black robe. Michael could see every luscious curve of her body. He knew it was meant to excite him, and it did. Man, it was exhilarating to feel like this!

The intensity of their sex moved to yet another level. Kristin was on top, and with each punishing bite to her nipples that Michael inflicted, Kristin punished him in return with hammering slams, one after another, evoking rasping grunts from both as flesh pounded against flesh. The fusion of pleasure and pain they had established took them to a newly-discovered, thrilling height, and Michael was enmeshed in the utter raw sensuality of it.

Afterward, as Kristin watched Michael straightening his tie in front of the mirror, she asked the question that had been on her mind since their first night together.

"Michael, what drew you to me, initially?"

Michael turned to her and looked into her always-mesmerizing eyes. He thought about telling her about her resemblance to Alison, but decided against it. "I've asked myself that same question. I still haven't come up with the answer. I guess on some level I sensed that sex with you would be fantastic. Who can account for that kind of instinct? It's as ancient as the mating ritual. It's like it's coded into our DNA. Does that make sense?"

"Perfect sense. The first night I met you, I left the fundraiser and sat in my car. For the first time in years, I had a deep, sexual urge. It shocked me, actually. That's when I knew I had to have you." At his questioning look, she added, "Sexually, I mean."

"I think we've proved our instincts were right."

"Oh, yes, definitely," Kristin laughed.

"Inevitable, then," Michael said as he shrugged into his jacket. And just like that, he had committed to ongoing adultery with Kristin Long.

She understood the message.

"I'll call you," Michael said, "but give me some time. Things are really heating up with the special session and I won't have a lot of opportunities for this over the next couple of weeks."

"I think my body could use a break anyway," Kristin replied, laughing. "This kind of sex—it's just so...*demanding* on my body. But it is so worth it. I think about it all the time, Michael. Do you?"

"I think about it, Kristin, sure." But Michael didn't want her to think it was meaningful for him, because it wasn't. He didn't really care how she felt. He had to get going.

Kristin had hoped he would say more about how special it was, but she let it go. There would be time for that in the future.

"All right then, I'll call you," Michael said as he reached for the door knob. He turned to face her. His expression softened. "Thank you, Kristin. It was terrific."

Then he was gone.

Kristin sat down on the bed and put her face in her hands. Oh God, I should stop this affair before I fall completely in love with him, she thought. She knew she was being used, but she was long past caring.

Michael's conscience was less troubled each time he had sex with Kristin. It was just that—sex—and now he was sure he could continue to compartmentalize it in his life. She was willing, flexible in her schedule, and on the same page that he was. She accepted this for what it was— fantastic sex that didn't carry any emotional weight.

Michael had never imagined having an affair, but that's what this was turning into. Had Caroline been with him more than with her father, it wouldn't have happened in the first place. But the opportunity and motivation were there, and so it *had* happened. He supposed those two things were why most affairs occurred. A man could get blindsided when he wasn't even looking.

When the elevator stopped on the third floor, Manny was waiting. He stepped in without looking at Michael.

Hell, Michael thought. He's pissed. I better talk to him. He probably thinks I'm a real bastard for screwing around on Caroline.

But Manny wasn't concerned about Michael screwing around on Caroline. He didn't think like that. In fact, he was surprised it had taken Michael this long to do it. He was pissed off, all right, but only because he thought Mike was playing it a little too loose. Mike needed his help with planning, and expecting Manny to make all the right moves to cover Mike's ass, with only moments of notice, put Mike in danger of being caught. Manny thought that the man who was like a brother to him didn't have the confidence or respect—he didn't know which—to trust him with handling the details.

Didn't Mike know that he had the strongest ally in the world in him? Manny was hurt to think Michael didn't realize it. If he was willing to lay down his life for Mike, wouldn't he be willing to help him with something as simple as an affair? Hell, every man screwed around on his wife. Manny's own mistress was a testament to that fact.

As they pulled out of the parking lot of the hotel, Michael leaned up and said, "Hey, Manny, I'm sorry if I've offended you. I really am. I know how much you love Caroline, and I know you must think I'm a bastard for doing this. I..."

"Mike," Manny interrupted him. "This has nothing to do with Caroline. You ought to know me better than that. I don't give a damn if you're seeing someone on the side, but I am pissed off that you haven't involved me in making the arrangements. You're not being smart about this. How is it that all of a sudden you don't trust your best friend to do what I've always done for you? Clear the path, look out for you. Or isn't that true anymore?"

So that was it. Michael realized that Manny was right. It had been downright callous of him not to let his best friend, and the man he trusted with his very life, be involved in this. He told Manny so.

Manny was somewhat mollified, but there was something more.

"What else, Manny?" Michael asked.

"Nothing else. I just don't want you to have any problems because of this, Mikey. You've got too damn much to lose. Just the protective nature in me I guess. You need my help with this."

Michael put his hand on Manny's shoulder. "Ah, Mann thanks. You don't know how much it means to me to have a friend like you. I mean that. I should tell you more often.

"Look," Michael continued, "this came about mainly because of opportunity. Caroline's being out of town so much allowed some things to happen that, frankly, I wish hadn't happened. She should be back for good in a couple of weeks, and I don't think I'll have any desire to continue this. I'll tell you, I appreciate your having my back more than I can say, but I also don't want to put you in a tough position."

"Mike, I love Caroline, but I'm here for you. You ain't gonna fool around anymore, good for you. But I'm here to make sure you don't get in trouble. That covers a lot of different territory. I'm also here to make your life easier. Just don't forget that again, okay?"

"You got it, Manny. Thanks."

Manny hesitated before asking, "Hey, Mike, how come you got involved with this particular broad in the first place?"

"Manny, she's not a broad." There was mild reproach in Michael's voice.

"Okay, this lady."

"Hell, I don't know how to explain it, exactly." Michael paused, looking for the answer which was important to him in a way that Manny couldn't know. "Have you ever met a woman who just knocked you on your ass?"

"Yeah, my momma!" Manny laughed. Michael laughed with him, though he felt a need to be serious. He wanted to understand his own feelings and to get them clear in his head and off his chest.

"No, really, Manny. I'm glad we're having this talk, because I'm having a hard time understanding this. All I can say is that from the first time I laid eyes on her, I wanted her. You know, she reminded me a lot of Alison." He didn't need to tell Manny who Alison was. "So I was temporarily thrown. It made me look at her in a way I normally wouldn't have looked at her—or any woman, for that matter. Then I felt an attraction for her, which surprised the hell out of me.

"I wouldn't have pursued it, though. She came after me. And I guess I just didn't have the strength to say no. I was flattered. And I admit I was *hot* for her."

"Something's changed between you and Caroline on that front?" Manny asked, knowing the question wasn't too personal. He and Michael had talked about everything over the years.

"No, not at all. That's the funny thing about it. And even though I've had some of the most exciting sex in my life with Kristin—that's her name—Kristin..."

"I know," Manny said casually.

Of course he would know, Michael thought.

"But even though it's been great with Kristin," Michael continued, "I'm still as turned on as ever by Caroline. Even more so. It doesn't make any sense."

"Sure it does," Manny countered. "I've never believed we were meant to be with just one woman from the time we say, 'I do.' It's just not natural. Why wouldn't we be turned on by more than one woman?"

133

"I guess you're right," Michael agreed, "but I feel guilty about it. Guilty as hell. How about you? You ever feel guilty?"

"At first I did. A little bit. Then I realized that nobody was getting hurt. The wife lives a good life, she's happy with the kids and the house, has just about everything she wants, including regular sex with me. So I figured, hey, if nobody's getting hurt, what does it matter?"

Yeah, what does it matter? Michael asked himself. "I'll have to chew on that one a while, Manny."

Manny was silent for a few minutes before he said, "Yeah, I guess you will, Mike."

17

MICHAEL WOKE UP and looked at the clock. It was a few minutes after midnight. He realized he had woken up because he was thirsty. He picked up the glass on the night stand and took a long drink of flat Perrier. He looked over at Caroline. He could see the outline of her perfect profile in peaceful slumber. The night light from the dressing room provided the faintest light, but it was enough for him to appreciate the beauty of those fine features.

What a great night of lovemaking they'd had. He felt a sharp pang of guilt at the thought of having fantastic sex with Kristin just the day before in Tampa, then making love to his wife this evening. And he had wanted her so damn much. Sitting next to his wife, he had felt his desire for her rise again and again throughout the evening, despite the endless, dull speeches delivered at the Chamber dinner. He thought it would never end. He hadn't waited until they got home. With the privacy window up, he had fondled and kissed and titillated Caroline in the back seat of the limo until they were both panting with desire. He was living out all kinds of fantasies. He smiled, despite his guilt. Man, it was like the high he had gotten in screwing Kristin spilled over to Caroline.

He thought about his lovemaking with Caroline. Sweet and tender, building to a frantic pace until she was emitting falsetto-like screams of passion. Quite certain they had woken the live-in staff, they had laughed in each other's arms afterwards—a good, hearty laugh—while Michael playfully shook his fist at the wall, as if to the other occupants of the Mansion, shouting in his best Italian-imitation accent, "My wife...she's an operah singa!"

He smiled at the recollection. How can I love my wife like this, he wondered with a sigh, and yet hunger after another woman so much? He didn't have any answers, because he was thinking with the wrong head. He let his mind wander to sex with Kristin.

What a sexual dynamo. Yes, she was new, and no doubt that was part of the excitement, but she was also the best damn sex he had ever had. Her luscious mouth, her body...able to take all the forceful fucking he had to give, and to give it back to him.

Michael felt another erection coming on. He turned to Caroline and pushed the sheet from her body. He put his mouth on her breast and began his seduction. He got the desired reaction.

Caroline moaned softly, opening her eyes to see Michael's head moving down her body.

As she parted her legs to allow his seduction, still not fully awake but deliciously aroused, she whispered his name with all the love she felt for him.

"Ah, my *sweet Caroline,*" came his muffled response.

Michael drank his coffee and read the Sunday morning papers with a mixed sense of well-being and worries...well-being in his cozy world with his beloved wife, worries that came with being governor. It was almost the third week in August, which should give him plenty of time to prepare for the special session that was set for October tenth. The tide was going against him at this point, however, and it was going to take a lot of effort and energy to turn it back.

He looked at the immediate itinerary that had been prepared for him, then at the short-term itinerary, which usually covered two to four weeks. Two more out-of-town trips over the next month, which he had precious little time for. One to Miami to cut the ribbon in front of a new office complex on Brickell, erected by one of his most important supporters, Rafael Medina; and another trip to St. Augustine to open a new historical museum. Plans also included meeting with key legislators in both areas, in an effort to enlist their support.

He was hoping Caroline could go with him. Traveling was harder on her than it was on him, but he loved having her with him. Seeing Kristin in Tampa for a quickie was one thing. Having his wife with him on a trip was another. Infinitely better. Maybe they could stay overnight at the Fontainebleau Hotel in Miami, order room service, take a walk on that gorgeous beach. Manny would, of course, have to stay within safe distance, which might not leave much room for spontaneous romance. It would still be nice, though. He made a note to ask her about it, but he didn't have to wait long.

She came into his office just as he finished jotting it down. She was smiling, and as he got up to come around the desk and hug her, she said, "These bags under my eyes are your fault, you know. So if I look dreadful today, you have no one to blame but yourself."

"You look gorgeous, sweetheart," he said sincerely.

"Well, I must say I feel pretty wonderful after all that delightful lovemaking. You, my darling, are better than ever. I didn't think that was possible."

Michael stood up and pulled her to him to make certain she didn't see the look of concern on his face. "Well," he said, stroking her soft hair, "even though the separation has been tough, I think it has made me want you more than ever."

He couldn't let her think that there could be any other reason for his heightened ardor.

To his relief she said, "I thought the same thing, and I'm glad we're back on track. It was trying at first." She stepped back out of his arms to look at him before she continued. "That's why I'm hoping you won't be too angry when I tell you I have to go back to Palm Beach today. We can look at the positive side of this...absence makes the libido grow stronger."

She could see Michael was keeping his annoyance in check. He could have such a temper, though he rarely displayed it with her, or anyone else for that matter.

"How long this time?" he asked tersely.

"Just a few days, I think. When I left yesterday, there were some problems brewing with the domestics, something to do with the 'round-the-clock nurses disrupting the household. The major-domo doesn't seem to be able to get it under control, so I really must go down. I need to make sure nothing interferes with father's recovery. Besides, you've been so busy preparing for the special session that I don't see that much of you when I'm here."

"That's true. But Caroline, I have two out-of-town trips planned over the next few weeks, Miami and St. Augustine. I want you to go with me."

"I'll certainly plan to, Michael, but you know how tentative this whole situation with father is. Are the trips that important to you?"

"Only in terms of wanting to be with you, wherever I go." Michael was speaking the truth. He always wanted her with him. Before, it was because she was the other half of him. Now, he had to admit that he also needed her as a shield to keep him from straying.

"St. Augustine isn't that important. It's a short car ride, two meetings, and a turnaround. But I was hoping," he continued, "that we could enjoy a nice romantic night in Miami at the Fontainebleau. We have an after-hours ribbon cutting downtown, and it would really be too late to come back to Tallahassee. That's on September eighth. Please circle that date in red and don't let anything else interfere."

"Well, that sounds nice. A romantic evening with room service on the balcony, a walk on the beach. Do I have it right?" she teased.

"You read my mind."

"Easy to do after all these years."

He knew that what she said was true. They seemed to know what the other was thinking much of the time. He wondered why she seemed to have no inkling of his affair. He was curious. He took a shot.

"I'm surprised you're able to even think at this point, with all you've had to worry about."

"You've noticed I'm distracted, then? I'm sorry, Michael. I'm trying to keep my head in the game."

"No, no," he protested. "That's not a criticism, just an observation. You've been stretching yourself pretty thin. That's why I think a nice evening away would be good."

"It will be. I'll plan on it. And thank you for thinking of it. You've been so supportive through all of this. I don't know what I would have done this past month if you hadn't been there for me."

Michael felt like a real shit. He knew he hadn't been there for her like he should have, as a faithful husband. She believed in him and gave him reason to believe in himself. He hugged her hard, and assured her that he would always be there for her.

18

DESPITE HAVING THE BEST home medical care his money could afford, not to mention a doting daughter, Pierce Fulton had suffered another stroke. It wasn't another cerebral hemorrhage, which almost certainly would have been fatal, but an ischemic stroke. Though not as severe, it was certainly serious. Pierce had spent another ten days in the hospital. Caroline was calling to tell Michael her father was returning home that day.

She had been at her father's hospital bedside much of the time, but now being at home with her husband was becoming more important than being at her father's side. She was weary, horny and lonely, she was saying to Michael, causing him to laugh. "I can cure all those ailments," he promised.

Her absence, however, had worked in his favor in terms of seeing Kristin Long. Twice he had gone to the apartment. The logistics of doing so were made much easier now that Manny was on board.

Sex with Kristin was becoming an addiction. He'd never used drugs, but he suspected this was what it was like. He wanted more of it. He wanted the high of it. He wanted the thrill of it.

He heard Caroline saying, "Michael, are you listening?"

"Sorry, Caroline. Got distracted for a second. What were you saying?"

"I was saying that on Friday I'm going to have Hanes drive me to Miami from here. It's only about an hour's drive, and it will save some wear and tear on me if I don't have to fly back to Tallahassee first. Where and at what time shall I meet you?" Caroline asked.

"That's going to work out just fine, Caroline. I need to be in Miami early on Friday. I have two different meetings set up with some legislators down there. I'm going to need their support for the special session."

"That's good Michael, but you didn't answer my questions—when and where?"

"Oh, sorry. Well, we have reservations at the Fontainebleau, like we planned, for Friday night. So why don't you meet me there around four o'clock? I'll be finished with my appointments, and we'll both have time to freshen up and make the ribbon-cutting by five thirty. It's on Brickell. That's only about fifteen or twenty minutes from the hotel."

"Sounds perfect. I'm really looking forward to spending a romantic evening with you. I need a break, badly."

"I'll bet you do. We should get back to the hotel by seven or so. They're just going to be serving hors d'oeuvres and cocktails at the ceremony, so we'll have dinner at the hotel. Room service, all cozy and romantic. Does that still sound good to you?"

"Absolutely wonderful."

"Say, since Hanes is driving you down, think he'd like a break, too? I'll get another room for him. I assume you'll be going back to Palm Beach the next day anyway, right?"

"Right. And if he stayed overnight, he wouldn't have to come back to get me. Why, Michael, that's a nice thought. I know he'd really appreciate it."

"Done. I'll have Lynn make another reservation."

"That's really so nice of you, Michael."

"Well, Hanes has been terrific during this time."

"He really has, Michael. What about Manny? You've booked a room for him?"

"Naturally. But I don't think those two will be going out on the town together, do you? I mean, my Brooklyn bodyguard with your father's British chauffer. Can you picture that?"

Caroline laughed with Michael at the image of those two men trying to find something to enjoy doing together.

Manny would be looking for topless bars, and Hanes would be looking for a four-star restaurant. No, they wouldn't have a good time together, but they could both have a break and each have a nice evening in Miami.

"Well, it all seems to be worked out. So I will meet you at the hotel at four o'clock," Caroline said. "I've missed you so much this week, Michael, but father's doing better. I'll go back to Palm Beach on Saturday, and then come home on Sunday."

"That's terrific news, Caroline. I've missed you, too. But we'll make up for lost time Friday night. And we'll talk in between."

"Okay, darling. Love you."

"Love you, too, Caroline."

The temptation was just too great to resist. It had been over a week since he had seen Kristin, and he wanted her again—badly. He blamed it on Caroline. Sure, she had to be there when Pierce went back to the hospital. But did she have to spend ten days there? She should have been here with me, Michael fumed.

It should be easy to meet Kristin in Miami. The timing could be worked out. His first meeting should be over by eleven, and he didn't have to be at the second one until two. That gave him three free hours. Hours he could spend with Kristin. He'd beg off any invitations for lunch.

He wondered if she would even do it. Why should she travel all the way down to Miami just to have a few hours with me? Maybe I'm asking too much of her. He decided there was only one way to find out.

Michael picked up his private line and called Kristin's number. There was no answer. He let it ring nine times, and wondered why she didn't have an answering machine. Not that he would have left a message, but it seemed everyone had a machine or a service these days.

He hung up the receiver and pondered his motives. Why *was* he so determined to see her again? He decided it was simply one thing— incredible sex. Even though sex with Caroline was still great, this was different. It was the most exciting sex he'd ever had. It was like she had lit a fire in him, and he needed to keep stoking it.

What was it Manny had said? As long as no one gets hurt, there's no problem. And why should anyone get hurt? Caroline would never find out. He'd make sure of that. Once Caroline was back for good, he wouldn't be going to Kristin's apartment here in Tallahassee. Too risky. Meeting her out of town was the perfect solution. He traveled often enough, and she seemed to be willing to travel to meet him.

He wondered how long she would be willing to do this. She might start making demands. If that happened, he would have to remind her where things stood. He would never consider giving her any rightful place in his life. If Kristin wanted to continue seeing him, knowing that, then fine. Otherwise, he would have to break it off. He was confident he would know if things started getting too sticky. He would know when to cut out.

He thought about what would happen if Caroline did find out somehow. He knew she would leave him, without a second thought. They had talked about how that could never happen to them, and if it did, then the relationship wouldn't be worth salvaging anyway. What they had was so special, so profound, that for one of them to cheat, something would have already have gone wrong in the marriage.

Michael realized that he had always thought this was absolutely true. Yet, here he was, having an affair, and it wasn't because anything had gone wrong with the marriage. He loved Caroline as much as ever. He would be with her for the rest of his life. In fact, life without her was unfathomable. So why was he having this affair? Back to square one.

It was the sex. That was all. He thought about how he felt about Kristin. He was hot for her, but there was no emotional element. She was beautiful and sexy, and he even admired her, but he had no feelings whatsoever for her. His love, even his simple affection, was saved solely for Caroline. Kristin was just an exciting piece of ass. Ah, but that mouth of hers. He had to admit her mouth was something special. She kissed with a lustiness he had never known. So nakedly passionate. And when she used that mouth on him...

Michael was getting excited, but he had no time to indulge that excitement now. He had to be on the golf course with three senators in less than an hour.

He called Kristin's number again, not really expecting her to answer, since only five minutes had passed. When she did, he was caught off guard.

"Kr...Kristin?" he stammered.

"Hi, Michael," she said, obviously glad to hear his voice. "How are you?"

"I'm fine. And you?"

"I'm fine."

Michael was trying to decide the best way to ask her to meet him in Miami when she interrupted his thoughts and asked, "Would you like to see me again, Michael?"

Relieved, Michael replied, "Yes. Yes, I would, Kristin, but it's going to have to be in Miami this time."

"Miami? Michael, why can't you just meet me at the apartment? Why do I have to travel to Miami?"

"Are you angry?" he asked, not able to ascertain from her voice how she felt.

Kristin checked her irritation before she answered, "No, I'm not angry. A little put out, though. I'm just wondering why we can't see each other here in Tallahassee more often."

"Caroline's coming back for good, Kristin, and the apartment won't be an option. We'll just have to meet on my out-of-town trips from now on. Do you have a problem with that?"

Kristin heard the cavalier tone in his voice—almost like, *take it or leave it.* It exasperated her, but casually she replied, "Not really. But why Miami?"

"I have some business down there. Caroline will be meeting me in Miami later that afternoon, but I'll have three hours free in the early afternoon, and I just couldn't stop thinking about spending that time with you."

Kristin was stung by Michael's casual reference to his wife's meeting him, even though she was pleased to hear him say he couldn't stop thinking about her. Although she was tempted to tell him she just wouldn't continue to be available for a quickie whenever he wanted it, she found she couldn't say it. After their amazing times together, she knew she would go anywhere to make love to Michael. Her body was craving his again. Oh, yes, she wanted to see him, but she wouldn't let him think it was always going to be so easy.

"That's fine, Michael. As a matter of fact, I was planning to go to Miami next week to visit the company in Miami Lakes," she lied easily. "I'll just move it up to Friday of this week."

"Perfect," Michael said with enthusiasm.

"So let's plan this," Kristin said. "Where are you going to be—what part of the city?"

"The first meeting will be in Coral Gables. That should end around eleven. The second meeting is at my hotel, the Fontainebleau, around two. So I'll be on Collins Avenue for the rest of the day. Could you meet me at a hotel in that area?"

"What about at the Fontainebleau?"

"No," Michael countered. "That's where I'm staying with Caroline."

Caroline again. Kristin ignored the reference and said, "I understand that. But it would be perfect from the standpoint of your not being spotted somewhere you shouldn't be. There are more than a thousand rooms there. You'll be a guest, so it won't be unusual for you to be around the hotel. If you walk into a different hotel just to meet me, there's a chance you'll be recognized." She paused and took a deep breath. "And I can leave before your wife gets there."

It was an excellent plan, Michael thought. She was right about all of it. He had been foolish to think that she might be a threat. She was obviously just as concerned about secrecy as he was.

"You are so right, Kristin. I'll have Manny call the hotel and ask for you to find out what room you're in."

Kristin had never formally met Manny, but Michael had told her that he was the one dropping him off at the apartment.

"You're so lucky to have Manny," she said with a sigh. "I wish I had someone like that to trust."

"Kristin, I hope you'll never talk to anyone about this."

"Of course not, Michael."

"Good. So, back to Friday. Think you can get an early check-in on Friday. Before eleven?"

"I'll go down Thursday afternoon, just to make sure. I'll do a late check-out on Friday. That way, there can't be any chance of the two women in your life crossing paths." There was a hint of sarcasm in her voice.

Michael paused. The two women in his life. Though technically correct, he didn't feel like he had two women. After all, Kristin was just..."Kristin, I'm really appreciative of the way you're handling this. You're really something."

"I'm glad you think so."

"I do. And I'm really looking forward to seeing you Friday."

"I'm looking forward to it, too, Michael."

"Okay, then, see you at the Fontainebleau. Bye, Kristin."

Michael was tempted to fuck Kristin again, but he was aware of his limits. If he was going to be able to make love to Caroline that night, which he certainly planned to do, he would have to hold back. He made that decision with regret. Hard to fathom, but the sex with Kristin had been the best yet. What was that song about hurting so good? He got it now.

"I better use your shower," he said as he rolled off the bed.

Kristin looked at Michael's magnificent body, and took his hand and pulled him back down to her for a kiss. She would have loved it if he had come back to her then, but he headed for the bathroom instead.

He stopped abruptly and turned around to her. "Come in and join me, why don't you," he said, abandoning his resolve against sex for a second time.

"Love to. Just give me a minute to put my hair up. Get the shower started."

Michael took in all of her lithe, beautiful body as she confidently stepped into the large walk-in shower. He picked up the lavender-scented bar of soap and sensually ran it over her breasts. Putting down the soap, he began to massage them, gently at first, then with more eagerness. He squeezed her nipples, hard, between his thumbs and forefingers, and was gratified to see them pucker in response. He moved his hands down her sleek sides and around to her buttocks. She put her hands on his shoulders for support as his strong hands massaged her buttocks and the insides of her thighs.

She pressed into him, rotating her slick breasts against his chest. Michael let out a groan, and then pushed her up against the marbled shower wall.

His lips traveled down her neck to her breasts. He sucked her taut nipples as his fingers slid into her. He loved doing this to Kristin. She was so tight and hot, and he really got off on how she responded to his avaricious explorations. She gasped and rode his fingers, but it wasn't enough to satisfy the deep need that only his cock could satisfy.

"More," she demanded in her sultry voice. Michael obliged by quickly flipping her around and bending her torso over the built-in shower seat. Kristin locked her elbows in anticipation of his impending forceful entry.

With her lovely ass in such an enticing position, Michael considered it...but he would save that for another time. Instead, he held onto her hips as he rammed into her eager vagina. Kristin yelped, and Michael heard both the ecstasy and the injury in her voice. Deeper and harder he went with each thrust, the new angle taking him to unexplored silken depths. Kristin moaned and rocked back into him to meet each demanding plunge. They became lost in the prolonged rhythm and escalated pounding, until they both cried out in orgasmic pleasure.

As he took a moment to catch his breath, Michael looked down at her tanned, glistening back, which was rising and falling with her labored breathing. His hands caressed the shapely curvature of her buttocks. She really was goddamned beautiful. He stayed inside her until their breathing calmed. God, but she was the absolute sexiest woman he had ever known.

He pulled her up and turned her around and covered her mouth with his, sucking the very last of her energy from her body. "That was god dammed magnificent."

"Magnificent," Kristin echoed, sighing deeply. She closed her eyes and leaned against the wall of the shower, letting the warm water run down her body.

"I can't seem to get enough of you," Kristin sighed.

"Christ, the feeling's mutual," Michael admitted, as he turned and began to soap off.

It dawned on him that he had no intention of ending it with Kristin. He supposed that he would keep on seeing her, just like this, whenever he could safely do so. When will it end, then? He couldn't see a reason to stop it, as long as he continued to be careful. And he really didn't want to stop it. It was just too damned fine to give up.

As he dressed, he watched her brush out her shiny, raven-black hair. He smiled as he compared that surprising shock of silver along the front of her hairline with her shocking wild-sex streak.

Fastening his cuff links through his French cuffs, he was reminded of the stud he had left at her apartment. He had not thought about it again after that first night, not until just last week, when he was going through his jewelry chest. He could have kicked himself for not remembering it either of the two other times he had been at her apartment. But hell, with everything else going on, including the amazing sex that took place when he was there, it really wasn't surprising.

"Kristin, the first night I was at the apartment, I lost a tuxedo stud. Did you find it?"

Kristin looked perplexed. "No, Michael, I haven't seen it. Did you lose it in the bedroom?"

"Yeah, I remember it hit the floor. Will you look for it?"

"Of course. But I've had a cleaning service in the apartment twice, so I hope it hasn't been vacuumed up."

Michael was distressed to think one of the four studs, a first-anniversary gift from Caroline, could have been lost to a cleaning service's vacuum cleaner. "Well, just look for it, please."

"I will. And if I find it, I'll give it to you the next time I see you."

"Thanks. By the way, did you get to take care of business while you were here?" he asked as he put on his jacket.

She hadn't really needed to take care of business here in Miami. She had dropped by the plant for a few minutes the day before, prior to checking into the hotel, but she had spent the morning in the room, waiting for Michael. But she didn't want him to know that.

"Yes," she answered, "although there really wasn't a lot of business I had to take care of. It's just a good idea for me to show up now and then— so my accountant and lawyer say—to let them know I'm still involved and interested."

"And are you involved and interested?"

"Sure. But I don't want to get bogged down in the everyday running of the operations. As I told you, I have some excellent people in place for that."

"No head for business, huh?"

"Actually, I met Ted because I was an accountant with one of the big eight accounting firms, and we were doing an independent audit of Pro-Long Plastics."

"I didn't know that."

"There's a lot you don't know, Michael, because you never asked. I have an MBA from Florida State. I double-majored undergraduate in accounting and finance." She smiled at him and said, "Impressed?"

"Am I *impressed?* Beauty, brains, sexuality beyond belief...Kristin, why are you wasting your time with me?"

"Why do you say 'wasting' my time with you, Michael? Because you aren't going to leave your wife for me?"

"I guess so."

"Have I asked you to?"

"No."

"And I'm not going to. I don't consider any hours spent being happy a waste. I'm only thirty-three years old, and I've already lost my parents and my husband. I've had too much sadness and loneliness, and I'm not going to throw away any kind of happiness that easily."

"God, you have been through a lot. I am sorry."

"Thank you. My biggest regret is not having a baby with Ted. I know if I had a baby, my life would be so much fuller. But that just didn't work out for us. I still have time. I'm sure I'll get married again someday and have a baby. I hope so, anyway."

"I know what you mean. A baby is something Caroline and I always wanted, too."

The mention of Caroline hurt Kristin, as it always did. She tried not to let it show as she said, "But you had a vasectomy. Why did you do that if you wanted children?"

"Because Caroline had three miscarriages and the doctor said it would be a bad idea for her to get pregnant again."

"Oh, I see. I'm sorry."

"Yeah. Thanks." His voice was subdued with a tinge of sorrow.

Michael sat down next to Kristin on the bed as he felt an unaccustomed sorrow come over him. It was a sense of sorrow for both of them, and he pulled her close, wishing he could do something to make this remarkable woman's life better. But, of course, that really wasn't possible.

19

MICHAEL REGARDED HIS wife's lovely features, enhanced as they were by the soft glow of candlelight. The hotel had indulged his request for a room service meal by candlelight, creating a romantic atmosphere and adding to the pleasure of dining privately on the balcony of their suite which, naturally, overlooked the ocean.

Michael Romano was betraying his wife, and his deception was becoming more abhorrent.

He loved Caroline. He adored her. Her happiness meant more to him than anything in the world. He would defend her, under any circumstances, more aggressively than he would defend himself. He would have killed with his own hands anyone who hurt her pride. Yet here he was, potentially the greatest offender.

He felt like a criminal. Her ignorance of the truth and her constant love for him were torturous. In the middle of a conversation, he would suddenly be stung by his guilt, and would not hear a word she was saying.

Nothing was worth this torture he grappled with. Nothing was worth the potential anguish for her. He would end the relationship with Kristin.

No more rationalizations. No more surrendering to lust. His life with his wife was the foundation of his happiness. Nothing else meant more, not even his political career. Here was the woman who had believed in him before he had given the world reason to think he was worth believing in. He owed her so much for where he was today, and he wouldn't repay that debt with pain.

"What are you thinking about, darling?" she asked as she reached for his hand, giving it an affectionate squeeze.

"I was just thinking about the first time I saw you, and how beautiful I thought you were. How I almost spilled your vichyssoise in your lap at the Palm Beach Country Club, I was so nervous."

"I don't think that would have cooled my attraction for you one bit. I remember how upset mother and father were that I was flirting with a waiter."

"I remember that, too. But I was flirting back. They didn't have much to say about it after that, did they?"

"Well, when they realized that you were at least a Columbia Law School student merely working in Palm Beach for the summer, they were a little relieved. *And*, a law student who spoke almost flawless French."

"God, I was just trying to impress you. I heard you using some French phrases at dinner and thought I'd serve up a few of my own. The look on your face was priceless."

"There you were, devastatingly handsome, extremely attentive, and you spoke French, too. Who *is* this man? I remember thinking. I was also thinking I was going to find out."

"Lucky for me, there were no clerking jobs that summer. Otherwise, Victor's family wouldn't have recommended me to the Club, and I'd never have met you. Remember that first night together, when we got caught making out in your cabana? I had waited there for you for almost an hour. I thought you weren't coming."

"Oh, I remember. But I also remember they were suspicious, and I couldn't get away for a while. They sent Hanes to find me—and he found *us*, in a passionate embrace. Father was so upset."

Michael laughed. "I think the best thing I ever did was standing up to your father that night. Remember how nervous we were, following Hanes back to the main house, and how you didn't want me to talk to your father, but I insisted? I wanted him to know that my intentions were honorable."

"He didn't exactly welcome you."

"He sure didn't. I remember being so overwhelmed when I walked into that house. And that was just the kitchen."

Michael squeezed her hand tightly and said, "It was the best night of my life, despite everything, because it was the real beginning of my life with you."

"What a summer of passion that was," Caroline sighed.

"It was a summer of fully discovering each other," Michael said, his voice reminiscent.

"And I loved everything I learned about you," Caroline assured him.

They had reminisced like this, saying these same words and feeling these same feelings, numerous times over the years. The romantic impact was always as strong, and the conversation often led to a phase of heightened emotional tenderness between them.

Caroline smiled. "No doubt father hoped that being separated that following year would cool things down. Was he ever wrong. It only increased my desire."

"Mine, too. I knew I had to do well, because I wanted to be able to write my own ticket, to practice law anywhere in the country—and I had my sails set for Palm Beach, and you. I was a book-cramming celibate that entire year. Well, except at Christmas," he teased.

"Didn't we set Palm Beach on its ear by getting engaged at Christmas and married that next summer? All I could think about my last six months in Paris was our wedding."

"Whoa, your wedding gown...you were stunning. When I was standing there, watching you come down the aisle, I was in a trance. I felt like I was looking at a fairy princess. The most incredible, beautiful woman I had ever met, who had actually consented to be my wife." He picked up her hand and pressed his lips to her palm.

"And my parents. They were a stitch, weren't they?" Michael continued, laughing. "Remember that tux I rented for dad? The tailors worked on it for days, and it still looked like dad had driven a truck across the country in it. And momma. Poor momma. So out of place. But your parents were so gracious to them. I remember that so well."

"Mother and Father were always such good, decent people."

"They sure were. You know, your parents, the way they handled everything, including my parents, really helped me appreciate what class was. It wasn't just having money, and being the crème-de-la-crème of Palm Beach society. It was the way they treated everyone with respect. It's a spectacular quality. It's what made me love them."

"Mother certainly loved you," Caroline said. "Before she died, she told me that she was so happy with the choice I had made. She said you were an honorable man who would always take care of me."

Caroline's eyes began to tear as she said, "Father loves you, too. He doesn't show it as easily as mother did, but he does love you. When he gets better, Michael, I think we should make a point of spending more time with him."

"Absolutely. He needs to know how much we care, though he's had plenty of evidence of how much you care these last couple of months."

Caroline nodded, and then looked out over the moonlight-illuminated darkness of the ocean. "I just wish we had been able to give them grandchildren. They wanted them so very much," Caroline said sadly.

"I know, sweetheart. If there's anything in my life that's been a letdown, it's that. But it wasn't anyone's fault. It just wasn't meant to be. And there are plenty of people who have kids but who are miserable with each other. Our marriage is the only thing in life that *really* matters." He kissed her hand tenderly.

"You're sure, darling?"

"How can you doubt it?"

"No regrets about not adopting?"

"None. We wanted our own children, conceived in our love, to add to our lives. We didn't *need* children to make our lives complete."

"I must say my life is totally complete with you, Michael. Maybe our love has stayed so fresh and exciting because we didn't have children."

"I've thought about that, too. About how we've showered all our love on each other all these years, and that's what's kept it strong."

Caroline smiled at Michael, a smile filled with love and warmth and devotion...and happiness. Then her over-sentimental mood lifted, and she said, "Enough of this. I want another glass of Champagne, and then I want one more, and then I want to make love to you. Any objections?"

"None," Michael laughed. Underneath the laughter he was wondering if he would be able to make love. It had been a few years since he had tried to make love three times in a day. He shooed away his apprehension, realizing it could only make matters worse.

Michael had no problem making love to his wife. It was tender one moment and tumultuous the next. It was the best lovemaking they'd had in a very long time. With all the amorous foreplay, it lasted for almost two hours, and by the time Michael's spent body was able to achieve orgasm, Caroline had enjoyed several. They had fallen asleep in each other's arms and stayed there through the night.

Caroline awoke before dawn, and she woke Michael with a kiss.

"If we hurry," she said excitedly, "we can be on the beach for the sunrise. We missed our moonlight walk."

They hurried out of bed and dressed quickly. Michael picked up a still half-full bottle of Champagne, and two glasses. Caroline's smile said she loved it. He rejected the idea of waking Manny to accompany them. The hotel beach would be safe.

They finished the warm, less-than-bubbly bottle of Dom on the beach while they dug their toes in the sand and watched the dawn of the new day. For Michael, it was a new day indeed. It was a night of a renewed love and promise to his marriage, to his wife. Michael had never felt so happy or so grateful for being alive. As he watched the morning tide come in, he thanked his Creator for it all. "Lucky son-of-a-bitch!"

Michael knew he couldn't just discard Kristin without an explanation. Though he felt he owed her nothing, nothing at all, he did feel that she could become bothersome if he didn't end it quickly and cleanly.

He picked up his private line, and when she answered, he was somewhat surprised, and yet glad, to find that her voice had no effect on him, and that her image in his mind was no longer one of a sexy siren.

"Kristin," he started, with no hesitation, "I'm calling you to tell you that I can't see you anymore." He hurried on before she could answer.

"I know I've said it before, and I haven't been true to my word. But I'm being completely honest this time, Kristin. I just can't see you again."

Something in his voice told Kristin that he was serious, very serious, this time. There was an unmistakable resolve in his tone. She felt light-headed.

"Why, Michael? What's happened?" she asked in a tremulous voice.

"Nothing's happened, Kristin. Other than my deciding that what I'm doing is loathsome. Loathsome to everyone involved, but especially to Caroline."

Kristin started crying then, not caring any longer that he knew how emotionally involved she had become. She had fallen in love with him, and now she was losing him. Misery engulfed her.

"But I love you, Michael."

Damn, that was the last thing he had hoped to hear. Although he had suspected that she was falling in love with him, he hadn't been too concerned. After all, she had always known the score. But it wasn't his problem anyway. Not really. She was a big girl, and she had always said she accepted it for what it was. She would just have to handle it.

"I'm sorry about that, Kristin. I tried to warn you against it."

153

"You bastard! How could you have warned me against falling in love with you, when it was beyond my control?" She sounded as if she were in real pain.

Michael said soothingly, reassuringly, "You'll handle it Kristin. You'll be fine."

He heard her sobs soften, and when she next spoke, she sounded almost normal.

"I'm sorry I called you a bastard, Michael. You're right. You did warn me. I just couldn't help falling in love with you. And I will get over it. I will."

So it was going to be okay. Michael sighed with relief, and with a subconscious movement, he crossed himself—something he hadn't done in years. Vestiges of his Catholic upbringing.

"I could say all kinds of things right now, Kristin, about what a terrific woman you are. But that wouldn't serve any purpose. I think it's best just to end it by saying goodbye, and me wishing you happiness."

"Yes, I think that's best." She took a ragged breath and then said, "I'll still donate the maximum to your campaign, Michael. I still believe in what you stand for, politically anyway."

Michael hadn't even thought about that. The money wasn't important; in fact, it would be better if she dropped out of the picture in every respect.

"Don't do that, Kristin. You did enough when you underwrote the event at the Ambassador. It's not necessary, and I wouldn't feel right about it."

"No strings attached to the money, Michael. Just take it."

"Well, think about it, Kristin. I appreciate your even considering it, but you might feel differently when you think again. If you do, I'll understand."

"I won't change my mind. It's okay. And Michael? Thank you for what you gave me."

This woman was too good to be true. What a class act.

"Goodbye, Kristin."

"Goodbye, Michael."

Good luck, lovely lady, he thought as he replaced the receiver. She deserved it.

Kristin hung up the receiver slowly. There was a slight ringing in her ears, and everything was out of focus. She put her head between her legs to stop the rush of blood that was making her dizzy.

Her breath came in short, painful gasps, and she desperately wanted to drive away the familiar, agonizing pain. She couldn't do it, no more than she could when her parents had died, nor when Ted had died.

She wondered how this could be happening to her again. What have I done, she wondered, to deserve such pain? What? What terrible force was out there, working against her happiness?

Kristin Long was one of those women who, despite being beautiful and desirable, had little experience with relationships. Her dating in college had been casual, and though she had lost her virginity at nineteen and had several lovers after college, she had not lost her heart until she was twenty-eight, when she met Ted. Hers had been a happy, secure world, with no need of a husband, until her parents died. The resulting vulnerability had led to loving and needing Ted, with whom she'd had only three short years. Two of those years were pained ones, as together they dealt with his cancer. And then, finally, ultimately, she had risen out of those murky waters and gasped for love in the element of Michael Romano, only to founder once again.

Each loss had left a deep scar, and she had no doubt that this loss would leave one of its own. Just as she realized that she had no control over the loss of her parents or Ted, she knew she had no control over the loss of Michael Romano. Nothing would bring him back. The pain of separation was, she understood for the first time, just as painful in life as in death. The loss of one who lived could be just as painful as the loss of one who died. How cruel life could be.

She would deal with this new loss, just as she had dealt with the others.

After all, what choice did she have?

155

20

MICHAEL WAS WEARY from the day-to-day battles he was fighting over the special session. September had been a grueling month of working with key members of his staff, and several supportive legislators, to finalize the bills.

Every newspaper in Florida was at his throat, as were legislators and his own staffers—Andy most of all. He knew these people thought they were right, but they weren't. This was an issue that had to be addressed now, while it was still hot.

It didn't hurt that the President of the United States had called him personally to encourage him in his quest. His call had bolstered Michael at a time when he was actually considering throwing in the towel, despite the months of work in crafting the bills.

Besides the moral obligation he felt for holding the session, there was the matter of pride. He hated to admit it, but to back down now would be a sign of weakness. He wouldn't do it. Besides the president's support, he still had the support of a tight group of conservatives who were donating at record rates to his re-election campaign. And even more than that, his family had been watching the national news regarding his efforts, and they had all called and written to encourage him.

He wondered again what effect a defeat at the special session would have on his chances of being re-elected. The polls supported the theory that he would be badly hurt if he failed to convince the lawmakers to enact stricter abortion regulations. But the session was only a week away, while the election was still a year away. He would have plenty of time to make up lost ground if things didn't go his way.

He re-read the last paragraph of the editorial in the *Miami Herald*. It ended with, "Governor Romano has created a lose-lose situation for himself."

Could that be true?

He had been certain that once he had answered the cry for the specifics of the laws he was proposing, and a price tag estimate, then the opposition would let up and he would be able to overcome their strong antagonism.

But that action had wreaked even more havoc. The price tag of over a hundred thousand dollars for the special session in the midst of an already tight budget brought out loud cries of dissension.

Even the unlicensed clinic crackdown, which had gained support and momentum, was being criticized. He had been able to close down six dangerous clinics in the state, and while that was viewed as positive, there was another side presently being touted.

The top abortion providers in the state had met and subsequently warned him not to get carried away and start cracking down on legitimate clinics. That was not his intention, at least not initially. Sure, he'd like to see every one of them shuttered; but closing down the bad ones, the medically unsafe ones, was all he intended for now.

He had a genuine desire to see life-threatening clinics shut down, and if that bolstered his position for calling the special session, and for enacting abortion restrictions, then that was fine. Those places had been dangerous and had deserved to be shut down. Even the top abortion providers had acknowledged that fact.

But now things had taken a decided turn for the worse. The Florida State Supreme Court, in a 6-1 ruling, extended a personal-privacy guarantee in the state constitution to abortion for adults, and applied it also to girls under eighteen. It struck down the state requirement that teenagers obtain the permission of a parent, guardian or judge before having an abortion. In doing so, it discouraged any efforts to make abortions more difficult to obtain, saying that such efforts violated the State Constitution's guarantees of privacy.

That was just fucking insane. It meant that even a thirteen-year-old girl could walk into an abortion clinic and get an abortion without guidance. And wonder if she walked into one of those hell-holes?

The State Supreme Court's decision had led to the worst battering he had taken yet. Cries to cancel the session had come from every corner of the state. But he had refused to back down. If anything, it meant there was more need than ever to adopt his proposals, especially stricter regulation of abortion clinics.

The President of the Florida Right to Life Organization, Pete Gordon, had been even more vocal than Michael had been about the Court's decision. Pete had been outraged, and like the governor, he was looking to the Legislature to restrict abortion. If they didn't, he threatened, his group would push for a constitutional amendment that would define life at the beginning of conception. Michael didn't think that had much of a chance of catching on, however.

His weariness settled upon him like a cloud of dust, and he couldn't brush it off. He needed to talk to Caroline. He needed to hold her, to get back in touch with their personal life, and with some happiness.

He buzzed her office, where he knew she was, and asked her if she could take a few minutes to walk around the grounds with him.

They walked in silence for a while. Caroline knew that when he was ready to talk, he would. She knew that just being with him was a help.

"What am I going to do, Caroline?" he finally asked, doubt and anguish filling his voice.

"You're going to do what you've always done, Michael. You're going to stick to your principles. If there's anything your past has taught you, it's that you've never failed when you've held to your moral convictions. You can't change that formula now."

He sighed deeply and nodded his head. He knew she was right. She had said what was in her heart, and in his. Sometimes in the face of strong opposition, one could lose one's footing. Her words had put him back on solid ground.

"Thank you, Caroline. I needed to hear that."

"I know."

"Let's walk a while longer, okay?"

"Fine. It's a beautiful day. I love this slight chill in the air."

Michael looked up at the leaves in the trees, which were beginning to turn. The sun was breaking through the branches and scattering its rays upon the cooling earth. He breathed deeply, and as he did, he regained some of his zest for life. It had been sapped from him lately, and he was glad to recover it.

"How's your father doing? Have you talked to him today?"

"I did. He's doing well. He's getting out of bed for a couple of hours every day for therapy, and a couple of hours for sitting in the library. He's actually moved into the modern age and is listening to books on tape."

"Really? Good for him. I'm glad he's doing so much better. He's a tough old man, you know? Even his speech is improving rapidly. He even told me a dirty joke when I talked to him the other night. It was a little hard to understand, but he got it across."

"Are you serious?" Caroline laughed softly.

"I am. He also told me that he knew how much you had helped bring about his recovery. You know what else he told me?"

"What, Michael?"

"I wasn't so sure I was going to tell you this, but I think it's something you'd like to hear. He told me that at one point, he wanted to close his eyes and just go to sleep forever. But then he looked over and saw you, and he didn't want to leave you. He said that because you were there, at that moment, he realized he had a reason to live."

"Oh, Michael. He really said that?"

"He did."

"That makes me feel so good. Thank you for telling me."

"You're welcome. Don't tell him I told you. I think he'll tell you himself soon enough. I really don't know why he told me instead of you. Maybe he just wanted to remind me of what's really important, and what's really worth living for."

He looked into her eyes to tell her that he meant her, that she was all that really mattered.

"Thank you, darling." She put her arms around him and hugged him tightly, letting him know that she felt the same way.

As they held each other close, they unknowingly had the same exact thought; that no matter what life brought, they had each other.

With the special session set to begin tomorrow, Michael felt heartened by the swell of support he had received.

Already more than sixteen thousand activists from both sides had flocked to Tallahassee, hoping to influence the state's lawmakers, with more expected. At least half of those were anti-abortion protestors. Tonight, more than eight thousand of them had marched to the Capitol, chanting and singing, "Jesus Loves the Little Children."

In less than an hour, Michael would be addressing his legislators and the pro-life activists in a televised speech that would reach millions of Floridians, and much of the rest of the nation via tomorrow's network news. Michael and Andy had brought in extra speechwriters to help make his historic speech one that would have maximum impact, and serve as a template for other governors who were pursuing stricter abortion laws in their states.

It was, in his estimation, a powerful speech, and Michael felt he was poised on the brink of making history. He acknowledged the opposition was strong, but his numerous meetings with the President of the Senate and the Speaker of the House had left him with the hope that the proposed bills would make it out of committee and onto the floor for a vote by the full Legislature. If that happened, he was confident new laws would be made.

Despite the pummeling he had taken over the last three months—from the first day he announced his intention to call a special session—Michael was hopeful. Momentum was swinging his way, and the swell of support from pro-life activists was getting the attention of recalcitrant legislators.

Michael called Caroline and asked her to join him. He then called key members of his staff, those who were strong supporters of his quest, and asked them to join him and Caroline in prayer.

With a concluding chorus of "Amen" to spur him on, Michael and Caroline left his office to take their place on the podium, and in history.

Michael's appeal was pitched to the political leaders of Florida's Legislature. The crowd of eight thousand that would cheer his every point was already solidly in his corner. Many carried signs with identifying slogans: "Choose Life" and "Stop the Killing" and "I'm Pro-Life." This was a pro-life rally, but his speech was meant to resonate with both the pro-life and pro-choice faction. But the jeering pro-choicers would not be present.

Michael looked at the crowd before him. Faces of all ages and all races were looking to him to save the lives of the unborn. The speech was to be a short one, only fifteen minutes long. In that amount of time he could hammer home his points and keep crowd enthusiasm at its peak.

Michael and his speechwriters decided to use hard numbers to create the impression that Michael's proposed laws had the support of the majority of voters. Though the polling questions had been massaged to evoke responses of agreement, that information was not shared with his legislators or the crowd. Instead, he focused on only four of the proposed fourteen laws that had polled in his favor.

Caroline stood beside Michael, slightly recessed and to his right. She smiled with pride at her husband. Michael looked not only confident and poised, but very handsome and powerful as he stood at the podium and waved to the crowd.

After thanking them for being there to support him, Michael began by informing the crowd that sixty-six percent of registered voters in the state of Florida were *in favor raising standards for abortion clinics.*

The crowd cheered its agreement.

"To the Florida Senate and the Florida House of Representatives, I ask you to listen to the sixty-four percent of registered voters who *oppose public funding for abortion.*"

Another raucous cheer from the crowd.

"Mr. President and Mr. Speaker," Michael continued, addressing the leaders of the Florida Legislature's Senate and House, "Seventy-six percent of Florida voters agree that *doctors should inform patients about the status of the baby prior to abortion,* and sixty-six percent *are in favor of viability testing at five months.*"

The crowd clapped and cheered.

"Hear the voice of the people of Florida!" Michael implored his Legislature. "Let the House and Senate have a full vote on all of these laws. Don't let parliamentary procedure deny a vote by *all* legislators."

The crowd roared its agreement.

Michael encouraged those in the crowd to take their message to their lawmakers. "Your presence here is a clear commitment to the future of the unborn."

"An unborn baby is a sanctified life."

Cheers of righteousness.

"An unborn baby has a voice that deserves to be heard."

Cheers of compassion.

"Unborn babies are in need of those who would speak on their behalf and ensure their protection."

Cheers of commitment.

"Now more than ever, we need strong regulation of abortion clinics. Inspections over the last few months have revealed appalling conditions in abortion clinics."

Boos for the appalling abortion clinics.

"Now, more than ever, we need reason and rationale to prevail. Last week's ruling by the Florida Supreme court means that a thirteen-year old can walk into a clinic and have an abortion without adult guidance or consent."

Boos for an atrocious law.

After dynamically delivering a few more similar and encouraging points, Michael concluded, "Thank you for being here to represent the unborn, who cannot represent themselves. I ask for your support and your prayers as I continue my efforts to encourage your legislators to defend the rights of the unborn by passing laws that protect them."

Cheering, clapping, whistling and gospel singing accompanied Michael as he stepped down from the podium.

He had done his best. Tomorrow would begin the test of whether his best was good enough.

21

CAROLINE WAS WAITING for him when he walked through the door. She had, of course, heard the news. The special session was over. Over and finished, and for Michael, the outcome had been disastrous.

They held each other for a long moment before he said, "Let's go upstairs."

They walked silently, sadly, hand-in-hand up the stairs to the salon. Michael was weary. Caroline was trying to be strong, though her heart was breaking for him.

"Less than thirty-six hours," he said, falling into a slouched position on the sofa. "Less than thirty-six hours is all it took to pound every single bill into the ground. All that work, all that hope. The wasted time and effort." He expelled a ragged sigh.

There were so many things she wanted to say, but none of them seemed appropriate. She had never, ever seen him this devastated, this wrung out. It hurt her deeply to see him like this.

"Shall I turn on the news?" she asked, knowing he would be better off facing up to what had happened, and being aware of the media slant, rather than ignoring it.

"Go ahead."

It was three minutes till six. They spent those three minutes holding each other's hand in distressed silence.

Terry Marcus, the Channel 5 anchorwoman, did the lead-in on the story, reporting stonily into the camera, "Abortion-restricting bills backed by Governor Romano failed to reach votes of the full Senate or House before an emotion-racked special session adjourned. Legislators met for twenty-seven hours over the past two days to consider fourteen restrictive abortion bills, but not one of them made it out of committee to face a vote of the full Legislature. Governor Romano's bills were crushed in lopsided votes of two Senate committees and a House subcommittee.

"Governor Romano, however, refused to admit defeat, even though critics lambasted him for wasting taxpayers' money and lawmakers' time. He stated that it was a matter of values and conviction, not a matter of politics."

"Turn it off," he said quietly.

Caroline turned the television off and turned to Michael, opening her arms to him. He moved into her embrace. She kissed his forehead, his nose and his mouth tenderly. He put his head on her shoulder and closed his eyes. They held each other in silence for many minutes, until he finally spoke.

"I need to go down and make some phone calls." His voice was flat, and it seemed an effort for him to get up.

She knew he needed to be alone.

"Would you like to have dinner up here later?" she asked, sitting up next to him now and rubbing his shoulders.

"Sure. Give me a couple of hours."

She watched him leave, and thought again how she had never seen him quite so despondent. She had thought he would be angry instead, and that he would want to vent his frustration to her. As well as she knew him, however, she realized she couldn't always predict how he would behave. He was normally quiet like this when he had much on his mind, and although the special session had been a great blow, at least it was over. Well, if there was one thing she had learned over the seventeen years of marriage to Michael, it was to be flexible.

The best thing she could do for him now was just to be there to listen when he was ready to talk.

With heavy footsteps, Michael made his way down the stairs and into his office. He sat down at his desk and put his head in his hands, trying to make sense of everything that had happened.

The truth be known, he was glad the session was over, despite the outcome. He was sick and tired of worrying about it, thinking about it, talking about it, and most of all, defending it. He didn't even want to think about pursuing it at the regular session in the spring.

He couldn't ever remember feeling so demoralized.

His private line rang, and he was tempted to ignore it. But anyone who had his private number was someone he should talk to.

"Michael Romano," he answered in a hollow voice.

"Oh, Michael, I'm so sorry." *Kristin.*

"Kristin, why are you calling me?"

"Well, to offer my condolences on the outcome of the special session, of course. But, Michael, I also have some news that I hope will make you as happy as it made me."

"What is it, Kristin?"

"I'm pregnant!"

Michael was shocked into silence. Myriad thoughts raced through his mind, the first of which was, *Did I hear her right?* Followed by, *It can't be mine.* That would be impossible. He'd had a vasectomy. And how did she get his private number? Wait, had he given it to her back in the summer?

Random and radical thoughts and questions pinged inside his head like a jai alai ball bouncing off a walled space. The one he kept coming back to was, *It can't be mine.*

Was this a trick she was playing, trying to pull him back into her life? It had only been what, a month since he had last seen her? How could she even know she was pregnant already?

Instead of verbalizing any of these thoughts over the phone, however, he knew he had to see her, face to face, to determine if she was telling the truth—and to shut down her scheme if she wasn't. He needed get to the bottom of it *now*, and he couldn't do it over the phone.

He realized quite a bit of time had passed since she had spoken, and he felt compelled by her eerie silence to say something.

"I'm at a loss here, Kristin. I'm stunned."

"So am I, Michael. But I'm also happy."

Michael couldn't reconcile her happiness with his alarm. "I need to see you, Kristen. I can't talk about this on the phone."

"I agree, Michael. When?" Kristin sounded anxious.

"Can you meet me at your apartment in an hour? Wait, do you still have it?

"Yes."

"Okay. I'll see you in an hour."

He hung up the phone with a sweaty palm and a thudding chest. Just how much more fucked up could this day *get?*

He took a deep breath to calm himself so he could think. He had to come up with an excuse for getting away. He and Caroline were supposed to have dinner together in about an hour.

He rang Manny in the garage apartment, a nicely-furnished and comfortable area where he stayed throughout the day and into early evening so that he would be available if Michael should need him.

"Manny," he began, "I know it's almost quitting time, but I need you to drive me somewhere. Can you stick around?"

"Sure, boss. Just give me the word when and where."

"I'll call you back in a few minutes."

He went upstairs to find Caroline. When he found her, she was doing yoga, something that, combined with acupuncture, had done much to relieve her migraines. She looked surprised to see him, but before she could ask why he was there, he said, "I have to meet with some people tonight."

"What? Who? Michael, I thought you wanted a quiet evening."

"What I want and what I'm going to get are two different things. Andy called to tell me there's an informal gathering of some of my biggest donors at Hugh Grissom's house. They've asked me to join them."

"Why, for heaven's sake?"

"Andy said they need reassurances. This defeat won't poll well for me, and that means their contributions may dry up. I need to talk to them."

Caroline sighed with exasperation. "Well, fine. How long do you think you'll be?"

"Shouldn't be more than an hour. I'll be back by eight or so."

Caroline stood up from where she had been sitting on the floor, reaching for a towel as she did. As she put it around her neck, she looked at him with an aggravated frown.

"Well, if you have to go, go. I was just looking forward to our first quiet evening together in weeks."

"So was I, sweetheart. But we can still have dinner up here in the salon, like we planned. It will just have to be a little later."

"Okay, Michael. I'm going to shower." She didn't try to keep the irritation out of her voice.

"I'll be back by eight," he repeated, moving towards her to give her a kiss. "I love you, Caroline," he said with more emotion than usual in his voice.

"You, too," she said over her shoulder as she headed to the shower. But she was pretty damned annoyed.

He told Manny everything on the way to Kristin's apartment. He needed advice. He was just so damn confused and distressed.

"But Mike," Manny said after Michael had finished, "how do you know it's even yours? You did get fixed a few years ago."

"That's the thing, Manny. Damn. Have you ever heard of anything like this? Having a vasectomy, and a woman getting pregnant anyway?"

"You're not gonna like this, but yeah. It happened to my brother Vinny. Seems something grew back together. His wife got fixed after that. Apparently, that one doesn't have the same chance of growing back together."

Michael was devastated. The implications! Like, why hadn't Caroline gotten pregnant? Blind luck, he supposed, considering how dangerous it could be for her if she had.

"And how can she even know she's pregnant already? The last time I saw her was only a month ago. How can she even know already?"

"Hey, they got tests now that tell a woman if she's a *day* pregnant."

"How do you know that?" Michael asked.

"I got six kids and you ask me how I know that," Manny answered with a hint of exasperation in his voice.

"Sorry, Mann, I'm just rattled. Rattled like I've never been rattled in my life. I just got my ass kicked by my Legislature, and now I'm dealing with a catastrophe."

Manny nodded and said, "A shit day, for sure." He said nothing more as he drove towards Bent Tree Apartments. As usual, they had brought Manny's innocuous black Olds. Michael had slid down in the seat as they left the Mansion just in case any press was lurking in the exit area behind the Mansion. Manny parked the car in front of Kristin's apartment. He got out and looked around.

"All clear," he said to Michael.

"Thanks. Wait here," Michael said as he got out of the passenger-side door.

"Where else?" Manny muttered in response.

Michael knocked at the door and held his breath. What to say? How to handle this?

"Come in, Michael," she said hesitantly, stepping back from the doorway.

"Kristin, I haven't got much time. Tell me what's really going on."

"I told you, Michael—I'm pregnant."

167

"But it can't…"

"Don't you *dare* say it can't be yours! It *is* yours, vasectomy or no vasectomy. You are the only man I've been with. *The only one.* Are you hearing me?" she shouted the last question at him.

He feared this could get ugly real fast. Michael wasn't going to let that happen.

In a measured voice he said, "I understand that I had a vasectomy almost three years ago. I understand that I've made love to my wife hundreds of times since then, and had sex with you… what, seven or eight times? Now if you were me, what would you believe?"

"I don't care what you believe. I know the truth. This baby is yours, Michael. No one else's. I won't let you shirk your responsibility."

Damn if she didn't seem to be telling the truth. Still, she wasn't going to push him into a corner that easily. If she was trying to intimidate him, she was dealing with the wrong guy.

"You're forgetting who you're dealing with, Kristin. I'm the most powerful man in this state. I could get six different guys to say they all screwed you."

"You bastard, you just try it. I'll file a paternity suit, naming you, *the most powerful man in this state*," she mimed sardonically, "as the father. There are blood tests, you know."

"Yeah, and I have type 'O' like the majority of the population."

"There are much more sophisticated tests available now, Michael, like DNA testing. I can afford to do anything I have to do to prove you're the father. You forget who *you're* dealing with."

He felt acute physical pain, as if he had been punched in the gut. A sense of dread overcame him as the truth of what she said hit home. She was right, and she was a lot tougher than he had thought possible. He had always been able to intimidate, to get people to back down. He realized that tactic wasn't going to work this time.

"Okay. Let's say it is mine. What can I do about it? I know you don't need child support, but I'll make any financial arrangements you think are fair. More than fair."

"You cold bastard. Your baby is growing inside me, and you're talking about, what, a trust fund or something?"

"What do you want me to say or do then, Kristin?"

"I want you to say you'll leave your wife and marry me and have this baby with me."

Michael was rocked to his core. The thought that she would want him to do that had never even entered his mind. He wondered how he could have been so dense about the obvious.

"Kristin," Michael said in a cold and resolute voice, "I can't do that."

"Why not, Michael? You said you've always wanted children. I can give them to you. You don't need your wife's money. I have plenty."

"Money? This isn't about money. This is about my life, about my marriage. And just what do you think this would do to my political future, for God's sake?"

"Ruin it, probably, but you won't need it."

"Kristin, do you really expect me to give up everything I have in life— for you?"

"I do expect you to, Michael. And not just for me, but for your baby, too."

"You're being entirely unrealistic. You know I can't do that."

"Can't, or won't?"

"Okay, won't. Haven't you thought of any alternatives?"

"Like an *abortion?* "Kristin spat the word at him.

Michael flinched as if she had slapped him. "Good God, no!"

"Well, don't you see? There are no alternatives, Michael."

"What about having the baby on your own and keeping me out of it."

"Well, wouldn't that be all neat and pretty for you? I won't do that, Michael."

"Kristin, look. What you're proposing is impossible. *Impossible.* Can't you understand that? You're planning to ruin four lives here—mine, Caroline's, yours, and that baby's."

"Not mine. And not the baby's. In fact, I'm only wanting what this baby deserves—his or her real father."

"You mean that, don't you?" Michael asked, his disbelief continuing to grow.

"I certainly do."

Michael sat down on the couch and put his head in his hands. Could this really be happening? This was worse than any nightmare, because it was real and he wouldn't be waking up from it.

He could feel himself on the edge of coming unglued. He struck from another angle.

169

"Kristin, I don't love you. Would you want to marry me, knowing that?"

"You'll learn to love me, Michael, as I love you. And once we have the baby, you'll love him, too. Our lives will be complete."

She had lost her mind. He could never do anything but hate her for what she was trying to do to him.

"It wouldn't work, Kristin."

"You'll have to make it work, Michael."

She was unrelenting. He couldn't believe it. He could think of nothing to say in response.

"Michael, you'll be ruined anyway."

"What are you talking about?" he shouted, jumping up from the couch. He thought he knew, but he couldn't believe it could be true.

"I mean that everyone will know it's your baby anyway. If I have to hire a lawyer and prove it through tests, I will. Be very clear on that, Michael. I will."

Michael felt trapped. Trapped in this pathetic apartment, having to endure her threats. Trapped with a woman who had no compunction about ruining his life over a pregnancy that should never have happened.

Bitterness encased him. Anger rose within him. The impulse to act upon that anger nearly overwhelmed him. Instead, with practiced determination, he backed down those dangerous feelings. He didn't want to think about the consequences if he gave into them. He had to leave.

He found his voice and said, "Kristin, I need time to think about this. The fallout from the special session is going to be huge. This was my one evening to try to relax before all hell breaks loose tomorrow, but instead, I'm dealing with this. Your timing sucks, by the way."

"Only because you choose not to be happy about it."

"Happy about it? No, Kristin, I'm not happy about it. And I refuse to deal with it right now."

"Well, then, when?"

"Christ, I don't know. You know, this could have waited. But no. You chose to tell me this on what has been the worst day of my life. You decided it's okay to wreak havoc in my already unbelievably complicated life."

"Honestly, Michael, I didn't think of it like that. I thought you would want to know. I thought you would be happy about it."

"Why would you think that, Kristin? Seriously?"

"You said you always wanted children, and I'm carrying your baby. Why wouldn't I think you'd be happy about it?"

"Because I'm married and I love my wife, that's why. And any plans for a baby didn't include you."

Kristin was deeply stung, but also angry. "Well then, why the hell are you here?"

"I needed to know the truth. And now I do. You're pregnant with my baby. Okay. But we don't have to make any decisions about it this minute."

"But we will have to make decisions, Michael...like how soon you'll tell your wife. And when you'll leave her. And when you'll resign."

Michael drew back in revulsion. "Are you out of your fucking mind? You've scoped out the future for us according to what you want, but you didn't consider me for a minute in doing so."

"I'm considering what's best for our baby, Michael. Everything isn't about you."

Michael shook his head in disbelief. "Kristin, I'm going to need time to process this. We'll discuss it. But I'm on the ropes right now. I've got a lot of other things to take care of."

"Just when do you think you'll be able to discuss it, Michael? It's not going away. I want to start my life with you as soon as possible."

She just couldn't see that there would be no chance for that. But he didn't have time to argue now. "Things should settle down by next week. I'll give you a call."

Kristin not only looked doubtful, she looked hostile. He suddenly realized that he had to ensure her silence between now and then, and the only way he could do it was by reassuring her. That way she wouldn't do anything crazy. Like tell anyone else.

With every shred of self-control he could muster, he pulled himself together and committed to doing what was absolutely necessary at this moment...telling her what she wanted to hear.

He walked over to her, and took her in his arms. He hugged her, hoping it was a convincing hug, because he wanted to keep her close so that she couldn't look at him. He didn't want her to see his face as he spoke. He knew he wasn't that good an actor.

"A baby, huh? Think it's a boy?"

She relaxed into him, hugging him back. "Oh, Michael, I hope so."

He kept her close as he said, "That could be...nice. Do you really think it could work, Kristin?"

"Oh, yes, Michael," she gushed, pulling back from him to look in his eyes. He pulled her back into an embrace.

"Maybe you're right," he said with just enough hesitation and sincerity to sound convincing.

Kristin pulled back and looked up at him, then broke into a big, bright smile that told him she was convinced. She tightened her arms around him and said, "I am right, Michael. You'll see. We'll have a wonderful life together."

"But not immediately, Kristin. Just let me get through this week, and I'll call you."

"Michael, can it be true? You'll really marry me?"

"I just need time to work things out," he hedged.

"You won't change your mind?" she asked, drawing away from him to look straight into his eyes.

He fought for enough self-control to be able to meet her now frosty, steel-gray eyes. "I just need some time to work out a plan, Kristin. Give me that time. And trust me."

"Kiss me, Michael. Kiss me, and show me that you mean it."

Nausea threatened, but Michael closed his eyes and imagined that he was kissing Caroline. Surprisingly, he wasn't repulsed. In fact, he found he didn't have to pretend to enjoy the kiss. He had forgotten what an enticing mouth she had.

Kristin was ecstatic. His kiss told her that he meant what he had said. He couldn't be lying, Kristin surmised, and still kiss her with such passion. She felt him drawing away now, but she wanted him to stay. She wanted him to make love to her. That's what it would be now. Lovemaking, not sex.

Michael knew what she was thinking. He had to get away. The worst thing that could happen now would be...

"Stay, Michael," she said. "Stay and make love to me."

"I can't, Kristin." When he saw her hurt and accusing expression, he quickly added, "God, I want to. There's nothing more I'd like right now than to be inside you," he lied convincingly.

"But Manny's waiting, and..."

"Manny?"

"Yes, and we have to get back. I've kept him later today than I should have, and people are expecting me. I know you can understand the pressure I'm under."

"Yes, I understand, Michael, but it will be hard for me to wait."

Say what she wants to hear, he had to command himself. "A week or so, Kristin. Then we'll work things out."

"Okay. One week, Michael."

Michael could hardly breathe. This charade was too much. He was going to lose it if he didn't leave right now.

He moved away from her abruptly, and then caught himself. He gave her another hug as he turned to open the door.

"I love you, Michael," she said as he was pulling the door closed behind him.

When he didn't respond, she told herself that he must not have heard her. Otherwise, she was sure he would have told her he loved her, too.

From the look on Michael's face, Manny could tell things hadn't gone well. Mike looked like he was going to be sick. Manny started to get out and help Michael, but Michael held up his hand to stop him. He got into the front seat next to Manny and slammed the door. "Fuck."

"Tell me."

"The bitch wants to marry me."

"Fuck is right, man. She's really pregnant?"

"She didn't show me any test results or anything, but she's way too excited about having a baby to be faking it. Plus, she threatened to have blood tests to prove it's mine, and I don't think she'd do that unless she really was pregnant with my baby."

"Man, Mike, this is bad. I'm sorry, buddy. What can I do?"

"Nothing right now. Just get me back to the Mansion. What time is it?"

"Ten 'til eight."

"Shit. Caroline's expecting me at eight. Get me back as quick as you can."

Manny didn't say anything else as he pulled out of the parking space and drove out of the apartment complex. When he turned onto the main road, however, he couldn't help but ask, "So what are you going to do?"

Michael was in a daze. He felt like he was in a nightmare he couldn't bring himself out of.

"Mike? Mike, snap out of it. What are you going to do?"

"I don't know, Manny. I just don't know."

"Mike, listen to me. For now, you gotta get control. We'll be back at the Mansion in a coupla minutes. You can't face Caroline like this. You're a wreck."

"I know, Manny. I just wish I had some time to fucking *think*."

"You don't, Mike. You've gotta keep cool, just until you can get away by yourself."

"That won't be until midnight...or later," Michael moaned.

"You can do it, Mike. You can do it. Now *man up*," Manny said harshly, giving Michael a hard punch on the arm.

It was the best thing he could have done for him. Michael took a couple of deep breaths as he rubbed his sore arm and forced himself to calm down. There. That was better.

"Thanks, Manny."

"It's okay. You'll be fine. You just remember—you're Mike Romano, tough guy from a tough neighborhood. Nobody or nothing has ever kept you down. You can handle this."

"I'm not so tough anymore, Mann."

"Sure you are," Manny said. "Now act like a man, for Christ's sake."

The feelings those words evoked in Michael were familiar ones. He *was* a man. He was Mike Romano. And he would handle it—somehow.

"You're the best friend I ever had, Manny. Thanks a lot."

"You bet," Manny said. He watched Michael walk towards the Mansion, and he was satisfied. Mike's walk was strong, sure. His shoulders were up. He'd be all right.

22

AT THE SAME TIME Kristin Long was reveling in the prospect of marrying Michael Romano, Jake Miller was reveling in the prospect of going to Florida to find his sister. Eight weeks post-surgery, and he was feeling great. He had attacked the physical therapy regimen, and it had paid off.

He was seriously ready for a change of scenery, and in less than a week he'd be on his way to Miami. He wanted some sun and surf to top off his rejuvenation tank before going to Tallahassee to meet her.

He wondered, yet again, if he should try to contact her before he showed up. And again, he weighed the pros and cons. If he called her first, it might save her some of the shock she was sure to experience in a face-to-face. But then again, he might not be able to convince her that he was her brother over the phone.

He could describe himself and give her some facts. Nah. For all she might know, he could be a psychopath who was trying to kill her or take her for some money. No. No reasonable woman would believe a stranger who called out of the blue.

Maybe he could write her a letter and send a picture. He could enclose copies of the documents Ackerman's Agency had given him. That would convince her. But she might say she didn't care, and didn't want to know him. If he showed up in person, he would be a lot more likely to win her over. He was pretty sure that would be the best way to go.

The worst that could happen was that she blew him off. The best that could happen was he'd get lucky and get laid in Miami before she had a chance to blow him off. He had always liked Miami. His parents had owned a condo on Bal Harbour's beach for years, and he had enjoyed a number of Christmas and summer vacations there while growing up. He was kind of sorry he had sold it after their deaths.

But for the first time in a long time, Jake Miller had something to look forward to.

Michael woke up and looked at the clock. It was just after two in the morning. He was surprised he had been able to sleep at all. He knew there was no point in trying to go back to sleep now.

He got out of bed slowly, careful not to wake Caroline. He had begged off lovemaking after dinner, saying he was just too tired and too stressed to make it good for either of them.

"Are you okay, darling?" Caroline asked sleepily as he was putting on his robe.

"I'm just going down to the library for a while to read until I get sleepy again."

"Want me to get up, too?"

"No, sweetheart," he said, leaning over the bed to give her a kiss. "I'll be back up soon."

She didn't respond as she rolled over and fell back asleep. He was relieved she hadn't insisted, because he needed time alone to think.

He poured a brandy when he got to the library, and sat down in his favorite chair, pulling an old Columbia Law School blanket over his legs to offset the chill in the room. They would have to turn on the heat soon.

The feeling of unreality settled over him again, and the disbelief that he was even in this situation made it difficult to think objectively. But that was exactly what he was going to have to do if he was going to find any solution to this problem.

He could not have imagined feeling more disillusioned or despondent than he had when the special session ended. And then Kristin Long had eclipsed all of that with her pregnancy.

Kristin wasn't going to let go of him. She had him in a vice-like grip that he could see no way out of. He realized that her unintended pregnancy meant his life, as he knew it, could be over. Everything just *gone.* Caroline, the governorship, everything he had lived and worked for. How to salvage it? How?

He went through the alternatives, one by one, forcing himself to think without emotion. He could tell Caroline the truth. If she really loved him, like he knew she did, she might forgive him. The fact that Caroline knew the truth would destroy most of Kristin's offense. But *would* Caroline forgive him? In reality, not likely.

But if he didn't tell her, Kristin would. He would definitely lose her in that case. At least if he told Caroline, he'd have a fighting chance. If Kristin knew that Caroline was standing behind him, she wouldn't have as much ammunition. But she could still file that paternity suit and destroy his political career. And she would very likely do that. How humiliating that would be for Caroline. He just couldn't put her through that.

With startling clarity, he realized that if the baby went away, then everything else would, too. But how? He couldn't count on a miscarriage, but the alternative that pounded at the back of his brain, begging for consideration, seemed too overwhelming to consider.

An abortion. She had used that very word when he asked her about alternatives. "What, an *abortion*?" But her tone had said, "Don't even think about it."

But there it was, an alternative too demanding to ignore. He was sickened by the possibility that he could even consider it. Hadn't he been repulsed earlier when she had bitterly thrown that word at him? But it was there, wasn't it, offering a solution to this whole damn mess? How could he ignore it?

He had to ignore it, because it was inconceivable that he could condone an abortion when rape or incest wasn't involved. Sure, termination of Kristin's pregnancy would give him a reprieve on life. But to take an innocent baby's life for such a selfish, self-serving purpose was despicable. And yet...

For God's sake, he'd just staked his political career on restricting abortions. No, abortion wasn't an option. She'd never, ever go for it anyway. And he wondered how he would live with himself if she did have an abortion at his urging.

Michael felt that the threads of his entire moral fabric were coming apart, unraveling at a pace that threatened to destroy everything he was, everything that he had built on and believed in.

But he had to admit that the threads had begun to unravel when he started an affair with Kristin Long. He had let his moral guard down from that very first night by going to her apartment. And he'd completely shelved his morals throughout the time the affair lasted. He was just a man, after all, and not immune to temptation, or the delight of forbidden fruit, or pleasures of the flesh. The pleasures he found in Kristin's flesh had overcome any moral misgivings.

But that didn't mean he had to continue sliding down the proverbial slippery slope. He could do the right thing, confess all to Caroline and just accept the punishment that resulted from it. What choice did he have, anyway? Kristin had threatened to ruin him, regardless.

If Caroline left him, which she would no doubt do, he could marry Kristin. Although only seconds ago it seemed inconceivable to him, he realized that it could very possibly be the only means of salvaging his frayed morals. He would be doing the right thing by living up to his responsibility to that unborn child. But it would be a heavy price to pay. A ruined marriage, a ruined career, a ruined life. After all, what kind of marriage would it be? Married to a woman he would always hate for ruining his life? That could be the worst fate of all.

"God, help me," he entreated out loud.

He put his head down and closed his eyes, praying for guidance. Many minutes passed. Nothing. With a sorrowful sigh, he concluded that he, and he alone, would have to find the solution.

Despite his attempts to obliterate it, the thought of an abortion gained ground, until he found he was actually contemplating how to bring Kristin around to the idea—how to make it her idea.

Ah, the ultimate irony. For months he had focused on little else but enacting stricter abortion laws. He had taken on the monumental task of beginning the fight all over again for the rights of the unborn. And here he was, determining that in his case, there might be a plausible reason to take the life of an unborn child. Had fate played the ultimate trick on him, or what?

He had hoped it would be just the beginning of stricter abortion regulations. He had seen this as a way of getting a toe-hold on the whole abortion issue, knowing that if he could get these bills passed, he could push for even more restrictions in the future. Restrictions that would get tighter and tighter until abortion was no longer a choice.

Choice. What a whole new meaning that word took on now.

And now here he was, facing the only viable choice for saving his marriage and his political career. What a grand plan the special session had seemed back in the summer. It had seemed so right, so inevitable. He truly believed he had been guided by some greater power into pursuing it. He had been sure that he was the man to finally strike the *Roe* decision off the law books forever, even if he had to continue the battle from the White House.

What he hadn't counted on was the number of people, women and men, who believed a woman should have the legal right to terminate a pregnancy for whatever reason she chose. His office had received over ten thousand letters and phone calls saying just that.

Yet he had brushed those opinions aside, looking down from where he was perched on his high moral ground.

In truth, in the recesses of his mind, he had envisioned himself as a moral leader of the nation through holding a higher political office. Yes, President of the United States. And if he had been successful this week, that was the path he would have followed. But what kind of leader was he, really, if he was willing to trash his convictions when faced with a personal moral crisis?

It dawned on him that he had been very lucky as a politician. He had made so few, if any, moral concessions. He had looked down upon those who had. But here he was, faced with a huge ethical dilemma, and he found he didn't have the integrity to face himself.

How quickly one's moral compass could turn a hundred and eighty degrees, he thought. It was easy to uphold those moral convictions so long as they weren't being tested in any serious way. But this was dead serious. Everything that defined his life was at stake.

Sacrifices were called for. He would sacrifice his principles even further and ask Kristin to sacrifice hers. He would ask her to get an abortion. It was a horrible thing to ask of a woman who was as pro-life as he was. And how in the hell did he hope to convince her? She wanted this baby, and she wanted the father that went with it. It wasn't going to be easy. Maybe if she believed that it would be as anguishing for him as it would be for her, she would consider it. And it would be anguishing for him. It was, after all, his child.

Who was he kidding? It couldn't possibly be as anguishing for him as it would be for her. It was *her* body, *her* conscience that he would be asking her to violate. No man could really empathize with that, no matter how much he thought he could.

But he had to ask her. He had to try. He would promise her anything. But what could he promise her? She didn't need money. She didn't hold office, so her reputation wouldn't be ruined. She owned her own companies, so she wouldn't be unemployed.

Trying to look at it from her point of view, he determined she had absolutely nothing to gain by aborting this baby, and a chance of getting everything she wanted if she didn't—including him.

An impossible situation. His body and mind were reeling from exhaustion. He didn't want to think about it anymore tonight. He needed to get some sleep. Maybe once the committee of sleep, as John Steinbeck had called it, worked on the problem, there would be a solution awaiting him when he woke.

23

THE HEADLINES IN every paper in the state of Florida touted his defeat at the special session. He forced himself to read every article, word for word. It seemed like fitting punishment.

They had reported his claims of "moral victory," even though critics pilloried him for wasting taxpayers' money and lawmakers' time. He hadn't given many quotes, however, except to say that if there was a defeat, it was in being able to continue to abort viable fetuses.

The vice president of the National Organization for Women cited the resounding defeat as a warning to other politicians who were considering restrictions on abortion rights.

The Senate President, a Democrat whom Michael had met with numerous times to enlist his help, had been quoted saying, "Our refusing to let this legislation come to the floor for a vote was a direct reflection of the will of the people of Florida. Nobody is pro-abortion, but they are pro-choice. It's a decision that should be left to the woman."

But the one that rankled him the most was the comment from Elaine Ferguson, the Democratic representative who had been one of the most vocal female legislators he had met with back in July. "All men and women who believe that government should stay out of their private lives are triumphant!" she had exclaimed to the media.

Now he would need to discuss with Andy the comments he would be making to the media.

He buzzed Andy to come on in, hoping that Andy would do most of the thinking for him today. He wasn't disappointed with Andy's suggestions.

"You must have been up all night, working on this," he said when Andy had finished.

"Just about. What you say now is going to be very important. The nation has its eyes on Florida, and you have to set the tone for the other states that are hoping to enact similar legislation. That means you have to be upbeat, and you have to sound confident about pursuing this in the regular session."

"I know. Now let's go over everything again. We only have a few minutes before the press conference."

Michael looked dignified and confident when he stepped up to the microphone. He did not smile, however, because he wanted everyone to be clear on the fact that he was not happy about how the lawmakers voted.

"I'm here to answer your questions, ladies and gentlemen," he started, making it clear that no speech was planned.

"Governor, how do you feel about the fact that this special session is likely to have cost two hundred thousand dollars—double what you initially projected?"

"The issue of life far overshadows the issue of the cost of the session," he said emphatically. "I think the people of this state will understand that I was trying to save the lives of thousands of unborn babies, and you can't degrade that by making it about the cost."

Caroline and Andy were sitting on the platform, behind where Michael was standing. They gave each other a barely perceptible nod, noting their mutual relief that Michael seemed to be calm and controlled.

"How will this defeat affect your relationship with the legislators, Governor Romano?"

"I don't expect it to affect the relationship one way or the other. We will continue to work together to enact laws that are beneficial to the state."

"Do you think, Governor Romano, that the legislators were sending you any messages in not giving you the victory you sought?"

"Their message was clear. They want no changes to Florida's current abortion laws. Failure to pass these bills was the result of the legislators' ability to use parliamentary procedure to block the advancement of the bills."

"Governor Romano, you know that the nation had its eyes on Florida and the outcome of the session because it was the first test following the Supreme Court's ruling in *Webster v. Missouri*. Do you think other states that are considering enacting similar legislation will reconsider?"

"There are similar battles being waged right now in a number of other states, including Pennsylvania, Virginia, New Jersey and Wisconsin. Those are all very different states, with different constituencies, and the outcome of those battles can't be predicted by the outcome of this one."

"Governor, what effect will the Legislature's defeat of your most hopeful bill—the one that would regulate abortion clinics—have on the future of those clinics? Will you continue your efforts to close down unsafe clinics?"

"The Senate did agree to establish a special study panel on abortion clinic regulation. My future actions will be guided by their findings."

"When do you expect to get their report on their findings?" the same reporter asked.

"As yet, there have been no specific members named to the panel, nor has a deadline been set for their recommendations. We can only hope that they will serve the public as well and as quickly as possible, considering they know of the need for better regulation of abortion clinics."

There. At least it was made clear that the Senate had to get that ball rolling, and that it going to be watched to make sure it did its job.

"Will you champion this cause into the regular session in March of next year, Governor?"

"We'll have to assess the public's desire for stricter abortion legislation over the next few months before I can make that decision."

Michael continued a show of confidence in answering the other questions that followed. They were all along the same line, but he answered them tirelessly until Andy stood up and, to Michael's relief, announced the end of the conference.

Michael was physically and mentally exhausted. He had held on tight, showing no weakness in facing the barrage of intimidating questions. The effort had been worthwhile, however. Everyone in his administration, plus Caroline, seemed pleased.

Caroline stood up and hugged him, silently conveying her approval. He needed it now more than ever.

24

THE DRIED BROWN leaves, which only last week had been golden and vibrant, skipped along the hard, dark ground, scattered by a cool autumn wind that signaled the colder weather to come.

It was growing dark, and Michael was chilled by the scene, though he sat in his cozy study where a warm fire burned. Tallahassee could get such surprisingly cold weather. At least it didn't snow. That brutal snow, those cold winters in New York. He shivered at the thought.

He rose to pour a Cognac, wanting to drive away the chill of the late afternoon. But the chill, he knew, had nothing to do with the weather. It came from within. It was the type of chill that was born from fear and that grew with every breath he took. His whole life was in the balance, and he didn't have a clue about how to tip the scales back his way.

How could things have gotten this far, he wondered. Why now? Why not twenty years ago, when nothing counted? If he had nothing to lose, he would have nothing to fear. But now he stood to lose everything that mattered to him. His wife, the governorship, his peace of mind. His life, as he knew it, was on the brink of collapse.

Why couldn't Kristin understand that? Why did it have to be all or nothing? Why was she so intent on ruining his life? She didn't see it that way, though, did she? She had plenty of money, she said. They could get married, raise the baby she was so determined to have, travel and live a good life.

But that's not what I want, Michael thought, his anger rising. I want my wife, my position in life. I want things back to the way they were, before Kristin Long came into my life and got pregnant. Who is this woman, to try to take everything from me? What makes her think she has any right to do this?

But hadn't he led her to believe just that last night? He had held her off for a week before "the talk" became inevitable. Sitting in that wretched rental where it had all begun, he had relented quickly enough when his segue into the possibility of an abortion caused her to become hysterical. She had cursed him and threatened to expose him as a hypocrite, and he didn't doubt for a minute she would follow through on her threats. She had really scared him. He had never seen anyone as livid as she had been.

And how had he handled it? Like the hypocrite she accused him of being. He had lied and told her everything she wanted to hear, until she had been convinced that he would do whatever she wanted.

He had even...

He cursed himself for his weakness and pretense. He had tried to stop her when she had unzipped his pants and gone down on her knees.

"No, Michael, let me," she had entreated. "I want to show you how much I love you."

And then she had taken his flaccid penis in her mouth and enchanted it with her gifted mouth. He had looked down at her raven-black hair, saw her head moving up and down, and felt a moment of revulsion, even as he grew hard. He had closed his eyes and imagined that Caroline, his beautiful, blonde Caroline, was doing all those magical things to his cock.

How fucked up was this, he had brooded in that moment. How many men fantasized about their wife while they were getting head from their mistress?

But Kristin's rousing mouth and intrepid tongue had captured him after all, and held him captive, until his body surrendered.

The memory brought anguish and shame. Michael was disgusted with himself and with his ineffectual defense against her allure.

But now, away from her, sitting in the chilled room, feeling trapped and fostering anger, he wondered how he had ever found her so attractive. Attractive enough to get him into all this deep shit. Why did she have to be so damn unreasonable about it?

Because she's having your baby, you asshole, he admonished himself. She wants your baby, and she wants you. And you're not going to be able to change her mind about that.

He had never given her any reason to think she meant anything to him. He had been careful not to promise her a thing. Why was she being so unfair about it? If she wanted the baby so damn bad, why couldn't she just have it and go on with her life? He couldn't stop the thought that it would have been better, infinitely better for him, if she had just agreed to have an abortion.

He let out a low, anguished cry at his dilemma. What has happened to me? he asked himself. Only a week ago, I knew exactly what I was about. Life was sacrosanct, and short of rape or incest or to save the mother's life, I couldn't have sanctioned abortion for *any* reason. But now?

If she had agreed to an abortion, he thought, my life could have gone on as before. Maybe not totally, but the matter of wrecking my entire life to accommodate her inconvenient pregnancy would have gone away.

Unwittingly, he began to acknowledge that abortion might be justified in certain situations. Like his terrible situation, where so much was at stake. You're a fucking hypocrite, he thought to himself. You never forgave Alison for aborting your child, even though she believed she had a good reason. Even one short week ago it would have been unthinkable to acknowledge that just because a pregnancy was unintentional or inconvenient, abortion should be an option, simply because a woman wanted one.

No, it was never, *ever* justified when a pregnancy was merely unintentional, or inconvenient. It was never right to kill an innocent baby. So why can't she just go ahead and have the baby, and leave me out of it, totally and forever? That would solve everything.

But she had zero incentive to do that. She's not some single-at-forty working woman responding to an urgently-ticking biological clock, he thought. She isn't poor and uneducated, breeding from ignorance or from lack of access to affordable birth control. She's a well-to-do, conservative woman who wants to have that baby because she loves me. And because she couldn't live with herself if she knew she had killed our baby.

Our baby. What a kick in the ass. Here I've wanted children all these years, Michael lamented yet again, and now there's a part of me, growing in a woman who isn't my wife. Someone I don't love. Could never love. What a cruel, sick twist of fate.

He thought about how life had always been so good to him. Too good, he supposed, because it was sure balancing the scales now. Wasn't this supposed to happen to other people? Hadn't he always played by the rules? Yes, he had, and the first time he stepped out of line, life had called a foul.

He recalled Caroline's words from the previous week, when they had been walking around the grounds. "You're going to stick to your principles. If there's anything your past has taught us, it's that you always win when you do that. You can't change that formula now."

Her words slapped him in the face like a torrent of cold rain. She had said it all. If he had only stuck to his principles, not changed the formula...

But he couldn't change any of that now. He turned out the lights and sought peace in the flickering shadows of the dying fire. He tried to pray, but his head was empty and his heart was cold, and prayer wouldn't come. It was as if his communication with God was cut off.

Although he was sometimes irreverent about it, he had always had a sense of God in his life. He didn't believe God could forsake him now. So he had sinned. Where was the forgiveness, where were the answers, that were supposed to come with repenting?

When contemplative time in stillness brought no answer, he thought: it comes down to counting on me—again. That's what it always boils down to...taking matters into my own hands. But what can I do? The problem is real, and it's not going away. Unless Kristin Long does.

The impact of that thought hit him fast and hard. He felt as if he had been sucker-punched by the idea. If she went away...

A peaceful feeling crept in as he let the thought of her being gone— just gone—sink in. Not there to threaten him or destroy him.

Michael's thoughts followed the thread. Kristin wasn't going anywhere. Not on her *own*, anyway. What am I thinking of? Death? She wasn't going to die. I don't want her to die, even if it would solve all my problems.

Or do I? I can't even think about it. He looked down at his hands. Christ, I'm shaking. Calm down. Just because you thought about it doesn't mean you really want it to happen...do you?

He was deeply shaken, and although he willed it, willed it very strongly, the thought would not go away. It was buried in his brain like a hatchet. If Kristin were gone...

He could make it happen. He had a way. He wondered if he would be able to live with himself if he knew he caused her death. He examined the flip side of that coin. Would he be any better able to live with himself if he destroyed Caroline's life? That's what he would be doing if she found out about Kristin.

And then he saw everything clearly. It came down to two choices: destroying Kristin Long, or letting Kristin Long destroy Caroline. It was no contest.

He could not see that a misguided mass of rationalization had brought him to this point. He was too definite, too relieved, and too clear on the end result to go about analyzing how he got there.

Yes, he thought more calmly now, the only way this whole thing would go away would be if Kristin went away. He was amazed at how calm his thinking was now. But, he thought, isn't that how I make all of my decisions, with calm resolve? Why should this decision be any different, just because it has to do with murder?

There, he thought. That word is out there, and I didn't go up in flames. Murders are committed all the time. Hell, I'm no stranger to murder, he reminded himself. I didn't grow up in Little Italy with mob wise guys on my back doorstep without knowing about murder.

He reproached himself. But you've always held yourself above all of that, haven't you? You, nor any of your family, ever let it soil your lives. So your father and his father managed to stay clean for all those years, even being right in the thick of it there on the docks during the worst union problems. And now here you are, the squeaky clean, successful one of the family, and you're the one who's going to get dirty. Real dirty. Murder is as dirty as it gets.

Murder really wasn't that hard to accomplish. And his own hands wouldn't be soiled—at least not directly.

He went into his office and flipped on his desk light and pulled out the bottom drawer of his desk. He removed the file folders stacked there and lifted the piece of oak that, to the normal eye, would look like the bottom of the drawer. It was a false bottom, however. And in the dark, compacted space under it was a custom-made strong box. Less than two inches high, it fit neatly under the false bottom.

Michael removed the box with what he thought were surprisingly steady hands and sat it on his desk. He had never thought that he would need to open it, to finger its contents or soil his soul. Not for this purpose anyway. But now that he had removed it, now that he had made his decision, he couldn't—no, he wouldn't—return it to its hiding place.

With the familiar calmness that he felt in executing a decision, he turned the tiny combination lock to the numbers that were written nowhere, but that were firmly fixed in his memory. The lock was a beauty. Specially made for this box, flat and polished, and designed so that it could not be opened by anyone other than the one who knew the five-digit combination. The tumblers had been silently synchronized so that it was ninety-nine point nine percent impossible for anyone to crack it.

The only other person who knew about the box, and knew the combination, was Manny. The man he trusted with his very life.

He acknowledged his paranoia in taking the extra precaution of using such a lock. Even if it was opened, and a person saw the contents, all he would see was a piece of paper with a phone number that led to a hang up. That person would also see a small, black-velvet drawstring bag, and in it he would find a ten-carat, pear-shaped diamond of very-near perfect cut, color and clarity. It was unset, because he hadn't decided on the setting. It had cost a quarter of a million dollars, and he was proud of the fact that the entire amount had come from his own personal funds. When he bought it, it represented most of his life savings, which had been invested shrewdly by Victor's own financial advisor years before. Michael's savings had grown from ninety-thousand to over half a million dollars by the time he purchased the diamond. He had bought it knowing he would never find another such perfect diamond at that price to give to Caroline on their twenty-fifth anniversary.

The diamond alone would provide plenty of justification to anyone who wondered about the security precautions taken.

Someone might wonder why he had bought it ten years before that anniversary, but when they saw the accompanying appraisal, they would understand the purchase and investment value of such a near-perfect diamond. Such virtually unflawed diamonds were rare, and this one could only become more expensive to acquire in the future.

The diamond and the appraisal were intended to be a diversion. Anyone who might get into the box would focus on the diamond, not the piece of paper with a telephone number that, even if dialed, would result in someone answering the phone, "Mario's Meat Market." It would be a dead end, a wrong number. Without the right words being uttered by the caller, nothing more would be uncovered.

He picked up the piece of paper cautiously. It was a scrap of paper, really, torn in half and revealing only half the name of a hotel's note paper on which it had been written.

Why didn't I just commit this number to memory? Michael asked himself. But he had asked himself that question when he first acquired it, and he answered it the same way this time: because I never wanted to have such a piece of filth in my brain and on my conscience, that's why.

He looked at the piece of paper objectively, trying to decide how it would look to just anyone who might find it. It looked exactly as it was supposed to—a scribbled number on a scrap piece of paper. However, the words that needed to be spoken when the phone was answered *were* committed to memory.

He picked up the receiver of his private line. He put it back down quickly. Just like that? You're going to make a call to have a woman killed, without even thinking about what to say?

The private line was as secure as any phone line could possibly be. Its existence in the phone company's records had been distorted and buried by a high-level contact, someone who had owed Michael a big favor for his advice in a not-so-legal legal matter.

Plus, no one would ever have access to his private line phone records. Who would want them? And he would have to be notified first, in any case, for it to be legal. People didn't know it, but a private line installed under an immunity clause was highly protected. Okay, so no one could trace it legally. What about illegally? No, no one would do that. Why would they?

What the fuck was all this stupid deliberation about the phone? Just make the call, he told himself.

He knew his call would be routed to Robert Lineo, Sal's son. He knew that the old man had left control of his empire in Robert's hands. Would Robert know about the ageless debt his family owed to Michael's family? He was quite sure Robert would. No explanations should be necessary. But wonder if they were? Would he have to go into any history, any details? Would he have to tell Robert that his life had been saved by Michael's grandfather? He hoped not. He didn't know that much about it, only what his father had told him two days before he died.

Michael sighed and sat back in his chair as he recalled the painful scene. He unwillingly pictured his father lying in the large master bedroom of the home that he and Caroline, with her money, had bought for his parents out in Westchester. They had never really liked the home or the community. There weren't a lot of poor Italian Catholics living there. But he and Caroline had wanted to take them from the inferior life they had led in Little Italy. Away from that small, dark apartment that breathed garlic and sweat from every porous plank.

He felt a sense of disgust at the thought of that place where he and his two brothers, along with their baby sister, had grown up. A two-bedroom tenement apartment, a virtual hovel. His poor sister had never had a room or even a bed of her own during all those years. Just a sofa bed, partitioned off from the living room by a curtain patterned with faded red roses. Poor Theresa. She had to mature in that tiny space until she was almost sixteen. He couldn't afford to move them until then.

She had been happy enough to move. And so were Greg and Jonathan. But his parents had missed their old neighborhood. So much so, in fact, that when his father died, Michael had moved his mother back to Little Italy. To much-improved conditions in a better section, it was true; but it was still that little hell of a place that he would like to forget.

Theresa had forgotten it. She had married a union welder, and they had managed, with Michael's help, to move into a fairly nice two-bedroom place on the Lower East Side of Manhattan. She was happy. Her husband was good to her, and their two little girls were the light of their lives.

His brothers had fared pretty well, too, but had not tried to escape their squalid lives as he and Theresa had. They had opened up a seafood storefront in Brooklyn, and while they earned a good living, they were still prisoners to their lives as twelve-hour-a-day laborers with large families to support. It was predictable, though, wasn't it, that they should end up selling fish? After all, that's how all of the Romano boys had started out, delivering fish for Cassio's Fish Market.

Michael thought about the different directions those jobs had taken him and his brothers. His brothers had aspired to nothing more than being in the business for themselves. But Michael had always known he had wanted more. What constituted the difference? He felt sure it was more than just his extraordinary intelligence. His brothers had been smart enough.

Well, you just couldn't discount fate, with some real ambition mixed in. It was fate that Michael had been the one to deliver the salmon to Edith Silverman that day, but it was ambition that had caused him to pursue their friendship. That had been the real beginning of his education, and of his desire to live a better life. Again, fate had been his friend.

Where are you now, my friend?

Michael shook off those thoughts and went back to the issue at hand. Calling Robert Lineo.

Where should he start? What should he say? He practiced it in his head. "Hey, Robert, this is Michael Romano. You know the grandson of Antonio Romano, the one who saved your head from being bashed in by the Bowers' mob. Yeah, that Romano."

He smiled to himself. No, no explanation should be necessary. He was sure that Robert would know all about it. After all, that's where Robert's family got their real start, by muscling in on a piece of the huge dollars that were generated on those docks.

That was putting it rather simply. Michael had been fascinated by the stories of the longshoremen, and, in his customary quest to learn, he had studied the history of the docks to better understand it.

The New York Harbor docks were a self-contained city/state, with seven hundred and fifty miles of shoreline, eighteen hundred piers, handling back then thousands of ocean-going ships a year, carrying over a million passengers a year and over thirty-five million tons of foreign cargo with a value of around eight billion dollars. That figure had astounded Michael. The seagoing treasury had been in the pocket of the mob, and the fight for control was one of the bloodiest in history.

At least ten percent of everything that moved in and out of the harbor went into the pockets of the mob. And if you were one of the twenty-five thousand longshoremen looking for work, as Michael's father and grandfather had been, either you kicked back to the mob's hiring boss, or they starved you off the docks. They had the absolute power to do it, too, because they were hired with the implied consent of "legitimate" shipping and stevedore officials.

Michael's grandfather had quickly learned the survival lesson of kickbacks, and it was on those dingy docks of Brooklyn that he had overheard the plan to kill Sal Lineo's son, Robert.

Michael's grandfather, Antonio Romano, had hung around one night on the pretense of repairing some nets, something he was pretty good at doing. In reality, he was hoping to pilfer some of the fresh fruit off the holding dock. Because he repaired nets, saving the bosses time and money, (after all, the money designated for repairs went into their pockets instead) they were pretty good about turning their heads to his minor pilfering.

That particular night, however, they must have thought he had left, or maybe it had been that the case of Scotch they had stolen had loosened up their tongues. Whatever the reason, Antonio learned of their plans to knock off Sal's son. It wouldn't work to go after Sal, they had said. That wouldn't be enough to convince him to quash his plans for muscling in on some of the take. No, they had to hit him where he really lived. They would kill his only son, the heir to his empire. Without an heir, the old man's ambitions might not be so great.

Although Antonio Romano was a brave man, he had been frightened by what he had heard. He was an old man at the time, fifty-five, and he had his own son, Michael's father, to think about. The son who worked along-side him on the docks. He also had to worry about his other six children, spanning two decades in age.

He knew that if they found out he had overheard, he was dead. His family, too. But he had been friends with Sal Lineo since before they had stepped off the boat at Ellis Island. Even though Sal had been almost twenty years younger than Antonio, they had become close on the long boat trip. When Sal had prospered, as Michael's grandfather hadn't, Sal had helped him. Not in any big way that could hurt a man's pride. But there had been produce and fish and even a Thanksgiving turkey left on their doorstep that had helped to keep Antonio's family from going hungry when he couldn't work because of strikes or rivalries. Michael's grandfather had been pretty sure that he hadn't been starved off the docks when others had because some money had been passed from Sal to one of the bosses. His grandfather had guessed about who his benefactor was in those cases, not knowing for sure, but confident he was right.

Antonio had sneaked away that night, not taking any fruit with him because he had to get away unnoticed. He had to warn Sal Lineo that his son's life was in danger. It could mean his own life, and his family's, but he had no choice. The man was his friend.

Sal Lineo had reacted swiftly and with previously underestimated strength. He had been holding his money and his power in reserve until the right moment, and that had been the right moment. He attacked before he could be attacked, and by catching the Bowers off guard, he had exercised enough muscle to not only ensure his own son's safety, but to get a piece of the action he had so strongly coveted. It was a major coup for Sal, and the real beginning of his massive power and fortune.

No one ever found out where Sal had gotten his information. Two days after the bloody battle, both of the dock bosses who had been overheard disappeared. No questions were asked after that.

Sal Lineo had been smart enough not to change his relationship with Michael's grandfather—at least not so the outside world would notice. Any noticeable change would mark Antonio Romano for death. But the Romano sons, and their sons, had gotten steady, good paying jobs at the fish markets, including Cassio's. Sam Cassio was a distant cousin of the Lineo family.

There was nothing strange about that. A friend's sons, and their sons, working for friends, doing an honest day's work for an honest day's pay.

Antonio Romano had wanted nothing. No handouts, no favors. But he was not so proud as to deny his family a decent living if they were willing to work for it. And when, two generations later, Michael's brothers had wanted to start their own little business, no one had stopped them. They might have, but a hand-to-mouth fish business was not going to put a dent in the Lineo family's fortune. So while no money had passed hands, benevolence had.

Yes, Sal's son Robert would know all about it. He would know about the promise his father had made to Michael's grandfather: that if he ever needed "help," that if there were ever a threat to him or his family, he would be there to take care of that threat.

Michael's grandfather had known the value of that promise, and while he nor his son, Michael's father, had ever had a reason to cash in on that promise, it was something of value to be passed on through the generations, as any family treasure would be. Michael had shuddered with repulsion when his father had told him about the promise. Michael was sure he would never need to rely upon it.

When he had told his father that, his father had looked at him with rheumy but shrewd eyes, and told him that a promise of such value was not to be taken lightly. He had seen, he said, a different side of life than Michael. And though he was so proud of his educated, respected and successful lawyer son that his heart could burst, he knew that his son did not know the true way of life. It had all gone so well for him, his father had said, gripping his hand tightly, but the tide could turn. So, just in case...

Michael had been too full of himself, too sure of the continuance of a charmed life, to realize what his father was talking about. He knew now, though. Kristin Long was a very real threat, one that could surely turn the tide against him. With a reinforced sense of conviction in his decision, he picked up his private line and called the never-before-used number of Mario's Meat Market.

The homicide detective picked up his ringing phone as he stubbed out his cigarette. "Harry Pickins," he said into the receiver.

"It's me," said a gravelly voice on the other end of the line. Harry sat up straighter in his seat, almost as if the caller could see him. He started to sweat.

"Yes, sir," he said in a choked voice.

"I need you to do something."

"Well, sure. What?

"Get me the M.O. on those hooker murders down there. There's been three of 'em so far, right?"

That's right. What do you need to know?"

"Everything."

"Everything?"

"Yeah. It would be good if you sent copies of the files."

Harry paused. This wasn't his case. And even though the department worked on the whole as a team, detectives usually didn't share specific file information. Sort of a way of keeping tighter control.

"That might be tough."

"Just do it."

"When do..."

"Yesterday."

Harry Pickens whistled silently to himself and wondered what this was all about. He knew better than to ask questions, though. He had long ago made his deal with the devil. There was no redemption now.

By four o'clock that afternoon, a Federal Express package containing every piece of police information about the three hooker murders was on its way to New York.

25

MICHAEL HAD GONE through the week with a mixture of dread and
fatigue. Every moment that Kristin Long lived was a moment in which
she could destroy him. He slept little as the week dragged on and he
waited to hear from Robert Lineo. He slogged through his days with the
added weight of the special session defeat and plummeting poll numbers
dragging him down. Caroline's attempts to comfort him were ineffectual.

Finally, on Friday, shortly before noon, his private phone rang. He
recognized Robert Lineo's gravelly voice immediately when he said,
"You've got to get her to Miami on Monday."

"Say what?"

"Just make sure she gets there somehow. By late Monday night, it will
be over."

Michael felt deflated and ecstatic at the same time. It was a strange
feeling.

"That soon?"

His question was met by a stony silence on the other end of the line.

"Just listen," Robert said. "Get her to check into the Sheraton Hotel,
Bal Harbour. Then arrange somehow for her to be on the beach behind
the hotel at ten p.m. Got that?"

"How am I going to do that?"

"Hey, if you want this taken care of, you'll figure a way. Ten."

"Okay. I'll take care of it," Michael said with a confidence he really
didn't feel.

Robert hung up on him.

Michael stared at the receiver after he had replaced it. All this week
he had struggled to get the shock of what he was doing out of his system.
Twice he had come close to relenting and calling it off.

But now that the call had come, he felt the shock waning. In fact, he was feeling relief. How empowering just to be able to make a phone call and have a situation taken care of. It gave him a boosted sense of power.

Now, how to get Kristin to Miami? He had talked to her only yesterday, buying time by telling her he would be back in touch today with a definite plan. That was as much time as she would give him, she said, before she found a way to tell Caroline herself. He thanked his lucky stars that Robert's time table was so attuned to his own. It was a good omen.

Michael contemplated the call he would have to make to Kristin to set the wheels in motion. He didn't think he would have a problem convincing her to travel to Miami to meet him. She had traveled to hotels for that purpose before. But so late at night? And how to get her on the beach behind the Sheraton at that time of night?

With a plan in mind that was shaky but still plausible, Michael called Kristin's number.

She answered on the first ring.

"Michael?" she breathed his name into the receiver.

"Yes, it's me."

"I've been waiting for you to call. What's going on, Michael?"

"What's going on," he started, feeling expansive and smug, "is that you and I will be meeting in Miami Monday night."

"What? Why?"

"Because," he lied in a soothing tone, "we're going to get a hotel room and make love and plan our future together."

"Oh, Michael, are you *serious?*"

"Very serious, Kristin."

"But why do we have to wait until Monday? And why Miami?"

"Because I have to be down there for several meetings on Monday, and I have a dinner with a big donor that's going to run late. And I'll need this weekend to get things...settled."

"You've told Caroline then?"

Michael deliberately and audibly sighed, like a man aggrieved, and said, "Yes. I'll tell you about it on Monday." He was pleased with how smoothly and easily the lies came.

Kristin started crying.

"What's wrong, Kristin?" Michael asked, more annoyed than alarmed.

"Nothing's wrong. I'm just so relieved and happy."

"We have a lot to talk about," Michael offered lamely in response.

"Yes we do, Michael. Where will I meet you this time?"

"The Sheraton in Bal Harbour. I'll be staying there, but I won't be checking in until late. Around ten."

"That *is* late."

"Can't be helped, baby." Michael controlled his gag reflex.

Kristin embraced the endearment. Baby. It sounded so loving.

Michael knew the next part of his plan was weak. He took a deep breath and said, "Say, I've got an idea. I'll have Manny get a great bottle of Champagne for us to share on the beach. Wouldn't a moonlight walk with Champagne be nice?"

"It sounds very romantic, but I can't drink now that I'm pregnant."

Damn! *Stupid mistake, Romano*, he scolded himself.

"Of course. Perrier it is, then. Is that good enough?"

"Good enough for what? What exactly do you have in mind?"

"You'll have to meet me on the beach at ten o'clock to find out."

"That doesn't make any sense, Michael. Plus it will be dark. I'm not sure it will be safe."

Expecting just such a response, Michael executed the next phase of his lie. "Okay, you caught me. I have a surprise planned, and Manny's helping me with it. And I'm not going to ruin it by giving you too many details. But if you don't meet me on the beach, then the surprise will be ruined. Will you trust me on this?"

"A surprise? Oh, tell me! No, don't. Okay, I'll meet you on the beach. But do you think I'll be safe?"

"Kristin, it's Bal Harbour, not Miami proper. Of course it will be safe," he said in an assuring voice. "Besides, as part of the surprise, I'll already be there, waiting for you. Now I've told you more than you should know."

Kristin was wondering what surprise Michael had for her. He said Champagne, didn't he? That usually meant a celebration. Could it be *a ring?* Could that be the surprise? How *romantic* that would be. Of course she would be there at ten. She didn't want to ruin his plans.

"Then I'll meet you on the beach at ten sharp," she giggled.

"Great. I'll see you then, Kristin."

"I love you, Michael."

For what he knew would have to be the very last time, Michael lied without compunction to Kristin Long. "I love you, too, Kristin."

Michael hung up the phone and felt adrenaline pumping through his body at an unchecked rate. He stood up and paced. Would it work? It had to. He would be safely tucked away up here in Tallahassee, and she would be waiting for him in Miami. He was sure every detail would be clean and well-planned, and that there would be no possible connection to him.

The surge of adrenaline receded almost instantly when Michael allowed a single sad thought to intrude on his consciousness.

A woman—and not just any woman, but a fine woman—was going to die for his mistake. Could he really do this? He had to. There was no other way. Anyway, he told himself, it was out of his hands. He couldn't stop the wheels from turning now.

Upon closer inspection of his conscience, he found he really didn't want to.

26

"**GOVERNOR ROMANO,**" the receptionist said, "Dr. Sanders will see you now."

A nurse was waiting for him inside the entry door. She led him to the doctor's office and said, "Have a seat and he'll be right in, Governor Romano."

Michael thanked her and took a seat. He was anxious, hoping that the story he would be telling the doctor would seem plausible. He had been required to think fast on his feet most of his life, but creating fictional reasons and excuses on what was becoming a frequent basis, was daunting.

"Hey, Michael, good to see you," Dr. Sanders said.

"Good to see you too, Oscar. How's everything? How's Margaret?"

"Oh, fine, fine. Whole family's fine. How's Caroline?"

"As a matter of fact, she's the reason I'm here."

"Oh? What do you mean?"

"Well, she's two weeks late with her period. She hasn't gone to her doctor yet, and I think it's because she has mixed emotions. I don't think she wants to get her hopes up, but at the same time she's afraid that if she is pregnant, she won't be able to have the baby. You know how women think."

"I wish I did," the doctor said jovially. A look of concern passed over the doctor's face. "So you're here because you're wondering if your vasectomy has recanalized?"

"Is that what it's called?"

"Yes. And it's been known to happen. A blocked sperm tube can reconnect on one or both sides after the procedure. It's also called recanalization failure."

"After nearly three years?"

"Even longer."

"Damn. Well, let's check me out, then."

"Sure. I'm going to need a sample of your semen so we can do an analysis to see if you have a sperm count. You shouldn't have any at this point, unless it has recanalized."

"What do you want me to do?"

"The nurse will get you a sample cup and put you in a private room. There are some magazines and video tapes."

"Christ, Oscar. Really?"

"Really. Then come back to my office here and wait. We should have the results in short order."

Oscar walked into his office and said, "Bad news, I'm afraid. You were right, it did recanalize. Caroline may very well be pregnant."

"God sakes, Oscar, what did the tests show?" Michael asked.

"First, you had a normal volume of ejaculation. Next, normal sperm count varies from 20 to 150 million sperm per milliliter. You're right in the middle of that at 70 million. You can make babies, Michael."

Michael groaned. In the back of his mind, he had hoped against hope that it hadn't happened. He knew he should have checked it out as soon as Kristin told him she was pregnant, but she had been so definite about it being his, and Manny had confirmed it happened with his brother-in-law. He hadn't considered a medical confirmation a necessary course of action until the middle of last night. He had awoken with a start, and with the clear thought that he should have been tested, for Christ's sake.

Michael had panicked, and lay awake the rest of the night. Then he had watched the clock in his office until it finally struck nine. He called the doctor's office and, not surprisingly, had been worked in.

And now here he was, on this, the morning of the day Kristin would die. Before her murder could become a fait accompli, he thought he would take one last shot at proving Kristin couldn't be pregnant by him. Then he *would* make a phone call to stop the wheels from turning.

"Do you want to reschedule surgery?" Oscar asked.

"Is it comp?" Michael asked, half serious. He didn't think he should pay again for a botched job.

Oscar laughed. "We'll work something out."

"Well, I guess I'd better."

"Okay, I'll have Doris schedule something and give you a call. Any rush?"

"Well, the sooner the better, I guess. If Caroline is pregnant, I won't need to be...potent. Is that the right word?"

Oscar nodded his head, and said, "Close enough."

"And if she isn't pregnant," Michael continued, "I don't want her to get pregnant. You know the danger."

"I understand. We'll get something set up as soon as possible."

"Good. And please don't say anything to Caroline one way or the other, okay? Either way, this is going to be hard for her to take."

Oscar didn't really understand what Michael was talking about, but he did understand respecting a patient's wishes.

"Sure, Michael. Hey, listen, I'm sorry about this."

"Is there a way to make sure this doesn't happen again?"

"I can cauterize it this time. Since you had it done, that's become a more commonplace technique because it's virtually foolproof."

Michael stopped short of saying that Oscar should have done that the first time.

"All right, but I'm not looking forward to more surgery."

"I don't blame you." What else could he say?

"So Doris will call me?"

"This afternoon."

"Good enough."

Michael stood to leave and extended his hand to Oscar. The doctor held on to it an extra moment and looked into Michael's eyes.

"Michael," Oscar started, feeling embarrassed, "I want to tell you that I'm sorry about the outcome of the special session. I know how much that meant to you."

Michael was touched. "Thanks, Oscar."

Oscar nodded, and Michael turned to leave.

"Give Caroline my best," Oscar said to him as he opened the door.

"Will do," Michael said, wondering just what the hell he was going to tell Caroline.

He told Manny everything the doctor had said on the way back to the Governor's Mansion. Together, they worked out what he would tell Caroline.

She was in her office when he got back to the Mansion. He gave a familiar rap at the door, to let her know it was him, and went in.

"What did the doctor say?" she asked as she stood to give him a kiss.

"Just that I'm run down, like I thought. No flu or virus, though." He paused, knowing that what he was going to tell her would be a big shock. She had been under the impression that he was going to the doctor for a general check-up, to see why he was feeling generally lousy.

"Well, that's good to hear. So what did he prescribe—R and R?"

"That's about the size of it. But listen, Caroline, there's something else he discovered. Quite by accident."

"What?" she asked, looking alarmed.

"Let's sit down," he said, taking her elbow and leading her over to the plush sofa in her office.

Caroline was more alarmed now. She had no idea what he had to tell her, but she could tell it was bad.

"There's nothing really wrong," he assured her quickly, wanting to dispel her fears.

She was relieved but still apprehensive. "Well, what is it then?"

"My vasectomy somehow grew back together. I have to have another operation."

Caroline was shocked, but also relieved that it wasn't something serious.

He expected her to ask how it came up, how the doctor discovered it. He was prepared with an answer meant to impart little information but leave her satisfied, if not confused. Suspected prostate problems, he would say. Tests for that showed this.

"How did that happen?" she asked instead. "How did it grow back together?"

He told her about recanalization, and then added, "They're scheduling me for surgery as soon as possible."

She took both of his hands in hers and looked deep into his eyes and said, "Don't have the surgery, Michael."

"*What?*"

"Just listen to me. You know I've always read a lot about infertility and miscarriages. I haven't stopped, even though I knew that I could never get pregnant again.

"And remember a couple of months ago, when I was over a week late with my period? I actually had fantasies about being pregnant, though I attributed it to stress with father."

"Caroline, I didn't know that."

"What was to know? I finally started, and I recall it was particularly painful, much worse than usual. I just figured my body was going through some more changes."

"I wish you had told me. And I wish you had told me you still read about these things."

"I know. But again, what was the point of telling you? It's almost like...I don't know, a compulsion. I hate to admit that. But listen, there's a technique used to prevent miscarriages. It really wouldn't have been the right treatment for me before, but I think it will work now.

"And, Michael, I have to tell you. More than once I've wished that you hadn't had the vasectomy. I've dreamed of being able to try again."

Michael was astonished. How could he be so close to his wife and not know that she was having such thoughts? He was sad to think that she had been dealing with those painful wishes all alone.

"I wish you had told me, sweetheart," he said, taking her in his arms.

"What good would it have done? But now, there's a reason to tell you. Oh, Michael, let's try," she entreated, hugging him tightly.

"Caroline, it could be dangerous," he cautioned her, pulling back to look at her so that she would fully understand the implication of what he was saying. "You know that. And what's this technique? What makes it okay to use it now, but not before?"

"It's hard to explain, but basically it had to do with the migraines I used to get. The treatment could have made them worse, but since I haven't had a migraine in over two years, I think I could do it now."

Before he could say anything, she rushed on. "Michael, please try to understand. This is like a miracle to me. I just can't throw away this opportunity. Not without talking to Dr. Sanford first, anyway."

"Well..."

"Please, Michael. Let's hear what he has to say about it. If he says there's any danger, any at all, we'll nix the idea. But he might just say that it's very possible, too."

"I want to be there when you talk to him."

"I would want you to be. I'm going to call him right now," she said, jumping up from the couch.

He grabbed her hand to stop her. "You're sure this is what you want?"

"Don't you?"

Yes. This is what he wanted, more than anything in the world. A baby with his beloved wife—but not at the risk of losing her.

"Of course I want it, too. But I'm worried."

"I told you. We'll hear what the doctor has to say, and then we'll make a decision."

"All right, then. Call him."

Caroline let out a little yelp and bent down to hug his neck. Michael watched her as she looked up the number and called the doctor's office. She looked radiant, more excited than she had looked in as long as he could remember. Could it be possible? Could they really have a chance at having a baby?

She looked over at him from where she sat at her desk and smiled. She was so damned happy. The hopeful look on her face took Michael's breath away.

"Yes, I'll hold," she said into the receiver.

"Isn't it strange, darling," she started to say, but was interrupted by the receptionist.

"Yes, this is Caroline Romano. I'm fine, thank you, Jean. I'd like to make an appointment to see Dr. Sanford as soon as possible. No, nothing's wrong, it's just...well, I don't want to go into it right now, but I do need to see him just as soon as I can," she finished with an unaccustomed assertiveness.

She looked over at Michael, as if to ask, "Did that sound okay?"

Michael smiled and nodded his head.

"Wonderful," she said. "Tomorrow morning at ten would be perfect. Thank you so much, Jean."

She threw up her arms after she hung up the phone, expressing a glee that Michael rarely saw.

"I'm sorry I didn't check with you about the time," she said, going back over to the couch. He stood up so that he could hug her as she reached him.

"I'm sure you knew I'd make the time," he laughed, catching her euphoria.

"I was pretty sure you would," she giggled. "Oh, Michael, I'm so excited."

"Let's not get too excited, sweetheart. We have to hear what he says."

"Oh, pooh," she chided, giving him a little push. "I'll be excited if I want to be."

He couldn't help himself. He laughed out loud and picked her up. He twirled her around, and dropped her on the couch, where he fell down beside her.

"Want to start trying now?"

"We can't. There's a lot to this. Now listen..." Suddenly what she was going to say to him earlier came back to her.

"Michael, isn't it strange that I haven't gotten pregnant?"

"I thought about that, too. It wasn't for lack of trying."

"Maybe I can't get pregnant anymore," she said gloomily, her happiness slipping away.

"Don't say that. It just hasn't happened yet. If everything checks out okay, we'll try, and try again. And don't forget, you've had a lot on your mind with your father and all. Lots of stress. That could be the reason."

"Maybe, I don't know." Then her happiness returned as quickly as it had left. "But like you said, if everything checks out okay, we'll try and try."

"We'll take a good, long vacation. We owe ourselves one, anyway. We'll hop down to St. Barths and spend a week drinking French martinis and trying to get you pregnant. How does that sound?"

"Mmmm...that sounds nice. But I'm not sure we'll be able to go away if I start the treatment."

"No? Why not?"

"Let's just wait and see what the doctor says."

"Okay. We'll take this one step at a time," Michael said, sitting up. "We'll see what he has to say, and then we'll see about St. Barths. See how cooperative I'm being?"

"Yes, darling," she laughed, squeezing his hand.

"I've got to go back to work now," he said, giving her a kiss.

"Me, too. Oh, Michael, I'm just so happy!"

"I'm happy, too, Caroline. Very happy."

Michael walked back to his office in a state of disbelief. How fucking crazy was it that, despite having a vasectomy, Kristin became pregnant and Caroline fantasized about becoming pregnant? If there were a silver lining behind the dark cloud that was hanging over him, this was it. To have a baby with Caroline would be miraculous.

He stopped in his tracks and looked at his watch. It was twelve thirty. In ten hours, Kristin would be...taken care of.

206

He shook off the macabre feelings brought on by that thought and went to his office. He tried to work, but his mind wouldn't change direction, no matter how hard he tried to concentrate. He got through two meetings and three long-winded phone calls, grateful for the temporary distractions they brought. Now that the time was ticking down, he was more anxious than ever. He looked at his watch again and saw it was four fifty-nine. Damn. Time was going so slowly.

He had called Oscar's office to postpone the surgery. He had vacillated all day between dread and euphoria. Would it all go as planned with Kristin? Would Caroline be able to have a baby?

But the problem with Kristin was the more immediate one, and it dominated his thoughts.

He had to get his mind off what was going to happen. He had made a decision and taken action. That was that. He wasn't going to change his mind. Especially now, with the possibility of having a baby with Caroline. How special, how complete his life would really be then. Their prayers answered.

At five thirty, when he could no longer stand the inertia that was trapping his body while fueling his thoughts, he went upstairs to work out, thinking that there was nothing like good, hard, physical exertion to clear the head.

An hour later, he had worked up a real sweat and felt much better. Caroline came into the exercise room, looking for him.

"What are you doing up here now?" she asked.

"Just felt like working out," he answered easily.

"This is an early day for you, isn't it?"

"I'm going to shower and go back down."

"Oh. How late will you be working?"

"Late. Past ten. I have some work to do and I need to talk to someone who won't be available until then." He knew he had to stay in his office at least that long. He was expecting a very important phone call.

"You're a little on edge over all of this talk of my getting pregnant, aren't you?" she asked with concern.

"A little. Just worried about you, but I'm also happy."

She smiled and walked over to him. She didn't want to hug him because he was still sweaty, so she leaned forward to give him a kiss.

"Okay. I'm sorry to have bothered you. I'm going to go write a couple of letters."

"You never bother me."

She smiled and said, "Can you take a break for dinner?"

"Sure. Let's eat around eight."

"Okay, I'll check in with you shortly before."

After she left, he showered and put on some jeans and a sweater.

When he got to his office, he tried to work but found that his thoughts were quickly returning to where they were before he had gone to exercise. He went into the library to find a book, knowing that if he could get absorbed in a good book, the time would pass a lot faster.

He would wait. He would read. He would have dinner with Caroline. And then he would wait some more.

27

KRISTIN STAYED IN her hotel room long enough to hear the promo for the upcoming ten o'clock news.

She flipped off the set and slipped her feet into her new Versace sandals. She looked at herself in the mirror again, and decided that the pink shorts and matching top were indeed flattering. After a brief visit to the Miami Lakes Pro-Long Plastics office that morning, Kristin had checked into the hotel and walked across the street to the Bal Harbour Shops. She wanted something with a *wow* factor for a special, celebratory evening on the beach with Michael.

The shorts revealed her shapely legs, and the v-neck, short-sleeved blouse accentuated her breasts without being too revealing. She decided that the eight hundred dollars she had spent on the designer outfit was justified. She picked up the matching pink cotton sweater, which had cost another five hundred, thinking that the beach might be a little chilly at night. Even in Miami, October evenings could be cool.

In a state of extreme happiness and anticipation, she headed to the bank of elevators, where she waited alone. On the way down, the elevator stopped on the fifth floor where a nice-looking older gentleman was waiting. When he stopped short at the sight of her before getting in, she knew she had the look she wanted.

She wanted Michael to stop short when he saw her, to catch his breath, to tell her she looked gorgeous; and most of all, to tell her that he loved her.

The man got out on the lobby level, but Kristin stayed on to descend to the basement level, which led out to the beach. There was no one in sight when she stepped off the elevator, and the starkness of the area, though well-lit, spooked her. She shook it off and resolutely headed for the beach. Michael said he would be waiting there with a surprise, and she was excited to see him.

She followed the sidewalk that ran beside the pool to the gate that opened onto the beach. She had been there earlier in the day, beckoned by the view from her room. The pool area was huge, and as beautiful as anything she had ever seen. It was like a tropical oasis. There was a large, meandering pool area with palm trees, a waterfall, a water slide and two whirlpools. She had continued out to the beach where she had enjoyed the feel of the warm sand under her feet and the afternoon sun on her shoulders.

When she had returned to her room, she sat on the large balcony, enjoying the view while sipping a glass of orange juice and wishing that Michael were with her at that moment. She had waited impatiently throughout the long afternoon and evening for ten o'clock, when she would finally be meeting him. Her excitement and curiosity about Michael's surprise caused her to quicken her step now.

She opened the gate that led to the beach, and then hesitated. The area was eerily quiet except for the sound of the waves. She wondered for a moment about the security at the hotel. She looked around for a security guard—or anyone else—hoping to find some comfort in their presence. There was no one in sight. Although she felt even more uncomfortable, she continued to walk toward the water, thinking the set-up might be a part of the surprise. She thought how glad she would be to see Michael, however, for more than just one reason. Where *was* he?

She spotted a man, walking along the shoreline, coming her way. From where she was, she couldn't see him well, but she thought he looked like an okay person. Undoubtedly he was a tourist, judging by the way his pants were rolled up and he was carrying his shoes in his hand. His presence brought her an unexplained sense of comfort.

Nevertheless, Kristin backed up a few feet so that she faded into the shadows under palm fronds. But the tourist didn't even look her way. He was looking out over the ocean, and he seemed to be absorbed in the beauty of the whitecaps breaking against the darkness of the ocean.

He kept walking until he was out of her sight, leaving Kristin alone again. She found that her fear of being alone on the beach was replaced by her fear that something was wrong. Could something have happened to delay him? Surely he would have called her at the hotel if that were the case. She'd give him five more minutes, and then she would go back to her room and ask to be connected to his room. He said he'd be checking in around ten.

She looked behind her at the lights of the hotel pool, and decided to head back that way. She might intercept him, but if not, she would go to her room and check for a message. She was only a few steps from the gate when she heard a rush of air and sand behind her.

Instantly, instinctively, Kristin knew she was in great danger, but before she could react, she felt a garrote bite into her neck. She tried to scream as the painful wire sunk into the soft skin of her throat with brutal force, but she was gagging and no screams would come. She struggled, falling to her knees in the sand. The wire dug deeper as her assailant fell to his knees with her, making it impossible for her to struggle any longer.

In that last second before her brain ceased to function, she had one clear, agonizing thought—*Michael!*

In the next split-second, both lives in Kristin Long expired.

The tourist with the rolled-up pants stopped in his tracks and did a double-take of the body lying on the beach.

From the way the body was sprawled in the sand, he knew that it was lifeless. He looked around, thinking he might spot someone else, but there was no one. He approached the body slowly, and as he got closer he realized it was the woman who had been standing alone on the beach earlier.

He had noticed her, and though he had felt compelled to look at her for some reason, had made a point of not doing so as he had walked by, sensing her nervousness and not wishing to add to it.

He knew she was dead, but he bent down and took her wrist to feel for a pulse anyway. Nothing. He stood up and backed away, knowing he could be destroying evidence. He shot towards the hotel to alert the manager and call the police. He looked around for a security guard on the way, but didn't see one. *Odd.*

He paused before opening the door, and wondered when the standing sign that said, "Pool Area Closed" had been put up. It wasn't there when he had exited the hotel earlier.

He hurried into the hotel's basement to catch the elevator up to the lobby. He approached the concierge, who was unoccupied at this late hour.

"Call the manager. It's an emergency," he said to the concierge.

"Is there a problem, sir?" The concierge looked genuinely concerned.

"There sure is. A big problem. Call the manager."

"Perhaps I..."

"Listen to me," the man said, gripping the concierge's arm tightly. "I said call the manager—now. Are you hearing me?"

The concierge looked at the man more closely, and decided he was not someone to be trifled with—he meant business. He picked up the phone at his desk and said quietly into the receiver, "Mr. Harris, I think you better come out here. There's a gentleman here who insists there's a problem he needs to see you about. Immediately."

The night manager of the well-run hotel did not ask questions. If there were a guest who insisted on seeing him immediately, then it was his job to oblige.

"I'll be right there," he said.

"He'll be right here," the concierge said to the man, taking in his entire appearance. He certainly wasn't a bum. He was clean-shaven and neat, and wore expensive clothes, although the bottoms of his slacks were wet and he had sand on his feet and shoes.

The concierge looked up at the approaching manager, and the man looked around to where the concierge was looking. The manager was approaching with a professional smile, which seemed to say, *How may I be of assistance?*

The man thought to himself that the manager's smile was going to be wiped away in a matter of seconds when he heard the news.

"I'm Andrew Harris," the manager said when he reached the man. "How..."

The man took his arm and led him aside, startling the manager so that he stopped in mid-sentence.

"There's a dead woman on your beach. You need to call the police." From the look of shock and horror on the manager's face, the man knew the manager had never dealt with a situation like this before. He was planted in his spot, with his mouth hanging open, unable to respond. The man gave him a push and said, "Call them—*now.*"

"Yes, sir," the manager said, "right away."

As the manager turned to go back to his office, the man said, "I'll come with you."

The manager nodded, and the two men quickly headed for his office. The manager picked up the phone on his desk and called 911.

"This is Andrew Harris, manager of the Sheraton Hotel, Bal Harbour. I have a man in my office who has just informed me that there is the body of a dead woman on our beach property."

He looked up at the man as he spoke, and the man gave him a confident nod, letting him know he was handling it just fine.

After thirty seconds or so of saying, "Yes," "No," and "I don't know," he repeated his request, in a terse but professional tone, to just send the police immediately.

The man said to the manager, "Tell her to tell the police you'll meet them on the beach."

The manager looked startled and repulsed at the same time, but the man gave him a quick, rigid nod of his head as if to say, *Tell her.*

The manager told the 911 operator, and then hung up the phone.

"Who are you?" he asked the man.

"My name's Jake Miller. I'm a guest at your hotel. I was taking a walk on the beach when I saw the body. Let's go."

"Do you think..."

"I think we better get there before someone else sees it. We need to make sure no one messes with anything."

The manager nodded, and they headed towards the elevators that would take them to the beach.

"Is it...awful?" the manager asked, dread in his voice.

"You can't see much, she's face down."

"You didn't check to see if she was alive?"

He didn't mention checking for a pulse. He'd save that for the police. "She's not alive."

"How can you be sure?"

"Because I've seen dozens of dead bodies. You get to know the signs."

The manager was suddenly gripped with fear. Jake read his thoughts and grabbed his arm before he could bolt.

"I was with homicide in New York City. You're safe. Ten people saw you with me. Nothing's going to happen to you. Now let's move," he finished, shoving the manager into the elevator.

The manager could tell Jake was telling the truth. He was greatly relieved, even glad that the man was taking control. He felt he had always

213

handled pressure situations well, but he had never had to handle anything like this.

The standing sign about the pool closure surprised the manager. "I didn't know anything about the pool being closed," he mumbled.

Jake was beginning to get the picture. He looked around the pool area and out towards the beach. "You don't have a security guard out here?"

"Of course we do. There's a guard on duty in this area twenty-four hours a day."

"Where is he?"

The manager stopped and looked around, but he didn't see anyone. Anyone at all. Usually there were a few guests milling around the pool at night, too. The whole area was deserted, and probably because of the sign, he realized.

"I...I don't know. Maybe he's down on the beach with the body."

"Let's hurry."

But there was no one on the beach. The woman's body was lying face down in the sand, exactly as before. Jake realized that perhaps only five or six minutes had passed since he had first seen her lying there.

"Oh, my God," the manager was saying over and over, burying his face in his hands.

It would do no good to tell the manager to get a grip. People were never able to get a grip at their first sighting of a dead body. Or the second, or the third...

Jake heard the sirens and put his arm around the manager's shoulder. "It's okay. The police are here. Don't lose it now."

The manager looked at Jake and nodded appreciatively. He thought that the man seemed very calm. But then, he had said he had seen dozens of dead bodies. The manager shivered at the thought.

"Police," he heard a voice shout. "Move away from the body."

When the manager didn't respond, Jake said, "This is Mr. Harris, the manager of the hotel. I'm Jake Miller. I'm a guest here. I found the body."

Two uniformed policemen approached cautiously. Jake would later think of them as the bald one and the tall one. Both officers made note of the authoritative way the man had spoken. Nevertheless, both kept their hands at their sides, close to their guns.

Jake nudged the manager and then raised his arms and took a step back, indicating to the manager that he should do exactly the same. The manager did, and when the two officers were within three feet of them, they ordered them to keep their hands up, and not to move. The officers frisked them, then told them to lower their arms. "Let's see some ID," the bald one said.

The manager showed them his driver's license and his business card. Jake showed them his New York driver's license. The cops shined their flashlights on the IDs, then on the men's faces. The tall officer who checked Jake's ID was studying it, looking from the ID to Jake's face, then again at the ID. When they were satisfied, the cops returned the IDs and turned their attention to the body.

The bald one bent down beside the body and turned it over. He shined his flashlight on the woman's slit throat and said, "Oh, Jesus."

The tall cop looked at Jake and the manager to make certain they weren't going anywhere, then bent down beside the other cop and the body. "Looks like those other three," he said more to himself than to the bald officer.

"Sure does," the bald one replied.

Jake had an odd sensation, and took a step forward very cautiously. Neither of the officers looked at him.

"Take a look at this," the bald officer cried.

"A flower," the other officer confirmed. "A rose, it looks like."

"What's up with that?"

"Beats me. But let's bag it and call for backup from Metro-Dade. I'll stay with the body."

The bald officer rushed off, and the tall officer shined his flashlight onto the dead woman's face. Her eyes were open. Strands of silvery-white hair, intermingled with darker ones, were pasted to her forehead. Incredulity registered on his face, and when he looked back at the New York man, open-mouthed, it was just in time to see the guy plant face down into the sand.

Jake came to a moment later. He knew he had passed out, and he was embarrassed and shaken. The manager was kneeling beside him, and the cop was on his radio, calling for an ambulance.

In his whole life, he had never passed out. He had been knocked out, and he had lost consciousness when he had been shot, but he had never passed out.

"I'm okay," he said.

The cop knelt down beside him now and helped the manager pull him to his feet. Jake felt disoriented, but otherwise he felt fine.

"I take it you know the woman?" the cop said more than asked.

"No. I don't know her. But I think she's..."

"What do you mean you don't know her? She's your ever-lovin' twin, mister."

"I know that."

"You're not making sense."

"It's going to take a while to explain."

The cop was understandably leery, and he said to Jake, "You'll have to come with us, anyway. You can explain at the police station."

Jake nodded, then asked, "Can I sit down?"

"Yeah, sure," the officer answered, looking back towards the hotel at the sound of the approaching sirens.

The manager didn't understand what was happening. He hadn't seen the woman's face. He hadn't wanted to look at it. But apparently the woman looked like Mr. Miller's twin, and that had caused him to faint and the officer to freak out. What the hell was going on? Oh, lucky me, he thought somberly. Why did I have to be on duty tonight?

He saw a whole battalion of people coming onto the beach then, including what looked like news people. He became even more despondent as he realized he was in for a very long night.

28

A FADED BLACK rag-top Caddy pulled up to the bus bench on Biscayne Boulevard that Virgil Carpenter had staked out for the night. Virgil the Vagrant lounged in a drug-induced stupor, caustically observing the parade of shiftless people who were staggering along Biscayne Boulevard, looking for someplace to crash for the night.

Virgil watched the car window slide down and was momentarily concerned that a gun would appear. Instead, the driver said, "Hey Virgil, how are ya, my man?"

Virgil walked over and peered in. He thought he recognized the driver, but in the dark, he couldn't be sure. "Hey man," Virgil said, "What's up?"

"Got some good shit here that I just scored. Care to take a ride and try it out with me?"

Never one to turn down drugs, Virgil said, "Sure man," and opened the car door and slid into the passenger seat. "Whacha got?"

"Got some rock, got some 'ludes. Either of those float your boat?"

"Both, man!" Virgil laughed.

Virgil was bad news, the driver of the Caddy knew, but only to unfortunate prostitutes. The Miami cops had been searching for him for a couple of months now, without luck.

Canvassing the crud that populated the miles of sidewalks hugging Biscayne Boulevard, the police had come up empty. But street people who wouldn't talk to the cops could be persuaded to talk to the Mob, which had a keen interest in finding the killer. After all, murdered prostitutes were bad for business.

The driver of the Caddy had been following his boss' orders when he flew down from New York to be on Biscayne Boulevard on this night, at this time, to ensnare Virgil Carpenter with the promise of drugs. Further north, he'd be picking up a Miami affiliate who was doing some other job for the boss. They'd keep Virgil drugged to the gills until the wee hours of Wednesday morning. Then they'd dump him on the beach in Bal Harbour—alive.

The driver didn't know why, and he didn't care. All he cared about was that Virgil Carpenter, the man who was his responsibility, was right where he should be—in the passenger seat of the Caddy, ready to party.

"Let's take a ride and get hiiiiigh!" the driver whooped. Virgil whooped in agreement.

At half past ten, when Michael felt he couldn't sit still a single moment longer, his private line rang.

"Yes," he said, sounding as if his voice had been pushed out of him.

"It's done."

He wanted to ask a million questions. Was he sure? How long ago? Was there any chance of...? But he knew that all he needed to know, all he would ever know, was just what the man on the other end of the line had said: it's done.

"Thanks," was his only response.

"We're even, Romano," Robert Lineo said. Then the line disconnected, and Michael sat with the receiver in his hand for what seemed like a long time.

"Michael," Caroline's voice called from his outer office. He quickly and quietly replaced the receiver.

"Are you coming up soon?" she asked, as she walked into his office.

"I am. I just finished with that call I was expecting."

She looked at the book in his lap and said, "You've been reading?"

"While I was waiting for the call," was his succinct reply.

That was odd. She thought he had been working. At dinner he had been distant, preoccupied. "What's wrong, Michael?" she asked him.

"Nothing's wrong," he said quietly, putting the book down on his desk and standing up.

"Oh. Okay. I thought maybe you were having second thoughts."

"About what?" he asked uneasily.

"About what?" she countered in disbelief. "About having a baby."

He smiled, as much to himself as to her. Of course that's what she meant.

When she saw his smile, she was relieved.

"I'm not having second thoughts, Caroline."

"Good," she sighed, walking to meet him as he came around his desk.

They hugged each other tightly and she said, "Let's go to bed. I'm tired and I want to snuggle with you."

Michael realized how drained he was. Going to bed with Caroline and holding her close sounded perfect to him at the moment.

He was hoping to get a better night's sleep, but he wasn't optimistic.

Jake looked at his watch. It was after midnight, and he was getting really tired of this.

"All right, let's go over everything one more time," the Metro-Dade detective said to him.

Jake sighed. "Look, I understand why you think you have to hear this over and over again. You're looking for holes in my story, thinking I might say something I didn't say before, or leave something out this time. Well, that's not going to happen. Now I'm tired, I've told you everything I know, and I want to get back to my hotel. You have what you need on record.

"And unless you plan to arrest me," he yawned, standing up, "I'm leaving."

"I'm the detective here, Miller. You're a witness. You'll repeat it as many times as I tell you to."

Jake laughed out loud. He was all too familiar with the intimidation routine. It wasn't going to work on him. "No, I won't. I've told you everything about me, about finding out about my sister, about my travel arrangements, about my involvement to the point of finding her dead on the beach, and staying there until the cops arrived. I've told you everything three times now."

"Just a couple more questions."

"What?" Jake asked, exasperated.

"You've never talked to the victim—never." It was stated more than asked. Jake was familiar with the routine.

"I've already told you: no."

"And you had no idea who she was before Officer Haggerty shined the light in her face."

"No."

"Well, don't you think it's strange that you were where you were, when you were?"

"Hell yes, I think it's strange," Jake responded with anger. "I think it's fucking insane. But that doesn't help us any, does it?"

"Help us?"

"Yeah, *us*. I want to know who did this, and it wasn't me. I think you know that, too. So while you're sitting here, harassing me, you've got a murderer out there whose getting colder by the minute. And if I were you, I'd be looking for that security guard who disappeared at a very inconvenient time."

The detective didn't answer. They were looking for the security guard, all right. He seemed to have completely disappeared, as a matter of fact. The detective thought Jake was telling the truth, but the whole fucking thing was just so weird. The guy had come down to Florida to find his long-lost sister, and he had found her dead on the beach. He had come down here to Miami before going to Tallahassee, where she lived, because he wanted a vacation before he saw her. So he said. But how did it work out that he was on that very beach at the very time she was killed?

It was too weird to be a coincidence, and yet the man's story jelled. Plus, what the man didn't know was that hers was the fourth in a series of identical killings. And he couldn't have known about the rose. No one knew that little detail except the few detectives who were handling the case.

"All right, buddy, I'm gonna let you go back to the hotel. But sit tight. We'll be in touch."

"Right," Jake said wearily, turning to leave.

"By the way," he said, turning back to the detective. "What did that officer mean by, 'It's just like the other three?'"

"One of 'em said that?"

Jake didn't want to get anybody in trouble. "Well, he didn't say it to me. He said it to the other cop. I just happened to be standing close enough to hear."

The detective nodded. "He didn't mean nothing by it. Nothing that would matter to you."

"Right," Jake said, thinking to himself what a jerk the guy was being.

"We'll be in touch," the detective said again as Jake left the room.

No shit, Jake thought as he turned to leave.

Michael spent an entirely sleepless night. He couldn't even doze, despite his mental and physical fatigue. He had to lie perfectly still, too, because he might wake Caroline, and she might start asking questions.

Throughout the agonizing night, he went over, time and again, everything that had ever transpired between him and Kristin. He went through numerous "what if" scenarios; but always, he came to the same conclusion—he had done the only thing he could have done.

Although he had reasonable fears, he intuitively knew that the deed had been done with no clues left behind. Besides Robert and his hit man, only two people in the world knew about Kristin—him and Manny. That was it. Robert was a non-factor. And he was pretty sure Kristin had told no one else. But what if she had? Still, no one could link him to her death.

He was here in Tallahassee when she was killed in Miami. He knew he was ninety-nine point nine percent safe. Those were pretty damn good odds.

He was relieved when the alarm finally went off at five-thirty. He could get up now and get on with his life. Free and unencumbered, except for the guilt he felt. He was hoping the guilt would dissipate in time. He could live with it until it did. He had to. A guilty conscience was the only price he expected to pay; and, considering the crime, it wasn't too awfully expensive.

Jake was lying on the bed in his hotel room, sipping his alcoholic beverage of choice, Dewar's neat. He had an unusual case of nerves.

Despite his earlier fatigue at the police station, he had found that he couldn't sleep when he got back to his hotel. Now, with the coming of dawn, his mind still raced with the recollections of the evening's events, and a deep, hollow feeling encased him.

He just couldn't believe his misfortune. He mentally recounted the sequence of events, trying to make sense of it, trying to find some justification for the disastrous events that had occurred in his life.

First was the premature death of his parents in a car crash. And how strange that Kristin's parents had been killed the same way a year after. Then there was his shooting. His promising career had been ruined.

Next, he had discovered the existence of a twin sister. That had been such good news. Additional surgery had kept him from getting to her sooner. He couldn't help thinking that if he had, somehow her death might not have happened.

And now, here he was, right in the middle of the investigation into her death. In a lifetime burdened with bizarre, this was the topper for Jake.

Not for the first time, Jake wondered just how much of a gift his special gift was. Though it had at times proven invaluable, tonight it had diminished in value.

True to form, he had relied on his intuition when he had decided to go to Miami first, instead of Tallahassee, as he'd originally planned. He hadn't really known why he had changed his plans. Now he understood. He had rationalized the change by thinking that she might not want anything to do with him, and then he wouldn't feel like a vacation.

So he'd decided to take the vacation first. He'd go to Miami, relax, get some sun, and shake out the kinks. Maybe even get laid. Then he'd go see her in Tallahassee. He imagined it was just quirky fate that had brought him to Miami at the time of her death. *But to the same hotel?*

Well, the hotel hadn't been an arbitrary choice for him. Because he had been to Bal Harbour often, he had just naturally booked a room at the Sheraton Bal Harbour, which was a first-rate hotel.

But what was she doing at the same Sheraton? He groped with several reasons in his mind before coming to the conclusion that if he knew that, he'd be a lot closer to knowing why she was murdered.

29

CAROLINE AND MICHAEL held hands as they left the doctor's office. They shared a state of euphoria which was only slightly dampened by the few complications that might arise.

"I'm going to be late for my lunch with Julia," Caroline said, looking at her watch. "I can't wait to tell her the good news."

"Are you sure you want to do that? Wouldn't you rather wait until it actually happens?"

"No way. Besides, she already knows we had this appointment, and she's waiting to hear the verdict."

"Okay, then. Whatever you think."

"Manny," Caroline cried as she spotted him stepping out of the limousine to open the door. "The doctor says we can try again!" She threw her arms around his neck and hugged him.

Manny was touched, but more than that, he was happy for Caroline. He gave Michael an odd look, which Michael couldn't read, then said to Caroline, "I'm happy for you, Caroline, really happy. Maria will be, too," he added, knowing his wife would indeed be happy for her.

Michael and Caroline chatted in the back seat of the limousine on the way to the restaurant. Manny tuned them out, respecting their privacy. Anyway, he had other things on his mind, like how Michael was gonna deal with the already pregnant woman in his life.

"Well, there are the normal concerns with a woman my age having a baby, especially with my history of miscarriages," Caroline said to Julia. Before she could continue, the waiter brought a bottle of Cristal Brut and went through the ceremony of opening and pouring it. He waited until Caroline had tasted it and nodded her approval before he placed it in the ice bucket stand next to the table.

Caroline sighed as she sipped it and said, "I'll miss this when I get pregnant."

"Small thing to give up, though, don't you think?" Julia responded, laughing.

"No, Champagne is not a small thing to give up, Julia. But I will, gladly," Caroline laughed, giddy with the prospect of becoming pregnant.

"You're only thirty-nine, Caroline," Julia said, picking up where Caroline had left off. "Lots of women have babies into their forties these days."

"That's what Dr. Sanford said, too, and I think he's hopeful. It's his job, though, to relate any danger, don't you think? I mean, he has to point out certain facts."

"Such as?"

"Such as, I have to realize that the blood vessels in my body have more wear and tear, and there's a greater chance for hypertension to occur."

"Which means what?"

"High blood pressure, possible diabetes. But that wouldn't normally happen until the last twelve weeks of the pregnancy."

"Caroline!"

"It's not that serious, Julia. My blood pressure is on the low side, and he says I'm in excellent physical shape. If my blood-sugar level is good, then there should be no problems."

"But if there are?"

"Look. At twenty-four to twenty-eight weeks into the pregnancy, he would do a screen of my blood sugar. If, at that time, he sees I've developed diabetes, he would put me on a special diet for a few weeks. If that doesn't work, he'll treat me with insulin."

"This sounds pretty serious, sweetie."

"Not really. If I can get that far into the pregnancy this time, I can deal with everything else. It's getting past the first three months that really matters."

"Would the insulin affect the baby?"

"Only in the respect that he might be bigger than normal, and I would have to have a Cesarean."

"Well, that's not so bad. I had one with my Allen, you know," Julia said, referring to her third and last child.

"I remember. So I can deal with those things, don't you think?"

"It sounds as if you're determined to," Julia laughed.

"Dr. Sanford said these complications might not occur at all, but if they should, they're controllable. Women who develop high blood pressure or diabetes deliver healthy babies all the time."

"He said that?"

"Yes."

"That's wonderful. But listen, get to the good part. What treatment are you going to use to help you get pregnant and carry the baby to full term?"

"Well, getting pregnant is just a matter of timing and luck. Do you know about luteal phase defect?"

"Luteal what?"

"Luteal phase defect. It's that time during the menstrual cycle from the time of ovulation to when my period starts. During that time, a hormone called progesterone is produced. When my period starts, it drops. In between, while I'm trying to conceive, the level of that hormone has to remain high enough to sustain the implementation and development of early pregnancy."

"In other words," Julia clarified, "if there's not enough progesterone, a miscarriage could occur."

"Exactly right. And there's something else, Julia. I think I was pregnant a month ago. I was more than a week late starting my period, and when I finally did, it was just terrible. I was in bed for a whole day. The more I think about it, the more I think I miscarried again. Very early in the pregnancy, though, if I'm right. Not like before."

"Oh, Caroline, how sad."

"I know. But at least I know I can still conceive and that now, with treatment, I have a chance of carrying a baby to full term."

"So how do you make sure you get enough progesterone?"

"Through daily injections."

"Ouch."

"Well, I could use vaginal suppositories or oral medication. All three are equally effective, Dr. Sanford said, but I think the injections are the surest thing for me."

"Didn't they have this progesterone three years ago?" Julia asked, referring to when Caroline had last gotten pregnant.

"Yes, and I knew about it. But the doctor and I discussed it, and we didn't think it would be the right treatment for me because of my migraines."

"But you haven't had migraines in quite a while. And what does progesterone have to do with migraines?"

"It precipitates severe headaches. And even though I knew about progesterone before my last pregnancy, I knew I couldn't take it because I was still having migraines. It's only been a couple of years since they've stopped."

"You started meditating to get rid of them, didn't you?"

"Yes, twice a day. And getting acupuncture—and it has worked."

"Great. So you're past that obstacle."

"Exactly. So there's no reason for concern now."

"Nothing else can go wrong?"

"Boy, Julia, if I had known you would be so negative, I wouldn't have suggested lunch."

"Caroline, you know I'm just concerned. I would be delighted for you if this happened. You know that. And you can count on my prayers to help."

"Okay, thanks, Julia. I appreciate that. But there is nothing else to go wrong, except not being able to conceive, or an undue amount of stress once I do. Other than that, all lights are green."

Julia leaned over and gave her life-long friend a hug. "Godspeed, love," she said with tears in her eyes.

"Thank you, Julia. I love you, my friend."

"I love you too, Caroline."

Jake picked up the phone on the first ring. "Jake Miller," he said, figuring it might be a call from homicide.

"Yes, Mr. Miller," said a voice Jake didn't recognize as the voice of Detective Robbins, the guy who had grilled him the night before. That was who he was expecting to hear from.

"I'm Detective Rick Givens, Metro-Dade Homicide. How are you today?"

This guy sounded nice, professional.

"So-so, detective," Jake replied honestly. "I guess you want me to come down for more questioning?"

"Actually, no. I'm calling to let you know that your story checked out, and that we won't need you anymore. You can leave Miami any time."

Just like that? Jake thought. Suddenly, he knew that Kristin's death had been linked to the "others" the bald cop had referred to.

"Then you have a suspect?" Jake asked automatically.

Rick Givens laughed. "I heard you were a detective. I expected that question. Now you know better than anybody I can't discuss anything with you."

"But I'm her brother," Jake entreated.

"Only by birth, according to the records you showed Detective Robbins last night. You have no legal rights to any information—which even if you did, I wouldn't give you at this time."

"Come on, give me a break," Jake pleaded.

"Can't do it," Rick responded resolutely.

"Just tell me if you have a suspect."

"I can't tell you anything. Anything more than you can read in the newspaper, anyway."

"Which reminds me. How did the press get a line on me? I took off with your detective before they could question me."

"Don't know. Probably the hotel manager."

Oh, right. "So just tell me this: Is her murder linked to the others?" Jake asked, trying to keep the detective talking.

"It's the same M.O. as three other recent killings, yes."

Big deal, Jake thought. This morning's *Herald* had said that. But were they *linking* her death to the others? Jake let out an exasperated breath. "You can't tell me anything more? Not even as a professional courtesy?"

"Look, Miller. You know the answer to that. First of all, you're a retired detective, so that severs any professional courtesy ties right there. But more than that, you know I'd have strong reservations about giving out any information, even to an active detective, from another city. There's absolutely no justification for it."

Jake knew everything the detective had said was true. He would do the same thing if the situation were reversed.

"I know you're right," he said, conceding. Then before he could stop himself, he said, "But maybe I could help."

Detective Givens smiled to himself, acknowledging that he had correctly predicted Jake Miller would offer that. It's what Rick would have offered if he was in Jake's shoes, so Rick couldn't blame him for it.

After all, according to what he had learned from the New York City Police Department that morning, this guy had been a true golden boy, top notch all the way around. That, along with the evident link of the woman's death to the others, had exonerated him of all suspicion—even if the whole thing was pretty damn weird.

"Thanks, but we have the investigation under control."

"I see. Well, if there's anything I can do, let me know. I'm going to hang around a few days."

"What for?" Rick asked suspiciously.

"Finish my vacation," Jake replied matter-of-factly.

"Right. Well, I'm sorry about your sister, but you can be sure we're doing everything we can here."

Jake had heard that before; in fact, he had said it himself hundreds of times.

"Thanks anyway, Detective Givens."

After giving it some thought, Jake dialed the number of the Chief of the Detectives of the New York City Police Department.

actual

30

MICHAEL PICKED UP the local section of the *Miami Herald* and read, for the fourth time, about Kristin's death.

"The body of a woman identified as Kristin Marks Long, who resides in Tallahassee, Florida, was found Monday night on the beach behind the Sheraton Hotel, Bal Harbour. She was a registered guest of the hotel.

Police have indicated that this is the fourth in a series of murders, though the victim did not fit the profile of the previous three victims, who were known prostitutes.

While the other murders occurred more than fourteen blocks south and west of the Sheraton, the particular method used to kill the victim was identical to the others, leading police to believe that all killings were committed by the same person. No further details were given.

In response to the rising concern about a killer whose victims can no longer be stereotyped, Metro-Dade Homicide Detective Rick Givens warned that all women should use caution when going out alone in the evening. Givens indicated that police were close to identifying the killer prior to this murder, and that their efforts would be escalated.

Sources have indicated that the victim's body was discovered by another guest of the hotel, Jake Miller, who is not a suspect in the crime. He did not return calls made to his hotel."

Michael had been right about Robert Lineo. He had done his homework about the murders and covered the bases, so that Kristin's murder was made to look like the others. He remembered reading about those murders. It struck him as kind of scary that someone could be murdered and that the true identity of the killer would never be discovered. But he had read that thousands of murders went unsolved. He had never understood that before, and had even been disdainful of the ineptitude of homicide departments in solving murders. Now he understood how it could happen.

The *Tallahassee Democrat* would no doubt carry the story in tomorrow's edition. He buried the *Herald* in the trash can and started out of his office to go see Caroline, who had buzzed him to let him know she was back from lunch. He was met by Manny, however, as soon as he opened the door.

"We gotta talk," Manny said.

Michael knew he must have seen the article, too. Michael should have sought him out before now to explain. But he dreaded the telling of it, and, in fact, had been avoiding Manny.

"I can't talk right now, Manny. I have to go see Caroline."

"I'll wait here."

"Look, I've got a full calendar today."

"You can spare the time."

"All right," Michael sighed. He'd have to face Manny sooner or later.

He spent ten happy, trouble-free minutes with Caroline, discussing everything again. During that time, he was able to put guilty thoughts of Kristin Long aside. But as he headed back to his office, where Manny was waiting, the burden of his guilt weighed on him heavier than ever. He expected Manny to understand, though he would also be giving Manny his own burden to bear in keeping his secret. But it would be a relief to unload his own conscience by sharing it with the one man who he could trust not only to keep a secret, but to protect and defend him, no matter what happened.

"What happened, Mike?" Manny asked from the armchair where he was sitting as Michael came in.

"You already know, don't you?"

"I want to hear it from you."

Michael's shoulders slumped, and his voice was ragged when he said, "Okay. I had it done."

"Shit, Mike. Why?"

"How can you ask me that question, when you know that she was planning to ruin my life?" Michael snapped.

"Yeah, but Mike—*murder?*" Manny whispered the last word.

"It was the only solution."

"I can't believe that. Who made the hit?"

"The Lineo Family. They owed me. Well, they owed my family. It goes back a ways."

"Holy shit! The Lineo Family? They're real dirty, Mike."

"I know that. But it was the only way I had to handle it."

"There had to be some other way, Mike. She didn't deserve to die."

"Manny, put yourself in my place, and tell me what you would have done."

"I wouldn't have done that."

"That's easy for you to say. You're not the Governor of the state of Florida."

"I don't care if I was the President of the fuckin' U.S. of A. I still wouldn't have done it."

"You've killed before, Manny," Michael said quietly, raising what he knew was a terribly dangerous and personal issue with Manny.

Manny's voice was icy cold as he replied, "That was self-defense, and you know it—*your* self-defense."

Michael nodded, acknowledging that Manny had saved his life. "So was this, Mann, in its own peculiar way."

The two men looked at each other, and in that instant both realized that a lifetime of trust had been destroyed. It could never be like it was before.

Neither could say why, or how, the instantaneous change had occurred. It simply had.

"I always said I didn't judge you, Mike. I guess I never really had to, since you never did anything that could be judged. Not even your affair with that lady needed judging. But this is something else, and you know it."

"Yes, it's something else, Manny, but I need you to understand it."

"I wish I could, Mike. But I don't think I ever will."

It was said with such conviction that Michael was devastated. His one, real, true, trusted friend in the world was turning away from him.

"I'm sorry you feel that way, Manny. Sorrier than I can say." Then, in a measured voice, he asked the question that had been in the back of his mind since the conversation had started.

"What are you going to do about it, Manny?" It was not a challenge; it was a question full of doubt and fear.

Manny gave Michael a hard look. He knew what Michael was asking. Would he tell what he knew? But Mike was safe, at least from him.

"I'm not going to say anything about it, Mike. I would never do that to you." He saw the relief on Michael's face, and for a moment he thought he was looking at a stranger. He no longer knew the man standing in front of him.

"But," he continued as he stood to leave, "I'm not going to stick around. I can't."

The thought that Manny would leave him had never occurred to Michael. Sure, Manny was upset—but quitting? "You can't quit, Manny," Michael croaked.

"I can't stay. I don't know you anymore, Mike. Maybe I never did. I just don't know," he finished, his voice trailing off sadly.

"Mann, please. We've been friends all our lives. We go back a long, long way. You've made it clear you would lay down your life for me. Damn, you've proved what you would do to help me. Don't desert me now, Manny."

"Don't say anything else, Mike. It won't make a difference."

Michael could not believe what he was hearing. This couldn't be happening on top of everything else. Manny gone? What would he do without him?

"Mann, I don't understand how you can just cut me off like this."

"You're just not the man I thought you were, Mike. The man I would have laid down my life for doesn't exist any longer."

"That's bullshit, Manny."

"Is it?"

"Okay, things went too far. But I'm still the same man I was. I had no choice, Manny, don't you see that? And besides, I need you now more than ever."

"Yeah, I guess you do. But I don't need you, Mike. Not anymore."

Michael acknowledged the finality of the friendship in that instant. He was crushed with regret.

"What are you going to do?" he asked Manny quietly.

"Go back to New York, probably. I've built up a pretty good nest egg. I can sell the house here, that'll give me more cash." He paused and then said in a heavy voice, "I guess I'll retire."

"No, you can't retire, Manny. You don't have enough money to do that. There are plenty of people in New York who need a good man like you."

"Maybe."

"No, definitely. You'll get the highest recommendation from me. You can still make a lot of money."

"I don't know..."

"Look, Manny. If I could talk you out of this whole thing, my dear friend, I'd give anything. But I know now that I can't. If you do decide to retire, I'll make it easier for you."

"I don't want your money," Manny hissed.

Michael was taken back. Manny must have thought he was offering him some sort of hush money. He hurried to correct Manny's misdirected thoughts.

"Manny, you've already told me you won't say anything. I know if I never gave you a cent, I could count on your word. I only wanted to make things easier for you. You've been good to me. Real good. I can't do anything that would ever really repay you. Money is just something I have a lot of, and I'd like to share it with you."

"No, thanks," Manny said resolutely, no longer angry.

"Okay. But the offer is always open."

When Manny didn't respond, Michael said desperately, "Manny, think about what you're doing. Can't we put this all behind us, just forget about it, and go on as before?"

Manny moved closer to Michael. Their eyes were level and locked when Manny replied, "You know the answer to that, Mike."

Yes, he had known the answer, but he had hoped that Manny might reconsider. What would he do without Manny?

Michael was suddenly very tired. He couldn't remember ever having been so damn tired. So much, so damn much to deal with. He thought that if he had known that he could lose Manny's friendship over this, he might not have done it after all. He was surprised that this man meant that much to him.

"When are you leaving?" he asked in a defeated tone.

"Just as soon as you can find somebody to replace me."

"That would take forever."

"I don't think so. I won't stay longer than a month."

Michael nodded, knowing Manny was being fair under the circumstances.

"Hey," he said in a final gesture of friendship, "I want you to know this. We were going to ask you and Maria to be the Godparents to our baby if that all worked out." He paused. "I guess that's out of the question now, huh?"

"It wouldn't be right, Mike."

Michael's audible sigh was filled with grief.

Manny stepped to the side to leave, but Michael couldn't let him go without telling him what he had wanted to say for many years. He put his hand on Manny's shoulder and said, "I love ya, Mann."

Michael saw the sadness in Manny's eyes before he dropped his head. With a shaking sigh, Manny nodded, then removed Michael's hand from his shoulder, and left.

31

JAKE WALKED INTO the modern, spacious lobby of the Metro-Dade police building. It was mid-morning, and it looked different in the daytime. There was the usual kind of bustling activity prevalent in any such station, but there seemed to be a relative order to affairs here.

He turned around in response to the whooshing sound of the automatic doors he had just come through. He saw two detectives escorting a sandy-haired, deranged-looking man wearing filthy jeans, ratty sandals and nothing else—except handcuffs. The guy was so bedraggled, he looked like he'd been fished out of the ocean. Wait...was that seaweed in his hair?

Jake stepped aside and watched as the detectives and their prisoner went through the electronically controlled glass doors off to the side. The prisoner turned around and gave Jake a dark look that Jake couldn't decipher, though he felt a spark of evil coming off the man.

He walked over to the counter that circled a good portion of the lobby. A uniformed cop greeted him with a professional, "Can I help you?"

"I'm Jake Miller. I have an appointment to see Detective Rick Givens."

"Just a minute," replied the cop, picking up an internal phone directory.

Motioning his head toward a clipboard on the counter, the cop said, "Go ahead and sign the log while I call upstairs."

Jake signed the log and then waited while the cop searched the directory for the right extension. He dialed a number, turning away from Jake to speak into the receiver.

He turned back around and said, "He'll come down and get you." He replaced the receiver and didn't look at Jake again.

Jake took that as his cue to move away, so he walked towards the doors he had seen the two detectives and the prisoner go through earlier. Beside the doors was a large plaque, with bronze plates naming the

Metro-Dade police officers who had been killed in the line of duty. He saw a date of 1953 on one of the plates, then various dates throughout the following decades, up to the current year. There weren't more than thirty names in all, and Jake thought that while that might not seem like many to outsiders, it was a powerful number in terms of the value of each of those lives.

He turned away from the plaque, thinking, *There but for the grace of God...*

He saw someone coming towards him on the other side of the doors. Rick? No. The man came through the doors, nodded and kept walking.

Practically on his heels, however, came Detective Givens. Jake knew it was him, of course, but as usual he didn't know how he knew, nor did he give it much thought.

He smiled at the man coming towards him, but the man didn't return it. Uh oh, Jake thought to himself. The man came through the door, and wordlessly extended the professional courtesy of a handshake.

"Good of you to see me, detective," Jake said amiably.

"Like I had a choice. Let's go get some coffee," was the curt reply.

Jake followed him down the corridor, and in an attempt to lighten up the detective's mood, he said, "Hey, this is a nice place. Looks new."

When he got no response, he asked pointedly, "Is it?"

"Just a couple of years old," Rick answered in a flat voice.

Jake made no more attempts at conversation as he followed Rick down the long hall to the cafeteria. He was pleased to find himself in a spacious, clean cafeteria that actually had enticing food smells. The smells made him hungry, but only coffee was offered by Givens, probably in anticipation of a short meeting.

He watched Rick Givens for a moment as he left to get their coffee, then sat down at one of the tables and looked around. He saw a rich blend of ethnic groups, men and women, who seemed to be relaxed and enjoying their coffee break. He knew that they had trained themselves to relax at these times, because they faced an inordinate amount of stress the rest of the time. The place had a good feel to it, and Jake recognized it for what it was: a police department, diversified in race and sex, yet cohesive in a way that only those who had seen that side of life could be.

He saw Rick coming back, and took the opportunity to size him up. It was a compulsive behavior in him, something that he had long ago been trained to do, but which had become, over time, as natural to him as breathing.

Detective Givens had a face which registered somewhere in the early forties, but a powerful body that a man in his early thirties would have been proud of. He strode towards Jake with a confident gait, and Jake correctly surmised that there was a nice guy under that tough exterior.

"Thanks," he said as Givens handed him the cup of coffee.

"Welcome," came the cool reply as the detective sat down.

Jake realized he was in a tougher situation than he had expected. He tried to put himself in Rick's place. Suppose the situation was reversed, and he was the one working a homicide case? Suppose a man who had for a short time been a suspect, then proved to be clean, had asked for information that was rightfully refused? Then the guy uses what had to be considerable clout to get the head of his homicide department to make a phone call to the head of your homicide department. Then your boss tells you to extend every courtesy to the man, as a result of that call. How would he feel about that?

Pretty fucking pissed, he had to admit to himself, which Detective Givens obviously was. Now, he asked himself, how can I turn that around? He decided that a direct, honest approach would be best.

"Detective Givens," he started, "I'm sure you're pretty unhappy about talking to me. Believe it or not, I'm sorry to put you in this position. I know that if I were in your shoes, I'd give a guy like me the most polite 'fuck off' that I could."

Rick hesitated before he said, "I've thought about it."

"I'll bet. Although I'm sure you'd put it in such a way that I would leave here with my tail tucked up my ass and not even know I'd been kicked."

There was a hint of a smile on the detective's face now.

Jake continued, "Then you could honestly tell your boss that you extended every courtesy to that pain-in-the-ass ex-detective from that great cesspool they call New York."

"You're reading my mind," Rick said. Jake could see him relaxing now. Not much, but enough to encourage him to continue.

"Understood. I'd do the same thing in your position. But you know what? It really wouldn't accomplish much."

Rick looked at him with expressionless eyes, saying nothing.

Jake plodded on. "I mean, think about it. We've got all these rules we live by, then some asshole like me comes in, and knowing better, asks you to bend them. But isn't that what cops do every day, anyway? Don't we often have to bend the rules, to get around the screwed up system, just so we can do our job?"

The detective nodded.

"So I bent the rules. That doesn't make me a bad guy, any more than it makes you a bad guy when you do it. It's all within the law. It's just how it's interpreted that makes the difference."

"I know what you're talking about," Rick said. "But what's your point?"

"My point is," Jake said forcefully, "that if there was ever a case where it might be justified to bend the rules, this just might be it. I am—was—a cop. Hell, in my mind, I'll always be a cop. Just because you don't punch a clock everyday doesn't mean you stop being one, I can tell you. I know about protecting information, and because I know that, I'm not about to abuse it.

"Maybe you think I'm just playing cop because I can't do it for real anymore. Maybe I am. But if that had been just any dead body I had found on the beach, I wouldn't be sitting here right now. But man, it was my sister. I know you must know the difference that makes."

Rick had been sizing Jake up while he talked. He liked the guy. He appreciated people who came at him straight on. He had always found he could trust those people. He knew he hadn't wanted to like or trust this guy. Maybe he wasn't being fair. The guy had a legitimate point. This was his sister, and he wouldn't be interfering if it wasn't. But he didn't have the right to interfere. Then again, what he had said about bending the rules was true. It could be done, if it was done cleanly.

"Ah, hell," Jake sighed, interrupting Rick's thoughts. "I don't know what I'm doing here. I know what I want to do—get any information I can about the death of my sister—but I also know a good cop like you isn't going to throw an open homicide file in my face for me to read. I sure wouldn't, if I was in your shoes."

His frankness caught Rick off-guard. He had planned to wait until this guy asked to see the file, then he was going to ream his ass, tell him there was no fucking way he could do that, that any decent detective ought to know that. He had gone over it in his mind several times, just exactly how

he would tell him, and how he would chew up and spit out this ex-
detective from New York... a grade three detective at that, though he
looked young enough to still be out on the streets, patrolling. But the man
had said it for him, neutralizing the effects of the bomb he had planned to
drop.

Again Jake interrupted his thoughts by saying, "I know what it's like
to work a case and have no definitive answers. I know how important it
is to keep every detail confidential. There's always the very real fear that
the least little thing leaked, no matter how innocently, can backfire on
you in a big way. Oh, yeah, I know about that."

Just as Jake hoped he would, Rick became interested. Curiosity was
stamped on his features as he asked, "What happened?" Rick knew he had
taken the bait, but he couldn't help it. He loved swapping stories.

Bingo! Jake thought. He had found a hot button.

Jake took a deep breath and concentrated on looking downright
morose as he spoke.

"There was a double murder up on the East Side. Rich yuppie couple
got it, both popped in the head with a twenty-two. There were no leads,
and I mean none. There was no evidence of forced entry, no burglary, no
murder weapon, no one unusual seen coming or going in the building—
which, by the way, seemed to have decent security, but no cameras. You
had to get past a doorman, who then had to buzz you through a set of
glass doors, to get to the inside elevator. If he wasn't there, you could use
a shunt key to open the glass doors, if you were a resident."

"But that's to get in. What about exiting?" Rick asked.

"Press a button on the other side of the glass doors, they open and
you walk out the front door of the building."

"So I'm going to assume you questioned the doorman on duty?"

"You know it. He didn't see anybody coming or going who shouldn't
have been coming or going. He swore only residents had been in and out
during that time, no visitors. He showed us the log."

"So what then?"

"Then we were told the dead woman's mother was a regular visitor,
but according to the doorman, she wasn't in the building the night of the
killing. She was home alone when we notified her, and she was
convincingly bereft. She said she'd been home all evening and hadn't
talked to her daughter. We gave her our condolences and moved on.

"A couple of months into the investigation, when the case was getting really cold, we found a tenant who had literally run into an older lady coming out of the building that night. He remembered because he had a taxi waiting for him while he ran upstairs to get his passport, and she had slowed him down.

"He couldn't describe her, other than she looked like she was the same age as his grandmother. He remembered she had on a heavy black coat, and she had a big black Chanel handbag with the double Cs on it. He noticed because he picked it up for her."

"Why did it take two months for the tenant to tell you about it?"

"Ah, good question. He traveled a lot with his job. He had been traveling between New York and Singapore, and points in between, during those two months. Plus he also had an office and apartment in California, so he just wasn't around to ask."

"And the doorman hadn't said anything about an older woman being there that night?"

"The doorman. What we found out was that he was a drunk who had a habit of disappearing into the storage closet behind the desk to take a nip. When we asked him if he had seen anyone fitting that description the night of the murder, he thought of the mother right away. But he couldn't be sure it was her, because he didn't see her going or coming. Drunk? Or couldn't remember? Anyway, he said he wouldn't have thought anything about her anyway, since she was on the list of who could come and go, and was often in the building visiting with her daughter. She wouldn't have signed the log.

"We figured the mother must have known about him slipping off to drink, and she waited until he disappeared to leave the building. Still, all we had was a vague description from the guy, and a mother who said she was home all night and seemed suitably bereaved.

"But we ran a check on the mother anyway. Turns out, she did a lot of gambling. All kinds of gambling. Horses—even football games—do you believe that?" he interrupted his story to ask the detective, who didn't disappoint him when he shook his head in amused disbelief.

"But mostly, she went to Atlantic City. Liked to play craps. She lost big, though, and was over two hundred thousand dollars in debt. Things began to add up, and even though we think we've seen it all, we're telling ourselves this sixty-eight year old woman couldn't have killed her own daughter for money, even though she was the contingent beneficiary of a million-dollar life insurance policy. Meaning, if the husband preceded the wife in death, or died at the same time..."

"Then the mother, the contingent beneficiary, got the million bucks," Rick finished Jake's sentence.

"Exactly," Jake smiled, playing up the camaraderie.

"We've always found money to be a pretty strong motive," Rick said.

"Yeah, well, but she was like *your grandmother*. Know what I mean?"

"I've got the picture. Go on."

"So this bereaved mother has no idea we've been checking her out."

Jake took a long swig of coffee, pausing deliberately for effect. He was enjoying himself.

"And?"

"And," Jake went on, "it just so happened that there's this new guy in homicide. Shiny shoes, shiny face—you know the type?"

The detective nodded quickly, growing a little impatient now. He wanted to hear this.

"He saw himself as a real hot shot. College degree, advanced pathology courses, and so on. Well, one day he just happened to see the file on my desk, and he gets curious. So this asshole just picks it up. I'm not even there..."

"You're shitting me!" the detective exclaimed.

"I am not. Now you know as well as I do that you just don't do crap like that."

The detective nodded his emphatic agreement.

"Well, it turns out this guy's mother knew the female victim's mother. They went to the same church. He had heard his mother talk about her. But for all his advanced education," Jake said scornfully, "he still hadn't learned that you don't discuss a homicide case with anybody outside the department, including family members."

Jake could see that Rick was now leaning forward in his chair in anticipation of the outcome of the story. He started to go on, but then stopped. He had an inspiration.

"Tell me what *you* think happened," he said to the detective.

Jake could see that Rick was mildly surprised, but delighted to be asked the question.

"Ummm, let's see," Rick pondered, obviously thinking it through thoroughly.

"Well, I'd bet that your new boy told his mother, who told her friend the gambler that the police were investigating her."

"Right," Jake said encouragingly. "But then what do you think happened?"

Jake knew it was a tough question, because there were so many turns the event could have taken. He was curious, though, to learn Rick's thought pattern. It would help him understand how to get the most cooperation out of him.

He watched the detective furrow his brow in concentration. A couple of minutes passed in silence as Rick weighed the possibilities.

Finally, Rick looked straight into Jake's eyes and said, "The old lady disappeared. You never found the murder weapon, the case was never solved."

Jake whistled softly, honestly impressed. "You're *good*," he said sincerely.

Rick was flattered. Even the best detectives rarely heard those words. "Thanks," he said with an unaffected modesty. "I suppose you looked high and low for the mother?"

"Yeah, but she had over a half million dollars left after paying off her debts, and that made disappearing easy for her. We hadn't identified her as a suspect, and the life insurance proceeds were paid to her in the meantime."

"So an insurance company will pay out on an unsolved homicide?" Rick asked.

"Once an insurance company is presented with a proof of loss for a death and has an identifiable dead body, they have to pay—unless the beneficiary is charged and convicted of the murder. But she wasn't even a suspect at the time, so yeah, she got paid out."

"Unreal," Rick said, shaking his head.

"Isn't it? But that's a perfect example of how information can be misused," Jake finished.

"That's for sure. I guess the new boy got busted back down to the streets, huh?"

"You got it. Leaving us with an unsolved homicide, because we hadn't been able to pursue it," Jake added. "I bet you guys have plenty of those, too, huh?"

"You're not kidding. Thousands of them, literally." He smiled at Jake, his hostility fading fast.

Suddenly, in one of those cool flashes of the meeting of minds, they exclaimed at the same time, "And they say you can't get away with murder!" The two men burst into laughter at the old, but still true, adage.

"Man," Rick said, finishing his coffee as the laughter died down, "you've got to be crazy to do what we do."

Jake heard the "we" and took heart. He was being accepted. It wouldn't give him carte blanche, but it was a fine start.

"Why else would we do it?" he replied, and the two men laughed again.

When they stopped, the two men looked at each other, each one assessing the other with new eyes.

"Look," Jake was the first to speak after the pause. "I can go to the medical examiner's office and pull the file. It's public record. I can read it from end to end, and I can find out how my sister was killed, but that's all it's going to tell me. You and I both know that there are things in our own files that are kept out of the medical examiner's report."

"Yeah," Rick agreed. "But you won't get to the file right now. Not until we say we're finished with the investigation."

"Aw, I can have somebody make a caaaall," Jake teased, drawing out the last word to emphasize the joke he was making on himself. His joke was taken in the right vein.

"Yeah, I guess you could make a caaaall, you jerk," Rick mocked in return.

Jake smiled at Rick and said, "But that's not going to help me, anyway. What we know—and the public doesn't—is that we always hold something back, even from the medical examiner; some important little detail or other that we'll use to nail the killer."

Rick nodded. "Something that only a few of us and the killer would know."

"A universal homicide investigation tactic," Jake acknowledged.

Rick nodded and looked hard at Jake, wanting to look into the man, to get the full measure of him. All of his training told him he should tell the guy to fuck off, as he had originally planned. But his instincts—and they were good instincts, he knew—told him that Jake was a straight-up guy who could be trusted. He also knew that Jake really expected him to bend the rules, though he would never ask him to break them.

Jake was, in turn, watching Rick, practically reading his thoughts, but not with the help of his sixth sense. It was more from knowing what he would be thinking if he was sitting in Rick's seat. He knew that the detective saw him as nothing more than an ex-detective, and as someone who he really owed no professional courtesy whatsoever, other than to respect his superior's orders to meet with him.

He also knew that Rick was tempted to tell him, nicely, to fuck off anyway. That a cop's files were damned-near sacred, not to be shared with any outsider, for sure. But he also was pretty sure he'd won the man's confidence, and that they were a kindred pair, related by a profession that only those who shared it could even start to comprehend.

Rick had made a decision, and was on the verge of telling Jake what it was, when Detective Robbins found him.

"Hey, Rick, hurry up, come on...you're going to love this!"

"What's up, Robbins?" Rick asked as he stood up. Robbins was real excited about something, and was on the verge of imparting what was obviously some dynamite news, when he spotted Jake. He stopped in his tracks.

"What are you doing here?" he challenged Jake.

Before Jake could answer, Rick said, "He's with me. What's going on?"

Mindful of not divulging too much in front of Jake, Robbins responded, "That suspect we brought in earlier is talking. And I mean *talking.* You'll wanna get up there."

Rick gave Jake a pointed look and said, "I gotta go. I'll call you later at your hotel."

Robbins turned around and gave Jake a look filled with disdain and distrust, before the cafeteria door closed behind him.

"Give me a run-down, John," Rick said to Detective Robbins as he fast-paced it to the elevators.

"The suspect we brought in earlier? We were getting him processed, going through the routine, hadn't even asked him any questions. Next thing you know, the guy starts talking. He *confessed* to the flower murders."

"What the fuck?"

"Exactly. We ID'd him. Name's Virgil Carpenter. He's been Mirandized and fingerprinted, and he's being run through the system now. But he's babbling about giving him a piece of paper to sign saying he 'killed the whores'," Robbins said.

"Damn, I wish I had been there."

"Well, you're here now. Let's see what else he has to say."

"Man, I hope this guy hasn't gone cold by now."

"I don't think so."

"Why do you say that?"

"He's rambling, like he's speeding or high on crack or something."

"Okay, okay. Which room is he in?"

"Number two."

"Who's with him?"

"Steve and Ralph."

"Good. Let's do this."

32

RICK WALKED OUT of the interrogation room, exhausted by the process, but elated by the outcome: a signed confession to all four murders. The white roses, the murder weapon of choice—a garrote, in all cases fishing line—and even the color of skin and hair of the prostitutes, had come pouring out of Virgil during the interrogation. It was almost like somebody shot him up with sodium pentothal—truth serum.

That last description, though, where Kristin Long was concerned, wasn't as strong. The victim had seemed puzzled about a fourth victim. And he had no sensible explanation of why he was up on Collins and 91st other than "some dangerous drug dude kidnapped me." *Riiight.* No memory of how he got blood on his shirt and in his hair. They were typing the blood against Kristin Long's, however, and Rick was one-hundred percent positive the blood types would match.

Virgil's confusion seemed to stem from "long dark hair." The third victim and Kristin Long both had long dark hair. Virgil had said the last one was better looking than the others. Rick looked in the file at the picture of the third prostitute. Not exactly a beauty, but not as ugly as the first two. But Kristin Long was beautiful. Virgil had been too doped-up and confused to make a distinction, Rick decided.

He also decided that if it wasn't for Jake Miller, he wouldn't even be questioning whether or not the information jelled where Kristin Long was concerned. He wouldn't care, since the confession held all the information the state would need to put Virgil away.

Rick reviewed the facts again. That morning, the Bal Harbour police had gotten a six a.m. call from one Millie Hawkins, who lived in an oceanfront condo on Collins and 94th. She was quite put out, she told them, to find a "drug addict" on the beach when she went out for her early morning walk. She didn't live in Bal Harbour, she had fussed, and pay the kind of taxes she paid, to find that kind of trash on "my beach."

Bal Harbour police were there in short order, and they found Virgil still passed out on the beach. He looked like he'd been tossed around by the waves and then unceremoniously dumped in the sand. Just another bum to be thrown into a cell, they thought, until one of the cops spotted what looked like blood on Virgil's shirt. Upon closer inspection, they saw there was also blood in his hair.

It wasn't a big leap to think he might be connected to Monday night's murder, and Metro-Dade had been called in. Virgil matched the ID the cops had gotten just two days before when they'd finally found the street vendor who had sold a "homeless drug addict" a single white rose on two different occasions. They'd been looking hard for him down on Biscayne.

And that was the other thing. The white rose that was found with Kristin Long's body. That was the one thing that wouldn't be known by anybody other than a very few cops and the killer. And Virgil had made a stink about "my slutty mom's thing for white roses" while admitting to leaving them with the bodies of the dead prostitutes. That was no damn coincidence. That was righteous.

Rick was fully convinced he had the right guy for all four murders. Damn fine detective work all the way around.

Jake was lying on the bed in his hotel room, yet again, waiting. He was unable to get involved in the book that was lying across his stomach. He had been waiting for almost six hours for Rick to call, but he knew it could be tomorrow or even next week before he did. Rick was under no obligation to call him, Jake admitted to himself, but he was still hopeful.

Twenty minutes later, the phone rang. "Rick?" Jake asked, picking it up on the first ring.

"How'd you know it was me?" Rick asked.

Jake smiled to himself. "You're the only person in town I know."

Rick laughed. "You need to get out a little more."

"Tell me about it," Jake replied good-naturedly.

"I thought I'd let you know, we've got a signed confession from the suspect. He killed your sister."

Jake felt all the air go out of his lungs. He couldn't breathe. *A signed confession?*

"You there?" Rick asked.

"Yeah, I'm here. Damn, that was fast. It's tight?"

"Air tight."

"I see. Well, Detective Givens, you must feel pretty good."

"I do."

"So you connected him to the flowers?"

"What do you know about the flowers?"

"I don't. The cops who were at the Sheraton questioned it. There was a white rose with Kristin's body. I saw it. Was there a white rose with the others?"

It would all be in the papers tomorrow anyway, so Rick had no problem with confirming the rose detail. "Yep, all four of them."

"And he confessed to all four murders, including Kristin's?"

Despite the niggling misgivings Rick had previously had where Kristin was concerned, he was confident he had the right guy for all four murders. "Yes, he confessed to all four murders."

Jake whistled into the phone then said, "You *did* have a good day."

"You could say that. Anyway, I just wanted to let you know so you can go back home and forget about this. He'll be put away for life—maybe even get the death penalty. So you don't need to be concerned with it anymore." It was more a directive than a suggestion.

"Just let me ask you one more thing," Jake said.

He heard the exasperation in Rick's voice when he said, "What?"

"Was your killer wearing filthy jeans, sandals? Had greasy blonde hair decorated with seaweed?"

There was a pause before Rick asked, "How did you know that?"

"I was in the lobby when they brought him in, right before you came down."

"Yeah, they brought him in through the front. That was him," Rick confirmed.

Jake took a moment to process that encounter. Though he had met the killer's eyes, he hadn't gotten any kind of a "hit" from him, just an impersonal confirmation of crazy, and bad news. Shouldn't he have gotten something if this was the guy that killed Kristin? Maybe that was stretching it, despite his intuitive talents.

"Hey, Rick, can I buy you dinner tonight?" Jake asked, surprising even himself with the invitation.

No way, Rick thought. He wasn't going to sit around with some stranger for hours, someone who would use the entire time to pump him for details about the interview with Virgil.

"No, thanks," Rick said simply, offering no excuse.

"Ah, come on. I've already told you you're the only person in town I know." After a slight pause he added, "I promise not to discuss the case."

Rick felt sorry for Jake. The guy obviously didn't know anybody, he had just lost his sister, and he was facing the prospect of what Rick knew would be a long evening of thinking about the murder. Still...

"You name the place," Jake urged. "The best in town, I'm buying." Jake was unaware of the loneliness that his voice conveyed.

But Rick heard it. He knew about those feelings. Ever since his divorce, he had been going home every night to his dreary, lonely apartment. He was supposed to have the boys tonight, but they both had a bug and their mom was keeping them with her. What else do I have to do, he thought. A good meal, paid for, in a good restaurant. Why not?

"All right, if you promise not to discuss the case."

Jake couldn't account for the happiness he felt at the prospect of not eating another meal alone. If that meant he couldn't discuss the case, he wouldn't.

"You got it," Jake readily agreed.

"Okay, you said I could pick the place, but I don't go to a lot of fancy restaurants. I'll have to let you pick." He thought for a second then said, "You sure you can afford it?" Rick knew disability pensions weren't that generous.

"I can afford it," Jake said simply. "I'm going to check with the concierge here at the hotel for a good restaurant. Can I call you back in ten minutes?"

"I'll be here."

33

THE SOMMELIER REFILLED Jake's wine glass with the 1976 Chateau Margaux. It was an excellent wine, but it looked like he was going to have to finish the bottle alone. Rick was sticking to beer. Both men were enjoying the fine food and swanky atmosphere of The Forge.

"So tell me, what do you do in your spare time?" Jake asked, hoping to get to know Rick better.

"Not much. But I do travel around to different parts of the country, giving seminars to cops from smaller cities who don't see the same kinds of action we do."

"I bet they're flabbergasted at some of the things you tell them, aren't they?" Jake asked.

"You're not kidding. I've even had some come down and spend a few days with us. Boy, was that an eye-opener for them."

"Tell me," Jake said enthusiastically.

"Well, I had this one guy, a lieutenant, in one of the classes I taught, and we always give 'em an invitation to come down and spend a week if they want to. I mean, book learning is one thing, but to live it makes all the difference in the world."

Jake nodded agreeably, and Rick went on.

"So this lieutenant said, 'Well, we don't get that many homicides, how about if I send down one of my guys.' I said 'fine,' so the guy came down from Brown County, Indiana. Got in around four o'clock. He said, 'Well, you get off at five, where are we gonna have dinner?'

"I said, 'No dinner. You came to see some murders. We got one body floating in the Everglades, and we got a migrant camp homicide. Which one do you want to go to first?'"

Jake laughed out loud and said, "I bet he almost crapped his pants."

"Almost," Rick laughed.

"So go on," Jake urged.

"Well, we went to both of them, and he ended up getting back in his hotel about eleven that night. The next day I had him down on Eighteenth Avenue—Central District—and we got rocked and bottled by the crowd. The following Wednesday I had him riding with another fellow and he got involved with our Swat Team in a big shoot-out at a Ranch House Restaurant. There were about, oh, a hundred and fifty rounds fired."

Rick took a swig of his beer and continued. "Then on Thursday, he went down to Homestead. They had a fire death, about five people dead in the fire. He got his picture in the newspaper with that one. Then on Friday I had him involved in a surveillance, and he ended up drawing down on the guy and almost had to shoot him. He had never had his gun out of his holster, then he gets down here and in five days he's had to draw down on two people."

Rick had told the story in one long, uninterrupted sequence, ignoring the fact that Jake was laughing so hard he had slid down in his chair and was gasping for air. He joined Jake in his laughter, and the two men drew the attention of nearly every patron in their section of the restaurant, as well as the miffed maitre d'.

"That's a great story," Jake finally managed, drying the corners of his eyes as he straightened up and attempted to regain his composure. "It's one for the books."

Rick had enjoyed telling the story again, and he appreciated Jake's laughter. He liked Jake. Jake was an okay guy. He might be from New York, but he wasn't a stuck-up asshole, as Rick had wrongly assumed all New York cops would be.

"Yeah, if I ever write a book, I'll be sure to put that one in there," Rick said.

The maitre d' had made his way to their table to ask if everything was okay. Jake and Rick looked at each other and burst out laughing again. The maitre d' gave them a scornful look and walked away.

"I'm going to have to give him an extra big tip," Jake said after their laughter had finally subsided.

Taking advantage of the opening he had just been given, Rick asked Jake the question he had wanted to ask all night. "You're on disability, right?" he started.

"Right," Jake answered, knowing what the second part of the question was going to be.

"So how can you afford this?" Rick asked, hoping Jake wouldn't take offense.

"I inherited from my parents. They died seven years ago."

"Hey, I'm sorry."

"No problem. I'd wonder the same thing if I were you."

Rick nodded and said, "You have any other brothers or sisters?"

"No."

"And no wife?"

"Never been married. You?"

"Divorced."

"Sorry."

"It's okay. I'm getting used to it."

"How long were you married?"

"Six years."

"Any kids?"

"Yeah, two boys. Good kids. She's doing a good job. I get them one night a week, and every other weekend. I miss them like crazy in between."

"That's tough. I've got some friends in the same position. It's not easy to keep a marriage going when you're a cop. Or so I've been told."

Rick changed the subject. "Hey, Jake, I want to tell you that I appreciate you living up to your end of the bargain, and not asking questions."

"I'm a man of my word," Jake said, holding his hand up in a boy scout-like oath position. "But I do wonder about just one thing."

"Ohhh no," Rick said, making it clear he wasn't going to talk about it.

"No, this isn't a big thing," Jake assured him. "I just wanted to know how you know for sure he's the one who killed Kristin."

Rick had been expecting this exact question. And it *was* a "big thing," despite what Jake thought. But he had decided, if pressed, he could give Jake a few specifics that would answer his questions.

"Okay, here are the facts, some you know. Each victim was found with a single white rose. At first, we thought it might be significant that it was a single rose, not a dozen like you'd think people would buy. But it turns out florists sell a lot of single roses, to a lot of different kinds of people, so it wasn't as simple as we thought it was going to be. Plus, a lot of people use cash, and there's a lot of employee turnover in those shops, so nothing was clicking. The ones that used credit cards or checks, we looked into them, but that was a waste of time.

"We expanded our area, and two days ago our guys found a street vendor who'd set up shop on Northeast Second who had sold two white roses to the same "homeless drug addict" as he put it, on two different occasions. He gave us a good description.

"So this morning, Bal Harbour police were called about a bum passed out on the beach in front of million-dollar condos. Two cops showed up, and they just thought he was a bum who somehow lost his way and ended up in Bal Harbour. They were going to take him in, but then one of them spotted some blood on him. Being smart cops, they called us, and our guys got there and saw that Virgil fit the description we'd gotten from the vendor.

"He started confessing before we'd even finished the booking process. So that's it."

Jake considered all that Rick had said. "Sounds like good police work. Again, congratulations."

"Thanks, I'm feeling pretty damn good about it."

"Just one more thing that puzzles me," Jake said, gauging Rick's level of patience.

Rick rolled his eyes. "You can ask, can't say I'll answer."

"You didn't find this guy on the beach until this morning. Where was he in between Monday night and this morning? Didn't your guys search the beach Monday night? And yesterday?"

"Yeah, sure. Problem was, there were no footprints—other than yours and the manager's—around the body, or leading away from it. You know the sand was all torn up around her body, from the struggle."

Rick saw Jake wince and said, "Sorry."

"Thanks, but no need to be sorry. Go on."

"I will say that's an odd part about this. No footprints in the sand going away from the scene, in either direction. Again, other than yours from your walk up and down the beach. Our guys looked for other footprints that night, went out about a half a mile in each direction with high-powered flashlights, but since there weren't any other than yours, they didn't go any further."

"So what do you make of the fact that it was almost thirty-six hours later that Virgil was found on the beach up there?"

"Gotta think drug binge, sleeping it off under a bridge somewhere, got confused, wandered around, wandered into the ocean. But look, we found him less than a half mile from where Kristin was killed. He was out of his normal hunting territory, true, but he was there."

"Sounds reasonable, but don't you wonder why Virgil would trek so far to kill again? And why on the beach, versus on the streets? Plus, I'd sure give a helluva lot to know why Kristin was even there on the beach, late at night, all alone."

"Lots of questions for a guy who wasn't going to talk about the case," Rick scoffed.

"Hey, would you really expect any less, considering what you've just told me? One question leads to another. I'm a detective to my bones."

Rick nodded and said, "Yeah, I get that. All right, look. Virgil wouldn't or couldn't tell us why he was up in Bal Harbour. All he remembered was getting in an old black car with a friend, a "dangerous drug dealer," as he put it, but he couldn't tell us that supposed friend's name, no matter how hard we pushed."

"Couldn't or wouldn't?" Jakes asked.

"The way he was dishing out details, he would have given us the name if he could have. No, he had no recall on that detail, but it answered our question about how he got up to the Bal Harbour area. But with all the evidence we had, it really didn't matter. And as far as I'm concerned, the white rose sealed it. No one, and I mean no one, outside of a select few of us knew that the three previous victims were found with a white rose.

"And there's one last thing I'll share with you, even though I shouldn't. The blood type found on his shirt and hair turned out to be the same as your sister's, AB."

"Well now, that's a damn compelling piece of evidence," Jake said.

Rick nodded his empathic agreement. "And why was your sister there? We'll probably never know the answer to that. I will tell you we found out that she was staying at the Fontainebleau Hotel back in early September. Maybe she just liked to stay in Miami luxury hotels that are on the beach."

"How'd you find that out?"

"The possessions we took from her room at the Sheridan. She had one of those pocket calendars in her purse. We called and confirmed she was

254

a guest there back in September, and were going to follow up, but then Virgil confessed."

He gave Jake a hard look and said, "And that's *it*."

Though he had more questions, like had they ever found the security guard, Jake just nodded his head and said, "Good enough. Subject closed. Thanks, Rick. I mean it."

Rick nodded and deliberately changed the subject. "So, when are you going back to New York?"

"Probably tomorrow."

"Well, it's been good meeting you."

"You, too. And if you're ever up in New York, you'd better look me up."

"Will do."

When they left the restaurant, Jake gave the maitre d' a twenty and an apology. He accepted both graciously.

When the valet drove up in Rick's car, Rick said, "Well, so long, Jake. Thanks for the good meal and good company."

"I enjoyed it," Jake replied, extending his hand. "Thanks for joining me."

He watched Rick drive off, then spotted his rental car coming around the corner. He took a deep breath, filling his lungs with the fresh salt air of Miami. He liked this city. It was clean. It was vibrant. In no way did it have the feeling of the lurking despair he sometimes experienced in New York. Despite what the media reported, Miami was the kind of city that, in most parts, one could walk around with no problem.

He had seen many people doing just that. People living life year around down here in the fresh air and warm sun, instead of fighting the pollution and cold of northern cities.

As he tipped the valet and got into the car, he decided he would come back to this special city, and soon.

34

CAROLINE HEADED STRAIGHT to Michael's office when she returned from her doctor's visit. She couldn't wait to tell him that she was ovulating, and that they needed to do something about it as soon as possible.

"Is he with anybody?" she asked Lynn, breathless from her hurried pace.

"No, he's alone," Lynn said, smiling at the governor's beautiful wife.

Caroline gave a short rap and went in. "Michael," she said, closing the door behind her, "I'm ovulating."

Michael laughed, caught by surprise at the unusual greeting, and said teasingly, "So what do you want me to do about it?"

She gave him a playful punch in the shoulder and said, "I want you to perform your husbandly duties."

"Now?" he asked.

"That would be great, if you can spare the time. I mean, we could try now, and we could try again tonight. Any objections?"

"None."

"Good. Let's go," she said, taking his hand to lead him out of his office.

"I just know we made a baby then," she said as she lay cradled in his arms.

"I hope so, sweetheart."

"But we'll try again later anyway, okay?" she asked.

"Fine with me," he laughed, swatting her gently on her behind and moving to get up.

"I've been meditating three times a day to relax, Michael. I've been 'programming' to make this happen. I feel as if my body is a fertile field. I just know it is!"

He looked at her mockingly, raising his eyebrows, and said, "A fertile field?"

"Don't make fun of me," she laughed, embarrassed. She pulled the sheet up over her head playfully, pretending to hide her embarrassment.

"Okay," he laughed, pulling the sheet off her face, "I believe you. I hope you're right."

"I am right," she said with conviction, wanting him to be as convinced as she.

"Good," he said, sounding convinced.

Satisfied, she rolled over on her side and watched him dress. "You're not going to shower?"

"No. No time. I'll be all right. I'm not seeing anybody else today, I just have some phone calls I have to make."

"Michael, you should have told me you were busy."

"And miss any opportunity to make a baby with you? No way."

She smiled at him and rolled over on her back. The smile stayed on her face as he came around to kiss her. She kissed him passionately and said, "I'm so happy."

"I am, too, Caroline. Want to have dinner out in the gazebo tonight? This weather is nice enough. I'm liking this warm spell."

"Let's do."

"Okay. I'll be back up around six. We'll have an early dinner—say, seven—and we'll get an early start on our evening."

"I'm so lucky to have such a virile husband," she purred, anticipating the evening of lovemaking which was to come.

"And I'm lucky to have such an enticing wife," he responded as he opened the door to leave. "See you soon."

Caroline stayed in bed, reflecting on Michael's behavior over the last couple of weeks. He seemed so edgy, so out of sorts, so...burdened. She wondered again what it could be. She was certain now that his strained behavior had nothing to do with their trying to have a baby. That had been settled. It was something else. What hadn't he told her?

Suddenly, it occurred to her that it must be because Manny was leaving. Of course. Why hadn't she realized this before?

She had been so sorry for Michael when he had told her. She had even sought Manny out herself, hoping to talk him into changing his mind. But he had been firm in his resolution to leave, telling her that Maria and the kids wanted to go back to New York, and so did he. Odd, Maria had never said anything about it before. Well, who knew what people thought?

Anyway, once Hanes started working for him, he would be fine. She had really done a job on her father, talking him into loaning Hanes to Michael. But her father rarely left the house anymore, and when he had asked a very bored Hanes if that was what he wanted to do, Hanes had jumped at it.

She hoped that was all it was. She searched her mind for other reasons. Ever since the special session, when things had gone so badly, he had been a different man. And the polls that had come out last week were discouraging. His popularity had dropped significantly. A vague uneasiness stirred in Caroline, but she couldn't put her finger on the source.

She decided that she would give him as much support as she could until he wanted to talk. If he ever did.

Michael did have a lot on his mind. Funny, he thought, attempting to put things into perspective—the defeat at the special session just didn't seem so important compared to the whole affair with Kristin.

Although the papers had reported that her killer had been apprehended and had confessed to her murder and three others, Michael found that instead of being relieved, he had become more and more consumed by guilt. He had no one to talk to about it, and at times he had become so overwhelmed, so anxious, that he had actually considered telling Caroline everything, just to unburden himself.

But reason and survival had won out each time, so he remained silent, except in responding to his conscience, which wouldn't quit condemning him. He argued with it, rationalized with it, agreed with it, and admonished it, on an alternating basis. But he couldn't ignore it.

His work had suffered as his energy was siphoned off by the guilt. Any energy he had left, any vigor he could muster after each round with his conscience, went into his demanding job and into his relationship with his wife. He fought hard to keep their marriage on an even keel, knowing if that suffered, he would have nothing left to hold on to.

His once close relationship with his best friend Manny had totally dissipated. Michael suffered acute emotional pain at that particular loss; but if he lost Caroline, he would be a defeated man. He wouldn't let that happen. Especially now, when so much was riding on their love, when they had a real chance of having a baby.

Kristin's death had been big news in Tallahassee, and Michael had been surprised at the swell of friends who had gone to the funeral. He had not attended himself, of course, but Les had; and he told Michael that it was one of the largest funerals he had attended in Tallahassee.

Michael had not known how significant she had been to others. In fact, he had really known very little about her. Apparently, she had been a real friend and a generous benefactor to a number of people and organizations. A fine woman, someone who would truly be missed.

But not by him.

Jake walked into the Tallahassee courthouse and asked a security guard where he could find the offices of the Clerk of the Circuit Court. The guard directed him to the third floor, pointing down the hall to an ancient elevator.

He was pretty sure Kristin's will would have been filed by now, given that it was more than ten days since her death. He wanted to see it. Perhaps it would give him some sort of clue about who really killed his sister.

After flying back to New York, he had spent a week with nothing but thoughts of Kristin's death to keep him company. Despite the confession, the rose, the blood, Jake felt that her real killer was still out there. If he was wrong, so be it. But he had to pursue it, if for no other reason than to satisfy his own doubts. It was also in his blood. He had to follow his instincts.

He realized that he was relying solely upon those instincts, but more than that, on his faith in those instincts. He had never been wrong before when his instincts were this strong. Sometimes, his conscience just wouldn't accept logic or reason or evidence.

He had shared every detail of the ill-fated trip to Miami with his former partner. Vic had listened and then suggested the most obvious thing in the world. "Okay, despite overwhelming evidence, you think somebody else is responsible for Kristin's death. So start by looking at motive—she was loaded, and she had to leave that money to somebody. Who would benefit financially by her death?"

Jake was ashamed he hadn't thought of the obvious himself. But instead of beating himself up over it, he hopped a plane to Tallahassee.

He walked up to the glass-enclosed area where a posted sign read "Clerk's Office — Public Records." A young woman smiled at him and said, "Can I help you?"

"Yes, please," he answered with a smile. "I'd like to see Kristin Marks Long's will. It should have been filed within the last few days."

"Kristin Marks Long?" the girl repeated, writing the name on a sheet of white note paper.

"Right."

"Just a minute," she said, "I'll see if we have it."

She handed the retrieved copy of the will to him with a pleasant smile. Jake returned her smile and thanked her as he sat down to read the will. As he read it, he gained a great deal of insight into his sister. What a generous, caring person she was. She had left most of her estate to the American Cancer Society. But it looked like she owned four corporations, and that she had made provisions upon her death for the "key employees" of each of those corporations to acquire them. If he was reading this right, then any one of those key employees was suspect. Jake couldn't be sure, though. He had no legal training. The will referred to "that certain Stock Redemption Agreement executed by me on March 11, 1987." The details didn't appear in the will.

So Jake would have to ferret out the details. No problem. He looked forward to digging in. And what better place to start than Miami, where one of the four corporations was operating?

After a fact-finding phone call to Kristin's attorney here in Tallahassee, anyway.

"Mr. Harrington," the attorney's secretary said, "there's a Mr. Jake Miller calling for you. He won't tell me what he wants, but—get this—he says he's Kristin Long's brother."

"*What?*" Allen Harrington exclaimed. "Is this a joke?"

"He doesn't sound like a joker. But what do I know?" the secretary laughed.

"Take a number, tell him I'll call him back."

"Sure you will."

"Just get a number, Anne."

Thirty seconds later, she buzzed him again. "He won't leave a number. He says he wants to talk to you, and if he has to come here to do it, he will."

"Oh, God," Allen groaned. "All right, I'll take it." Obviously, he was going to have to be the one to get rid of this prankster.

"Allen Harrington," he said tersely into the phone.

"Mr. Harrington," the caller said, "My name is Jake Miller, and I want to state up front that I am Kristin Long's brother, but that I have absolutely no interest in her estate, other than an interest in understanding certain provisions in her will."

"Kristin didn't have a brother," the attorney said emphatically.

"Yes, she did, but she didn't know it," Jake corrected him. "If you'd like verification, you can call Detective Rick Givens at Metro-Dade Police Department in Miami. I'll give you his number."

That got Allen Harrington's attention. A crazy caller wouldn't be giving out the name and number of a detective for the purpose of verifying his relationship to Kristin. No, that would be the act of a very sure man, one who was apparently telling the truth.

"You've seen Kristin's will, then?" Allen asked.

"Yes. And I have a few questions that I hoped you'd answer."

"What are you really looking for here, Mr. Miller?" the attorney demanded.

"Just a few answers, that's all," Jake said, trying to keep the contempt for the attorney out of his voice.

"The will is indisputable," the attorney said, trying to intimidate Jake.

"I'm not looking to dispute it," Jake reassured him.

"Well, what are you looking for then?"

"Just a few answers about her corporations," he said in a controlled, measured voice.

"What do you want to know?" the attorney asked warily.

"I'd like to know about the Stock Redemption Agreement. Can you give me some details on that?"

"Absolutely not," the attorney answered in a clipped voice.

"Why not?" Jake asked.

"Because that Agreement, unlike her will, is not public information. It's protected by the client-attorney relationship."

Inwardly, Jake moaned. He wasn't going to get a damn thing from this guy. True to form, however, he tried again.

"Can you just tell me if any one of those corporations is more valuable than the others?"

"No."

Damn. Even that would have helped. Who had the most to gain, was what he wanted to know. That would have given him a start.

"I see." It was on the tip of Jake's tongue to thank the attorney, but for what? But he didn't have to deliberate about it any further, because the attorney said, "Fine. Goodbye, Mr. Miller," and hung up before Jake could reply.

35

JAKE HURRIED INTO the building where Pro-Long Plastics, Incorporated, was housed. He was ten minutes late for the appointment he had set with the CEO of the corporation, Dale Walsh. Although directions weren't normally a problem for him, the warehouse district in Miami Lakes had really been confusing.

"Sorry I'm late," he offered the apology along with his hand to Dale Walsh, upon being escorted into his office by a secretary.

Dale took his hand and decided that any doubts he might have had about the man being Kristin's brother were dashed. The man was practically her twin, right down to the silver shock of hair and the silver eyes. His heart sank.

"No problem. Have a seat," he said, motioning to the chair beside which Jake stood. He came from behind his desk to sit in the chair next to Jake's, turning it so that he could face him. Jake turned his chair inward as well.

"I had no idea Kristin had a brother," Dale said.

"Neither did she," Jake answered.

"Oh?" Dale asked, obviously surprised.

"No. I learned about her only a few months ago. We were twins, separated by adoptions. I came down to Florida to find her, to let her know. I never got a chance."

"That's a sad story, Mr. Miller, I'm sorry for you."

"Thank you." Jake was sizing up the man, listening carefully to the intonations in his voice and watching his face. He could come up with only one feeling: he was talking to a decent guy.

"And what a shock that had to be for you. Of course, it was a terrible shock to all of us."

"I'll bet," Jake replied in a noncommittal voice.

"Yes. Kristin was a wonderful woman. She always took good care of her employees, just as her late husband did. But you must know that, because you told me on the phone that you had read the will, and that's how you found me. You must be curious about the stock purchase?"

"I am," Jake said, appreciative of the man's frankness, especially in view of the fact that he probably thought Jake was going to dispute the transaction somehow. He decided to let him know right up front that wasn't his intention. But he would not let Dale Walsh know that he was, to Jake, a suspect in the murder of his sister, since he stood to gain by her death.

"Dale...may I call you Dale?" he asked, feeling comfortable with the man.

"Please do," Dale answered, smiling.

"Dale, I want you to know that I have no intention of disputing any part of Kristin's will. I'm a wealthy man in my own right, and I have no interest in any part of her estate."

The play of emotions on Dale's face was genuine. He was greatly relieved, and he didn't try to hide it. Jake knew then that the man was an open book, there for the reading just by gazing upon his face.

"Frankly, I'm very glad to hear that," he said, leaning forward and lightly tapping Jake on the knee with the pen he'd been fidgeting with.

"I thought you would be." Jake smiled at him, liking him even as he suspected him. "So, can you tell me about the stock purchase?"

Dale wondered why he would want to know about it if he had no interest in the stock himself. He didn't ask Jake that, though. If he wanted to know, and it had nothing to do with his wanting to screw up the deal, then he would tell him everything. After all, this was Kristin's brother.

Before Dale could start, however, Jake said, "I'm sure you wonder why I want to know?"

Dale answered with a shrug and said, "If you want to tell me."

"I know nothing about my sister. I never got the opportunity to find out anything about her while she was alive. I'm simply curious to know how she thought, what kind of business woman she was, that sort of thing," he finished with a shrug of his own.

"I understand," Dale said. At least he would pretend he did. "Let me tell you this about her. She was a generous, kind, considerate woman. She was beautiful, inside and out." He bowed his head for a moment, and when he looked back up at Jake, it was with moist eyes. "I'll miss her. To tell you the truth," he said, blushing slightly, "I had a little bit of a crush on her—but don't tell my wife that."

"No, I won't," Jake laughed.

"She was just that kind of woman," Dale explained. "A real charmer. And she didn't even have to try to be."

Jake was caught in the drift of the emotion. In a soft voice he said, "Thank you for telling me that about her."

Dale nodded, then gathered himself and said, "But about the stock purchase. After Ted died, leaving her in control, she came to me and the other chief executive officers and asked for suggestions about how she could ensure our position in the company if anything happened to her.

"It was a little shocking, I'll tell you. She was so young, but then so was Ted when the cancer got him..." his voice trailed off momentarily.

"Anyway," he resumed, clearing his throat, "we came up with a plan. It's called a bootstrap purchase. Her accountant and lawyer put it together."

Jake nodded, and Dale continued. "An agreement was drawn up. In effect, it said that upon her death, her estate would sell ten percent of the stock of each company to its CEO for cash, or cash and a note. Kristin was the one-hundred-percent stockholder of all four companies at the time of her death," he added, looking closely at Jake to make sure he was following him.

"I'm with you so far, I think, but let me ask you. These were four separate companies, not just branches of one corporation?" He at least knew enough to ask that question.

"Right, four different markets, four different types of products. No one CEO could cover everything, and Pro-Long wanted the employees of each company to feel it was their business, not just part of a big, impersonal holding company."

Jake seemed to be following, so Dale continued. "Let's focus just on my company to make it simple. I have the right to buy ten percent of the stock. That leaves the estate with the other ninety percent, but needing liquidity to pay estate taxes. So there's another party here—the companies, which are a part of Kristin's estate." He paused and asked, "Are you following this?"

"I think so. Go on."

"Okay. So, using just my company again for simplicity's sake, my company will buy the estate's ninety percent of its stock, so that the only stock left outstanding would be the ten percent I am buying."

"You mean that ninety percent would just—disappear?"

"Well, yes, but my company has to pay for it, and the deal is for the purchase price to be paid out over ten years so my company can pay it out of earnings and doesn't have to go into debt. And the estate can elect to pay the estate tax on the shares over ten years, so it works out."

"Why didn't you get a bargain price for your shares? I mean, where's the bargain?" Jake asked.

"We'd have problems with the IRS if I didn't buy at fair market value, for the same price the company is paying for the ninety percent. We're working with the lawyer and an appraiser to determine that number right now."

"What happens at the end of that ten years?"

Dale smiled, glad to deliver the clincher. "My company has paid off its debt to the estate from earnings. I've paid off mine out of my salary, which remains the same, except for normal annual raises. Though that means I will have less personal income for ten years.

"But, at the end of that time," he paused for effect, "the ten percent I bought is the only outstanding stock, which means I'll own the entire company."

Jake thought he understood. To be sure, he asked, "So it will take you ten years before you own this company free and clear?"

"Exactly."

"And you'll be getting a company for one-tenth of its value?"

"Now you've got it. That's the bargain you were asking about; but remember, it's paid for out of earnings. When Kristin was alive, she could have taken out the earnings as dividends, but now they'll be diverted to pay off the note. That means I have to work hard to grow the company and increase earnings. While the company is paying off the note, I won't get the benefit of the earnings, but in the end I'll own the company."

"Wow," Jake said. "Sounds like she set you up with a sweet deal."

"Indeed," Dale said, glad that Jake had seen that point.

"That was a pretty nice thing for her to do," Jake mused.

"That's what I was saying about Kristin. She cared about people. She was a class act."

"Sounds like," Jake said. He had just learned that nobody was going to get rich quick through Kristin's death. It would take ten years of continuing to run the companies, and a lot of hard work, to make sure the companies were profitable so that the debt could be repaid from those profits, and the CEO's salaries. Not a strong motive for murder. Not strong at all. If someone killed for money, it was because they knew they could benefit immediately, not ten years down the line after working their butts off.

Jake dismissed Dale as a suspect. Any thoughts he had of pursuing this lead with the other executives were now gone. There wasn't enough motive, on any of their parts, to bother.

"What kind of a boss was she?" Jake asked, wanting to learn still more about Kristin.

"A hands-off boss, actually. In fact, before her last visit here, she hadn't been down since early September. She said she trusted us to handle everything. I don't think any of us disappointed her. The corporations are all very profitable."

Something struck a chord in Jake. "Was her last visit on the same day as..."

"Yes. And even then she offered an excuse for being here, like she felt she was bothering me. She said something about being in town anyway to work on something for the governor's re-election campaign and..."

Jake's ears started buzzing, a distracting low hum, and he didn't hear the rest of what Dale was saying. What was happening? What was it? The governor? What about that caused him to have this reaction? Was it...?

"Jake? Jake, are you okay?" he heard Dale ask.

"Sorry. I'm fine," Jake answered, trying to bring his mind back into focus. "What did you say about the governor?"

"What? Oh, just that she was in town to do something with his re-election campaign."

"Did she say anything else about him?" Jake asked cautiously.

"Well, yes," Dale answered. "She was actually quite excited about being involved in his re-election. She said she had gotten to know the governor well, and planned to contribute to his re-election campaign personally and through the corporations. I thought she was going to ask me for a personal donation as well," Dale concluded.

"But she didn't?"

"No. She left it at that. But you know, she looked really pleased, really happy to be involved in something. I don't think she's been involved in much since Ted's death. It was nice to see her excited about something again."

Jake stood up and said, "Well, thank you, Dale. I appreciate your time." It was abrupt, but necessarily so.

Dale's surprise at the brusque ending to the meeting showed, but he shook the hand Jake offered and said, "You're welcome, Jake. And I'm sorry you never knew Kristin. I think she would have liked to have known you, too."

"Thank you," Jake replied in a detached voice. He hurried out of the office, out of the building, to the refuge of his rental car. He had to be someplace quiet. He had to be alone to process his thoughts and feelings.

Sitting in the car, Jake contemplated all that he had learned, and determined that there were two courses of action he had to follow, one after the other.

First, he would find a way to talk to the man charged with her murder, Virgil Carpenter. He didn't know how, but he'd figure that out later.

Second, he'd find a way to talk to the governor. He had no idea who the governor of Florida even was. Whoever he was, Jake thought, he figures into this somehow. But how?

36

"HEY, RICK, how ya doing?" Jake asked the Metro-Dade detective.

"Jake? Is that you?"

"Sure is."

"Where are you?"

"At the Fontainebleau Hotel. Just sitting here sipping a Dewar's, looking out at the ocean. It's a nice place."

"No doubt. What are you doing back in Miami?"

"I'm investigating my sister's murder."

"Jaaake!" Rick exclaimed, his voice thick with exasperation.

"Yeah, I know. Just listen. I need your help."

"With what?"

"I want to talk to the guy you've got locked up for her murder."

Rick laughed out loud and said, "You've got to be kidding."

"Not kidding."

"No way, Jake."

"Why not?"

"How can you ask me that? You're not some idiot off the street, you're a detective, for Christ's sake."

"So? I repeat, why not?"

"Because I said so."

"Come on, Rick. Help me out here."

"No way."

"I'll buy you dinner again."

"I can't be bought," Rick said, his tone lightening slightly.

"Okay, okay. Then just do this for me. Tell me the name of the assistant state attorney prosecuting the case."

"Fuck you."

"I didn't ask for that. I asked for a name."

"Jake, what's this all about?"

269

"Just following my instincts."

"Shit."

"Come on. What have you got to lose? Look at it this way. If you've got the right guy for Kristin's murder, I'm not going to blow your case by just talking to him. But if you don't, I can help you find the right guy."

"And you think you can find that out just by talking to him?"

"I do."

"You're nuts."

"Granted."

"Jake, we have his confession. It's so airtight, you couldn't punch a hole in it with a bazooka."

"So what have you got to worry about?"

"I don't know. But you scare me."

"Just give me the name of the assistant state attorney."

"I'd say you'd have to worry about the public defender more."

"First things first. The ASA. Who is he?"

"She," Rick said, then hesitated, annoyed yet intrigued. He remembered what Jake's captain in New York had said about him. That he was "uncanny" when it came to figuring the ins and outs of a homicide case. The best. But the case was already figured out. He didn't want Jake screwing with it.

"Okay, who is *she*?"

"No."

"Rick, please. I'm not going to screw up your case. I promise."

Rick felt he still didn't know Jake well enough to trust him completely. "How do I know that?"

"Because anything I find out will be strictly for my own information. You'll proceed just the same, under your current assumption that you've got Kristin's killer. If I come up with anything concrete—and I mean dead certain and indisputable—to the contrary, I'll bring it right to you. Then you can do whatever you want with it."

"Let me get this straight. You want to talk to the suspect, and then go off on a manhunt of your own if you don't think we have the right guy. Have I got that right?"

"Yes."

"But you're saying that, even if you do come up with something else, I can totally ignore it, and you won't pursue it with the state?"

"You have my word of honor."

"But why do you want to talk to Virgil?"

"Oh. Just to satisfy my own curiosity. Is that good enough?"

"Not by a long shot."

"But you'll arrange it?"

There was a long silence.

"Rick? Still there?"

"I'm thinking."

"Who's the assistant state attorney, Rick?"

"She's gonna think we're both crazy."

"I bet she already knows that about you. She'll figure that's why we're friends."

Rick laughed. "You're probably right about that."

"So, are you going to call her for me, or not?"

"Now you want me to call her for you? Damn, you're a pushy son-of-a bitch."

"Thank you. It's a quality I know you appreciate."

The two men laughed, acknowledging their growing friendship.

"All right," Rick said. "I'll do it. But she's no pushover, let me tell you. All I can do is ask her to see you. I'm not even going to say why. That's up to you."

"Fair enough. Thanks a lot, Rick."

"Yeah, but you better not screw me over on this, Jake."

"I promise not to, Rick. Believe me."

"Okay. Her name is Leslie Sherwood. I'll give her a call, and call you back. I'll let her know she can expect to hear from you. As I said, though, the rest is up to you."

"Great, Rick. I really do appreciate it."

Rick grunted and said, "Yeah, yeah," and hung up on Jake.

Jake went through the security area of the Dade County Courthouse and then rode the escalator to the sixth floor, where he would need to check in for his appointment with Leslie Sherwood.

He walked up to the glass-enclosed office work area, and said to the woman standing there, "My name's Jake Miller. I have a ten o'clock appointment with Leslie Sherwood."

The woman nodded and picked up the phone, calling what he supposed was Leslie's extension. When she put down the phone, she said,

271

"Her secretary will come out and get you." She nodded towards some electronic glass doors off to his left.

Jake thanked her, then stepped away to wait by the doors. What an old building, he thought. No older than New York City's, though. What a shame that assistant state attorneys, and the entire host of state employees, had to work in such dismal surroundings, and for half the money they could make in private practice. He knew why they did it, though. Mainly because they saw lots of action, especially in a big city, and because they had a calling of sorts to keep the wheels of the justice system turning.

Besides, after a few years as an assistant state attorney, they could practically write their own ticket if they decided to move into a private law firm. Many of them did that, but quite a few stayed put. For the most part, they loved their jobs.

He saw a woman coming down the hall towards the doors where he stood. They made eye contact, and when she opened the door, she said pleasantly, "Mr. Miller?"

"Yes."

"Follow me."

Jake was led through a maze of offices, twisting corners that held surprises at each turn. He wondered how they had fit so many offices into such a small area. It was a virtual miracle of design and architecture.

The secretary stopped at the last door at the end of a hall. Jake had no idea where he was. He knew he couldn't retrace his steps if he tried. The secretary motioned with her hand, and he followed her directions into Leslie Sherwood's office.

He stopped short the moment he stepped into her office. He was looking at one of the prettiest women he had ever seen. He knew his inertia was due to his surprise, rather than her beauty. He hadn't known what to expect, exactly, based upon Rick's description of her being "no pushover," but it certainly wasn't this.

She was smiling at him, and he propelled himself forward. "One foot in front of the other, one foot in front of the other," his mind directed him.

"Hi," she said in a friendly but professional voice, "I'm Leslie Sherwood."

Jake shook her extended hand and said, "Jake Miller. Nice to meet you." The warmth of her hand stayed with him after he had withdrawn his.

"First, let me say I'm so sorry about your sister." Rick had told her about Jake's relation to Kristin Long, and that he had some questions. Leslie had read the statement he had given to Metro-Dade homicide the night of the murder, and wondered what kind of follow-up questions he might have.

"Thank you." Jake was at a distinct disadvantage. He had been caught off guard by her unexpected good looks. He was staring at her, taking in her long blond hair, her healthy-looking tanned skin, and her intelligent blue eyes.

"So what can I do for you?" Leslie asked, getting down to business.

"I, uh, I...I'd like to ask your permission to question Virgil Carpenter."

Leslie was startled. Rick had said nothing about that. He had told her Jake was an ex-detective from New York, and asked her to extend some professional courtesy for reasons that Jake himself would explain. That was all. So what was going on here?

"What are you talking about?" she asked defensively.

"Gee, I'm sorry," Jake said. "I know I caught you off guard. I was just giving as direct an answer as I could to your direct question."

Even though she wasn't smiling, she wasn't hostile, either. Jake kept staring.

Leslie was becoming uncomfortable with the way this man was staring at her. She was quite accustomed to gathering admiring looks, but this man was too much.

Seeing her discomfort, Jake said, "I apologize for staring. I just didn't expect you to be so pretty." He hoped he hadn't sounded condescending. Many professional women didn't like to be told they were pretty. They preferred to be recognized for their brains.

But Leslie Sherwood wasn't like that. She was a woman who was perfectly at ease with being both beautiful and brainy. It had always worked to her advantage. Anyone who had underestimated her brains because of her looks soon found out they were mistaken. And if her looks, along with her knowledge of the law and her prosecutorial skills, worked to her advantage, so much the better. She made no issue of being told she was pretty. In fact, she was always flattered, no matter how many times she heard it.

"Thank you," she said, something she had learned to say long ago in response to a compliment. To refute it or to take offense would only be ungracious, and it would make the person giving the compliment uncomfortable.

Jake breathed a sigh of relief. She hadn't been offended.

"Now let's get back to what you were saying," she said. "What is this about your wanting to question Virgil Carpenter?"

It was her turn to watch him now. She liked what she saw. He was extremely handsome, even with glasses. He looked athletic and powerful, but not hard. On the contrary, there was a very confident but pliable quality to him, she decided. And that odd streak of gray in his hair was disarmingly attractive.

Jake explained, starting with his accident, and how it led to his finally taking the initiative to find his sister. He continued to tell her how, with that knowledge, he had come to Florida to find her, and how he had found her dead body instead.

"How terrible for you," Leslie said sympathetically.

Jake nodded in acknowledgment of her sympathy, then went on to explain his dealings with Metro-Dade homicide and Rick, up to this point. He ended his explanation by saying, "So Rick called you, and here I am."

"I simply don't understand why you want to talk to Virgil, Mr. Miller."

"Please call me Jake. The bottom line is, Mrs. Sherwood..."

"It's Miss. And call me Leslie."

Pleased, Jake said, "Leslie. Anyway, Leslie, I'm just trying to find out more about the sister I never knew." He withheld the truth that he was tempted to tell her.

"You won't find it out from Virgil Carpenter," she said, seeing through his explanation.

He met her eyes evenly and said, "You're right. I'm sorry. I was skirting the truth."

She nodded knowingly, but without condemnation.

Jake plunged in. "So here it is. Some of it may alarm you, but I think being truthful is the best way to help you understand."

"Okay," she said, not afraid of the truth, as he suspected. She had heard everything in her eight years as an assistant state attorney.

"I just have a hunch...no, it's more than a hunch," he started, not sure how to explain it or how much to say. Suddenly, he knew he could trust her with the *real* truth. He'd start with a condensed version.

"Leslie, I have a strong sixth sense." He looked into her eyes expecting to see a skeptical look, but it wasn't there. She was looking at him passively, calmly, waiting for him to go on.

"I was at Metro-Dade homicide when they brought Virgil in. He walked right past me. He looked me in the eyes. Now if he had been in any way connected to my sister's death, I would have known it. I would have felt something. But I didn't. Not a thing." He stopped to let that sink in for her.

Leslie wondered what she was supposed to think about this. Did he expect her to believe him? She made sure her practiced face remained passive. She would give him the courtesy of hearing him out. Then she'd find a way to get rid of him.

"Go on," she said.

"That's why I have to talk to Virgil myself. I've got to validate the blank I drew when I saw him. Believe me, I hope I was wrong. I'd like to go home and forget all this. But I can't, not yet. I have to talk to Virgil, so that I can get past this, quit playing cop, and go on with my life—or so that I can find her real killer."

Leslie began to wonder if he was all there, mentally. He wanted to...what? Validate a negative? He didn't get the right, or in this case, the *wrong* vibe from Virgil, so he was pursuing other possibilities? Even though they had a signed confession? This whole thing didn't set well with her, not in the least. Still, there was something about him...

"Tell me more about your sixth sense," she said, hoping to get a better glimpse into the man. If she didn't like what she heard, she could at least have this friend of Rick's thrown out with a clear conscience.

Jake had never told anyone the absolute truth about his sixth sense. There had been those in the department who speculated about it, but in general his talents were referred to as "strong intuition" or "great instincts." But Jake had never verbally validated it. Should he tell her? He knew that he had no chance of getting to Virgil unless he did.

He started slowly, giving her a few examples of different events that had occurred throughout his professional career that were all related to his instincts and intuition.

As she listened, Leslie's doubt turned to intrigue, then, finally, to unintended belief. Surely no one could make up all of that.

"And you really believe you would have known if Virgil had been the one who killed your sister? It works like that?"

"Pretty much all the time."

"When's my birthday?" she asked playfully.

"I can't tell you something like that," he laughed. "I'm not a fortune teller, or a psychic. Things just come to me." He stopped short and then said, "Like your black and white dog with a red collar."

Leslie physically jerked in her seat. Quickly deducing that Rick couldn't have told him that, since he didn't even know Leslie had a dog, she said, "Well, you got that right."

Jake nodded and said, "Sorry, I don't mean to pry into your private life. In fact, I try not to do that with people. I deliberately block those things, figuring it's, well, disrespectful."

Leslie smiled, appreciating that particular point of view. It was a decent way to handle his...*gift*. They looked at each other for a long moment.

Leslie had an airtight case, one she could prosecute with no problem. Although she believed Jake, even liked him, she didn't want her case disturbed.

"I've got a solid case here, Jake. I don't think I want you fooling around with it. If I thought there was any reason to doubt that Virgil killed your sister, I might consider it. But I don't. I have a signed confession."

"I'll tell you what I told Rick. Anything I learn from Virgil will be strictly for my own knowledge. I'll sign anything I have to, to that effect. And unless I come up with something different that's really concrete, you won't hear from me. Even then, I'll let you make the decision about what to do with anything I give you. You can ignore it, and I won't say a word to a living soul, or you can use it.

"The guy needs to be put away," he continued. "I know that. And because I know that, I would never do anything to jeopardize that happening. You can trust me on this, Leslie," he said, removing his glasses so that she could see the truth he spoke, in his eyes.

She was startled by his eyes. The glasses he wore were slightly tinted, and they hadn't allowed her to see the magnificence and depth of his eyes. She felt herself drawn to him as she read the truth in his eyes.

Leslie hesitated a moment more before she said, "I'll call the public defender and see what I can do."

"Thank you," Jake said with genuine gratitude.

37

JAKE WALKED OUT of the Dade County jail feeling dirty, like he needed a shower. He had talked to dozens of killers over the years, and he always felt the same—polluted somehow by breathing the same air.

Virgil was no different from other killers in that respect. Jake had long ago become convinced that anyone who killed was crazy. It took a twisted mind to kill—except in self-defense. And Virgil's mind was definitely twisted. Virgil's public defender, Tom Maxwell, could plead insanity at the sentencing hearing in an attempt to avoid the death penalty, but even if he succeeded, Virgil would be put away for a very long time, and rightfully so. He had killed the other three women, no doubt about that. But he hadn't killed Kristin.

Tom had stayed with them throughout the interview. Although he had reluctantly—very reluctantly—consented to Jake's talking to Virgil, he knew there was nothing Jake could do to help or hurt Virgil. Virgil's signed confession made that issue moot.

Jake wasn't going to tell Tom that Virgil was confusing the third prostitute with Kristin. If the police and everybody else couldn't see that as clearly as he could, that was their problem. Though he was a little surprised that Rick hadn't seen it.

Of course, he had to admit that he had the ability to see it more clearly than they did, but he wouldn't tell them that, either.

No, he had found out what he wanted to know. Virgil Carpenter had not killed his sister. That fact left him with a clear path to follow, starting in Tallahassee with the governor of the state—Michael Romano.

Jake unlocked the door and walked into his hotel suite. He was glad to have seen Virgil and found out what he wanted to know, but he was growing weary of hotels, even one as beautiful as the Fontainebleau. He had something else important to do before he left, however, and a well-placed call to Rick Givens could make that happen. But first he had to call Leslie Sherwood and thank her.

He thought about how hard Leslie had worked to get the public defender to consent to her odd request. Jake had listened as she skillfully cajoled him into it, without revealing the real reason. Jake had been impressed. He hadn't been privy to Tom's end of the conversation, but he knew by one of Leslie's responses that Tom had taken the "What's in it for me?" attitude.

Leslie had mentioned another case, and referred to a plea bargain that Tom had been pushing for. She had assured Jake later that she hadn't committed to anything she wouldn't have done anyway; but he wasn't convinced.

He had thought about her often since he met her. Time and again, he had reached for the phone, wanting to call her and ask her to have lunch or dinner with him. And it wasn't solely because he was lonely and hungry for company, though he was. It was because he wanted to know her better.

He was attracted to her, and in no small way.

He had refrained from calling her only because he didn't want to mix business with pleasure up to this point. Now he had an excuse for calling her: to let her know about his interview with Virgil. He grew excited as he anticipated hearing her voice again.

She took his call right away. He took it as a good sign.

"Hi, Jake," she said warmly.

"Hello, Leslie. How are you?"

"Swamped."

"Oh. Well, I won't take up much of your time."

"No, that's okay. I have a few minutes. Tom called me, said you talked to Virgil."

"I did."

"Well?"

"Well, I told him I didn't have any ideas. But I do. I'm not going to take up your time now to tell you about them, though. I'll just say that I don't think Virgil killed my sister, though I'm convinced he killed the others."

"What? What are you saying?"

"Nothing right now, Leslie. Go ahead with the case just as it is."

"I don't understand."

"I don't expect you to. But I promised you I wouldn't jeopardize your case, and I won't. That's all that really matters right now, isn't it?"

Leslie was intrigued. She had been thinking about Jake quite a lot. She had even hoped he would call her, maybe ask her out. When he hadn't, she had assumed he wasn't interested in her. But she was interested in him, and she was especially interested in his sixth sense. She knew he had relied on it to draw whatever conclusions he had.

"I guess so," she said finally. Taking a breath and a chance, she asked, "So, how much longer are you going to be in Miami?"

Jake wished he could stay longer, and maybe even take her out. He thought that she might want him to. It was with real regret that he answered, "I'm flying out later this afternoon."

"Oh," she said faint disappointment in her voice. "Back to New York?"

"No, I'm going to Tallahassee."

"Tallahassee?"

"Yes. Just going to check on a few things about Kristin's estate."

"I see," she said, not really seeing, because she was remembering what he had said about not wanting any part of her estate. But she wouldn't probe any further.

"Well," he said, "I want to thank you for all your help."

"You're welcome." She waited hopefully for what he would say next.

"Well, so long, Leslie. I'm really glad to have met you." He wanted to say more, wanted desperately to ask her out, but he had something more important to do right now, and he couldn't let anything interfere. And he couldn't insinuate that there could be more at a later time. Depending on what he found out, he didn't know where things would end up.

"It was my pleasure," she said graciously.

"Mine, too. Goodbye, Leslie."

"Goodbye, Jake."

Now for one final thing before he took off. He needed to see the autopsy report and talk to the medical examiner. Maybe there was a clue there.

He picked up the phone to call Rick Givens. He smiled as he thought about how much fun he and Rick had at the Miami Dolphins game the previous night.

Still, Rick wasn't going to be too happy about this request. Before he could decide how to get Rick to help him get to the medical examiner and Kristin's autopsy file, he heard Rick's voice answer, "Detective Givens."

Jake took a deep breath and started talking.

Jake wound through the streets of Miami, maneuvering the rental car around the numerous cars parked against the curbs where "no parking" signs were clearly posted. Just like all big cities, he thought. No one pays attention. As in New York, people parked wherever there was a space, illegal or not.

He was following the directions that David Fells, the Deputy Chief Medical Examiner, had given him that morning. He read his scribbled notes again, and continued driving until he saw the sign for Jackson Memorial Hospital's emergency center. Okay, he was on the right track. He slowed down to look at the hospital.

He knew this was where the medical examiner's office got most of its business. Every homicide and accident victim was taken there first, since it was the county hospital. He had heard of Jackson Memorial, of course, even in New York. It had the reputation of being a top-notch hospital, one of the very best in the nation, despite crippling understaffing and inadequate funding.

Rick had told him that one night in February of the previous year, there had been eighteen homicide and accident victims treated in the emergency room. He was upset by the thought of the sister he never knew being taken here as just another victim. He felt his anger at the loss start to rise, but he fought it. Not now. He had business to attend to first.

He continued up the street, following Tenth Avenue around the curve, and saw the three-story brown building the medical examiner had described. "Sure looks a lot nicer than New York's big body bag," he said out loud to himself.

He pulled up to the entrance gate and pressed the intercom button. A soft female voice said, "May I help you?

He told her who he was and who he was there to see. There was no response as the arm lifted to allow him entry. As he pulled into one of the numerous available parking spaces and walked towards the building, he silently thanked Rick once again for his help.

The medical examiner had agreed to see him early this afternoon, which should leave Jake time to drop off the rental car and catch the last flight out of Miami to Tallahassee. He had his packed bags in the trunk of the car. He was ready and anxious to follow up on Governor Romano.

He walked up the curved steps, taking note of the modern structure. From a technological standpoint, the Dade County Medical Examiner's office had the reputation as one of the best facilities in the world, but he hadn't guessed that the structure would be so modern and so clean. He had always hated going to the ME's office in New York. He could smell that place fifty paces from the front door. He detected no odor whatsoever here as he walked in.

A woman sat at the receptionist's desk in the spacious and modern area. Jake introduced himself, and then waited as she called Dr. Fells' secretary.

"Have a seat," she said. "His secretary will let him know you're here."

Jake didn't have long to wait. Dr. Fells appeared on the circular staircase that led down to the lobby area where Jake waited. When he reached the bottom, he extended his hand and said, "Jake Miller?"

"Yes, hello, Dr. Fells. Thanks for seeing me," Jake responded, shaking his hand.

"No problem. Follow me," he said amiably.

As Jake was following him up the stairs, the doctor turned to him and said, "Rick filled me in. He must think a lot of you. He's never asked me to do anything like this before."

"Rick's a great guy," Jake said.

Dr. Fells nodded and said, "That he is."

As they reached the top of the stairs, Jake said, "I'll try not to take up too much of your time."

"Not a problem. I've set aside as much time as you'll need. Come on," he said, indicating that Jake should follow him.

Jake looked around at the clean and modern facility. "How long have you been in this building, Dr. Fells?"

"Call me David. About six years now."

"Six years? It looks brand new."

"Yeah, we make an effort to keep it looking that way. After that dump we were in before, we felt we were given a real break here. We take care of it."

"What I'd like to know," Jake said, "is where you put the smells."

"Unbelievable, huh?" David said. "We have a special ventilation system. It's designed to recycle the air at a seventy-five percent old air, twenty-five percent new air rate, so that a totally new supply of fresh air is circulated every hour. Hell, you have to be standing a foot from a cadaver in this place to even smell it."

"I've never seen anything like it," Jake said admiringly. "The ME's office in New York is a real stink-hole. It took me months to get used to it."

"I imagine it did," David said as they reached his office. "Have a seat."

After they sat down, David continued the conversation. "One of the doctors got smart one day and took a political hot shot to the old place. The guy had made a mistake by asking how things were going. Dr. Sims told him the place literally stunk, and then showed him what he meant." He smiled and said, "Sixty days after that grand tour, we had approved funding for this." He waved his arm to indicate that he was talking about the new facility.

"Nice going," Jake laughed. "How many autopsies does your office do a year?" he asked.

"Close to three thousand. We were just shy of that last year."

Jake whistled. "That's a lot of bodies. What's Dade County's population?"

"About one point five million."

Jake did some quick math in his head and said, "Geez, you guys have a heavier load, percentage wise, than we do in New York."

David nodded his head, as if he were already aware of that fact.

"Hey," Jake apologized. "I'm sorry about the 'we' and the comparisons. It's just always interesting to me to learn what other cities are doing."

"I know what you mean. I'm the same way. But it's a sick statistic to want to compare, huh?" he joked.

"You said it. Anyway, Doctor..."

"David."

"Sorry. David, like I said, I don't want to take up too much of your time—though if you can spare a little extra later, I'd really like a tour of this place."

"Glad to."

"But first," Jake continued, "may I see the file on my sister?"

"Got it right here," David said, pushing the folder across to Jake. "Like I said, this isn't ordinary procedure, so I'd appreciate your keeping this whole thing to yourself."

"Done."

"Good. Now this is the original file. It includes the computer report that summarizes the police investigation. I don't have to tell you not to remove anything, I'm sure."

"That's understood," Jake assured him.

David knew Jake would need some time to collect himself once he saw the file. He decided to leave him alone with it for a while.

"Look," he said, "I've got a few things to do. Take your time, look it over. I'll be glad to make copies of anything you want, or answer any questions you have, when I get back."

Jake nodded his thanks and waited until David left the room to open the file. Years of being a homicide detective had taught him to be indifferent to just about anything; but as he started reading the file, he was shaken. This was his sister, and though he never knew her, at this moment he felt her loss as keenly as if he had.

Slowly, he went through the familiar contents of the file. The body diagrams, the rap sheets, the property receipts, notes of conversations, histologic sections, X-rays, the photographs...he wanted to turn past the pictures, but he forced himself to look at them. He was saddened as he carefully studied her face and body. She was very beautiful. He saw past the slit throat to the face and eyes so like his own. Even though he could look at her naked body clinically, he still had to admit that she had a beautiful one. He put the photos aside and looked at the next report, which was her personal doctor's medical record. "My God!" he exclaimed out loud. She was pregnant. Why hadn't Rick or anyone else told him?

He answered the question himself by admitting that he wouldn't have wanted to be the one to tell him if he were in Rick's place. His unmarried, socialite sister—pregnant. No matter how lax morals had gotten, that was still something that could be embarrassing to discuss.

Pregnant. Jake continued reading Kristin's doctor's report until he found what he was looking for. Kristin was in her first tri-mester of pregnancy, estimated at six weeks. He flipped to the ME's report, and saw that the fetus had been estimated at eight weeks, though there wasn't an autopsy report on the fetus in the file.

284

He then flipped to the ME's list of medications that was provided by Kristin's personal physician. No birth control pills. Could she have gotten pregnant on purpose? Maybe to trap a man?

What a chauvinist you are to even think that, Jake Miller, he reproved himself.

It occurred to him that hers could have been an unplanned pregnancy, that it had been an accident, and that there was some man out there who was responsible. In a flash, his mind registered a single, crystal clear thought: the governor.

Jake clutched the file and waited for some kind of validation to occur. Nothing.

"You okay?" Jake heard David's voice from what seemed far away. He looked up to see him standing in the door of his office.

"I'm fine," he said, knowing he didn't sound that way. The fetus. What happened to... "David, she was pregnant."

"I had a feeling no one told you about that. I'm sorry."

"It's just that...hey, was there an autopsy done on the fetus?"

"No."

"Why not?"

"Nobody asked for one."

"Yeah, but..."

"Look, Jake. We had a prominent, wealthy, Caucasian woman who was brutally murdered. Normal autopsy procedures and protocol were followed, even though the killer confessed. But because we had a confession, we didn't need to follow through on it. The cost of more sophisticated testing wasn't justified."

Seeing Jake's distress, David said, "Jake, she was murdered in exactly the same way as three other women I autopsied. There were no discrepancies in the method. The only difference was, the other three were hookers. But she was a stranger in a strange city, and things happen, especially to naïve tourists.

"We chose not to blemish her stellar reputation by making her pregnancy known, since the fetus didn't figure into her murder."

"Maybe it did," Jake said quietly.

"What do you mean?" David asked.

Jake knew that anything he might say now would sound totally crazy. So he said simply, "Never mind. You're right."

The doctor nodded and said, "The pathologist did blood type the fetus, though." He stepped over to where Jake sat and flipped to a page in the file, then pointed to a notation at the bottom of it. It read, "Fetus blood type 'O'".

Big deal, Jake thought. The most common blood type in the world. Jake stood up. "You've been great, David. Thank you."

"I take it you don't want that tour?"

"Not this time, thanks."

"I understand," David said. And he did. Jake had just had a big shock, and he needed to recover from it. "Let me know if there's anything else I can do."

"I appreciate that. Thanks again." Jake shook the doctor's hand and left.

As he left, Jake wondered why he had drawn a blank after his initial thought about the governor and Kristin's baby. No validation at all. Was he wrong? Was he just trying to make things connect? Why was he even going to Tallahassee?

Jake questioned his reliance on his instincts. When he thought about it, he thought it was really sort of preposterous to implicate the governor. There didn't seem to be anything about this Romano guy to be suspicious of, from what he could determine.

To alleviate his boredom and get a head start, he had gone to the Miami Beach library and looked up everything he could find on Michael Romano. He was a clean guy, well respected. Poor boy makes good and all that. All the way from Little Italy to Palm Beach, via New York University, Columbia Law School, and marriage to a wealthy Palm Beach society girl.

After a short stint with a prominent Palm Beach law firm, he had begun a fast-paced rise in politics, starting as a state representative, and fortuitously moving into a state senate seat that had been vacated upon the premature death of a long-term, well-loved Republican senator. Romano had done some fine work during his two terms as a state senator, successfully heading up important committees, which gave him a lot of visibility. Although it wasn't specifically implicated anywhere, Jake had deduced that the money and influence of his wife's family had paved the road to the Governor's Mansion.

And that was another thing. The governor seemed to be happily married, according to a high society magazine article he had read. Had he been obsessively following a single, thin thread to the governor based upon that one-time psychic flash at Pro-Long Plastics? He realized he had.

Maybe he should skip Tallahassee, let it go. After all, what was he out to prove, really? That he was a better cop than Metro-Dade's cops? That his intuition never failed him? That his sister...*his sister*. What about her?

He had a vague sense of her, feeling a connection to her that he had never felt before. But now he knew so much more about her. And he missed her, even though he never even met her.

"Okay," he said out loud, as if he were addressing her. "I'll go to Tallahassee. I'll find out the truth about Michael Romano. For you, sis."

38

JAKE WAS HOMESICK for all the comforts of his apartment in New York. I'm sick of hotels, he thought as he sat in his suite. At least in Miami he had a great view. Here in Tallahassee, his room overlooked a parking lot.

He jumped to grab the phone when it rang. "Vic?" he said when he picked it up.

"Yeah, how you doing, Jake?"

"Not bad. What did you find out?"

"Nothing much. I ran a complete check on the entire Romano family, starting with Michael Romano. They're clean, Jake."

Jake's shoulders sagged in disappointment at Vic's words.

"But," Vic continued, "I asked a friend who has age-old connections in the neighborhood where Romano's from, Little Italy, to ask around. One thing came up, but I don't know if it's going to help you."

"What?" Jake asked eagerly.

"There was a solid but unclear connection with Sal Lineo, years ago, something to do with the Longshoremen and Antonio Romano, Michael Romano's grandfather."

"Lineo had a big piece of the docks, didn't he?" Jake asked, encouraged.

"Still does. But nobody in the Romano family is with the union now."

He gave Jake the background information on Michael's siblings, then added, "Are you going to tell me what this is about now, Jake? I've violated the files around here, ya know. I deserve an explanation."

"Still following up on what we talked about. The money angle didn't pan out, but I promise to tell you everything later, Vic. Just trust me for now. But based on what you just told me, I need your help again."

"Yeah? What now?" Vic asked with a touch of impatience.

"Can you check with OCCB for the names of Lineo's known hit men?"

"Oooh, big one. You know our organized crime unit plays it real close to the chest."

"I know, but I got a feeling about this. When you get that, I need a follow-up to it."

"What?" Vic asked, becoming worried now about the depth of the water Jake was asking him to dive into.

"When you have the names, call the airlines and see if they have any of those names on their manifest for October twenty-third, or for the days bracketing that date. And leaving from either airport in New York, going to Miami. Check Jersey, too."

"That's easy. It's getting the names to check that's going to be tough."

"Somebody in OCCB must owe you," Jake said, knowing Vic kept those tabs better than anyone else in the New York homicide department.

"Yeah, somebody does. But I'd be using up a big one for this."

"I know, Vic. You know I'll make it up to you, somehow."

"Yeah, sure." Vic's voice oozed sarcasm.

"Then you'll do it?"

"You know I will."

"Great. Thanks, Vic."

"But I won't have anything for you before tomorrow."

"No problem."

"Okay. I'll call you tomorrow."

"I appreciate it."

"Yeah, sure," Vic said again, and hung up.

Jake was nervous as hell, and he was afraid of screwing up because of it. He had never done an illegal breaking and entering, yet here he was, in his dead sister's house, and it wasn't by invitation. But he wasn't going to start at square one with the Tallahassee police department, trying to get the same favors from them as he had from Metro-Dade.

If he could get a grip on his nerves, he could be in and out of here in no time. He knew what he was after. He just had to find it.

This is it, he thought, as he entered what looked like a home office at the end of a long corridor. The house was huge, so it had taken longer than he had anticipated to find her home office. He was disappointed that it faced the street, distant though it was. He wouldn't be able to turn on any lights, even if he closed the curtains, which he did. He'd use his flashlight to find what he was looking for.

Jake sat down at Kristin's desk and turned on the flashlight. The first thing he spotted was her calendar. He didn't have to wonder why it was still here, instead of in an evidence locker. With Virgil's confession, further investigation into Kristin's life wasn't necessary.

It was a day planner, the kind that lay open with succeeding days on either page. It was turned to October twenty-second and twenty-third. He sighed deeply, remembering that October twenty-third was the date of her death. He pulled the calendar to him to read what was written on that page.

There was a notation of a flight number for eight a.m. on the twenty-third. She had drawn a small arrow and written "Miami" under it. Underneath that, he saw the words: Sheraton-B.H. resv. #33601. There was another reservation confirmation number for Hertz.

Skipping down a couple of lines, he saw that eleven a.m. was circled. Dale's name was written next to it, confirming her trip to Pro-Long plastics that day.

There was nothing else on the page, no mention of any re-election campaign meeting, as she had told Dale. Jake knew, from what Dale had said, that she hadn't made the trip to Miami just to visit Pro-Long Plastics. She went to Miami for another reason—to see the governor, all right, but not at a campaign event.

He flipped the page and saw that she had written the flight number next to four o'clock, for her return to Tallahassee the following day. He had a moment of gloom in realizing the return ticket was never used.

He continued to flip backwards through the pages of the calendar. She had a number of scattered appointments filled in, but there were no references to Romano.

He stopped on the page for Tuesday, October tenth, where he saw the name "Dr. Yates" written next to ten a.m. He recognized it as the name of her personal physician, the one whose name had been on the medical reports in her autopsy file.

He couldn't recall any specific date that he had seen on that report, so he did some quick math in his head. He concluded that, based upon the fact that she was six weeks pregnant, according to her doctor's report, and eight weeks pregnant, according to the medical examiner's report, October tenth must have been the day she found out she was pregnant. October tenth to October twenty-third was exactly fourteen days.

He felt he had missed something in between those dates. He went forward again, and spotted what he had indeed missed. It was at the very bottom of the page for October seventeenth. There he saw a single abbreviated word, "apt." with a tiny heart drawn next to it. Nothing else.

He looked at the surrounding pages, more carefully this time, for a similar notation, but he didn't see anything. Damn. Whose apartment did she go to? It didn't jibe with his suspicion of the governor, who, of course, lived in the Governor's Mansion. But maybe Romano had an apartment, too. A place to carry on affairs. Some married men did that. But wouldn't he be taking a big risk, doing that? After all, he had a pretty high profile. Maybe it was under someone else's name. Whose? A friend, maybe? A staff member?

In a clear, startling flash, he had it. It was under her name. She had rented an apartment, to be discreet. It made perfect sense. Somebody might recognize the governor if he had come here to Kristin's home.

She must have a lease somewhere, or at least a canceled check, Jake thought. He searched the top of the desk, but there was nothing to give him any clues there. He tugged at the top desk drawer, and was pleased to find it wasn't locked. It was one less thing he'd have to break into.

He pulled it all the way open, sliding the chair back to accommodate the extension of the drawer. He fingered through the papers he found there, until he spotted a rubber-banded stack of bank statements. He opened the unsealed flap of the one on top and pulled out the contents. Canceled checks were wrapped inside the statement. He quickly flipped through them, looking for one made out to an apartment or a company. There was nothing like that, though.

He went as far back as June before giving up. He re-banded the statements and returned them to where he had found them. He slid the chair back up to the desk and pulled out the large bottom drawer on the right side. He saw some well-organized files there. Shining the flashlight on the tabs, he thumbed through the files until he saw one labeled "Receipts." He plucked it from the drawer and laid it on the desk to open it. There it was—a cash receipt. It was made out for eight hundred and seventy-five dollars. At the top was the name, "Bent Tree Apartments," and it was dated August eleventh. Underneath was a small check mark inside a box which said "cash," denoting a four-hundred dollar security deposit and four-hundred seventy-five in rent. Next to that was written H-9. The apartment number.

The name on it was Angela Marcus. Of course. She had combined her middle name with her altered maiden name—Marks, Marcus—and rented the apartment for cash under that false name.

He removed a note pad and pen from the inside pocket of his jacket and wrote down the name and address of the apartment complex. He trusted his memory, but he trusted ink even more.

He closed the file and put it back in the drawer. He still hadn't found what he was looking for, though, which was a link to Michael Romano. He thumbed through the rest of the files, but didn't see anything that looked like it held any answers.

He closed the drawer, and was about to open the bottom drawer on the other side of the desk, when he realized he hadn't finished with her calendar. He looked at his watch. One twenty a.m. He'd been here almost an hour.

He knew it was a long time to be in a house that had been broken into, but he wouldn't leave until he found something—anything—that would link her to Romano.

He turned the pages of the calendar back past October seventeenth, the point at which he got sidetracked looking for the apartment information. He continued past the tenth and the doctor's appointment, on back through October and into September. Oddly, there was very little activity in September. And then he landed on Thursday and Friday, September seventh and eighth. Another flight number on September seventh, plus the words, "Font. Blu Hotel resv. #988760," along with another Hertz reservation number.

So okay, Kristin had been in Miami in early September. He had learned that from both Dale and Rick. Rick had said she stayed at the Fontainebleau around that time. And that was the last time, before the day of her death, that she had visited Pro-Long Plastics, according to Dale.

So what was she doing at the Fontainebleau? He didn't buy Rick's simplistic theory that she liked luxury hotels on Miami's beaches. She was there for a reason. Something to do with the governor's campaign? Or something to do with the governor himself?

Jake wrote down the dates and the information, including the hotel reservation number.

He continued to flip back through the pages, taking him into August.

Jake realized he was getting into the time frame when Kristin would have become pregnant. He counted back from October tenth. Six weeks would have been around August twenty-eighth. And there it was, "apt." on August thirtieth.

So the apartment was being used for an affair after all.

Same notation on August twenty-third, "apt."

He continued turning back through her calendar, stopping on August eighteenth. She had flown to Tampa, and stayed at the Omni Hotel. Of course, there was a Pro-Long company there, too, so it could have been business.

The governor of a state traveled around that state a lot. Maybe Kristin met him in both Tampa and Miami. It felt right. Then again, maybe he was just hoping he was right, making it fit with his suspicions.

Still, if he could find out whether Michael Romano had been in Tampa and Miami on those dates, he'd definitely be on to something. He picked up his pen and wrote down the information pertaining to the Tampa trip.

August fifteenth. Leon Cty Rep Pty, Hyatt. Noon was circled. Tallahassee was in Leon County. It was a meeting of the county Republican Party. The governor would be there, for sure.

When he got to Saturday, August twelfth, he saw something that made him catch his breath. She had written the words, "Preston, Ambassador Hotel." Underneath it she had written, "Governor Romano," and had underlined it twice. Finally, the name he was looking for.

He looked at it again, trying to determine if the name of the place was "Preston Ambassador Hotel", or whether it was just "Ambassador Hotel" and Preston was the name of someone she went there with.

He decided that the latter must be the case. He could verify the name of the hotel by looking in the phone book when he got back to his room. Then who would this Preston guy be?

A fly in the ointment at this point, he decided. Maybe this Preston guy could tell him something, though. He jotted down the information. Maybe she has an address book here somewhere, he thought, scanning the desk. He didn't see one.

He looked at his watch and saw that it was two-fifteen a.m. Better get out of here, he thought. He wasn't totally satisfied, but he had enough to get him started. If he really had to, he could come back, but he had stayed too long already. One thing he had learned for sure, being a cop—the longer you stayed in the wrong place, the greater your chances of getting caught.

He returned everything to its original position, and quickly glanced over the desk. He was satisfied that it look undisturbed.

He stuck the pad and pen in his pocket as he stood up and pushed the chair back under the desk. He opened the curtains and then hurried out of the office and down the corridor, through the hall and kitchen and out the back door.

His heart was pounding, and he surmised, not for the first time in his life, that it was a lot more comfortable being on the right side of the law.

39

THE DEEP SOUTHERN voice that answered the phone said, *"Tallahassee Democrat."*

"Could you please connect me with the Political News Department?" Jake asked.

"Just a moment, please."

The phone rang three times before someone picked it up and said, "Earl Wallace."

"Is this the Political News Department?" Jake asked.

"Yes, can I help you?"

"Yes, Mr. Wallace. My name is Toby Graham, and I'm a student at Florida State University. I'm doing a term paper about political campaigns. I wonder if you could give me some information."

"Sure, what do you need?" the reporter asked. He got these calls from students all the time.

Jake was calling this particular department because he knew that, as in New York, the governor's itinerary was given out to the newspapers on a daily basis. It allowed them to plan their coverage of any significant events. Knowing that, he had decided to bluff his way through this.

"I'm researching Governor Romano's re-election campaign efforts. He was in Tampa on August seventeenth and in Miami on September seventh. Do you have any information that would tell me if he was in those cities to do campaigning, or to enlist support for his special session?"

"Hmmm. Let me see if I have anything," Earl Wallace said. He didn't bother to ask the student any questions. He had learned that could lead to a whole lot of talk that he didn't care to get into.

Jake heard the clicking sound of computer keys in the background, along with the hum of newsroom chatter.

"We have limited info about what the governor did on those trips," Earl said with a slight southern drawl. "But on the Tampa trip, he was doing a ground-breaking ceremony. Let's see..."

"And that was the eighteenth of August?" Jake asked in a matter-of-fact voice.

"Right," Earl said distractedly. "Umm, I don't see anything in Miami on September seventh."

"Did I say the seventh?" Jake asked. "Sorry, I meant the eighth."

"The eighth," Earl repeated, and Jake could hear the click, click of the computer keys.

"Yes, here it is. Something about a ribbon cutting ceremony on Brickell Avenue in Miami," Earl said.

"Sounds like those weren't campaign trips, more like official-function trips. Good. That's what I needed to know. Thanks," Jake said, prepared to hang up.

"You might check with the Tallahassee bureaus of the *Tribune* and the *Herald* if you want details," Earl suggested, referring to the Tampa and Miami newspapers.

"That's a good suggestion, thanks. I appreciate your help, Mr. Wallace."

"Anytime," Earl drawled and hung up.

Jake was bolstered by the information he had gotten. He had placed the governor in both of those cities on the same days as Kristin. The pieces of the puzzle were coming together.

Now he had to place the governor in the same hotels. He'd have to run another bluff—an illegal one—to do that. He'd identify himself as one of the governor's staff people. If anyone questioned it, he'd just hang up.

He decided to use a pay phone in the lobby for the calls. He didn't think the hotels would bother to check the phone records to see where the call came from, even if they did suspect something. After all, hotels got thousands of calls. But right now, he couldn't be too careful.

From the lobby pay phone, he called information for the number of the Omni Hotel in Tampa. He already had the number of the Fontainebleau.

He called the Omni first. "Omni Hotel," the operator said.

"Reservations desk, please."

There was a click, then a man's voice said, "Reservations."

"Hello. This is Toby Graham, Governor Michael Romano's administrative aide. The governor stayed in your hotel on August eighteenth of this year. We're searching for a lost brown leather portfolio, and we're calling all the hotels at which the governor has been a guest over the last few months. Could you tell me if anyone has turned it in?" It was weak, but hotels probably got these calls all the time. Maybe not months later, but it wasn't unheard of.

"The eighteenth of August?" the man confirmed.

"Right."

"Just a moment, please."

When he came back on the line, the man said, "I'm sorry, sir, but our records don't show that the governor was a guest at our hotel on that date."

Damn! Jake thought. Strike one. "Oh, I may have your hotel mixed up with the Omni in Miami. Sorry to bother you. Thank you, anyway."

"You're welcome," the man said. Jake started to hang up when he heard the voice entreating, "Sir, sir?" He was tempted to hang up anyway, thinking the guy might start asking him questions.

"Yes?" Jake said, hoping he didn't sound too hesitant.

"My manager just told me that Governor Romano was in the hotel that day, though he wasn't a hotel guest. He was here for a meeting."

"Oh, right, of course, that's why the Omni is on his schedule. I've been calling so many places, I'm getting confused. Anyway, since we've established he was there, could you check and see if the brown leather portfolio was found?" Jake asked, continuing the ruse.

"Of course. One moment please." The man put him on hold and came back after a couple of minutes.

"No, sir, we haven't had a portfolio of that description turned in. I'm sorry."

"Nothing to be sorry for. Thank you for your help," Jake said in a polite, official tone and hung up. He hoped no one there would ever call the governor's office and ask for a Toby Graham. But it didn't matter if they did. They'd never find out about him.

Still, he had confirmed an important suspicion. This was great. Now, to call the Fontainebleau.

He gave the same story to the woman who took his call there, and was told that yes, she certainly remembered that Governor Romano was a guest there the night of September eighth, but that no portfolio matching that description had been turned in.

She asked for a number where he could be reached if it should turn up. He made up a number, using only the correct area code, and thanked her. When he hung up, he leaned against the wall of the phone booth and let out a deep sigh. Now he was getting somewhere.

Michael answered his private line and said, "Michael Romano."

"Do you know who this is?" the caller asked.

He immediately recognized Robert Lineo's voice. "Yes," he answered, his throat tightening.

"I just wanted to let you know that someone has been asking around about you up here."

"What? Who?"

"A cop."

Michael's heart lurched. "A cop? Who?" he repeated the question.

"Don't know for sure. I can't get anything else on it, but I thought I'd let you know. Forewarned is forearmed," Robert snickered.

Michael felt like reaching through the phone and punching the fucker. "Can you find out?"

"Maybe I could, but I won't. I don't think it's anything you need to worry about. You're squeaky clean, Governor Romano," Robert sneered.

"Well, what am I supposed to do about this?" Michael asked, distressed.

"Nothing. I'm just letting you know. Stay cool. If anything comes up, I'll take care of it. No way anybody can connect you to anything."

Michael was a little relieved, though not completely assured. However, he knew Robert had told him everything he was going to tell him. The nasty son-of-a-bitch.

"Thanks," he said simply.

Robert didn't respond before Michael heard the line disconnect.

He hung up the phone and looked at his shaking hands. His hands never shook; but then, nothing this nerve-wracking had ever happened to him before.

He was going to have to believe that what Robert had said was true. No way could anyone connect him to Kristin's death. But his hands were still shaking.

When Vic hadn't called by noon, Jake got antsy and decided to check out the apartment Kristin had rented. He asked the desk clerk for directions to the address he had found in the phone book for Bent Tree Apartments.

When he pulled into the complex, he rolled down the car window and asked a student where the manager's office was. The office turned out to be an apartment, where the manager also lived. The man who answered the door looked startled when he saw Jake.

"You're her brother!" he exclaimed.

"Angela Marcus," Jake confirmed.

"The papers used a different name."

"Yes," Jake said, seeing the man was getting nervous. He extended his hand and said, "I'm Jake Miller. Can I come in?"

"Oh, sure. Sorry," the man said, not taking Jake's hand but opening the door wider and stepping back so he could enter.

Jake saw that the living room had been converted to an office.

"I'm Bill Hale," the manager said. "I'm sorry about your sister."

"Thanks. You rented her the apartment?" Jake asked him.

"Yeah. Back in August. I didn't know who to call to return her security deposit," Bill Hale lied.

So that's why he's nervous, Jake thought. "You can keep the security deposit, Mr. Hale." He knew the manager's bookkeeping would reflect a cash refund, and that the refund would go straight into his pocket.

"Well, I appreciate that. After all, I didn't have any notice," Bill said, justifying it to himself more than to Jake.

"I'd just like to collect her things," Jake said.

"Oh, sure. Not much there, though. Just a few clothes and some toothpaste and stuff. No food." He paused as he looked at Jake closely and said, "She didn't live there, you know."

"I know," Jake answered him, knowing that neither of them would openly speculate on it.

The manager nodded and said, "Come on. I'll take you over there."

"Can we walk, or should we take my car?" Jake asked.

Bill thought about it and said, "It's not far, but if you're gonna be taking her stuff, you might as well bring your car to put things in."

They drove around the complex until they got to the building. Jake pulled into the parking spot the man pointed out.

He knew that the manager was being cooperative because he was being allowed to keep the security deposit.

Jake wanted to ask Bill some questions, and one in particular—like did he ever see anyone else at the apartment with Kristin? That was really why he had come here, but he'd need to get a better feel for Bill before asking him.

Bill led him into the bedroom and opened the closet. "That's all there is," he said, pointing to the few clothes hanging there. He turned around and pointed to the bathroom. "The rest of her stuff is in there."

"Mind if I do this alone?" Jake asked disconsolately, playing on Bill's sympathy so that he could be alone to search the room.

"Not at all," the manager said. He walked out of the bedroom.

Jake took the few clothes out of the closet and put them on the bed. He walked over to the dresser and pulled out the top drawer. He picked up the silk bras and panties he found there and threw them on the bed, too. Bill Hale had either forgotten to look in the drawers or had planned to give the expensive underwear to someone. Probably a pretty tenant, Jake chuckled to himself. The other drawers were empty.

Of course, Jake had no real use for any of Kristin's personal effects, but it gave him the excuse he needed to search around.

He walked into the bathroom and gathered up her toiletries, including a toothbrush, toothpaste, deodorant, powder, lotion, and an expensive bottle of perfume. He'd leave that for Bill Hale to make the best use of. He was disappointed not to find any male toiletries.

He stepped back into the bedroom and saw that a pair of panties had slid from the bed to the floor. He put the toiletries on the bed and bent over to pick up the panties. Something shiny caught his eye. He picked up the shiny object that was on the floor, partially hidden behind the leg of the dresser.

He recognized it as a tuxedo shirt stud, and he knew, without a single doubt, just who it belonged to.

He stuck it in his trousers pocket and went out into the living room. "Mind if I check for a bag to put the stuff in?" he asked Bill, who was sitting quietly on the couch.

"No. Here, let me help you," he volunteered, getting up.

"Here's one," Bill said pulling a brown paper bag from under the kitchen sink. "I don't see anything big enough to put the bedspread and sheets in, though."

"Mind if I leave those?" Jake asked.

"You don't want 'em?" Bill asked, surprised. Jake could see him ticking off the value of them in his head.

"No, I can't use them."

"Okay, sure, leave 'em," Bill said, with just a hint of greed in his voice.

When Jake had gathered up all her things and put them in the car, with Bill's help, he put his hand in his pocket and pulled out a folded stack of bills. He took a hundred-dollar bill from the top and handed it to Bill, saying, "I appreciate you taking care of my sister's things."

Bill hesitated before taking it. "You're real generous, Jake. Thanks." He glanced at the car and said, "I'll just walk back. I need to check a couple of things along the way."

Jake nodded, thinking that the manager didn't want to take a chance on being asked any questions. He obviously didn't know anything, and was afraid Jake might want his money back if he couldn't answer them.

That was okay. Jake had already found out more than he had ever hoped for.

"Hey, Jake," Bill said as Jake was getting in the car. "Your sister was a real nice lady. I'm sorry."

Everyone who knew her said the same thing about her. She was a real nice lady. "Thank you," Jake replied, and closed the car door.

Jake could hear the phone in the hotel room ringing as he unlocked the door. He slammed the door behind him and dashed for the phone.

"Hello?" he said breathlessly.

"What's wrong with you?" Vic asked.

"Just hustling to catch the phone."

"Oh. Well, listen, you're gonna be happy with what I found out," Vic said in a self-congratulatory tone.

"Tell me," Jake said, falling back on the bed.

"I don't know what you're up to, but whatever it is, you're on the right track. Filo Marcheso—also known as Tony Marcheso. Does that name mean anything to you?"

"No, but is he one of Lineo's men?"

"He sure is. *And*, he flew into Miami on October twenty-second and back out on the twenty-fifth. Those dates are smack dab around the time of Kristin's murder, aren't they?

Jake whistled and then said, "They sure as shit are. Great work, Vic. I owe you—big."

"I know that, and I'll remember it." After a pause he said, "When are you going to tell me what this is all about?"

Jake thought about it and made a decision. "Soon. I'm coming back to New York tomorrow. In fact, can you come over tomorrow night? I've got to talk to you about this. I need you to help me sort some things out."

"Well, sure," Vic said, glad that he was finally going to find out what was going on.

"I'll call you when I get in. Plan to get there around eight. We'll get delivery from that Japanese place you like."

"Sounds good, I'll be there."

40

"**YOU DON'T HAVE SHIT HERE,**" Vic Salinas said, leaning back into the sofa cushions and taking a swig from the beer bottle he was holding.

Jake was exasperated, even though Vic was only confirming what he already knew.

"But you'll agree that it looks like they were having an affair?"

"Yeah, so? That's a long way from murder."

"But there's the Lineo connection," Jake pleaded for Vic's agreement.

"Can't prove a fucking thing," Vic replied resolutely.

When he saw the defeated look on Jake's face, he added, "You've done a good job here, Jake, figuring all this out. And it all adds up, but not to murder. Not from an official standpoint, anyway," he said, after taking a few seconds to reflect on it.

"I can't just let this go," Jake said.

"You're going to have to. Who's gonna listen to you? You're talking about the damn governor of the state of Florida. That, plus the fact that the police have a signed confession from a killer, would only get you thrown in a looney bin."

"What about phone records? The lines in the Governor's Mansion? All of them? Those records might show calls made to Lineo."

"No good, Jake."

"Why not?"

"Too much heat on the privacy issue. Obligation to disclose access to records. You know that," Vic replied.

"What about an illegal access? You must know somebody who..."

"No, Jake," Vic said with unchecked irritation. "Are you stupid, or what? Do you really think that an illegal access could be done on the phone lines in the Governor's Mansion? Think, Jake!"

Jake knew every word Vic said was true. He sat back on the couch and leaned his head back, exhausted and disappointed.

"Besides, you don't think any number that would show up could be traced to Lineo anyway, do you? If he even made the call, it went to some obscure place, not to Robert Lineo's home or office."

"I know you're right," Jake said dispiritedly.

"Sorry, buddy. I wish I could tell you something you wanted to hear, but I've gotta be honest with you."

"I know that, Vic. That's why I wanted to talk to you. I needed a gut check. I can trust you to give me that."

Vic nodded and said, "Hey, I'm hungry. You ready to order?"

"Sure. Let me get that takeout menu. We'll order and you can catch me up on what's been happening in the department."

"Fine," Vic said, glad Jake seemed willing to put this behind him.

But Vic was wrong.

Caroline came out of her meditative state, pleased that the headache that had begun earlier was completely gone. She had been able to control them well enough until now, although the progesterone was causing them to threaten more frequently.

She could handle it, though, she told herself. Only two more days until she was supposed to start her period, then she'd know for sure what she had already guessed. Two more days. It seemed like forever.

Les rapped on Michael's office door and rushed in, not waiting for an answer. "Chuck Garner has thrown his hat into the ring. He just made the official announcement."

Michael nodded solemnly at the confirmation of the rumors that had been flying for the past three days.

"It's a little later than you predicted," Michael said. "But I guess that means Florence is going to be fine?"

"The word is her cancer is in remission," Les answered.

"I'm glad to hear that," Michael said sincerely.

"Me, too." Les rushed on, "We have to work with Andy and adopt a new media strategy to get the polls turned around."

"Any updates?" Michael asked apathetically.

Les wondered again what was bugging Michael. He couldn't believe that the big drop in his popularity polls after the special session could bother him that much. There was still plenty of time to fix that.

"Just slightly," he answered. "Only forty-two percent, down from forty-three percent, said they were less likely than before to support your re-election. The percentage of those most likely to support you is still the same, twenty percent. But that leaves thirty-eight percent that aren't committed. That's a big number, and we can work on it."

Les expected Michael to ask him how, but Michael said nothing.

"Hey, it's not that bad, Michael. This is normal. It's only been a little over a month since the special session. We've got almost a year until the election. People will forget by then."

"Not if Chuck Garner is in the race as the Democratic candidate. He'll pound me with it."

What was with him? Les wondered. Where was his fight, his competitive spirit? This wasn't normal—or good for the Party.

"Michael, what's bugging you?" Les asked the direct question out of exasperation.

"Don't bother me, Les," Michael responded, though without rancor.

Les was even more confounded. He had never heard Michael sound like this. "Okay," he said, "When you're ready to hear my ideas, give me a buzz."

When Michael didn't respond, Les shrugged his shoulders and walked out.

Michael watched him go, then got up from his chair and stared out the window. Bleak, bleak, he thought. An ugly day. They all seemed that way lately.

A cold wind slapped Jake in the face as he came out of Bloomingdale's He was tempted to turn around and step back into the warm store to slip on one of the sweaters he had just bought. Instead, he hailed a taxi and headed home.

When he got there, he dropped the shopping bags on the sofa and went into the kitchen to get something to eat. What goodies did Lucy fix today, he wondered, opening the refrigerator.

He saw a roast with potatoes and carrots on a platter, covered with plastic wrap. He touched it, and was glad to find that it wasn't thoroughly chilled yet. He could eat it without heating it up.

He watched television as he ate, but his mind wasn't on the program. He looked around his empty apartment and sighed. It was a deep, lonely sigh. I have to get out of this rut, he thought. But where to start?

Leslie Sherwood. He had thought about her often since he'd returned to New York. He wanted to call her, but he couldn't think of a legitimate reason to do it. She had seemed interested, though.

But I live up here, and she lives down there, so what's the point? He asked himself despondently.

He knew he had to shake off his depression. He just couldn't find a way to do it. Ever since Vic had helped him realize how futile his efforts had been, he had sunk into deeper and deeper lethargy.

Perhaps he could call Leslie and just run it by her, he thought, for what must have been the tenth time. But he rejected the idea quickly, as always. Vic was right. He'd be heading to the looney bin.

A thought struck him from out of the blue. It was a riveting thought, causing him to bolt from the couch and pace his floor with eagerness.

He'd take it to the governor himself. He'd get the son-of-a-bitch to confess.

Whoa, now, he told himself. Michael Romano isn't stupid. He'd never confess. But maybe he could shake Romano. Maybe he could get him to stumble. Was it worth a try? Thinking he had nothing to lose, he answered the question with a fist pump and a resounding "Yes!"

Caroline practically ran down the hall to Michael's office, where she knew he was waiting for her. She merely waved at Lynn as she passed and flung open his door.

Michael looked up and saw his beautiful wife rushing towards him with her arms outstretched for an expectant hug. The jubilant look on her face could mean only one thing.

"Yes?" he shouted the question, jumping out of his chair to meet her.

"Yes!" she exclaimed as she flung herself into his arms. They hugged each other tightly, their euphoria washing over them like a warm wave.

"I can't believe it," Michael cried. "Are we blessed, or what?"

"Lucky, lucky, lucky," she laughed, flinging her arms out and throwing her head back. "Of course," she laughed, "timing was everything. We knew when I was ovulating, and we certainly did everything we could to increase our chances," she laughed again.

Michael pulled her to him even more tightly and buried his head in her neck. Caroline felt his body shaking, and when she pulled back, she saw he was crying. Crying like she had never seen before.

Overwhelmed herself, she hugged him as tightly as she possibly could; and these two lucky people showered all of their love upon each other with their tears.

When he woke up, Michael thought he must have been dreaming about a bird singing, but as he continued to lie there, he heard it again. He realized it had awakened him.

He got up and walked over to the window, where he opened the drapes only slightly, not wanting to wake Caroline. What he saw caused his heart to soar.

It was one of those rare, exquisite days. The sun was shining and the air actually *looked* crisp. Everything was in sharp focus, clean and clear and sparkling. He opened the curtains a little more and raised the window.

He reveled in the invigorating magic of the air he breathed. Gently, miraculously, his burden lifted. He felt purged, pure, and fully alive. He felt that God had forgiven him, and had sent him a child and this special day to tell him that. In a state of overwhelming gratitude, Michael fell to his knees and solemnly thanked his Creator.

41

JAKE SAW WHAT he had been watching for all week long in the *Tallahassee Democrat.* The governor was going to be addressing the Businessmen's Club of Tallahassee at a luncheon that day. It was being held at the Hyatt Hotel. Perfect. A public place, where Jake could get to him.

He arrived twenty minutes earlier than the time the luncheon was scheduled to start, and was surprised to see the number of people who were already assembled. Everybody seemed to have a drink in their hand. He had hoped to get there early enough to get the layout of the place to determine how he might best approach Romano.

He was counting on Romano's surprise at seeing Kristin's twin brother to knock him off balance. He hoped it would give the governor enough reason to at least notice him.

Jake ordered a Dewar's on ice and mingled with the crowd in the lobby, trying to look nonchalant, but he couldn't help noticing that several people were staring at him. He braced himself when one of the men who had been staring at him broke off from a group and walked towards him.

Jake met the approaching man's eyes with a look of comfortable self-confidence. The man's eyes met his with a question, so that when he reached Jake he said, "Excuse me. I guess you noticed us staring?" He nodded his head in the direction of the group he had just left.

"Well, yes," Jake answered in a guarded voice.

"I'm sorry. My name is Patrick Lambert," he said, extending his hand.

Jake took it and said, "Jake Miller."

"Nice to meet you, Mr. Miller. Please forgive us for staring, but we couldn't help but wonder if you were related to Mrs. Long—Kristin Long?"

Jake was momentarily taken back by the stranger's question, though he supposed he shouldn't have been. After all, he was her twin.

"Well, yes," he said, his voice faltering slightly. "I'm her brother."

"Her brother? Why, Kristin never mentioned that she had a brother."

"Then you knew her pretty well?"

"Of course. We were all terribly sorry about her...death."

"Thank you," Jake said automatically.

"Do you live here in Tallahassee?" Patrick Lambert asked.

Jake had regained all his composure by now, so that he answered agreeably, "No, I live in New York City. That's probably why Kristin didn't talk about me. We hadn't seen each other in...many years."

"I see," Patrick said, though the look on his face said he didn't. "Then you're down here for..." he left the statement open for Jake to complete.

Nosy son of a bitch, Jake thought. Then he had an inspiration.

"I'm here because I know it was my sister's wish to support Governor Romano in his re-election bid. I plan to see that her wishes are carried out—with my own funds, of course."

Patrick Lambert smiled an expansive smile and put his hand on Jake's shoulder. "Well, that's fine of you, fine of you," he said condescendingly.

Jake wanted to knock the man's hand off his shoulder, but he smiled and asked, "Do you know the governor?"

"Michael?" Patrick used the governor's first name casually for effect. "Sure. Would you like to meet him?"

Jake felt like he had just been handed the world's most expensive gift on a platinum platter.

"I certainly would. I'd like to let him know he can count on some sizable contributions from me," Jake embellished, now that he knew which buttons of Patrick's needed pushing.

"Well, here he comes now," Patrick said, putting his arm around Jake's shoulder and pulling him towards the lobby door that Michael had just entered.

"Michael! Michael!" Patrick shouted over the crowd as they moved towards the governor. Jake saw Michael Romano and a man who looked to be his bodyguard, based on the way he walked close to the governor while scanning the crowd, turn their heads in unison towards the summoning voice.

In a shattering instant, Jake's eyes locked with Michael's, and Jake not only saw, but felt the man's fear. Every fibrous nerve in Jake's body snapped as he absorbed the dark force of the man who had killed his sister. He was being propelled by Patrick's hand on his shoulder towards a man who was rooted in his place by terror. Jake was emboldened by Romano's fear. By the time he reached Michael Romano, however, the governor had begun to recover.

"Hello, Patrick," Michael said calmly, looking at Patrick Lambert now. Jake saw the glisten on Romano's brow as he heard Patrick saying from what seemed far away, "Michael, I'd like you to meet Jake Miller. He's Kristin Long's brother, and he wants to talk to you about some hefty campaign contributions."

Almost imperceptibly, Michael relaxed. Just a little. Jake saw he was looking at him expectantly now. He summoned control, smiled, held out his hand and said, "It's an honor to meet you, Governor Romano."

From the look of relief that passed over Michael's face, Jake knew he had sounded convincing. Romano didn't suspect a thing. Michael returned the smile as he shook Jake's hand. "Thank you, Mr. Miller. And let me say, I'm very sorry about your sister."

You maggot, Jake thought. How cool he was to be able to lie so easily, to express what anyone else would have perceived as sincere sympathy. Jake had to look away, had to take a moment to control the anger that was rising within him.

Michael watched the man closely. He interpreted Jake's reaction as grief, and wondered again why Kristin had never mentioned him. In fact, she had told him she was all alone in the world. Had they been estranged?

With difficulty, Jake kept his voice controlled and said, "Thank you. I know my sister planned to support your re-election campaign. I'd like to talk to you about carrying through on that."

Michael let his guard down completely then. His initial shock at seeing the male incarnate of Kristin Long passed when he heard what the man had to say.

"Why, certainly," Michael said, pleased at the prospect of the contribution. More than that, he was relieved. He had nothing to fear from this man. The feeling of dread that had hit him upon seeing Jake had now evaporated. "Why don't you call my office, and we'll arrange a meeting."

Jake didn't want to wait. He had to get to Michael Romano now if he was going to be effective.

"If you can just give me a private moment of your time right now, Governor Romano, I'd appreciate it. I have to leave town this afternoon and I'll be gone for some time." Though he wasn't sure why, he knew he shouldn't mention New York.

"Well, fine," Michael said after a short pause. "Let's step over here." He pointed to an alcove several feet away from the body of the crowd.

The bodyguard started to follow them, but Michael said, "Everything's fine, Hanes. Get Caroline into the banquet room, please." Jake looked over to where Michael had motioned his head when he mentioned Caroline.

He saw a strikingly beautiful blonde woman talking with some people. As Jake looked at her, their eyes briefly met, and she gave him a perfunctory smile. Her eyes then moved to Michael's face, and she gave him a smile that rocked Jake with the amount of the love he saw in that smile. He looked at Michael and saw him return that love in his own smile. For the briefest instant, Jake second-guessed himself. Then Romano said, "Over here," and Jake's certainty returned.

He followed Michael into the privacy of the alcove until Michael stopped and turned to him. Jake felt his hatred rise up in him, so that when he spoke, his voice was pure venom.

"I know about you and my sister," he hissed. Michael's eyes widened with alarm. Jake rushed on, "I know about Tampa, the Omni. I know about Miami, and the Fontainebleau; the apartment at Bent Tree; the pregnancy." He took a deep breath to deliver the final blow. "And I know about Robert Lineo."

Michael felt as if the ground beneath his feet had shifted. His heartbeat accelerated to an intensely uncomfortable rate. He was caught up in a torrent of panic. But then, from the depths of that fear rose his strongest instinct—an instinct born in the streets of the Little Italy—survival. And survive he would.

Jake watched every one of those emotions pass over Michael's face, and with genuine astonishment, interpreted the final one accurately. Michael Romano was a fighter, a survivor. In that bleak moment, Jake knew he had lost.

"You...don't...know...shit," Michael said slowly, deliberately. "Because if you did, you wouldn't be talking to me. So I'll tell you this, and you'd better listen up. Don't come near me again. If you do, you'll be sorry. I guarantee it."

Jake hated the man, but he wasn't intimidated by him. "Does that mean you'll have me killed, too, Romano?" he asked in a voice filled with a malice that matched Michael's.

Michael kept his voice pitched low. "I don't know what you're talking about. And neither do you. Now get out of my face, you motherfucker!"

He gave Jake a poisonous look and then adjusted the features of his face into neutral nonchalance. He turned and walked confidently towards the crowd that awaited him.

Jake bowed his head in defeat, and walked out of the hotel lobby.

So that's who was asking around about me in New York, Michael thought as he walked into the banquet room. Who else could it have been? The asshole sure knew a lot—but not enough. And he never would.

Michael was relieved; but more than that, he felt exuberant, powerful. He had squashed the guy like a bug. He knew he'd hear no more from him, and he knew that his survival, and even his continuing success, was perpetually assured.

What Michael Romano couldn't know about Jake Miller was that his instinct to survive was equally as strong. But the difference was, what coursed through Jake's veins was pure and proud. What coursed through Michael's was poisoned and arrogant.

Jake's desire to bring down Michael Romano was undeterred, despite his failure to shake the man. The need for justice on his sister's behalf was stronger than ever. He would find a way, if it was the last thing he ever did.

When the idea came to him, it was so simple that Jake almost dismissed it. As he studied it from every angle, however, he could find but one defect in it: he would ruin an innocent person's life. But the possibility of ruining the guilty Michael Romano's life more than made up for it. After all, Michael would still be alive. His sister would always be dead.

Jake spotted the governor's beautiful wife coming out of the restaurant. She was laughing along with another pretty woman, and as the sun danced off Caroline's laughing face and shining hair, he thought he had never seen anyone quite so lovely.

Before her chauffeur could get out of the limousine to open the door, Jake stepped out from behind the corner of the restaurant where he had been waiting, undetected, since he had followed her there. He assumed a purposeful stride, and reached her just as she had kissed the other woman's cheek and turned towards the limo.

"Mrs. Romano!" He sounded surprised and happy to see her. She looked up to see who had spoken her name, putting her sunglasses on at the same moment.

He was gambling heavily on the fact that she would be the consummate politician's wife, pretending she remembered absolutely everybody. From the smile she gave him, he knew he had won the bet.

Caroline did remember him, but she couldn't place him. He was different enough to be remembered, with that hair and those eyes. In fact...

"How are you?" he asked as if they were friends, though he was careful not to be too friendly or come too close to her.

"Hello, I'm fine. And you?"

"Fine, thank you. Did you just have lunch here?" he asked, looking at the restaurant.

"Yes," Caroline said a little hesitantly, looking for Hanes from the corner of her eye. When she spotted him, she relaxed a little.

"Well, I was thinking about having lunch here myself. Is it any good?" he asked, trying to put her at ease with the small talk.

"Yes, quite good actually. I'm sorry," she said with an apologetic smile. "I know we've met, but I don't remember your name."

He admired her honesty. "Jake Miller," he said.

"Oh, yes, Mr. Miller," she said, trying hard to recall.

"Don't worry," Jake said. "You know, you're rather well known, so it's easy for me to remember you, but I certainly don't expect you to remember me."

"I apologize," she said with a relieved smile, "but you're right. There's only one of me, the governor's wife, and thousands of..."

"It must be pretty trying sometimes," Jake said kindly, relieving her of the burden of finishing what could be an embarrassing admission.

"Well, yes, sometimes; but I do enjoy meeting people," she responded warmly to his graciousness.

Hanes was watching the interaction, but he wasn't particularly concerned. He had seen Michael with the man the other day, and although

313

he couldn't hear what she was saying, he could see that Caroline was at ease. He assumed she knew the man also.

Jake knew that was what the bodyguard was thinking without even looking at him. It was exactly the scenario he had wanted to create.

"Well, Mr. Miller, it's been nice seeing you again, but I really must go." She turned slightly, ready to leave.

"Just one other thing," Jake said entreatingly, before she took the first step.

"Yes?" She was looking at him through the sunglasses so that he couldn't see her eyes. He decided it was just as well. He wasn't sure he wanted to see this lovely lady's eyes when he said what he had to.

"It's about your husband." Her head came up slightly at the mention of Michael.

"Oh, what about him?" she asked, growing a little impatient now.

"Just this: He had an affair with my sister, Kristin Long. He got her pregnant, and when she wouldn't have an abortion, he had her killed."

"What?" Caroline mumbled, feeling faint. "You're cra..."

"Not crazy, Mrs. Romano. Here," he said, holding out his hand. "Your husband left this at her apartment. In the bedroom. You might want to give it back to him."

As if in a trance, she looked down at his hand, and saw what she instantly recognized as a tuxedo stud she had given Michael on their first anniversary. It was one in a set of four, and there were no others like it in the world. They had belonged to her father. He'd had the black jade set in eighteen-karat gold. Each one had been engraved on the back with a tiny "F" for Fulton. Her father had given them to her, along with the matching cufflinks, in a moment of mad generosity, knowing she admired their unique quality and beauty. He had also known that she coveted them for Michael. They had been her father's favorites. And then they had been Michael's favorites.

When she didn't hold out her hand to take it from him, Jake reached for her hand and placed the stud in it. From the corner of his eye, he saw Hanes moving towards them then, so he pumped her hand as if shaking it, and said loudly, "It's been a pleasure seeing you again, Mrs. Romano."

He dropped his voice and said quietly, sincerely, "I'm sorry." With that, he turned to leave, passing Hanes from three feet away as he turned left on the sidewalk. He held up a hand to Hanes in greeting, keeping up the friendly pretense.

Hanes didn't know what to think, but he could see that Caroline was not well, and that concern overtook any other thoughts. When he reached her, she leaned into him for support. He put her in the cooled limousine, and then looked around for the man; but he was gone.

"I'll have you home in a jiffy, Miss Caroline," he said in his clipped British accent.

"No hurry," she replied quietly.

42

WHEN SHE WAS very certain Michael was asleep, Caroline crept out of bed and walked softly across the bedroom. She opened the door to Michael's dressing area and went in. She closed the door behind her, then put her ear against it and listened for sounds of his stirring. When she heard none, she walked over to his dressing table and turned on the light. She didn't think enough light would escape to wake him.

With a sense of dread, she opened his jewelry chest and saw what she had hoped not to see. Three black jade studs, not four.

She closed the box and leaned against the wall, finding it hard to breathe. She slid down the wall, buried her head in her lap, and sobbed quietly.

No wonder the man had looked so familiar. He had a twin sister, and Caroline recalled seeing her that day Michael had rushed over to her at the Billiard Club. A fanatic. That's how Michael had explained her. She had been suspicious at that time. How had she missed this?

She also recalled seeing that same woman's picture in the papers when she was murdered. She had tried to place her then, hadn't she? There had been some talk about it for a while, but Michael hadn't seemed interested or concerned.

But that murder had happened in Miami, she tried to rationalize. Michael had been here, in Tallahassee. He couldn't have done it. He *couldn't have.*

From somewhere deep inside her, a voice whispered to her: yes, he had done it. Not with his own hands, no. But he was responsible.

Now she understood. It answered a question she had chosen to bury, for a reason she couldn't pinpoint. How did he find out his vasectomy had reversed itself? When she had thought to ask him, he had said it was by accident, something about checking his prostate. But something had always tugged at her subconscious. A doubt, an apprehension...

With a sharp snap, the pieces fell into place. He had gone to the doctor to confirm that he couldn't have gotten that woman pregnant. And he found out just the opposite. So he had her...*killed?*

She saw it all clearly. The woman must have threatened Michael with exposure. With no other way out, Michael had somehow arranged for her to be killed. She knew he had grown up around the docks and the mob, and she could only surmise that he had some kind of connection there. The woman was brutally murdered on a beach in Miami, Caroline recalled. She shuddered as she thought of what Michael had set in motion.

And now here she was, pregnant as a result of all that deceit. Oh, God, she thought. I love him so much, and I know he loves me. How could he have done this?

Who *is* this man I'm married to?

Caroline stayed in Michael's dressing room a long time. When she finally stood to leave, she looked at her reflection in the mirror and said, "There's a way to fix this. There has to be."

She turned off the light and went back to bed, back to her lying, deceiving, immoral husband.

Jake stood at the window of his apartment and watched the snow fall on a city decorated in holiday splendor. It was so beautiful, too beautiful not to be shared.

"I'm lonely," he said aloud, surprising himself.

He reflected somberly on spending Christmas alone. Even if he did go to Vic's house for Christmas dinner, he would ultimately be alone.

He thought about Miami. It was probably eighty degrees down there and it wouldn't feel like Christmas at all.

Well, what was so important about that?

What was Christmas supposed to be about anyway? Sharing it with someone you cared for, he decided.

He picked up the phone and called the number he had resisted calling for so long. When he heard her voice, he knew he had made the right decision.

"Hi, Leslie, it's Jake. I'm thinking about coming down to Miami for the holidays. Would you like to have dinner?"

If he could have seen her eyes, he would have compared them to the sparkling holiday lights in Rockefeller Center.

"I'd love to!" she said.

"And so, ladies and gentlemen, I am withdrawing my candidacy for re-election as governor of the state of Florida. I promise to serve you faithfully and well throughout the remainder of my term."

Michael turned to Caroline, who was sitting on the platform from which he had just announced he would not run for re-election.

She smiled at him, then rose and walked over to where he was standing. He kissed her, ignoring the media's cries of "Governor! Governor Romano!"

"No regrets, Michael?" she asked him.

"None. I want what you want—to live our lives around ourselves and our child. I won't miss this. Thank you for making me realize it."

"You are so welcome."

"Michael," Caroline asked, "are all the packages in the car?"

"Yes, they're in the car," Michael answered, coming up behind her and giving her a kiss on the neck as his hands reached around her to touch her stomach, where their baby slept.

"There's just been so much to do," she said, slipping out of his embrace to put another shirt in her suitcase.

"Are you feeling okay?"

"I'm fine, Michael," she answered, knowing he lived in a state of perpetual unease where the baby was concerned. She had repeatedly assured him that all was well.

"Your father will be so pleased, sweetheart. You've done everything possible to make this Christmas special for him. Especially this," he added, moving close to her and patting her stomach tenderly with his strong and loving hands.

"Yes, it was better that we waited to tell him," she said. They had agreed that they wouldn't tell Pierce Fulton the news until they were confident that she could carry the baby to full term.

"Now," she said, "I want you to shoo, so that I can get your present wrapped before I have to leave."

"You're sure you don't want me to come down to Palm Beach with you now?"

"No, Michael, I told you there will be millions of things to do to get things ready for Christmas Eve dinner. We'll be entertaining eighteen people. You'll end up getting bored, as always, and driving me crazy. You'll be down in two days."

"All right," he laughed. "I'll be back to help you take the rest of your things down to the car."

"I'll call you when I'm ready."

Michael kissed her on the cheek and left. He had already decided that this was the merriest Christmas of his life, and he wanted to do something very special to celebrate it.

He went into his office and sat down at his desk. He pulled out the bottom drawer, then picked up the false bottom and pulled out the strong box hidden there.

He admired the diamond again as he picked it up from the box and laid it aside to wrap it. He would let her decide on the setting. He couldn't wait to see her face. She had seemed so sad lately, and he had caught her crying more than once. Raging hormones, she explained. Perfectly normal, her doctor had said. He hoped this gift would drive away the blues.

It suddenly dawned on him that he should give it to her now, right this minute. That would certainly lift her spirits. He wouldn't even bother to wrap it. It was perfectly wrapped in its own beauty.

He dashed out of his office with the diamond in his hand and ran up the stairs. He stopped short outside the door of their bedroom, however, remembering that she had sent him away so that she could wrap his gift.

He tapped lightly on the door and said, "Hide everything. I'm giving you ten seconds, and then I'm coming in."

"No, Michael!" she exclaimed, slight exasperation in her voice.

"One, two, three..." he started, laughing.

"Wait," she yelled through the door.

"Four, five, six..."

"You're impossible!"

"Seven, eight, nine...ten!" he yelled as he burst through the door, laughing.

"You just wanted to see your present," she scolded him.

"Au contraire, ma chère, I wanted you to see *your* present." He smiled and then held out his palm for her to see the small black velvet bag lying there.

She gave him a questioning look, then took the small bag and opened it. She shook it once, and the magnificent diamond fell into her palm.

"Oh, Michael, it's absolutely gorgeous."

"What? I don't even get a kiss for it?"

"Yes," she said, moving into him slowly. Her soft kiss was a short one. "Thank you, Michael."

"You're welcome, my love. I thought you would want to select the setting," he said.

"Oh, yes," she said quietly.

"So you like it?" he asked.

"Michael, it's beautiful. It's stunning. It's perfect, actually," she said with a curious smile.

"You won't have a present to open Christmas morning now, you know."

"That won't matter."

"Good," he said, gathering her closer to him.

That was a fabulous dinner," Michael said as he sat down on the sofa in the library. "I'm stuffed."

"Let's go for a walk on the beach," Caroline suggested.

"It's kind of chilly out there," Michael protested mildly.

When she gave him a sharp look, he said, "Oh, all right," pretending to give in unwillingly. He was actually thinking that he might be able to seduce his wife and make love to her on that wonderful private beach. It had been weeks since they had made love. He had of course agreed with her that they needed to take every precaution to make sure she didn't lose their baby, but now she should be past the dangerous stage.

"I thought you were going to tell your father about the baby tonight," he said, as they started down the path to the beach.

"Not tonight," she said.

"Fine, your decision. Hey, why don't you give me a hint about my Christmas present?"

"No."

"No? Just no?"

"That's right," she answered. She kicked off her shoes as they reached the beach. Looking at the blanket he had thrown over his arm, she said, "Why don't you spread that out so that we can sit down."

"I thought you wanted to walk," he chided, though he was secretly pleased. Maybe she had lovemaking in mind, too.

"Not yet."

"All right," he smiled and flipped the blanket out over the sand.

When they were seated, he leaned over to kiss her. She stopped him.

"Is something wrong, sweetheart?" he asked.

"Yes, Michael. Something's wrong."

"What? Did I do something?"

"Yes."

"Well, tell me."

Caroline didn't answer right away. He watched her as she bowed her head and took a deep breath, seeming to steel herself for what she was about to say. An alarm went off in Michael's head. Had something happened to the baby? Before he could gather his courage to ask, she turned to face him. In a voice Michael had never heard her use, a voice filled with a contempt he didn't know Caroline could even harbor, she said, "You got Kristin Long pregnant. And you had her killed."

"Wh...what are you talking about?" his voice caught in his throat as he spoke, so that his words sounded false even to his own ears. He was flooded by a wave of disbelief and alarm. This isn't happening, he thought. How did she know? An image of Jake Miller popped into his head.

She ignored his question. Her next chilling words drove reality all the way home for him. "I'm divorcing you, Michael. You'll go back to Tallahassee tonight, and I'll stay here. Your bags are packed and in the car. I never want to see you again." Her icy voice cut even deeper into his heart.

He was on the verge of denying it—everything—but he realized the futility of that. Instead, he had to make her see how wrong it would be for her to leave him.

"Caroline, you can't leave me! What about our baby?"

Caroline paused for a long moment, and then whispered in a voice replete with sorrow, "There is no baby, Michael. I had it aborted."

The screams caught in his throat, so that when they finally escaped, he sounded like a wounded animal, one that was caught in a trap and fighting for the last scrap of life.

Caroline, alarmed by his screams, started to rise. "Caroline, no!" He grabbed her by the shoulders and held her in place. "Tell me it's *not true*," he demanded. Michael was beyond any shock, beyond any grief he had ever felt. This couldn't be happening, not again. Maybe Alison could have aborted his baby, but not Caroline. Not his *wife.*

His pain was greater than any he could have imagined himself capable of bearing. The slicing pangs in his chest, his excruciating shortness of breath...these were elements of anguish he never knew existed.

"It *is* true, Michael," Caroline yelled back, shaking free of him and looking away from his tortured face. "Do you really think I could have your baby, after what you did? The...baby," Caroline's voice was straining against a suppressed sob, "...the baby was conceived in love. And I have no love for you any longer."

She turned to face him. "How could I? While I was doing all I could to make sure my father didn't die, you were fucking another woman. And you got that woman pregnant, Michael. How could I *ever* forgive you for that? And the rest...well, it's really too *horrible* to contemplate."

Caroline felt the full measure of her revulsion towards him rise up in her. It was that revulsion, that loathing, which had driven her to tell him his baby had been aborted. She knew she would never rid herself of him, that he would never leave her alone, if his child were anywhere on this earth. "But, our *baby!*" Michael wailed, as he dropped his head in his hands and began to cry.

Caroline ignored his tears. "It's all gone now," she sighed, emotionally exhausted. Then, gathering strength and determination, she delivered another crippling blow.

"I've had a lot to accomplish in these past few weeks. I wanted everything in place before I told you, so that you couldn't fight me.

"The will and trust agreement have been rewritten. You're no longer a beneficiary. All of our money is now in my name. It was always mine, anyway. I've left one account with the equivalent of what you've earned over the years, a little less than a million dollars.'"

"Caroline," he pleaded through tormented sobs, "Please forgive me. Please, *please* forgive me, and I'll forgive you for aborting our baby, and we can..."

"Forgive me? Forgive *me*, Michael? Oh, how big of you. You are such a hypocrite! I don't need your forgiveness. What you want, what you think... it means *nothing* to me," Caroline spat the words at him.

"Do you hate me that much, Caroline?" Michael asked in a disbelieving and anguished voice.

"I do hate you, and can you blame me? We had everything, but that wasn't enough for you. You thought we didn't make love these last few weeks because of the pregnancy. But I couldn't stand for you to touch me, ever again, in that way.

"Anyway, none of that matters now. It's done." She stood up and looked down at him. Her voice filled with chilling resolve as she delivered the final blow. "But there is one more thing. If you ever try to run for any political office again, I'll use everything I have to destroy you. I'll expose you for the hypocrite you are."

"Don't do this, Caroline!" he futilely pleaded as he sprang up from the blanket to reach for her.

She stepped back quickly, out of his reach, and tossed a small, unwrapped box onto the blanket. "Here's your Christmas present."

And with that, Caroline turned and walked away.

"Caroline!" He screamed after her. But she didn't look back.

Michael looked down at the box on the blanket. He picked it up slowly and removed the top. He let out a roaring, pain-wracked cry at the sight of the black jade tuxedo stud.

A cold wind blew over him, chilling him all the way through. Michael looked out to the ocean, from where the cold wind had blown.

He saw that the tide had gone out.

EPILOGUE

"BUH UH DA," the beautiful baby girl with the blonde hair and silvery gray eyes said to her father.

"What did she say?" Jake asked Leslie.

"She said she loves you," Leslie answered, smiling at him as she looked up from the Sunday morning *Miami Herald* she was reading.

"Ah, that's what I thought she said," Jake laughed.

"There's an article here that says Michael Romano will be joining the law firm of Dumas and Simpleton in Gainesville."

"That's his third firm in four years. He won't last there, either," Jake said in a sharp-edged voice.

"Hard to believe he was once governor of Florida. What a shame," Leslie sighed and shook her head.

"He got less than he deserved," Jake said coldly.

"You're right, I know. But I've always felt so bad for his wife."

"Yeah, but she's okay. I'm glad she found someone else. Those two Palm Beach fortunes combined. Can you imagine all that money?"

"We're not doing so badly," Leslie reminded him, looking around their comfortable Miami bay front home and feeling especially blessed.

"True. And when I finish law school, we'll be doing even better."

Leslie smiled and came to join him and their baby girl, Kristin. She sat down on the floor next to Jake. Kristin toddled over and put her arms around her mother's neck.

Leslie hugged her daughter tightly and said, "I'm so lucky."

"We're both so lucky," Jake said, leaning over to kiss her, then Kristin. Corby, their black and white Springer Spaniel, joined the love fest. Jake laughed and stroked his head.

Kristin picked up her Raggedy Andy doll and shook it at her mother.

"Ub ah da?" she asked.

Leslie laughed, then looked at Jake and said, "She's wondering where Raggedy Ann is."

"Well, where is she?"

"I hid her. Kristin was pulling out that red hair. She didn't seem interested in pulling out Andy's hair. Who knows why the difference? Anyway, I tucked poor Ann away for a little while. I'm hoping that phase will pass soon."

"Ug ad ub," Kristin said, and toddled away. Leslie and Jake watched her as she crossed the room and stopped at Leslie's Queen Anne desk. She tugged at the bottom drawer with determination until it opened. She reached in and pulled out the doll, then looked at her parents triumphantly and exclaimed, "Og de tug!"

"How did she...?" Leslie started to ask, then stopped and looked at her husband.

With a resigned shrug, she returned his knowing smile.

CAROLINE WATCHED FROM BENEATH the cabana as her son ran toward the ocean, leaping into the frothy waves as they broke onto the shore. She looked over at her husband, who was dozing with a book lying open on his chest. Marc was a handsome man, a good man, a man she had known most of her life. Marrying him had steadied her world, and she loved him more each day.

Her father was standing close to the shoreline, leaning on his angel of a caregiver, Arial, while waving his cane back and forth, calling out for his grandson to be careful. Stephen raised his small hand in a salute, then dived into a wave.

Though he suffered from dementia, Pierce Fulton seemed imbued with better health and a happier demeanor since she, Marc and Stephen had moved back to the States and moved into the estate with him. They were a happy family.

With a soft grunt, Marc awoke and turned his head to look at Caroline. Their eyes met, and they smiled at each other. He reached for her hand. She took it. He squeezed. She squeezed back.

Caroline rose and walked toward the shoreline to join her son and her father. "Grand-père! Maman! Voir ce que j'ai trouvé!" Born in France and raised there for the first three years of his life, Stephen spoke French as a first language, though he was equally proficient in English.

Her athletic, dark-haired boy ran toward them, his face splashed with a bright-white smile, eager to share what he had found.

Pierce, still leaning on Arial, dropped his cane and shaded his eyes to watch his grandson approach. "What is it, Michael? What have you found for me?"

Caroline tensed. Her father's dementia was getting worse. "Non, je m'appelle Stephen, Grand-père!" her son exclaimed with a giggle, then opened his hand to reveal a shiny pink and white shell.

Caroline bent down to look. Stephen wrapped his free arm around his mother's neck and leaned into her body. "For you, Maman. Do you like it?"

"It's beautiful, Stephen. I love it. *Merci.*" She kissed his warm, salty cheek and tousled his hair.

His vivid blue eyes sparked with delight. Despite having her eyes, he looked so much like his father. Anyone who saw him would know who that was. But here in their luxurious, private enclave, that never had to happen. And when Stephen was ready to start school, they would return to France where he would be enrolled under his adoptive father's last name.

The sun went behind the clouds, and a chilling breeze caught Caroline by surprise. She stood and looked around. A vague discomfort caused her to shiver. Then the sun broke through the clouds, dispelling her uneasiness. As she took her son's hand and walked back toward the house, she assured herself she and her son were safe. No one, not even Michael Romano, could penetrate her walls and her world and take her son from her.

But she couldn't resist looking over her shoulder and scanning the beach, and the horizon, one more time.

ACKNOWLEDGMENTS

My thanks to the Metro-Dade Police Department, Miami-Dade Office of the District Attorney, Miami-Dade Office of the State Attorney, and Miami-Dade Medical Examiner's Office for being so generous in sharing their time and knowledge with me.

I appreciate permission granted by author Jonathan Dudley to use excerpts from his book, *Broken Words: The Abuse of Science and Faith in American Politics.*

Many thanks to my sister, Sandy, my niece, Stacy, my long-time and very dear girlfriends, and my generous author friends who have encouraged me when I needed it most. Rochelle Weinstein, a special thank you for your wisdom and support. Ann-Marie Nieves, you are a brilliant PR agent.

Most of all, my love and thanks to my husband for supporting me in every way while I endeavored to complete and publish this long-term project.

ABOUT THE AUTHOR

Following a successful career in banking, Rebecca Warner pursued her lifelong dream of writing.

Her first novel, *Moral Infidelity*, won the *Readers' Favorite* Bronze Medal in Thrillers. Her second novel, *Doubling Back to Love*, was included in *Goodreads'* third most popular romantic anthology of all time, *Peace, Love & Romance.* Her most recent book, *My Dad My Dog*, has been an Amazon #1 bestselling book in all three of its categories.

When she's not writing, Rebecca enjoys reading and exploring the great outdoors around Asheville, North Carolina, where she lives with her husband and their feisty Blue Heeler.

Visit her website at www.rebeccajwarner.com
Email Rebecca at rebeccawarnerauthor@gmail.com

NOTE FROM THE AUTHOR

Word-of-mouth is crucial for any author to succeed. If you enjoyed *Moral Infidelity*, please leave a review online—anywhere you are able. Even if it's just a sentence or two. It would make all the difference and would be very much appreciated.

Thanks!
Rebecca Warner

NOTE FROM THE AUTHOR

We hope you enjoyed reading this title from:

www.blackrosewriting.com

Subscribe to our mailing list – *The Rosevine* – and receive **FREE** books,
daily deals, and stay current with news about upcoming releases
and our hottest authors.
Scan the QR code below to sign up.

Already a subscriber? Please accept a sincere thank you for being a fan of
Black Rose Writing authors.

View other Black Rose Writing titles at
www.blackrosewriting.com/books and use promo code
PRINT to receive a **20% discount** when purchasing.

CPSIA information can be obtained
at www.ICGtesting.com
Printed in the USA
LVHW100931100122
707889LV00014B/302

9 781684 339334